City of Buried Ghosts

CITY
OF
BURIED
GHOSTS

CHRIS LLOYD

CANELO

First published in the United Kingdom in 2016 by Canelo

This edition published in the United Kingdom in 2019 by

Canelo Digital Publishing Limited
57 Shepherds Lane
Beaconsfield, Bucks HP9 2DU
United Kingdom

A CIP catalogue record for this book is available from the British Library.

Print ISBN 978 1 78863 557 8
Ebook ISBN 978 1 910859 84 1

Look for more great books at www.canelo.co

Printed and bound in Great Britain by Clays Ltd, Elcograf S.p.A.

For my mum and dad, Averil and Mervyn Lloyd.

He wanted to close the man's eyes.

Only they don't slip shut like they do in the movies. A gentle glide of the hand over the eyelids and the light is out forever, the sightless searching accusation gone. The face calm and at rest. Because the eyes don't close. Not easily. Not if you don't want to feel the shape of the eyeballs roll softly under your fingertips. Not if you can't bear to pinch the edge of the thin fleshy lid between thumb and finger and coax it down and hope it stays.

He gave up but the eyes kept pulling him back. They stared up at him through the torrential downpour, oblivious now and forever to the heavy rain pounding at them. The sudden summer storm that beat at his own bare head, that drowned out any noise that he'd become used to. The angry clattering of the branches on the pine trees, the creatures slinking through the dead needles on the ground, the endless sweep of the sea hidden beyond the headland, brushing in and out along the small, sharp stones of the little beach.

He felt like the rain was hammering him further and further into the shallow trench in the ground. He looked at the hole where he stood. The unbidden and surprising thought that it wasn't a trench he could use.

He thought of turning the generator off to kill the light, but the fear of the dark that would envelop him was too great. Instead, he reached forward and angled the light away from the man's face. It shone down the small incline to another clearing below, further from the headland.

1

He looked at the pool of light cast into the dark wood and turned back to look once more at the eyes of the man lying in the trench.

He'd made his decision.

Chapter One

'So why exactly are we here?'

Elisenda could hear Àlex grunt at her question.

The mosso, a uniformed caporal, signalled for her to go with him to the middle of the small boat.

'Not because I don't want him hearing us,' he explained, gesturing at the grey-haired and grizzled man steering the craft, 'but because we'll never hear ourselves speak over the engine.'

Elisenda followed him to the thinly-cushioned bench towards the front of the boat. The water was slapping against the sides but these wide-bottomed llaüts, once the work horses of the coast, now fine and polished play-things, stayed calm in the choppiest of seas. The one they were in was firmly stuck in the work horse breed, its captain a retired fisherman with a rock-hard gut straining at the buttons of an ancient nylon shirt. A smaller, clinker-built dinghy was tied to the stern and tugged in its wake like a reluctant child. Elisenda flicked an oily rag off the bench but chose not to sit down anyway, decades of grease and grime ingrained in the plastic-covered foam sheet. Instead, she leaned against the short mast supporting the long yard, the other end of which rested on the crutch near where the boat's owner stood. Even here, the noise of the diesel engine, hidden away in what would once have been one of the fish holds, was loud enough to make them have to raise their voices. Holding on to the yard for balance, Elisenda was surprised to see a sail furled up along it. Most llaüts had long ago given up any pretence of being a sailing boat.

'What do you do when you need a proper boat?' Àlex asked grumpily, following them.

The caporal shrugged. His name was Fabra and he'd been stationed at the Mossos d'Esquadra police station in Palafrugell for three years, he'd told them. He had the tan and the physique of someone who lived and worked by the beach, Elisenda thought, even now in February.

'The Salvament Marítim boats if it's anything urgent or more remote,' Fabra told Àlex. 'The dive team from Sabadell if they've got to go underwater.'

'Sabadell,' Àlex muttered. The dive team for the whole of Catalonia was based inland.

'Urgent,' Elisenda murmured in an echo of Àlex's tone. She glanced at her sergent and raised an eyebrow.

'In cases like this,' Fabra continued, 'we get one of the local sailors to help out. Senyor Ferran here keeps his boat in Palamós but he's almost always on hand.'

'Palamós?' Elisenda asked.

'We have a station open there in the summer. I've been seconded there for the last two years. That's how I know the local fishermen. I'm in Palafrugell for the rest of the year.'

'I miss working,' the old captain grumbled loudly, his voice deepened by decades of after-lunch cigars, his ears flapping.

Fabra led them further away, towards the front of the boat. So, not because of the sound of the engine, Elisenda thought.

'Normally we'd get to where we're going by 4x4 and then walk,' he explained once they'd settled again, 'but the storms this month have washed away part of the track, so we're having to go by boat.'

'Where is it we're going?' Elisenda asked him.

'An archaeological dig a few coves to the north. The senior archaeologist called to say she'd found an anomaly. Two bodies buried on the site.'

'An anomaly?' Elisenda questioned.

Àlex sighed and sat down on the triangular bench in the prow. 'Bodies at an archaeological site?'

'I visited the site when she called,' Fabra explained. 'She reckons something's not right with one of the bodies. I couldn't see any difference, but she said that it needed to be examined.'

'What state are the bodies in?' Elisenda asked him. 'Any clothing? Are we likely to get DNA, fingerprints?

Fabra stared back at her. 'They're just bones, Sotsin-spectora.'

Senyor Ferran at the rear of the boat called something out. Fabra grimaced in apology at Elisenda and made his way to the captain.

Elisenda turned to stare at the dark grey rocks of the coastline being slowly eaten up as the llaüt cut through the sea, running parallel to the shore.

'Bones,' she finally muttered.

Àlex looked up at her, the old anger in his face. 'Another non-case, Elisenda. That's how we're seen now.'

She could only close her eyes to hide her agreement. She held her head back, the winter sun warming her face, the wind flailing her long hair behind her in fine brown tendrils, and wondered how long she'd be allowed to keep her unit together. In case she didn't need one, Àlex's hoarse voice was a constant reminder of the events of the autumn. The death of one of her team, Àlex nearly dying, both at the hands of one of their own. And Elisenda's team was still paying for it. Distrust at her experimental Serious Crime Unit now allied with increased scrutiny and a lack of will from their seniors to trust them with a major case.

'We're still wounded,' Elisenda murmured now, wryly, in echo of the reasons she'd been given for the last four months of stagnation and excuses. She opened her eyes and was shocked at the cerulean beauty of the Mediterranean sky.

'And we'll stay that way until they let us repair ourselves,' Àlex replied, the anger in his voice straining the vocal chords damaged by the rope that had cut into his neck.

Elisenda had to look at the wake from their boat rolling to the shore to gather herself. Àlex's changed voice could still make her want to weep. The sound of the engine shifted down and she could feel the llaüt pitch towards land. Relieved, she paid attention for the first time to where they were. The captain slowly steered into the mouth of a small, elongated cove, carefully avoiding the rocks that emerged from the water a few metres offshore. Elisenda simply stared at the tiny sandy beach and the three old fishermen's huts nestling under a low cliff. Electric green pines seared through the proud blue of the sky, the trees' gnarled brown trunks clinging precariously to the grey rock.

It was a beautiful scene she didn't want to see.

'Where is this?' Àlex asked.

'El Crit,' she replied.

The Scream.

–

Despite the bright sky and the sunlight, there was still a chill in the air. The breeze that had made the sea so lively seemed to be redoubling its efforts to whip the dark sand up around Elisenda's ankles. They'd had to row into the shore from the llaüt in the dinghy, Fabra expertly guiding the shallow-draughted boat through the under-water rocks, but they'd then had to jump from the llaüt onto the beach, and all three of them, Elisenda, Àlex and Fabra, had splashed in the tiny laps of water brushing the sparse pebbles. Elisenda could feel the sharp grains of sand stinging her calves, the bottoms of her trousers clinging damply to her legs. Seawater had seeped in through the stitching of her shoes, making her feet slide about inside them. It made gripping the steep steps climbing up to the small headland from the beach that much harder. She turned to see Senyor Ferran down below, checking the diesel tanks on his boat, a lighted cigar in his mouth.

'We might be walking back,' she muttered to Àlex. He looked to where she was gesturing and shook his head in annoyance.

Caporal Fabra led them up the uneven steps terraced roughly into the hillside, the path turning back on itself again and again to negotiate the sharp ascent. Only the sound of the breeze whistling softly across the water past the sharp rocks into the cove could be heard. Otherwise it was silent. No cicadas, Elisenda thought to herself. She only knew the beach in the summer and was used to its heat-filled sounds of insects chirruping and bathers splashing.

'Is that the only way back?' Àlex asked her, looking out to sea.

'There's a dirt track, but Caporal Fabra said it was impassable. And you can only get so far by car anyway. It's still a bit of a hike from there. Sea or land, it's much of a muchness.' She turned to smile at him. 'That's why it's so good in the summer. So don't tell anyone about it.'

He smiled back at her, a rarity these days. Elisenda sometimes forgot how much it softened his features, took the rough edge off the anger coiling below the surface.

'Nudist, mind,' she added.

'We could have a unit outing here, then. Bring Inspector Puigventós along. Make a day of it.'

Elisenda carried on walking and tried not to laugh. For one moment, she'd caught a fleeting glimpse of the old Àlex.

'Just along here,' Fabra twisted to tell her.

The steps levelled out under a canopy of pine trees, the ground carpeted with soft and shifting dried needles that felt comforting underfoot, even through her wet shoes. To the right stood a cluster of holm oaks, the bark flaking off in thin layers like ancient scrolls. To the left, the sea, down below them. A cruise ship way out on the horizon, no doubt heading for Barcelona. Elisenda smelt the sweet scent of the pines mingled with the sunlit salt aroma of the Mediterranean. She took a deep breath and followed Fabra to a cordoned-off area in a small clearing.

A woman looked up from a trench and saw them. She jumped nimbly out and walked towards them, placing a small trowel in a jacket pocket and clapping dust from her hands. She was taller than Elisenda, and had long, unruly hair barely restrained by an elastic band. More grey in it than Elisenda had realised from a distance. The woman wore linen trousers and a light cotton jacket despite the February chill.

'Doctora Fradera,' she introduced herself. 'You must be the police from Girona.'

'Sotsinspectora Elisenda Domènech and Sergent Àlex Albiol,' Elisenda introduced them.

'Only I do hope it hasn't been a wasted journey.'

Elisenda stifled a sigh.

'So why exactly are we here?' she asked.

Chapter Two

'This is the first body we found,' Doctora Fradera explained to them.

She'd led them back to the trench and was kneeling alongside a brown and mottled skeleton. A spike was buried in the fragile bones. Both Elisenda and Àlex had recoiled when they saw it. Rusted and brittle, it protruded from the front of the skull, closing a cold and shocking triangle with the empty eye sockets.

'How old is it?' Elisenda asked her, recovering from the sight.

The archaeologist gently flicked some of the earth from the cranium. 'At this stage, my best guess is about five thousand years.'

Elisenda looked down at the older woman in the trench. She could feel Àlex standing next to her getting restless. 'There is a reason for our being here?'

The archaeologist didn't seem to have heard her and pointed to the spike. 'We think this is an execution. We're not entirely sure. Until we remove the skeleton and get it back to the laboratory, we won't be able to tell if the spike was inserted ante or post mortem.'

Despite herself, Elisenda's curiosity was piqued. 'And if it's post mortem?'

Doctora Fradera gazed at the skull before answering. 'Display. Or so we think. What for, we don't fully know. The thing is, in these cases, we've normally found the head severed from the body, which rather bears out the display theory. But that doesn't appear to be the case here. Initially, I can't see any sign of the individual having been decapitated, either before or after death. It's really very odd.'

'So why exactly have you asked us to come here?' Elisenda was finding the archaeologist's extemporisation irritating to have to follow, especially when she was beginning to suspect it was going to turn out to be a wasted journey. Àlex had already taken a pace back from the side of the trench, his face cold.

'And what is also interesting is that there is evidence of its having been found before and left here,' Fradera carried on talking, apparently oblivious to the Mossos. 'Markings around the body would indicate that an earlier dig found it but chose not to remove it. But that's not so unusual. They may have left it undisturbed for subsequent digs to find. Subsequent dating techniques. It does happen.' She looked up at Elisenda. 'Interesting, don't you think?'

'Yes, I do,' Elisenda answered honestly. 'But I don't see why you brought us all this way to see it.'

Fradera climbed easily out of the pit and walked purposefully away. 'Oh, it isn't this one. That's over here. Sorry if I stink, by the way. It gets awfully hot digging in these trenches.'

'For Christ's sake,' Àlex muttered.

Elisenda raised her eyes at him and set off after the archaeologist, deep in thought. She suddenly had the feeling that the woman did have something that was worth bringing them all the way out to the coast from Girona. Erratic she may be, but she had an evident intellect, and her care for the skull showed an awareness of her subject, if not of other living beings. Somehow Elisenda couldn't see her jumping to a wrong conclusion. She caught up with the archaeologist as they began to descend gradually through a thicker clump of pines, heading away from the sea. Àlex was five paces behind. Elisenda caught him gazing intently from side to side, checking the scene, searching for anything, no matter how much he felt it was a waste of time. The old Àlex slowly coming back, she thought, tucking the idea away in a faintly optimistic drawer.

'Only you here, Doctora Fradera?' she asked.

The archaeologist threw a glance around at the quiet scene. 'What? Oh yes, just two of us working on the dig at the moment. My colleague's gone into Palamós. No money for any other archaeologists, funding's been cut. You know how it is these days.'

'I do indeed,' Elisenda replied, heartfelt.

'And it's too early in the year for students to come and help out. Pity. They're free and glad of the experience. We'll have to wait until Easter for that. If we're still going, that is.' She suddenly swerved. 'Mind the dog shit, disgusting people leaving it there like that. It's just over here.'

Elisenda sidestepped and looked back at the first trench, some thirty metres away. 'Why so far from one to the other?' she asked.

'The settlement's much bigger than we first thought. The trench back there is on the site of an earlier dig, in the 1980s, when the belief was they were dealing with a much smaller site. We've sunk a couple of pilot trenches further afield to get some notion of the extent of it.' She stopped and oddly lowered her voice. 'If we can show some evidence of a more major find, not even the lot in power now could cut off the funding. The tight-fisted bastards would have to let us carry on.'

'A dig in the 1980s?'

She carried on walking. 'There've been several over the years. The first one in 1908, another one in the 1930s before the Civil War, then nothing until the 1980s. They pulled the plug on that one because of funding. And other issues, as far as I've heard. And now us, going the same way unless we can prove greater cultural significance.' She suddenly stopped on the edge of a much smaller trench cut through the dry earth, the pine needles swept up into a high pile a few metres away from it. 'Here's your man. Mind you don't fall in.'

Elisenda looked down at a straggle of bones, lying sad at the bottom of the pit. From the size and shape of the pelvis, clearly visible in the light brown soil, even she could see that it was a man. Years of attending post mortem examinations had taught her that. Otherwise, she felt it looked similar to the first body, except that it wasn't fully exposed, as though it had only been half excavated. Àlex came alongside her and looked down into the trench.

'What makes you say we're dealing with a modern body?' Elisenda asked. She noticed that Doctora Fradera didn't step down into the trench this time.

'Without a proper examination, I can't know for certain, but the colour and texture of the bone is different. And I found fragments of fabric. They're badly

13

decomposed, but they look to me to be non-natural, not the weave we get from natural fabrics.'

'You haven't cleared all the earth away, I see.'

The archaeologist nodded. 'The moment I suspected it wasn't as it should be, I stopped.'

'Thank you, Doctora Fradera, you were quite right to stop.'

'Who else has seen this?' Àlex asked.

'My colleague. He stayed here while I went along the cliff path to get a phone signal. You can't get one here. There's a house just a few hundred metres to the southwest, you can get a signal near there.'

'Is there anyone living in the house?' Elisenda asked her.

Fradera considered that for a moment and shook her head. 'Empty for the winter, I think.'

'Did your colleague touch the body while you were phoning?' Àlex added.

She looked down at the trench, scanning. 'I wouldn't have thought so. It certainly doesn't look like he did.'

'The bones look like they've been pushed together,' he insisted.

'No, the body was probably placed here curled up.'

'Was that usual practice among the original people? The Iberians?'

'Indiketa,' Fradera specified. 'We don't know. We've found bodies buried in all sorts of different ways, so I couldn't say if this was unusual. But this is.'

Carefully, she finally stepped down into the pit, pulling a brush from her jacket pocket.

'If I may?' she asked, looking up.

Elisenda nodded at her to go ahead. The archaeologist brushed some of the dry earth away from the skull. Elisenda and Àlex had to walk round to the other side to get a better view.

'I'd only just started removing the soil here when I noticed it. It's why I stopped.'

She took the brush away and the two Mossos saw the beginnings of a spike emerging from the skull. As the body was on its side, they hadn't seen it before.

'A spike like the first one,' Elisenda murmured.

Fradera shook her head. 'The first one, along with all the other skulls like this that we've found, has a round-headed spike, like a giant nail. Look at this.'

Elisenda and Àlex peered in. Through the dirt, what appeared to be a hole was visible in the spike.

'I'd say it was a mattock, wouldn't you?' the archaeologist asked. 'A modern one.'

Chapter Three

'I'm not fucking going back in that sick bucket bobbing about on the fucking ocean. Tell them to clear the fucking road by the time I finish.'

'Have you worked with Albert Riera before?' Elisenda asked the judge.

'More times than I care to remember. One day I hope to be good enough at my job to be that rude.'

Elisenda decided she liked the court official, an earnest young man with dark-rimmed spectacles that looked too big for him, like adults' glasses on a child's face. They were standing to one side of the clearing where the second trench lay, watching the spectacle of the pathologist's arrival through the pines from the beach below.

'Jutge Rigau,' the judge had introduced himself when he'd arrived, shaking the dust from his neatly-pressed trousers. 'Please call me Pere.'

'I can tell you're a judge,' she'd replied. 'The bottoms of your trousers aren't wet.'

He'd had the grace to look sheepish, which had endeared him immediately to Elisenda.

'I drove. I didn't know about the land slippage on the track here. That's why it took me so long. I've had to walk through the woods for the best part of an hour.'

'Have you come from La Bisbal?'

Rigau nodded. 'This comes under our judicial area, so we're dealing with it, not a judge from Girona.'

Elisenda smiled to herself and thought of Jutgessa Roca, one of the Girona judges that she usually had to contend with, a stickler for form and oblivious to suggestion. 'I'm sure I'll get over it. No court secretary?'

'No need for us both to come all the way out here. I'm just present because I'll be instructing the investigation, so I want to get an idea of the scene.'

Elisenda nodded and liked him even more. When a body was found under suspicious circumstances, protocol had it that the judge, the court secretary and the pathologist had to be present to permit it to be removed. In practice, it was usually done by just one of them, usually the pathologist. The judge being there without the other court official showed an interest in the content, not the form.

As it happened, Jutge Rigau had only turned up a few moments before Albert Riera and his shell-shocked entourage had arrived from Girona, by sea as Elisenda had done.

The whole of the machinery had been set in motion the moment Doctora Fradera had shown them the mattock embedded in the skull.

'It's a common tool,' she'd explained to Elisenda when Àlex and Caporal Fabra had gone off in search of a phone signal, 'but they're also used by archaeologists. From the size of this, it looks like a hand mattock, a smaller one.'

'So a tool that would have been ready to hand during a dig?'

'Very much so. But nowadays the handles are made of fibre glass. This looks like an old-fashioned wooden one. The handle's gone, but you can see the hole where it should be. There are fragments that look like they could be wood.'

'In which case, a tool that could have been in use in the 1980s dig.'

'Or even earlier, the 1930s. We won't know until we can date the skeleton properly.'

Elisenda had waited deep in thought until Àlex had come back to tell her that he'd spoken to the forensic medicine service in Girona and the judicial service in La Bisbal.

'But it's going to be some time before they get here,' he commented. 'Caporal Fabra has called the Policia Científica in La Bisbal. They're sending a team.'

'So we wait,' Elisenda had replied.

In the meantime, Fabra had climbed down to the beach to let Senyor Ferran know that they were going to be some time.

'He wanted to come up to see for himself,' Fabra told them when he returned. 'I said he should go back to Palamós and we'd call him when we were ready. I've arranged for him to bring the pathologist from Girona when he gets here.'

'Wise move,' Elisenda replied.

Àlex quickly grew restless and began to search the area around the earlier trench. He knew not to contaminate the murder scene, but was impatient to get on with the investigation.

'Not that there'll be much left uncontaminated,' Elisenda commented.

Fabra went with him, while Elisenda stayed near the second trench. Doctora Fradera brought out a couple of

18

battered folding canvas chairs and she and Elisenda took one each.

'This would be the Indiketa tribe, wouldn't it?' Elisenda asked. 'The settlement? I heard of them at school, but I know very little about them.'

'None of us knows a great deal about them.' Fradera sighed and gestured around her. 'This rather sums up our relationship with so much of our past. This dig has been started and stopped three times before we got here. The way things are going, it will soon be stopped for a fourth time. If it's not a lack of funding, it's a lack of political will that has constantly hamstrung research.'

Elisenda nodded. She felt this conversation was for another moment. For the present, she simply wanted more of an idea of the context. 'Can you give me some idea of the Indiketa, Doctora Fradera? I need to have some idea why a thirty- or eighty-year-old murder would have happened precisely in this place, especially when there are such similarities between the victims.'

'In a nutshell,' Fradera said, taking a deep breath, 'the Indiketa were an Iberian Celtic tribe, we think stretching from what is now Tarragona and northwards along the coast as far as here and up into the Pyrenees. You're from Girona, I take it. We think they may have inhabited that area too, along with the Ausetans. They are your ancestors.'

'This is pre-Roman, isn't it?'

'Indeed. Our earliest records are from the sixth century BC up until about the first century BC. They traded with the Greeks and then the Romans. They were eventually subjugated by the Romans in 218 BC but rebelled in 195 BC. That was put down by Cato the Elder as part of his campaign in Hispania. With the customary cruelty we expect of Cato.'

'War feeds itself.'

Fradera looked surprised. 'Very good. Yes, that was Cato the Elder who said that. It was to justify the severity of his repression. And it's been used as justification ever since. He also said that he had destroyed more towns in Hispania than he'd spent days in the country.'

'Could the original killing in the first trench have been Roman doing?'

'Unlikely. The Indiketa weren't averse to a spot of cruelty themselves, both on the battlefield and to their prisoners. Anyway, I'm certain that that killing pre-dates the Romans. No, I think we can assume that it's entirely in the family.'

Elisenda turned to look at the second trench. She could just see part of the bones over the lip of the pit. 'So, I wonder if this one is, too.'

She was aware of Àlex approaching where they sat. He was accompanied by a man wearing glasses that crowded his face. She stood up as the man shook the dust from the bottoms of his trousers. He looked hot and was carrying his coat over his shoulder.

'Jutge Rigau,' he told her. 'Please call me Pere.'

He was quickly followed by the Científica forensic investigation team from La Bisbal and a few moments later by Albert Riera. With his soft, white hair and neat goatee beard, his bird-like hands and his waspish manner, the pathologist most resembled an avuncular demon. Elisenda and Jutge Rigau watched him now as he finished his tirade against the sea and set to work in the trench.

'You, archaeologist,' he barked. 'Come here. I'll need your expertise.'

Doctora Fradera had looked dumbstruck at Elisenda.

'He's recognised your expertise, Doctora Fradera,' Elisenda reasoned. 'I'd say you were winning.'

Two of the Científica team, anonymous in their forensic whites, began their visual search in the area around the trench, while the other two assisted Riera and Fradera in gently scraping the earth from the bones. They looked at their colleagues like they'd drawn the short straw.

'Carefully with that brush, you numskull,' Riera told one of them. 'You're not scratching your balls.'

They had.

'I have to agree with your opinion, Doctora Fradera,' Riera finally grumbled after much of the bones had been revealed. 'This is modern.'

Fradera picked up a piece of fabric that had been hidden under the earth. 'And this is man-made.'

'You're very skilful, Doctora Fradera.'

'I know.'

'That amounts to flirting in Albert's book,' Elisenda whispered to the judge, who stifled a laugh.

'I'd like to start moving the body,' Riera told Rigau. 'Do I have your consent?'

'You do.'

'Not that I give a fuck. I'm moving it anyway.'

'Quite right too,' the judge replied, a grin on his lips. Riera looked up at him nonplussed.

'You learn fast,' Elisenda told him, impressed. Being overly polite was often one of the ways to take the wind out of the pathologist's sails.

Riera called for a box and the team in the trench began to lift the bones carefully out and place them inside. As they removed the parts of the rib cage, he and Fradera suddenly stopped.

'Well, that settles that,' Riera said, carefully picking up an item. He showed it to Elisenda. 'A Sony Walkman, if I'm not mistaken. With a cassette still in it.'

'So, not the 1930s then,' Elisenda replied.

El Crit, 1981

Everyone on the coach craned their neck to see what the hold-up was. Noticing the movement, the student took off his earphones and looked out through the windows on the other side of the aisle.

A dog was lying on the road, where the dozen or so lanes after the toll booths merged into the three lanes of the motorway. Blood was pouring from its mouth, but when a man from a car tried to approach it, it growled and he had to back off.

'Abandoned,' the student heard one of the other passengers decide. 'Someone must have dumped it there and another car's hit it.'

'Some people,' someone else commented.

His neighbours started telling each other stories of people abandoning dogs on main roads and in the woods, but the student didn't join in. He looked at his watch and wondered how late this was going to make him. Tugging at his shirt front to fan himself in the June heat, he took the letter out of his rucksack and read it through again, even though he knew what it said by heart.

He was disturbed again by someone in the coach quietly jeering. He looked up to see a green and white Guardia Civil car draw up and two cops trying to shoo the dog to the side of the motorway.

'Bastard Guardia Civil,' a young man said.

'Occupying troops,' his girlfriend added, an epithet often applied indiscriminately to both the Guardia Civil and the Policía Nacional.

'Lock them all up with Tejero and throw away the key,' an elderly woman chipped in.

Others joined in, talking heatedly about the attempted coup the previous February, when Tejero and other Guardias Civiles stormed the parliament in Madrid, although they all made sure that the two policemen outside the coach couldn't discern any gesture or look that would be likely to antagonise them. They spoke in low voices, not willing to close the sliding panels at the top of the windows in the hot summer sun.

The student sighed and looked at his watch again. The coach had already been late leaving Barcelona. At this rate, it was going to reach Palamós at least an hour after it should do.

Putting the letter back in the rucksack, he searched through one of the pockets for a moment before finding what he wanted. Taking out the most recent album by Orquesta Mondragón, he swapped over cassettes and put his earphones back on, closing his eyes and turning the volume on his Walkman up as loud as it would go.

Chapter Four

'That's the one with *Caperucita Feroz*, isn't it?' one of the Científica from La Bisbal had asked. 'That's one of my mum's favourites.'

'Oh, do fuck off,' Riera had replied.

'Orquesta Mondragón,' Elisenda explained to Jutge Rigau.

'I know, I'm a fan.'

'Very retro.'

After the Walkman had been found in the trench, the senior Científica officer had opened the device and taken out the cassette that was still inside it. Holding it gently in his gloved hand, he'd announced the name of the band.

'And the album is called Bon Voyage,' he'd added.

'That came out in 1980,' Rigau had announced, impressing everyone.

Elisenda turned to Doctora Fradera. 'Do you know the dates of the dig in the 1980s?'

'I know it closed down in 1981, in June or July I think. As far as I'm aware, it had only been in operation for less than a year.'

'That gives us a time frame,' Elisenda replied.

It was late afternoon by the time the last of the teams had left the scene. Jutge Rigau had signed the order for the body to be removed from the scene, and four porters from the Institut de Medicina Legal in Girona had carried the man from the second trench in a box past a silent assembly through the trees to their van.

Satisfied they'd completed their inspection of the scene, the Científica team had also returned to the clearing beyond the blockage on the track to retrieve their vehicle for the drive back to La Bisbal. Albert Riera had refused point-blank to return by boat and had tramped through the darkening pine trails with Jutge Rigau and Doctora Fradera. The archaeologist had left her car a short distance from where the judge had parked, she said, to the side of the track near the blockage.

'Good,' Riera had replied. 'We can talk old bodies.' He turned to Rigau. 'And you can drive me on to Girona from La Bisbal, young man. The round trip won't take you long. And you might learn something.'

'I'm sure I would,' Rigau had replied, 'but I have no intention of driving you to Girona.'

'I do like that judge,' Elisenda whispered to Àlex.

In the end, Doctora Fradera offered Riera a lift. 'I live in Girona,' she explained. 'It's no trouble.'

Elisenda decided to return by sea, so Caporal Fabra had gone to call Senyor Ferran, who'd returned in his boat to take them back to where she and Àlex had left the pool car in Llafranch. Back on dry land after the short journey along the coast in the deepening gloom, Elisenda and Àlex found the car and headed for Girona, with Àlex at the wheel.

'We'll have to stop in La Bisbal,' Elisenda decided, calling the station there to tell them to expect them. 'This is an old case. It will come under their local investigation team's jurisdiction.'

'You don't think it'll be given to us?'

'It shouldn't. Is it a serious crime, do you think?'

'Is anything?' Àlex replied, the dark fog evidently back in place.

Elisenda watched him drive. The shell was there. The lean face and dark, probing eyes, the powerful body kept in reserve under layers of tended clothes. But the spirit and the humanity, what it was that made him Àlex, was no longer shining through. He was anger without a just outlet. Wounded, she thought to herself again. My whole team is wounded and I've got to hold it together. And what's worse is that we're seen to be wounded.

'Who knew a judge born after 1980 would like Orquesta Mondragón?' she finally commented, breaking the silence of the lonely road they were on.

'Who knew Albert Riera would?'

Àlex laughed for a brief moment, then fell silent again, concentrating on the road. They passed empty crop fields and darkened woods and drove through quiet villages, the lights on in the houses behind shuttered windows, the main streets devoid of people, unknown lives come and gone in the trace of a headlamp.

A sergent met them at the station in La Bisbal, a purpose-built and angular smoked glass and concrete construction on the edge of the town, built when the country had money for such things and the newly-formed Catalan police force was striving every way it could to present a modern image, a break from the policing of the past. When the Mossos d'Esquadra had progressively taken over functions from the old Spanish police forces, they'd been determined not to use any of the vacated stations, setting themselves up instead in temporary or semi-permanent homes or building new ones.

'They get a nice new station,' Elisenda had commented to Àlex as they'd parked outside. 'We're still stuck in Vista Alegre.'

Àlex had simply grunted. The Mossos in Girona had been supposed to be moving to a spanking new building on the border with the town of Salt, but the recession had hit and the plan had been shelved indefinitely, the new station unbuilt.

The sergeant introduced himself as Jaume Poch.

'I'm the head of the Local Investigation Unit.'

Elisenda explained about the body at the scene at El Crit beach. 'It's a cold case, well over thirty years old. We were called as they didn't know what they were dealing with when the message came through, but your team will be in charge of the investigation. If there's anything we can do to help, just call.'

'Thirty years old?' Poch commented. 'I'll check missing persons from that time.'

'Good luck with that,' Elisenda told him. The perception of policing at that time and the not always happy changeover from the Spanish police to the Mossos meant they were always battling against a void of information.

He gave a wry laugh. 'If we can find an identity and if there's family still alive, then we can pursue it, but I might not be able to give it top priority. Not initially, at least. Budgets.'

Elisenda nodded. 'As I say, if you need any more information from us, let me know. Your Científica team here will be handling that side of it.'

Poch checked his watch. 'They're still not back from the scene.'

'The track was blocked,' Elisenda explained. 'They had to leave the vans a long distance from it.'

They took their leave and continued the journey to Girona, driving into the city alongside the Ter river through the Pedret part of town. As they crawled in the evening traffic, Elisenda watched the lights come on as the restaurants and bars on the pavement opposite the river began gearing up for a quiet midweek evening. In her youth, there'd been just one disco and one late-night bar stuck out in what seemed the darkness on the edge of town. The first time she'd gone to the bar, she'd been startled as her friends knocked on a grim and battered door until a face appeared at an iron grille before letting them into a wondrous cavern of shattered tiles, jazz and liberation. It was still there, but sanitised, no longer mock-forbidden and no longer alone. Other bars had come in its wake, restaurants too, some of them in buildings that had been around at the time the cathedral was built, one even involved in its construction, the lime kiln used to make the mortar hidden quietly proud among the cocktail movers and shakers.

She turned to look at Àlex. He'd remained taciturn for most of the drive.

'If you want to get a bite to eat, Àlex,' Elisenda suggested, gesturing at the restaurants to their left. 'Chat.'

'If it's all right with you, Elisenda, I'd like to get home. See my boys before they go to bed.'

'Of course.'

He dropped her off on Plaça Independència and she watched him drive away along Carrer Santa Clara to take the car back to the pool at Vista Alegre. The shops on the narrow street were closing, owners and employees gathering outside, lowering the shutters and talking in that way of people who spend all day together but barely know each other.

'Wounded,' she muttered to herself, crossing the square and heading for the Pont de Sant Agustí, the footbridge leading over to the old town and home.

On the other side, she turned left at the small crossroads everyone called the Quatre Cantons, the four corners, and glanced as she often did at the ornate iron and copper outline of the four rivers that met in Girona sunk into the road surface. It was modern, not from her childhood, but from her daughter's. Lina had loved running her feet along the contours every time Elisenda had brought her to Girona to visit her parents. She still found it odd that her daughter had been more Barcelona than Girona, her accent like her father's, not her mother's. Elisenda had sometimes felt with guilt that she didn't belong in her married family, perhaps why she and her husband had divorced, why her daughter used to look forward so much to holidays with her father after they had. And why her daughter had died in her father's plane five summers ago, Elisenda thought with a start. She slowed her pace along the narrow Carrer Ballesteries, where she lived. It curved gently to the right, following the line of one of the earliest city walls, part of which still stood further along on the opposite side. Her road was essentially without the true city, the narrowest of strips trapped between the original town and the river. Always an outsider.

Inside the deeper gloom of her building, she punched the timer switch on the landing lights and climbed the stairs to the top floor, the loud ticking counting down the seconds until the staircase would be pitched into blackness again, growing heavier and more insistent as she trudged the last flight to her apartment.

She went into her flat, dropping her keys on the small hall table, and leaned heavily back against the door, pushing it shut. Without taking her jacket off, she dropped to her haunches, slowly slipping to sit on the floor, barely inside her apartment.

'Home,' she whispered.

Exhaling deeply, she pulled her knees up to her chest and folded her arms over them, using the cradle she'd formed as a rest for her head. She clenched her teeth to make sure she wouldn't cry and dug her nails into the scuffed and faded leather of her jacket sleeves. The day's mask had finally fallen.

Awaking with a start, she saw that over an hour had passed. She was ravenously hungry. Standing up stiffly, she arched her back and stretched her arms, then walked though her flat, turning on all the lights. In silence, without music on as she usually would, she fried a piece of frozen fish and served it with some salad. Half an hour later, she hadn't touched it. She had sat at her kitchen table and stared at the lives being lived in the flats and restaurants on the opposite bank of the Onyar; people talking and children being read to, waiters and chefs clearing up in weary conversation, televisions flickering in the dark and lights coming on in kitchens as dishwashers were loaded before bed. The buildings slowly being turned off for the night, the reflections dying in the river.

Picking up her plate, she scraped the cold food into the recycling bin and turned the light out, for once not taking it downstairs for the nightly collection.

Chapter Five

Elisenda could feel her body temperature rising for the third time since the small hours of the morning.

She'd had a nightmare. She'd fallen asleep quickly but had woken before the dawn, her sheets soaked in sweat, her face burning. Kicking the covers off in fright, she'd scrabbled to find the switch on the bedside lamp, her breath in short panics. There'd been a woman in her dream. Standing in the middle of a lonely beach. She was crying out. Elisenda had recognised the beach as El Crit. The Scream. At first, she hadn't known who the woman was until she'd turned to face the headland up above her and the moonlight had illuminated her face. It was Elisenda, but different. Shaking, she knew with horror that it was how she would have pictured Lina as an adult. Ripping the thin material of the sheet in her need to get out of bed, but refusing once again to allow tears to come, she'd got up and hurried through the apartment, turning all the lights on. The fish from the previous night was beginning to smell of decay.

The sun hadn't risen high enough to break over the top of her building and shine on the opposite bank, but the river was reflecting growing pinpoints of light as the lives on the other side began to wake up. In the fake electric glow of her own gloom, she'd heard singing. Gentle enough for her to turn her head to listen for the source. She'd opened the French window onto the balcony, but the voice wasn't from outside. Drawn back in by the sound of a lullaby she'd sung to her daughter as a baby, she'd roamed her apartment, but Lina was nowhere in sight, not even a shadow of her dancing in the light unfolding like a morning flower outside the kitchen window.

Defeated, she'd thrown on her running clothes and had followed the sunrise around the city walls, totally alone, working her lungs and legs harder and faster. It was her punishment. She'd run among the strewn boulders of the Torre Gironella, where she'd watched Àlex almost die, and clung to the base of the medieval stone as it curved around the old town. Where the walls ended, near the river, she finally stopped, her heart racing, her calves and shoulders on fire, and lay down heavily on the grass slopes of the small Foramuralles park. Rolling over and on to her knees and hands, she was sick, but there was little food to come up and her throat burned with the dry pain.

A café was open on Plaça Vern as she walked past, pulling air into her lungs, and on impulse she went inside and took a seat at the polished zinc counter.

'You don't look so good, Elisenda,' the owner, a slight woman who'd gone to school with Elisenda's mother, told her.

'I hate running, Enriqueta, that's all.'

While Enriqueta quietly served other early risers and set about preparing dishes for the day, Elisenda wolfed a Manchego baguette, the bread liberally smeared with tomato and doused in olive oil, the semi-cured cheese cut thickly and layered generously between the soft morning bread. Enriqueta gave her a couple of doughnuts on the house to go with her coffee.

'You spoil me,' Elisenda told her.

But it was at the third time of her body suddenly rising in temperature that Elisenda felt anxious. She'd gone home from Enriqueta's café and showered and was now at Vista Alegre. At the morning meeting with Inspector Puigventós and Sotsinspector Micaló, the first the head of the Regional Investigation Command and her immediate boss, the second her equal, and head of the Regional Investigation Unit, which dealt with the crimes in the Girona region that Elisenda's unit didn't cover. In theory, at least. She was having to keep her anger in check.

'It's a cold case, Xavier,' she argued one more time to Puigventós. 'La Bisbal is perfectly capable of taking it on.'

'I'm sure they are,' Puigventós replied, 'but I've decided that your team is going to be in charge of it. You and Sergent Albiol attended the crime scene yesterday, you are already up to speed with the case.'

'We attended the scene because the station in Palafrugell thought it was serious. It's a cold case, Xavier, not the sort of investigation my team was set up for.'

Puigventós considered his words before answering. 'Elisenda, a lot of things have happened that your unit was not prepared for. One of our own, someone we sat with every day, killed a fellow police officer, and we didn't see it coming. This is a way back. This is a murder investigation. It might be over thirty years old, but it's still a murder. Still a serious crime. Exactly what your unit was set up for.'

Elisenda sat back, deflated. 'I'm not happy with this. We need a real investigation to ensure the survival of the unit.'

'There's no doubt about the continued existence of your unit, Elisenda. You must be aware of that. You have all the proof you need.'

I do, Elisenda thought, and it doesn't make me any happier.

'We're all under scrutiny,' Micaló finally said. 'Not just your team, but all of us. It's in everyone's interest for your unit to take on this investigation, get a result.'

'With none of the media harassment we've had lately,' Puigventós added. 'I agree with Roger, we are all in the spotlight. And not just with the media, but with the Mossos and with the whole of Girona. If we get a result on this, with none of the pressure of a live threat to the public, we will be restoring so much confidence in the Mossos, in us.' He looked at his watch before continuing, the meeting running over its normal fifteen minutes. 'Which brings us neatly to the next point. Low-level crime. We're in an unusual situation since the killings of the autumn. The public has lost a lot of confidence in us, and the degree of petty incidents that the whole matter caused has not diminished entirely. As I've been taking over a lot of the work that would normally be done by the head of the Local Investigation Unit, I've decided to go after minor crimes to make sure we nip in the bud a lot of the sort of offences that are an issue with the public.'

'Is Intendent Moner in agreement with this?' Micaló asked him.

'I've spoken to him and he accepts my arguments.'

Intendent Moner was in charge of the Girona station of the Mossos. Normally, the head of the Local Investigation Unit would report to him and merely coordinate with Puigventós, who ran the Regional Investigation

Command and reported to the Criminal Investigation Division in Sabadell rather than to Moner. Under usual circumstances, Puigventós dealt with criminal cases for the whole of the Girona police region, but the vacuum left by not having someone in charge of the local unit for the city meant that Puigventós had been forced to go outside his remit and take on much of this work.

'It's an unusual situation, I know,' Puigventós continued, 'but until a replacement is found, it's how we'll have to carry on for the time being. This low-level crime initiative shouldn't affect your unit so much, Elisenda, but I wanted you to be aware of it. Roger will be much more closely involved.'

Elisenda nodded her agreement thoughtfully. Amidst the complicated hierarchy of the various departments, her own Serious Crime Unit still often seemed to be the dog in the manger, a misunderstood outsider both within Vista Alegre and within the Criminal Investigation Division. She watched Puigventós shuffle papers on his desk, his usual unwitting signal that matters were at an end. Low-level crime, she mused, standing up. She followed Micaló out of the room and along the corridor, knowing she now had to convince her increasingly disenchanted team that they would be taking on a case from over thirty years ago.

Chapter Six

'They've given us the cold case, haven't they?' Àlex asked her.

Elisenda signalled for him to come into her office and close the door.

'I'm going to need your help on this,' she told him. 'Montse and Josep are not going to take it well. I need you to be upbeat about it.'

Àlex flung his arms out wide. 'Upbeat? They're killing us.'

Behind Àlex, beyond the interior window occupying the top half of the wall separating her fish bowl from the main room, Elisenda could see the two caporals seated either side of a desk. The only other two members of her team, they were pretending not to be paying attention to what was going on in Elisenda's office.

'Be with me on this, Àlex.'

He looked at her and sighed. 'All right. But how much longer can we go on?'

Privately, she had to agree with him. Privately, too, she was disappointed. Her Àlex would have kicked and railed at the latest order from above and done as he'd pleased regardless. This Àlex went along too willingly. He was easy, but she liked him edgy. It made him a better sergent to her sotsinspectora.

He opened the door and beckoned Montse and Josep in. They entered without a word and took a seat each. Àlex leaned against the wall, his arms folded, a tic in his cheek giving away how much he was having to hold his frustration in. More tentative signs of the old Àlex fighting his way back, Elisenda thought.

'The death at El Crit beach,' Elisenda began. 'How much do you know?'

'Àlex told us, Elisenda,' Montse replied. 'We're happy to take the investigation on.'

'We thought it would be assigned to us,' Josep added. 'We're okay with it.'

Elisenda looked from one to the other. Josep towering over Montse, despite hunching his shoulders, his mousy hair again wilfully losing its battle with a comb. Montse seated lightly on her chair, compact and strong, fibre and muscle relaxed. Elisenda caught a slight downward movement in Josep's eyes. Not so okay with it, she realised. That was as good as it got lately, she knew, but she also knew that they would do everything they could to solve it. For themselves and for their dead colleague. On that score, she had other news to break to them later. She was dreading it.

'Well,' she went on, 'it is our investigation now and we're going to make sure we nail it. The first thing we have to do is ascertain the victim's identity. It's more or less certain that he died in 1980 or 1981, but we'll know for sure later today when Riera carries out the post mortem. Àlex, I'd like you to attend that.' Because if anything can bring you back from your inertia, she thought, it's Riera's goading.

'What makes us think it dates from that time?' Montse asked.

'A Walkman was found in the trench where the body was buried, with a cassette from 1980 still in it. Científica are checking on the model to see what years it was in production. Also, it was found underneath the body. It seems highly unlikely that an item from that era would find its way underneath an earlier body. So I think we should work on the assumption that this murder does date from that time unless we get any evidence to the contrary from Riera.'

'What sort of person would have had a Walkman in those days?' Josep asked.

'Young, I'd presume,' Elisenda replied. 'Riera should give us an accurate age range, but we can start on the assumption it was someone in their late teens or early twenties, would you say? The problem being that finding missing persons records from that time isn't going to be easy. Different times...'

'...different police,' Montse finished her well-used sentence for her.

'Smartarse.'

Montse grinned at her. Elisenda relaxed and let the others speak, their interest in the case rising.

'Police records will certainly be difficult,' Josep agreed. 'Our best bet is probably newspaper archives. I'll get on to them.' He sat more upright in his chair, not appearing to mind for once being the tallest person there.

'And I'll take police records,' Montse offered, 'but I don't hold out much hope.'

'If the killer is still alive,' Elisenda reminded them, 'they're going to be in their mid-fifties at least. We also need to check other incidents around the same time that might have a resemblance. The murder appears to resemble a ritual form of killing used by the Indiketa, the tribe that lived in that settlement. Therefore, the killer would in theory be someone who is aware of the practice, conceivably an archaeologist, although their custom of inserting spikes into the skulls is very widely known.'

'I remember more being discovered a couple of years ago,' Àlex said. 'There was a news report on it. But would ordinary people have known about it back then?'

'Possibly,' Elisenda answered. 'I remember two of them in the museum in Ullastret when I was a kid. We'll check up on it, though. But first, I'd like Josep and Montse to get out to El Crit, familiarise yourselves with the scene and the lie of the land. The head archaeologist, Doctora Fradera, mentioned a colleague. See if you can speak to him.'

The other three made to get up, but Elisenda waved at them to stay.

'There's just one more thing.' She chose her words carefully. 'The process to find a new member of the team is going ahead. I'm supposed to be looking at the candidates for the job.'

Her words were met with silence. She looked from one to the other, their faces numb, the enthusiasm of the last few minutes instantly tempered.

It was Àlex who spoke first, his damaged voice all the more stark. 'We understand that, Elisenda. We knew it had to happen.'

'I'm sorry,' was all she could say. 'I don't want to have to replace him either.'

Staring into the middle distance, Àlex followed the pathologist along another shorter corridor to an ante-room. He didn't even smile to himself at Riera's frustration at his not taking the bait. Unknown to him, Elisenda's plan to draw his old self back was going badly wrong.

Doctora Fradera was waiting for them in the ante-room, accompanied by the assistant who'd given Riera the folder. Deep in affable conversation with the archae-ologist, the young man immediately hushed when the pathologist entered the room. Riera took a look through the contents of the folder, half a dozen pages dense with text.

'Sergent Albiol,' Àlex reminded Fradera who he was as Riera read the notes. 'Of the Mossos d'Esquadra. I was at El Crit yesterday with Sotsinspectora Domènech.'

'Right.'

He could see she didn't remember him.

Riera finished reading and handed the folder back to the assistant without acknowledging him. 'This way, Doctora Fradera,' he invited the archaeologist into the examination room. 'I carried out a preliminary investiga-tion this morning. I'd simply like to ask you to corroborate my findings.'

Àlex followed, standing a short distance from the two of them. He was quite relieved to be forgotten as it allowed him to engulf himself in his thoughts. He stood and stared at Riera as he worked. He had to admit that he was an exceptional pathologist. A pity, then, that Àlex should find him so objectionable a man.

Riera called him over. 'You can tell Elisenda that Doctora Fradera and I are in agreement regarding our findings. Everything indicates that time of death would be

43

at the time the discovery of the Walkman would suggest, the early 1980s. As for his age at time of death, we would place him in his mid-twenties. Much of the fusing of the skull and the pelvic region was complete or almost complete, so I would say that mid-twenties is fairly accurate. He also had dental work that's in line with Spanish dental practices of that time. Other than that, there are no distinctive signs, no fractures.'

'The murder weapon?' Àlex asked.

Riera pointed to the mattock protruding from the skull. 'What do you think, Sergent Albiol?'

'The murder weapon, Doctor Riera,' Àlex insisted.

'It's a mattock,' Fradera answered, gesturing to Àlex to take a closer inspection. 'If you look here, you'll see that the pick end is what entered the victim's skull. The hole where the shaft would have gone still has wood fragments in it. That also dates the tool to the time we say. A modern one would have a fibre glass handle. You can see the adze, the end we use for scraping, protruding from the wound.'

'You would say it's most likely a tool used by an archaeologist?' Àlex asked her.

She looked thoughtful. 'They are used in other fields. Farming, forestry as well, I think, but it is definitely a tool that an archaeologist would use.'

'How much force would it take to penetrate the skull to that extent?'

'Considerable,' Riera spoke. 'The angle of entry would imply that the attacker was right-handed and standing directly in front of the victim.'

'Man or woman?'

Riera considered for a moment, but Fradera answered before he could. 'Either, I would say. I use a mattock in my work. They are light and balanced. This one would have been a little heavier because of the wooden shaft, but nonetheless, they're tools that are extremely wieldy and that can exert a great deal of force. We have to break some very tough soils in our work, Sergent. It really wouldn't take much effort with a strong downward swing.'

'Yes, I think I would agree with that, Doctora Fradera. There are also no other blows elsewhere to the body. It would have been a single movement.'

'Done in anger,' Àlex muttered, more to himself.

'You really miss nothing, do you, Sergent Albiol?' Riera commented. 'Despite your new-found calm.'

A darkened candle flickered somewhere inside Àlex.

'No, Doctor Riera, I don't. And one day this calm will go and you will make one comment too many. Make the most of it while you can.'

Àlex turned and walked out of the door of the examination room and began to walk along a shortening corridor.

—

Elisenda was sorely tempted to keep her foot on the accelerator and carry on driving. She was on the same road through the Pedret suburb that she and Àlex had driven along the previous evening, this time heading back in the direction of the coast.

'I want to see the sea,' she murmured to herself, impatient behind a slow-moving Mercedes. 'Only without the spikes and the skeletons.'

Instead, she turned left almost immediately after leaving the city centre on to the tree-lined road that ran parallel to the main route out of Girona. The building she was looking for stood out, the most elegant in a short staccato row of simple nineteenth-century houses, incongruous amid the functional render and aluminium of car repair shops and industrial glaziers. Parking in front of the austere gateposts either side of the entrance, she went in and showed her ID to the guy at the reception desk.

'I don't suppose Doctora Fradera is here?' she asked him.

He checked but doubted it. 'I saw her leave a short while ago. I don't think she's come back.' There was no answer on the internal phone and he shook his head.

'No worry,' Elisenda said. 'I'm interested in the records of an archaeological dig in 1980 to 1981. At El Crit.'

He thought for a moment and picked up the phone. 'I'll ask someone in Admin, see if they can put you on to the right person.'

After a few minutes, she was shown up to a room on the first floor. A slim woman in a snug blue dress and low heels that clopped on the tiled floor came up to greet her. Her hand hovered constantly near her nose, clutching a paper tissue.

'Gemma Cardoner,' she introduced herself. 'Don't come too close, I've got a streaming cold.'

'Hot whisky and honey,' Elisenda suggested.

'Does that work?'

'No, I just like the taste.'

Gemma laughed but burst immediately into a coughing fit. Out of guilt, Elisenda reached into her bag and handed her a small packet of tissues.

'The El Crit site,' Elisenda said, once the other woman's throat had calmed down. 'Do you have any records of the 1981 dig that I could look at?'

'I thought you'd be here about that. Everyone in the Archaeology Service has been talking about it since Doctora Fradera told us this morning.'

Oh good, Elisenda thought, but hardly surprising. 'How much has she told you?'

'Just about the body found there. A recent one, but done up to look like an Indiketa killing.'

'I see.' She preferred to say nothing more but registered the archaeologist's interpretation of it. 'So, would you still have the records of the 1981 dig here?'

Gemma nodded enthusiastically. 'Any records will be here in the new wing.' Elisenda had seen the low building with odd arrow-slit windows tacked on to the original house, forming a courtyard used as a car park. 'Not computerised, I'm afraid, and it might take me some time to dig them up, but I'd be more than happy to hunt them out.'

'Would there be any point in my looking for them?'

Gemma let out a small laugh. Elisenda worried she'd start coughing again. 'You'd never find them, I'm sorry. At the time of the dig, the municipal archaeology service would have been based in the Casa de Cultura, in the city centre, but we're now over two sites, this one and the museum itself. What we have will be here, at the Archaeology Service, but most of the material is boxed up. The files we keep here are pretty extensive. I can start trying to track them down this afternoon.'

'That would be very useful, thank you. How long do you think it might take?'

'I can't really say. I might be able to get something to you by tomorrow morning, but I can't really promise. I have a general idea where they'll be stored, but it'll still take some searching.'

'Thanks, I'd be really grateful.'

Elisenda left Gemma eagerly anticipating looking for the records and returned to her car for the drive back to Vista Alegre.

'Everyone wants to be a detective,' she muttered on the traffic-light crawl back into the city centre. 'Just try and make sure your cold keeps off till tomorrow.'

Montse and Josep had also driven through Pedret, but unlike Elisenda, they'd carried on the same road, Montse at the wheel for the half-hour's gently swooping drive to Palamós, where Senyor Ferran was waiting for them with his boat. Most of the journey had been in silence. His seat lowered as far as it would go, Josep had surreptitiously studied Montse's profile as much as he could. She had steadfastly concentrated on the road.

'Everything all right?' Montse had asked him.

'Just wondering what we'll find,' he'd replied.

From the busy fishing harbour in Palamós to the beach at El Crit, and then up the steep steps to the headland and the archaeological site, Caporal Fabra had accompanied them, making any further conversation impossible. Both relieved and frustrated by that, Josep wondered how Montse felt about it. Since Pau's death, he had no idea any more. He put that out of his mind as they walked through the pines and holm oaks framing the cleared area of the dig.

A man with a wide moustache and a small pointed tuft of hair on his chin, like an old-fashioned grandee in a black-and-white film, looked up, startled by their approach.

'Caporal Capdevila,' Josep introduced himself, showing the man his ID.

'Caporala Cornellà,' Montse gave her name.

The man in the trench appeared relieved. He got to his feet and directed himself at Josep rather than Montse, which annoyed Josep.

'You're here about the other skeleton,' the archaeologist guessed.

'Pardon me, your name is…?' Josep asked him.

'Doctor Llàtzer Bosch.'

'Doctora Fradera isn't here, I take it?' Josep asked.

'She's in Girona. I'm also a senior archaeologist on this project. How can I help you?'

'You seem nervous, Doctor Bosch,' Montse commented.

Bosch pointed down the gentle incline to the new trench, cordoned off with tape. 'Dead body found over there. I've already had the press here today. One or two ghouls as well. Wouldn't you be nervous?'

'You must be used to bodies.'

Bosch waved the trowel in his hand vaguely at the Indiketa skeleton in the trench he was in. 'I'm used to bodies like this. No matter how much respect I feel for them as people who once lived, they're still thousands of years old and far removed from today. I know where I stand. I'm not used to bodies like that one down there.'

'We understand you were with Doctora Fradera when she found the other body,' Josep continued.

The archaeologist shook his head. 'That's not entirely accurate. I was up here, working in this trench. The trench down there is Doctora Fradera's idea. She found the body and called me over.'

'Was this once she realised there was something wrong?'

'No. The first time was when she'd just discovered it. I think she felt the need to justify digging so far from the main site, so she showed me the body to try and prove her point.'

Josep and Montse didn't need to look at each other. Both knew the other had picked up on the barb in the archaeologist's words.

'The first time?' Montse questioned him.

'I went back to my own work. Then she called me over again when she found that the body wasn't what she thought it was.'

'And who alerted the Mossos about the discovery?'

'Doctora Fradera did. She went to phone. You can only get a signal down the path a way, near a house at the end of one of the tracks from the main road.'

'And you stayed by the other trench?'

'No. I've got work to do. I came back to this trench and carried on working. But no one came here. Look around, it's pretty isolated at this time of year.'

'You don't agree with the second trench, Doctor Bosch?' Josep asked him.

Bosch shook his head in irritation. 'As I say, look around you. What on earth is an important find like this doing with just two archaeologists? If you go off scratching around all over the place, of course no one's going to have any confidence in funding you.'

'Have there been any other archaeologists working on this site?'

'Couple of students last summer. Another one for a short time in the autumn. That's it.'

Josep thanked the archaeologist and asked if he was based in Girona.

'I work out of the Archaeology Service on Carrer Pedret, like Doctora Fradera, but I live in Palamós.'

On the drive back to Girona, Josep commented: 'Not a happy couple, are they? Fradera and Bosch?'

Montse stared at the road. 'No, they aren't, are they?'

'They don't communicate.'

'No.'

Montse dropped Josep off by Plaça Catalunya and took the car back to Vista Alegre. He watched the tail lights disappear over the bridge and turned away to walk down Plaça Pompeu Fabra as far as the modern bar on the corner opposite the Casa de Cultura. Ten minutes later, his girlfriend of one month walked in and kissed him.

'Hi,' she said, her smile warm.

'Hi.' His smile was less certain.

Chapter Eight

'You look dreadful, Eli.'

'So good to see you, too, Catalina.'

Elisenda stirred her large white *café amb llet* with one hand, taking a sip of water with the other. Enriqueta brought her and her sister another *xuixo* each, still warm from the morning's delivery, the confectioner's custard oozing richly out over their fingers already coated with oil from the sugared surface of the doughnut-like sweet. The owner stopped to fuss over Catalina.

'How long to go is it now?' she asked.

'Three more weeks yet.'

'And she'll be two weeks overdue,' Elisenda commented. 'I was. Our mother was. Now it's your go.'

'I only said you looked dreadful, Eli.'

'Big mistake.'

Elisenda recalled another night searching through her flat, pulled out of bed by the spectral sound of a lullaby floating in and out of her mind, teasing her from one room to the next. Another uneaten meal in the kitchen bin and another morning punishing herself running through the dust and stones outside the city walls. The one moment of happiness was now, meeting her younger sister for breakfast. She could see her sister wasn't satisfied with her answer.

'I'm OK, Catalina. I just didn't sleep too well.'

But even Elisenda had to admit that Catalina's long brown hair looked fine and glossy, whereas her own, worn equally long, had suddenly gone straggly. Her sister's dark eyes weren't underpinned by the bruised tiredness shadowing her own. Her face was slender where her own had become gaunt. She's eight months pregnant and she looks less wrung out than I do, Elisenda was shocked to realise.

The day's newspaper was on the next table over from them. Catalina had been reading it when Elisenda had turned up. She gestured to it now, affording her older sister some relief.

'That thing out on the coast is grisly, isn't it? We used to go to El Crit when we were kids. You still go sometimes, don't you? In the summer?'

'It's in the papers already.' Elisenda sighed. She picked the paper up and quickly scanned the story. The bare facts as they knew them, little more. 'It's my investigation. I'll be going back out there later today.'

'Is that right?' Catalina scanned her sister's face, her eyes red and puffy, her cheeks pinched. A thought occurred to her. 'Why don't you stay at the beach house? It's not far from El Crit. It's nearer than Girona, anyway. Stay there the nights you need to. It would be good to have someone there at this time of year.'

'Wouldn't Sergi mind?'

Catalina's plush holiday home overlooking the sea was one of Catalina's husband's greatest joys, the proof when he'd bought it that he'd made it.

'It's not his to mind. It's mine too. I'll bring you the keys later today. It'll do you good, Eli. You need to get away from Girona for a bit.'

Elisenda looked back at her sister. She could see the worry in her face and was alarmed for the first time.

'All right, Catalina, I'll do it. Thank you.'

After walking with her sister to the bus stop, Elisenda showered and dressed at home and went to Vista Alegre, where she was immediately waylaid by a request from Puigventós for her to go and see him. When she got to his office, he handed her a large pocket folder.

'Candidates,' he told her. 'For the new caporal in your unit.'

She looked at it, not wanting to open it to see inside.

'They're the top ten selection procedure passes for caporal,' he continued. 'Go through them and bring it down to a shortlist of five, which we'll discuss.'

'Right,' she replied. She took the folder back to her own room and put it away in a drawer without opening it. 'But just not now,' she muttered to her empty office.

Before she could do anything else, her mobile rang. It was Gemma Cardoner from the Archaeology Service, telling her she'd found the boxes with the records for the 1981 dig.

'That was quick,' Elisenda told her when she got to the Archaeology Service on Carrer Pedret.

Gemma led her into the new wing to where a large cardboard box was sitting on a table. 'It's like a mystery,' the young woman replied, her voice thicker with cold than the previous day. 'I love puzzles. I wouldn't have stayed away today for the world.'

'Well, thank you, but you really probably should go home now. You sound terrible.'

'It's the dust.' Gemma gestured to the store rooms beyond the anteroom where they were standing. 'It gets everywhere. Luckily, it was easy to find in the end. Everything's stored chronologically, so it only took me a few minutes yesterday to locate all the boxes and a quarter of an hour this morning to separate it.'

'Separate it?'

Gemma lifted the lid on the box. A stack of folders like the one Elisenda had just hidden away in a drawer came almost all the way to the top. 'These are the daybook of the dig and the written reports of the findings, along with forms and details about the project. Staff, timetables, funding, that sort of thing. All the artefacts that were found are in a couple of dozen other boxes, which I've put to one side in the store room. If you need to see them, let me know.'

Elisenda stared into the box for a moment, considering. Logically, anything removed from the dig would have been prior to the body being buried there. 'We shouldn't need to see the artefacts, I wouldn't have thought. It's the records of the dig itself that are important. Can I take this away?'

'Of course. You'll have to sign for them, but I've already got clearance.'

'Great. If I find we do need to look at any of the finds, I'll call you. Thanks again for your help.'

'I enjoyed it.'

'Now go home.'

Carrying the large cardboard box into Vista Alegre from the car park below ground, Elisenda ran into Mosso

Paredes walking along the corridor. He offered to help carry it for her.

'No, it's fine, thanks, Francesc. How are you getting on?' She'd first met Paredes at the time of the killings shocking the city the previous autumn.

'Getting the feel of Girona, thank you, Sotsinspectora.'

'I hear you went walking all over the city when you first got here.'

'Wanted to get to know my new home,' he told her. 'The good bits and the bad.'

From the tabs on his uniform, she could see that he was still at the rank of mosso. 'When are you due to take your caporal's exams?'

'Next year would be my first opportunity.'

'OK.' She studied him walk off and carried on her own way to her office. The other three were in the outer room, each working on a computer. She asked Montse and Josep for their impressions of the crime scene.

'There's no love lost between the two archaeologists,' Montse commented. 'Doctor Bosch, the one we spoke to, didn't seem to agree with Doctora Fradera's extending the area of the dig.'

'Did Doctora Fradera have anything to say to that?'

'She wasn't there,' Josep told her.

'She was at the post mortem,' Àlex explained. 'Riera invited her. For her expertise.'

Elisenda looked surprised. 'Unusual. What did their joint expertise find?'

Àlex told the other three members of the unit of the conclusions reached by the pathologist and the archaeologist at the previous afternoon's examination.

'And did Riera behave?' Elisenda asked him when he'd finished.

'Like a prick. Nothing new. Nothing I can't handle.'

'Good,' she replied, taking a surreptitious look at him. Therapy by Riera, she thought, having to restrain a laugh, instantly feeling alarmed by that, the same way Catalina's concerned look earlier had shocked her. She gathered herself quickly. 'OK. Initially, I don't see that either Fradera or Bosch would necessarily be involved in the killing, but we'll need to check them out. Bosch would be too young, I'd reckon, but Fradera would roughly be the right age.'

'But why she'd start digging precisely there if she had any involvement is doubtful,' Àlex argued.

'There's involvement and there's involvement. Was she specifically looking for our guy for some reason? We'll keep an open mind.'

'One thing struck me as odd,' Montse said. 'The distance to the new trench from the old one.'

'Fradera said that they now thought the site was more extensive than they'd initially presumed, but that had occurred to me too,' Elisenda agreed. 'Either Fradera was looking for the body, or she was genuinely wanting to extend the site and came across it by chance. That also raises the question of why the killer buried the body there. If it was at the same time as the archaeological dig, there would have been a lot of activity going on. Burying the body would have been risky, unless it was someone on the team who thought at that time that the dig wouldn't ever extend that far. First of all, we need to find out who was on the team working there in 1981, and we need to check up on missing persons from that time.'

She hefted the box she was holding. 'This might help with some of that. They're the records of the 1981 dig.'

Leaving the two caporals in the outer room, she asked Àlex to come with her into her room to start looking through the folders. They'd only been going for ten minutes, when Àlex suddenly exclaimed.

'Got it.' He showed a file to Elisenda. 'Personnel list. Names and dates of archaeologists and volunteers who worked on the dig between May 1980 and June 1981. Including addresses. This is exactly what we were after.'

Elisenda took a look at it. The list ran over two pages. 'Just over a year, then. Quite a few more people working on it than the one now, though.'

'Yeah, but only four full-time archaeologists on the project. The rest were students who worked on the site for short periods, mostly the two summers and Easter 1981.'

'We split them into the archaeologists and the students?' Elisenda suggested. 'Of the archaeologists, three were men. That narrows it down slightly.'

Àlex took the pages back and counted. 'And eleven male students.'

'The man in the trench could be either or neither, but I would say that there must be some connection with the dig. It's too much of a coincidence, otherwise, that someone should randomly choose that spot to bury a body killed in that way. Also, with this number of people working on it, say a quarter of them at any one time, there'd also have been a lot of activity. Someone from outside the dig would never have chosen that as the ideal spot to bury a secret.'

'They found an open trench and took advantage of it? That doesn't work, as the body would have been found during the dig, and the dig didn't extend that far then, anyway.'

Elisenda rummaged through the contents. 'We'll need to check the exact location of the trenches in the 1981 dig. We only have Doctora Fradera's perception for that.'

Àlex laughed wryly. 'Doctora Fradera's perception.'

They were startled by a knock on the door. Josep walked in, stooping his head instinctively but needlessly under the door frame. Montse followed him in.

'Newspaper from June 1981,' he announced. 'An Esteve Mascort went missing. An archaeologist from Girona.'

Àlex turned the list in his hand back to the front page. 'Esteve Mascort. Worked on the site from September 1980 to June 1981. We have our man in the trench.'

'Or the man who put him there,' Elisenda countered.

Chapter Nine

Elisenda drove along the dirt track through the woods. Caporal Fabra from Palafrugell had told her that the council had cleared most of the blockage away and the route was passable, but the road was still pitted with holes and crumbling in parts. Crossing a slippery patch of shale that sent the wheels spinning helplessly if she drove at anything above ten kilometres an hour, she now found the path gave way to a section where the grooves made by vehicle wheels had worn the track down so much she was having to fight to balance the car between the central ridge and the verge on the left-hand side.

'Next time I'm taking the boat,' she muttered.

She passed where the track had evidently been damaged by the storm and saw an uprooted tree dragged to the side, clean cuts made by a chainsaw through the slender trunk to be able to move it. The compacted earth of the repair to the surface was a different colour, lighter and with more loose gravel, its texture more mobile under the car until it settled. Large rocks had been stacked up to one side, ready she imagined to be taken away.

She hoped her meeting with Doctora Fradera would be quick so she could negotiate the return journey in daylight. Looking up, peering through the thick trees, she could see the light in the sky was already getting weaker.

There were no clouds, just a blue winter sky descending through the spectrum as the afternoon wore on. She knew the track, had taken it many times on hot summer's days, but the fading light and the changes since the storm had turned it from a road of familiar anticipation to one of snarling challenge.

She'd been reliably informed by someone at the Archaeology Service that the archaeologist would be here all day. After Josep's news of the missing archaeologist in 1981, she'd asked him to find out what he could of the other members of the team at the time.

'Many of these addresses will be out of date by now,' she'd told him. 'Find out where they are now. Arrange interviews with each of them.'

She'd got Àlex to chase up the students. 'That'll be harder as they seem to be more of a fluid population. In those days, students would have had to study archaeology in Barcelona, not Girona. You might find some of them are from Girona, working on the dig back home as a summer job, but others might be from Barcelona or elsewhere. It might take some tracking down.'

'If they were students at the time,' Àlex had pointed out, 'the addresses we have might be their parents'. It's possible the families are still there.'

Montse had been looking at the personnel list. 'It says here that Esteve Mascort lived here in Girona. In Sant Narcís.'

'Yes, I'd like you to check up on him. See if there's any family surviving. Wife, children, parents. This list doesn't give ages, so we've no idea what we're looking for.'

Elisenda felt a thud on the underside of the car, bringing her back to the moment. In the side mirror she saw a large stone tumble away into the trees.

'I'm definitely coming by boat next time,' she said, swearing. It was her own car she was using, not a pool one, as she'd be spending the night away. Catalina had dropped off the keys at Vista Alegre, which had decided Elisenda to sleep at her sister's beach house in La Fosca.

The track came to an end and she left her car in a small turning area cleared of trees and stones. Two other cars were parked there at an oblique angle to each other, a blue Seat and a silver Peugeot. She recorded both registration numbers just in case.

The walk to the headland overlooking El Crit was as she remembered it from cicada-serenaded summers, although now in February the sunlight searching through the pines wasn't the crystal white and cerulean of August but a thin shroud of cobalt deepening into an overwhelming Prussian blue. A light wind blew through the long fingers of the pine needles, which flexed softly at her as she passed.

The second car evidently belonged to Doctor Bosch, as both archaeologists were at the site when she emerged into the clearing. She introduced herself to Bosch and asked them if either of them had known anyone who had worked on the dig in 1980 or 1981.

It was Bosch who answered first, with a shake of his head. 'I was still at school then. I didn't know anyone.'

'And you, Doctora Fradera?'

'That was my first year at Barcelona University. I knew of some students in the years above me who worked here in the summer, but I didn't know them. As far as I know, no one in my year did.'

'And you didn't, even though it was close to home?'

'I helped out at the Ullastret settlement.' She gave a wry laugh. 'It was easier to get to.'

'Did either of you know of an archaeologist called Esteve Mascort?'

Both archaeologists shook their head. 'He's had nothing published that I know of,' Fradera replied. 'I don't know the name.'

'Did he work on the dig back then?' Bosch asked. He waved generally towards the second trench. 'Do you think that he's…?'

'We're looking at various possibilities at the moment,' Elisenda told them. 'Has the trench there been left undisturbed?'

She began walking in the direction of the cordoned-off area where the body was found, the two archaeologists tagging along with her. When they got there, they both looked carefully at it. Elisenda had asked for a pair of Mossos to be put on guard duty for the night, but Puigventós had vetoed it on budgetary grounds. And because he felt that the scene had been fully inspected and cleared. Elisenda still wasn't happy with that.

'No,' Fradera finally answered. 'It all looks as it was. Neither of us has touched it.'

Elisenda heard a very faint snort from Bosch. She looked at him but he had recomposed his expression.

'You have something to say?'

An unfriendly smile floated across Bosch's face. 'Only that I would be very unlikely to touch it. It's entirely Doctora Fradera's domain.'

'And I haven't set foot in it since yesterday,' Fradera rejoined.

All the while she listened, Elisenda scanned the trench, the imprint where the body lay curled up still visible.

'Can you tell me the significance of the spike? Is it punishment? Ritual?'

Again, Elisenda heard a low noise from Bosch as Fradera began to speak.

'That's something of a problem, Sotsinspectora Domènech. The more we find, the less of a pattern we can establish. It was once thought that they were ritual killings. That is possibly how the 1981 team might have construed them. But subsequent investigation has shown that the spikes were administered post mortem, with the head severed from the body.'

'They're trophies,' Bosch interrupted. He sounded irritated. 'Enemies killed in battle, their heads displayed.'

'Displayed?' Elisenda asked.

'The spikes are inserted through the front of the skull and they emerge at the base of the neck. We've found them near walls. We think they were hung there, nailed to the settlement walls as trophies.'

'We can't say that with any certainty,' Fradera objected. Bosch shook his head angrily. 'They might be trophies, they might be deterrents. Enemies in battle, possibly. But maybe also criminals. Their heads displayed as a warning to the people of the settlement.'

'They were a warrior people,' Bosch insisted. 'They fought a war against the Romans. These are trophies of enemy invaders.'

Fradera looked at Elisenda and sighed. 'And we now believe that there might be more to it still. Not a deterrent or a punishment, but a sign of veneration.'

'Listen to yourself, Mireia,' Bosch argued. 'A spike through the skull? Veneration? That is just not possible.'

Elisenda realised she was walking into an argument that had no end, so she began to head the two archaeologists away from the trench and back towards the centre of the dig. As she left, Fradera slipped her a card.

'I sometimes work at Ullastret. If you'd like to come and see me there one day, I could explain a bit more about what we think this ritual means.' She cast a glance over to Bosch, who was packing his tools away and putting a small number of bagged items in a box, ready to leave while it was still light enough. 'Without interruption.'

Elisenda thanked her and walked off through the trees. Looking back, she saw Fradera go to the furthest part of the trench from Bosch and start to examine something on the ground, already engrossed. Neither of them spoke.

Deciding not to wait for them, Elisenda set off inland towards the clearing where she'd left her car, regretting not having brought a torch. The wind had picked up and the needles on the trees pulled at her hair as she walked past, the dead ones on the ground curling under her feet. The sun had all but set in front of her, the dark coming in quiet waves from the sea behind her, forcing its way past, obscuring the path. Unwittingly, she quickened her pace when she heard a sound behind her. It caught her up.

She turned to see a face up against hers. She felt a hand on her shoulder.

'I forgot my torch,' Bosch told her, breathless from catching her up. 'Sorry if I startled you.'

Elisenda let her breath out in a long sigh. She moved to one side on the path and let the archaeologist walk alongside her. Her hands were shaking.

'I usually bring one,' he explained, 'but I left it in my car. Gets quite spooky, this walk in the evening. I normally try and leave earlier but we got a bit caught up, didn't we?'

'Does Doctora Fradera normally leave after you?' Elisenda could see her car up ahead in the gloom.

'She has very little concept of time. She's often leaving it until it's dark before she comes away. There's nothing I can say. But she doesn't appear to have the same irrational fears as the rest of us. Too scientific.'

Elisenda let him speak, suddenly aware that the discovery of the body in the second trench had frightened him.

'Irrational fears,' she agreed.

'One can only hope they stay irrational.'

'You were putting something in a box. Back at the dig.'

'Just a couple of finds from today. Shards of pottery. I leave them with Doctora Fradera and she takes them back with her to Girona to leave at the Archaeology Service.'

'You never leave any artefacts here?'

Elisenda heard rather than saw him shake his head. 'No way of keeping them safe. This is a more isolated site than most, but things can still go missing. Thieves sometimes target ongoing digs.'

'You couldn't put in a security guard overnight?'

He laughed. 'Budgets again. If we paid a security guard, there wouldn't be enough money left for more than one archaeologist to work here.'

Back at their cars, he offered to drive ahead as he knew the track better.

'Follow my lights. I've done this route so many times, I've found the easiest way through.'

Agreeing, she followed him and had to admit that the ride was far less bumpy and uncomfortable than going the other way had been.

'No one's ever entirely an arse,' she said to the night as Bosch led her to the main junction where the asphalt started. Waving, he accelerated away on the same road towards Palamós.

Turning off for La Fosca, to the north of the town, she drove through narrow streets equally as lonely as the path through the pines. Catalina's house was at the end of a pockmarked road, the surface torn by tree roots and verges fraying into the dust. Unable to use the remotely-controlled garage doors and get into the house on the landward side because the electricity was turned off, she parked at the foot of the steps to the side of the building. Taking an overnight bag and a bag of shopping out of the boot, she climbed the stone flight, which led to the path running in front of the house. It was one of four on a low and rambling headland overlooking the sea, fifty metres inland from the old coastguards' trail that now ran the length of the coast. She could hear the sea down below, see the phosphorescence on the small waves borne in by a more benevolent breeze than the one just a few coves to the north. A small path led through low palms and light gravel to the seaward door. Finding the right key, Elisenda opened the door and fumbled around in the hallway for the mains switch. Flicking it, she felt along the wall to the light switch and snapped it on.

Turning to face the room, she let out a gasp at the sight of a roomful of huge white figures below, beyond the three tiled steps into the living room, facing her, marching slowly in time towards where she stood.

El Crit, 1981

It was a ghost town.

The student had got off the coach in Palamós at Plaça Catalunya, near the seafront, but there'd been no one waiting there for him as planned. He hadn't been surprised. The coach had got in nearly two hours late.

He found a call box on a main road a short walk from the square, but there'd been no answer to the number on the letter. It was gone eight and all the shops away from the beach and the port were shut, but the cafés and restaurants were open. He could hear the sounds of life down by the sea, but he was hot and tired and his rucksack was heavy. Sweating in the hot evening air, he decided to walk. Checking a second letter in his bag, he went into a café to ask for directions. *The Birdy Song* was playing when he went in. Two small children, a boy and a girl, were frantically doing all the moves, their parents watching them indulgently. He was sick of it. It was the only song you'd heard all summer.

He told the waiter the address he was looking for, and the man, an old-school type baking in white shirt and black waistcoat, went out on to the pavement with him to show him the way. The student thanked him and set off along the main road, heading away from the sea, looking for the turnoff to the right that the waiter had described. He had *The Birdy Song* in his head, so he hunted out his Walkman and put Orquesta Mondragón back on, a feeling of relief when the frenetic chorus of *Caperucita Feroz* filled his mind.

It was when he found the road to the right that he was supposed to take that he stopped in his tracks. It was a ghost town. Used to Barcelona with its noise and movement, it was so odd to find himself just metres from cars and people and lights but engulfed in a bygone street of low buildings and village quiet.

He walked on as instructed and found the crossroads. To the left, the hospital, looking rundown and disused in the humid evening. To the right, the strange ground-floor turrets with eye-level gun slits of the Guardia Civil barracks. He walked past it on the opposite side of the road, the only other person in sight a single guard standing on duty at the gate midway along the block. Counting off the numbers, he found the house he wanted. On the same side as the Guardia Civil but another street over was a row of tiny houses, an incongruous village street in a thriving beach town.

'I thought you wouldn't be coming,' the elderly woman who opened the door to him said.

'The coach was late. And there was no one to meet me.'

'You'd better come in. I can warm your meal up.'

After he'd eaten, a plate of boiled Swiss chard in olive oil and garlic followed by grilled hake, he paid the woman the first month's rent.

'I'll be here until the end of September.'

The woman didn't have a phone in the house, so he walked down to the main road to ring again. She told him of a quicker route and it took him just a couple of minutes to get there, but there was still no reply.

Going back to the elderly woman's house, he went into the small living room at the front of the house to wish her goodnight.

'I live alone,' she told him. 'I've been a widow for nearly twenty years. I like the company and I can do with the money.'

So he stayed up with her for a time, watching an episode of *Cervantes* on a tinny-sounding black and white television in the corner of the room. When it finished, he went upstairs to the room he was renting and lay awake on the bed in the stifling heat until he finally found sleep.

Chapter Ten

After the first moment's shock, Elisenda doubled up with laughter, a release of tension, the first deep laugh she'd given for months.

Drying her eyes, she descended the three steps into the open living room and began removing the dust sheets from the army of furniture standing patiently in waiting. Carefully, knowing what was underneath, she pulled the cover from two huge terracotta vases either side of the short staircase, the rough surfaces of both stylishly held together by a straggling line of giant rusting staples. Then came two large bronze figurines on tall display tables. She examined the two statues, reproductions of Roman goddesses. Sergi's taste, not hers, she hoped not Catalina's.

Turning lights on as she went, she went through the living room, kitchen and the bedroom she was going to be using, folding the protective sheets and storing them in the hall cupboard. When she'd finished, she turned to look at the result. The expensively-tiled floor could do with a polish after months of the house being empty, but the room looked welcoming, despite the taste in statues. It was bigger than her whole apartment, with three large cream leather sofas to accommodate the summer's heat.

'That's going to be chilly now,' she said out loud.

They were arranged in a horseshoe around a wrought-iron and mahogany coffee table the size of a double bed. Elisenda knew the ornaments that would be placed on it when the house was in use were stored in another cupboard somewhere, as were many of the other trinkets from the half-empty shelves along one wall.

'They can stay there.'

There was an unused chill to the house. A fireplace was set into one wall in case Catalina and Sergi ever decided to use the place in the winter, which they rarely did, but there was plenty of wood and kindling stacked up to one side of it. Finding firelighters and matches in a kitchen drawer, Elisenda quickly had a fire going and stood warming herself in front of the warm radiance. Over the crackling of old logs, she could hear the sea outside the house, some fifteen metres below, the winter waves shushing in and out over smooth pebbles and sand. She found it soothing.

'Food,' she told the large room, which echoed back at her.

She'd brought some dried pasta, tomatoes, garlic and olive oil, and she made a bowl of macaroni in the splendid kitchen. Coming back into the living room, she glanced at the huge dining table near the French windows leading out on to a terrace, but decided it would be too lonely. Instead, she ate supper standing by the window at the front of the house, looking out through the dark at the sea, occasionally focusing on her blurred reflection in the costly double-glazed expanse. She felt strangely less lonely and exposed in this empty house with just the sea for company than she'd felt lately in her small flat in the centre of Girona surrounded by people and noise.

'Wonder if Sergi'd agree to a swap,' she asked herself, laughing momentarily at the thought before giving a deep sigh. 'Wonder if I would.'

She loaded the bowl and pots and pans in the dishwasher but realised she had no tablets for it, so she turned the lights out on it all and made up her bed with the bedclothes in the wardrobe, switching off all the lights in the house as she retreated through the rooms.

The alarm on her phone woke her the next morning. At first disoriented, she realised with a shock that that was simply because she'd slept through the night. She got up to open the shutters and then hopped back into bed for two minutes, gazing out at the sea in the distance. On the upper floor and at the front of the house, the bedroom had an unbroken view of the horizon. Two small fishing boats were anchored some distance out. She could see movement on each one, slow in the padded cold.

Stretching slowly and enjoying the sensation of having slept through the night, she suddenly lost the moment. She hadn't seen Lina in the dark. And she felt relaxed because of it, happier than she had done in years. But that immediately brought its attendant guilt flooding in and she quickly got out of bed and showered, unable to find tears in the scalding water coursing over her head and face.

Checking on everything, she took the back stairs down to the large double garage, which was at a lower level than the seaward side of the house. Stacked along one wall, she found two bright yellow sea kayaks. She'd forgotten about them. They were Sergi's fad of two years ago, used obsessively all that summer and left to gather dust the next. Checking her watch, she saw that she had two hours before she needed to be at Vista Alegre, so she carried one of the kayaks, along with all the accoutrements, outside the garage and along to the left of the house where the cliff dropped to the level of the sea and there was a path leading directly onto the beach.

She soon found her stride, the years of hateful jogging through the stones of Girona having kept her muscles strong, and she rowed north from La Fosca. Her punishment for a night's unbroken sleep. She glanced from time to time at the electric green and age-old grey of the shoreline swooping by to her left and saw that it was no punishment at all, so she quickened her pace, the sweat pouring from her head, soaking her face and neck. She could feel her T-shirt sticking to her shoulders.

Finding the rocks at the entrance to El Crit, she slowed and steered for the beach. A small boat was moored beyond the rocks. Scraping the bottom a couple of times, she managed to reach the beach, pulling the kayak up out of the water.

A man was watching her.

He was in his sixties and wiry, with greying hair riding back from his tanned forehead in tight waves and fibrous skin pulled taut over his cheek bones. He was wearing a wetsuit and must have swum from the small boat anchored a short way out.

'Good morning,' Elisenda called to him.

Without smiling, he grunted something back at her.

'Your boat?' she asked.

'Uh-huh.'

'I thought I'd be the only one out so early,' she persevered.

'Cleaning the beach,' he told her gruffly. In one hand, he was holding a spike from an underwater spear-gun, jabbing with it at a tangle of nylon netting on the beach until it caught. He showed her a sack with bits of plastic and ring-pulls in and scraped his trophy off into it. 'They get washed up here.'

She left him picking through the sand and stones and climbed the compacted earth steps up to the headland, walking the short distance to the dig. Neither of the archaeologists was there.

Moving quietly through the site, her feet in trainers no longer leaving wet prints, she looked first at the original trench, which stretched from east to west through most of the clearing. An extension to it ran off at a right angle to the north. She could see that all the bones of the Indiketa body had been removed. She'd seen Doctor Bosch placing the last of them the previous afternoon in tissue paper in a couple of boxes.

At the other end, where Doctora Fradera had been working, she saw a straight line of stones at the bottom of the trench, evidently once a wall. There were other darker stretches of earth that the archaeologist had obviously been working on, but she could see nothing to tell her of their significance. Crouching down, she saw something brightly-coloured emerging from the soil. She recognised it as a shard of pottery, its clean appearance incongruous amid all the brown dust. Not wishing to touch it, she thought it strange that Fradera wouldn't have boxed it up with other finds the previous evening.

From the beach, she heard a small engine start up. Hurrying to the headland, she saw the man she'd seen earlier, now back in his boat, slowly chug away, heading north towards the beaches of Palafrugell. The sound of the motor drifted in on the breeze, long after the boat had disappeared, but when the noise finally faded to nothing, a shock of silence overran the clearing. She went down to the newer trench. The trees were still, the light wind in the cove and on the headland somehow not falling again to the lower level further inland, where the forest was more dense. It was both numinous and unsettling, like an abandoned church.

She roamed the paths and trees around the settlement, trying to get a picture of it in 1981, to work out what might have happened, and where the original dig fitted in with all of it. Finishing, she left and made her way back to the house in La Fosca for a second shower and a quick breakfast before the drive into Girona. She turned the car radio on and felt more awake than she had in months.

'Any views on the list of candidates?' Puigventós called through to her when he arrived.

She looked at the closed drawer. 'Narrowing the field down,' she told him.

Going out into the main office, she saw Àlex working on a computer.

'Tracking down the students,' he explained. 'I'm focusing first on male students working on the dig in summer 1981. There were five, two addresses still valid and the parents still alive. I've called numbers for both. No reply at one, the mother at the other said her son was a teacher in Barcelona, so he's not our man, but I've got his details to interview him later.'

'Good work.' She felt sad for the first time that morning on hearing Àlex's voice. Like the way he worked now, the timbre was still the same, but it had been weakened, lost its edge. 'I wanted to ask you something, Àlex. You know Mosso Paredes, don't you? Any thoughts?'

Àlex looked frankly at her. 'You want him for the team. Yeah, he seems good, but he's only a mosso. I thought we were after a caporal.'

'We are. I'll have to see what I can do.'

At another desk, Montse put her phone down and looked at Elisenda.

'That was the wife of Esteve Mascort, the missing archaeologist. Widow,' Montse corrected herself. 'He was declared dead in 1991. She still lives at the same address in Sant Narcís.'

'Good. Have you made an appointment?'

'She didn't want to see us.'

Elisenda turned to face Montse.

'Is that right? Meet me with a pool car outside. She's not getting any choice in the matter.'

Chapter Eleven

Ferran Arbós had an agreement with his neighbours. He didn't make a noise before they set off for work at eight-thirty in the morning, and they didn't object when he ignored them or told their children to get lost when they came around selling raffle tickets to pay for the end-of-year school trip. They all shared a peaceful village between Palafrugell and Palamós that most outsiders only knew as some vague place that flashed by to the side of dual carriageway linking the two towns. Older drivers remembered it as somewhere inconvenient you had to slow down on the fast main road before the new one was built.

He lived on the edge of Vall-Llobrega furthest away from the noise of the traffic. It was why he'd moved there when he'd retired. The quiet, the gentle hush of narrow streets meandering gently through old village houses and smart new villas behind their stone walls and careful lawns, hidden from fast cars by tall and implanted palms and pines.

In fact, the noisiest part of the village was the room where Ferran Arbós sat now, quietly whistling an old Catalan sea shanty to himself about someone's grandfather who went to Cuba. Most of the villagers had gone to work, certainly the ones in the other modern houses on the one-sided street facing the low foothills of the Gavarres mountains in the distance. The others in the older houses were still here, working in the fields or at home, but far away enough not be disturbed by him.

In an airy room tacked on to the side of his house, well-lit and warm in the winter, baking in the summer were it not for the air conditioning, he looked at a piece of stone and considered it. A shape was forming in it. A hollowed-out circle, with a stylised sailing ship at its heart. He selected a round-headed chisel and struck it with the mallet in his hand, chipping at the surface of the round, smoothing it. With the noise of the stones spattering the floor and the effort of the short, sharp blows he was giving, he stopped whistling. Pausing to consider his work, he forgot what tune he'd been playing in his head. He found he did that a lot these days, since retirement, despite the surprising new turn his life had taken as a sculptor exhibiting in local galleries.

The usual hush between hammer blows was broken by another sound. He looked up, unsure of what he'd heard. It sounded like one of the doors in his house, one that he'd been meaning to oil for weeks. He'd probably forgotten to shut it, like so much else he forgot these days.

Putting his tools down, he wandered off to the room where the door was. It was closed. He turned and went back to his studio, tutting at himself for imagining things. Sitting down on his stool in front of the chunk of stone, he reached for the hammer and chisel, but they were nowhere to be found.

Looking around, he tutted at himself one last time in irritation, trying to remember where he'd put them.

Chapter Twelve

They went on a curious tour through a potted history of Girona's new town, crossing the river from Vista Alegre and following Carrer Emili Grahit to the end.

'I saw photos of Emili Grahit not so long ago,' Montse told Elisenda as they waited at the lights at the junction with Carretera Barcelona. 'It was all dirt, with trees down the middle. You could see cars pulled up between the trees, parked.'

Elisenda looked in the side mirror at the wide avenue teeming with cars and modern apartment blocks. 'I've seen those pictures too. They'd probably only be from about the same time as Esteve Mascort went missing.'

'Hard to believe now.'

Past the concrete railway bridge, they both entered a Girona that had changed in their recent lifetime when the high-speed train line had been brought into the city. Once a simple two-lane road, Passeig d'Olot was now a bustling central artery, with filters and junctions and traffic lights.

'Still lousy for traffic,' Elisenda commented.

They turned left on to Avinguda Sant Narcís, getting deeper into the suburb of the same name, where more of the city's history paraded by on either side of them. To the right, low terraced houses built in the early twentieth century, to the left, the taller apartment blocks of the 1960s and 1970s. The right painted white, the left in muddy pastels. As they drove further into the neighbourhood, the buildings on the right gave way to the more utilitarian apartments of the post–civil war period. The left was filled with new car parks and modern commercial and residential blocks, built in the last few years.

The street they wanted dated from yet another snapshot in time, when part of Sant Narcís was designated a garden suburb in the 1950s for the immigrant workers from southern Spain looking for jobs in Catalonia. Low whitewashed houses, some with the rarity of a garden, that had once been homes for the poor were now rather more upwardly mobile, even if they'd never become entirely fashionable.

'Number eighteen,' Montse said, looking for somewhere to park.

Standing outside a whitewashed house with a smart red-brick porch, she rang the bell. The door opened and a trim woman in her late fifties wearing a long chunky pullover over a tight black skirt answered.

'Senyora Eulàlia Esplugues?' Montse asked.

The woman sighed. 'I said I didn't want to see you.'

'Caporala Cornellà, we spoke on the phone. This is Sotsinspectora Domènech.'

The woman went to close the door. 'I've got nothing to say.'

'We believe your husband's body has been found,' Elisenda said before Eulàlia Esplugues shut it completely. 'He was murdered. We can interview you here or at the police station.'

The woman hesitated, a look of shock on her face. 'Murdered? I thought the bastard had just left me.'

Elisenda and Montse exchanged a glance as Eulàlia Esplugues invited them in. Crossing the small hall into the kitchen to the right of the front door, Elisenda saw that little of the original interior of the house remained. The left-hand side was designer-rustic open plan, with La Bisbal tiled floors and a large open fireplace in the corner of the room, next to sliding glass doors leading out on to a terrace and a small garden beyond. In the past, the lounge would have been divided into two tiny rooms. Ahead, a pared-down blond wood staircase with no banisters rose steeply to a semi-landing under a high window. It wasn't a long drop to the floor, but it gave a dizzying feel. The whole of the downstairs was painted a dazzling white.

Esplugues led them into the kitchen, which occupied the whole of the right-hand side of the ground floor and was dominated by a huge central fireplace, open either end. Rows of pipes ran under the grate, supplying hot water and heating to the rest of the house, Elisenda presumed. Wood and kindling were arranged in the hearth, but no fire lit. The woman showed them to a table and put a smoke-blackened aluminium *cafetera* on a modern stove at the far end of the room. She was obviously calming herself after the news. Elisenda signalled to Montse, who carried on making the coffee, and invited Esplugues to sit down.

'I appreciate this is a shock, even after all this time,' Elisenda told her, 'but we need to ask you some questions.'

Esplugues gathered herself. 'Not really a shock. I never thought I'd see him again. I hoped I'd never see him again. But I didn't think he was dead.'

'Hoped?'

She let out a small laugh, filled with bitterness. 'He was a complete bastard. A womanising, self-centred, philandering piece of shit who made sure I never had enough money to do anything.'

Her vehemence took Elisenda by surprise. 'But you were still married when he went missing?'

'Only because there was no divorce at that time. If there had been, I'd have divorced the bastard within a year of marrying him. Your only recourse in those days was legal separation, and believe me, that was firmly stacked against the woman. Or get the church to have the marriage annulled, which would have meant that my son would have been regarded as illegitimate. I wasn't going to allow that.'

Montse brought a tray with the coffees over and set it down on the table.

'So his disappearance must have been a great relief,' she commented, taking a seat.

'Not really. The exact opposite, in fact. I was counting down the days. The divorce law was about to be passed and was supposed to be coming into effect that year, 1981. In the end, I could have filed proceedings in the August, and we'd have been divorced by the following summer. As it was, I had to wait ten years before I could declare him dead. All the time, worrying he was going to come back, unable to get married again.'

'Do you know of anyone who would have wanted him dead?' Elisenda continued.

'Me for one.'

'Should you have a lawyer present, Senyora Esplugues?'

She looked shocked but waved the suggestion away. 'Why? I don't need one. It's just a thing you say. I sometimes felt I could happily have strangled him because he made my life such a misery, but I would never have done anything. Least of all with the possibility of divorce just around the corner. If you're looking for people who would have wished him harm, I've no doubt there were plenty of husbands around at the time who could cheerfully have seen him dead. Maybe some other poor woman or two who'd also believed his lies.'

'Do you know of anyone in particular?' Montse asked.

She shook her head sharply. 'I never wanted to know. I didn't want to have to see someone in the street or in a shop who I knew was laughing at me. This is Girona we live in.'

'Does your son live in Girona?' Elisenda wanted to know. 'We still need to identify the body we've found to make sure it is your husband, although everything points to it being him.'

'Why would you want to see my son? I don't see how he could help.'

'DNA. We'd like to take a swab from him to match it with the body. That way we'll know for certain that it is your husband.'

Esplugues stared at Elisenda for a while, seeming to be wrestling with something. Elisenda kept quiet, not wanting to put her off saying whatever it was she had to say. Eventually, the woman gave a little laugh, more ironic this time.

'You can take a DNA sample if you want, but it won't do you any good. He's not my husband's son.'

Elisenda and Montse looked at each other.

'Two could play the little games my husband delighted in. And before you ask, the real father died some years

84

ago, of a heart attack. We were never together. He was married too.'

'Right,' Elisenda said slowly, digesting what she was hearing. 'Do you know of any of your husband's living relatives we could test?'

'His father's still alive. He lives in a home.'

'His mother?' Montse asked, writing down the name of the nursing home.

'She died just a few years after my husband went missing.'

'Do you still have any photos of your husband?'

'Do I look like I would?'

Elisenda thanked the woman and got up to leave, after first asking Montse with a glance if she had any further questions. The caporala gave a slight shake of her head and they allowed Esplugues to show them to the door.

'I'd really like my son to be kept out of this,' she told them quietly. 'He doesn't know about his real father.'

Elisenda nodded, considering. 'I'm sure there's no need for it to come out.'

She and Montse walked back to the car in silence and got in.

'Girona back then sounds quite a soap opera,' Montse commented.

Elisenda laughed wryly but sat deep in thought.

'Did you notice one thing she didn't ask? She didn't seem curious about where her husband was found. Or how he died.'

Chapter Thirteen

'We're going to have to organise getting a DNA sample from Mascort's father,' Elisenda told Montse in the car on the way back to the station. 'But to do that, we first have to tell him we believe we've found his son. It's going to have to be done very delicately.'

'I'm OK to do it, Sotsinspectora.'

Montse waited like a runner on the blocks to cross the Onyar back to the east side. Drumming her fingers lightly on the wheel, she took the first half-opportunity in the flow of cars to accelerate quickly into the fray of the large Plaça dels Països Catalans roundabout.

Elisenda studied her. 'OK. Take Josep with you.'

She watched Montse consider her answer as she waited impatiently at the next set of lights. 'I'll need to take someone from Científica with me to take the swab. I think any more than two of us would be too much for the father if he's elderly.'

Elisenda had to agree. 'OK. Arrange it with the nursing home. If they have any objections to us taking a swab from the father, let me know and we'll get an order from Jutge Rigau.'

Montse snatched a glance at Elisenda and laughed. 'A judge?'

'Seriously,' Elisenda told her. 'He actually seems keen on letting us do our job. We also need to take a close look at Eulàlia Esplugues, see how much water her story holds. We should also check up on her son's real father. See what he was doing in 1981.'

Back at Vista Alegre, Elisenda left Montse to park the car and went to the Serious Crime Unit office. Josep was in front of his computer.

'I've found the woman and one of the men from the 1981 dig,' he told her the moment she walked in. 'The man lives in Barcelona and is retired. He left the project in February 1981, but he might still be of interest. The woman was there until the dig was wound up. She's one of the curators at the City History Museum here in Girona.'

'Good news. Arrange times to visit them with Àlex. Don't let them know we're going to be paying a call on them.'

Her phone rang and she held a hand up to Josep in apology.

'*Elisenda*,' the person at the other end said. '*Pere Rigau.*'

She was about to comment on talking about him only a moment ago, but a note in his voice told her not to.

'*There's something I think you need to see.*'

She listened in silence as he spoke.

'I'll be with you in about thirty minutes,' she finally said, hanging up.

Montse appeared along the corridor, and Elisenda was on the point of telling her to get the pool car back out, but another thought occurred to her.

'Josep, have you seen Àlex?'

'He's having a coffee.'

Elisenda called his number and he answered immediately, telling her he was just walking into the building.

'Jutge Rigau has just called,' she explained to the three other members of her team when Àlex arrived a few moments later. 'I get the feeling our case is about to be taken up a notch, so I think we should all see what Jutge Rigau has just told me about. Anything you have pending with the Mascort investigation, put on hold until we get back.'

She told them more of what the judge had said on the phone as they drove along the same road leading northwest towards the coast that she'd got used to taking the last few days.

'It looks like the victim was staged,' she ended.

None of the others spoke.

'Vall-Llobrega,' Josep read on the sign as Montse raced down through the gears to come off the dual carriageway. 'I don't think I've ever stopped here.'

'No real reason to,' Montse replied, glancing at him next to her in the front seat and quickly looking back to the road.

They cruised past narrow old village houses into a street of modern, moneyed villas, where a blue, red and white Seguretat Ciutadana car was blocking one side of the road, a mosso on duty controlling who went in and out. It was Caporal Fabra from Palafrugell. He called them through.

'Bad business, this,' he told them.

Another patrol car and a Científica van were parked outside a house, a second mosso at the gate. A small throng of elderly ladies in nylon housecoats and whiskery men in wrinkled jackets and allotment trousers stared at the house without expression, stepping aside grudgingly to let Elisenda and her team walk past.

Jutge Rigau was waiting for them in the garden, pacing slowly by a squat olive tree reaching up from of a bed of dust and coarse gravel. Sergent Poch from the Local Investigation Unit in La Bisbal was with him. Both were wearing forensic whites, unzipped and with the hoods down, their masks hanging around their necks. A third man, also in whites, was sitting on the edge of a large flower tub filled with weeds, his body rocking rhythmically back and forth, his eyes closed.

'Thanks for coming, Elisenda,' Rigau told her. He looked pale.

Elisenda introduced the judge and Poch to the others in her team. They'd already met Àlex, who stood apart from the small group, staring at the front door into the house. A white-suited Científica came out of the building, looking at the screen on his camera, clicking through the images. He looked up and saw the newcomers, but turned and went back inside without a word.

Rigau introduced the man sitting a short distance away as Joan Culell, the court secretary. Culell looked over and nodded his head in greeting but didn't get up.

Elisenda asked if the forensic doctor was here.

'Inside,' Rigau told her. 'Riera.'

'You'd better follow us,' Poch told them.

Elisenda and her team pulled on their white overalls and blue gloves and drew a deep breath before entering. A path had been marked through the hallway and along a corridor where they could walk. Elisenda had barely enough time to register the surroundings. Old but good quality rustic furniture with some antiques that looked to be genuine and books and papers stacked untidily on shelves. Clean but not necessarily cared for.

They passed a living room where a uniformed mossa was comforting a middle-aged woman in a housecoat and carpet slippers who was sobbing uncontrollably onto her shoulder.

'The cleaner,' Poch explained in a whisper. 'She found him. He lived alone and she comes in once a week.'

'I'll want to talk to her after,' Elisenda told him.

The sergent from La Bisbal nodded and showed them in through an open door into a room that looked like it had been added to the house at a later date.

'A studio,' Poch told them. 'He was a sculptor.'

A shocked gasp rolled in a wave from the mouths of Elisenda and her team as they entered the studio, Elisenda in the lead, Àlex at the rear.

'His name was Ferran Arbós,' Jutge Rigau told them. He looked at the notes on his tablet to tell them. Elisenda guessed it was to avoid having to see the scene that lay out in front of them. She could scarcely blame him. 'He was a sculptor, exhibited locally with some success.'

Without taking her eyes off the man standing falsely opposite them, Elisenda asked him if there was anything to connect the man with the archaeological dig at El Crit.

'Nothing specific that we know of. But he took up sculpting after he retired. Before that, he was a curator. It appears he worked for various museums, including projects relating to Iberian sites.'

Elisenda nodded slowly, all the time studying the man.

He was pinned to the wall.

Between a metal shelf cluttered with tools and old pots and a cork board with faded photographs and newspaper cuttings, Ferran Arbós was held heavily on the tips of his feet, staring emptily at his viewers in one last exhibition.

'It's his own chisel,' one of the Científica told them.

Mirroring the round pin through the skull of the first body at El Crit and the mattock through the second, the head of the wooden end of a chisel was jutting from the forehead of an elderly man. The other end was embedded in the wall, securing him in place. It was supporting the entire weight of his body, holding him unnaturally on his feet, his arms hanging limply at his sides, his head tilted slightly forward as though he'd simply nodded off to sleep.

'Display,' Elisenda murmured.

His features were hidden by a torrent of blood that had flowed down his face and chest and legs to a pool that was drying on the floor at his feet. Pieces of stone from a sculpture he'd evidently been working on glinted like teeth in the congealed mess. His eyes remained open behind a frail curtain of crimson tassels hanging from his brows.

'So what was your crime?' Elisenda asked out loud to the dead man before she could stop herself. She looked at Josep and Montse and knew they were also seeing the awful crimes they'd witnessed the autumn before.

Glancing over to Àlex, she saw him slowly clench his fists, a nerve in his cheek flickering with nascent rage. It was the one sign of good in a room stolen by evil.

Chapter Fourteen

'Jutge Rigau insists that you lead the investigation.'

'So do I,' Elisenda told Puigventós.

'Is your team ready for it, Elisenda? I have my reservations.'

'We're more than ready to take it on, Xavier. We need it so we can heal.'

After a show of reluctance, the inspector finally agreed to the Serious Crime Unit taking the investigation. The two murders committed over thirty years apart were too obviously connected for him not to.

'You will come under a lot of scrutiny, you realise,' he warned her.

'As I say, I think that's what we need.'

Elisenda had gone to see Puigventós the moment she and her unit arrived back at Vista Alegre. The judge had consented to the body being removed long before Riera and the Científica had finished their examination of the scene and had returned to La Bisbal, evidently to start the wheels in motion for Elisenda's team to be given the investigation.

Elisenda had spoken to the cleaner but got little out of her. Arbós had no visitors and kept very much to himself.

'He wasn't popular in the village but he was always decent to me,' the woman had told her. 'He always paid on time.'

'Was there anyone in the village who wished him harm?' Elisenda had asked her.

'Not like this.'

Elisenda was inclined to agree. To her, it was more obviously linked to the victim having some sort of connection to the El Crit dig, but she knew they had to question the neighbours to cover all angles.

She rose now to leave Puigventós' room, but he had one last parting shot.

'The candidates. Have you decided on the shortlist?'

'Getting there.'

'Well, please get there sooner, Elisenda. The panel interviews are scheduled for next week. We have an inspectora from Barcelona coming. Please don't make me waste her time. In light of the situation and experimental nature of your unit, the procedure has been adapted to suit you enough as it is. Don't do anything to make me have to change that.'

'I'll try not to, Xavier.'

Back with her own team, she wanted to talk to them about how the new investigation was going to tie in with the cold case.

'They're obviously connected until we prove to ourselves otherwise,' she began. 'In that case, I want us all to work simultaneously on both killings so we have a clear picture of the parallels that we find. Josep's already tracked down two of the archaeologists from the 1981 dig, so he and I will interview the guy in Barcelona. Montse and Àlex will see the woman here in Girona. Besides that,

Josep will carry on looking for the other two archaeologists from the 1981 team and Àlex will continue to chase up the students who worked on the dig in 1980 and 1981. Montse, you keep looking into Esteve Mascort, check up on the wife, get the DNA swab from the father.'

'Shouldn't we be focusing on the Arbós murder?' Àlex asked.

'We are. But I have the feeling that they are so intertwined that we need to solve the past to solve the present. And vice versa.'

'The past again,' Àlex muttered, voicing all their thoughts.

'As for the present case, Àlex, I want you to look into the victim. Find out everything you can about his work as a curator. I think that's where we're going to find the connection with the 1981 victim. I'd say we can assume the first victim is Mascort, although we still need to keep an open mind on that until it's confirmed, so we should be looking for any connections between him and Arbós. And any links between Arbós and anyone involved in the 1981 dig. We also need to question Ferran Arbós's neighbours. I don't think we'll find our answer there, but someone might have seen or heard something.'

'Do we think Arbós is responsible for Mascort's murder?' Àlex asked. 'And this is revenge?'

'It's the same doubt as with the Indiketa skulls,' Elisenda said, nodding. 'Is this display or deterrent? If it's display, Arbós's killer somehow knows or suspects that Arbós killed Mascort and is exacting revenge, like-for-like. And if it's deterrent, Mascort's killer is still alive and is sending out a warning through Arbós to anyone else who may have been around in 1981 about what could happen to them if they speak out.'

'One killer or two, in other words,' Àlex commented.

'Why wait over thirty years?' Josep wanted to know.

'Because Mascort's body has been found,' Elisenda suggested. 'And the killer is now covering tracks they never thought they'd have to cover. Anyway, it's all good supposition. Initially, we'll work on the basis that it could be one of those, and we'll narrow it down as we learn more.'

She watched them all get up to leave the room once they'd all been allocated their jobs and her eyes went to the tightly-closed drawer where the candidates' applications remained unread. She really didn't want to have to look at them now, not when her team were more united and motivated than they had been at any time since Pau's death. For a fleeting moment, she missed his unique blend of logic and imagination. She was seeing more and more how, in the team as it stood, Josep was taking on a large part of the organisation and doing it well and Montse's ability to see less obvious paths was increasingly coming out. And Àlex. Àlex was a wounded version of himself, his passion and sharp mind numbed by what had happened to him, but she could see the wounds beginning to heal.

'It's your job to make sure they all mend fully,' she told herself.

More than ever, she didn't want a new member of the team to disturb the fragile balance of that process.

—

Unknown to her, Montse had one of Elisenda's moments when she couldn't face going home. Still living with her parents, given the difficulty of getting a mortgage these days, she'd left the nursing home where Esteve Mascort's father was cared for in need of some time to herself. Returning the pool car to Vista Alegre, she'd walked along the river in the evening gloom to +Cub, at the start of Carrer Albereda, where she sat at a table with her back to the window onto the small square, one of the bar's special gin and tonics with herb-infused ice cubes in front of her.

'His hearing is poor,' the nurse at the home had warned her. She and the mosso from Científica who'd come with Montse to take the sample had accompanied the man in light blue uniform and clogs along a hushed and institutional corridor. 'You'll have to speak up.'

The nurse had left them in Esteve Mascort's father's room, where Montse had sat down on a chair she'd pulled up in front of the father.

'Senyor Mascort,' she said, repeating her name to him three times, each one increasingly louder.

He'd looked at her, a smile on his face, trusting.

The hardest part was having to tell him in a raised voice, shorn of dignity or compassion, that they believed that they might have found his son.

'I'm afraid he's dead,' she'd repeated a fourth time, having to shout to get through to the frail man in cotton pyjamas buttoned to the throat.

His face had folded. Tears formed in his eyes and quickly began to stream down his cheeks. He crumpled further into the well-worn high-winged chair, his clenched hands shaking in his thin lap in grief.

'He was all I had left,' the old man said, his voice failing on every word.

Montse had leaned forward in her chair and held him, his face against her neck, the bones of his shoulders frail in her arms.

The nurse had returned when they took the DNA sample, to witness that it was done with the elderly man's consent. The Científica officer quickly took the swab from inside Senyor Mascort's cheek, who barely moved or reacted while he was doing it, and nodded to Montse that he was done.

'Thank you, Senyor Mascort,' Montse had said, although he didn't hear her, his eyes focused on the darkened window in front of him.

With the lights from the square casting her shadow over the table, she took a long sip of her gin and tonic, the herbs both soothing and stimulating. She wondered, not for the first time, whether to try and find a flat to share, not out in the Santa Eugènia suburb where she'd grown up but in the city centre. And not with other cops, but with people with whom she could switch off and talk running and cooking and the trivia of everyday nonsense rather than the minutiae of loss and evil.

She only noticed the guy at the next table when he spoke to her. Good-looking in a cleansed and moisturised sort of a way, he wasn't her usual type, if there was such a thing. He asked if she wanted another drink and what she did. She lied on both counts, saying yes to a drink and to working in an office. When he asked her if she wanted to go for dinner, she sighed and reached for her coat.

'Maybe another time,' she told him.

–

Five minutes' walk away, Josep sat in the same bar as the previous evening and waited for his girlfriend. He had reacted less at the time than the others to the scene in Vall-Llobrega but it had not left his memory for one moment since seeing it. Nursing a small beer at the bar, he sat hunched more than was usual even for him, his long legs crossed over on the stool, cramped against the counter, his shoulders pulled in, trying to take up as little space as he could.

'Hi,' his girlfriend said, cooler this time, her eyes searching his.

'Hi.'

'Do you want to go for dinner?'

He sighed. 'Do you mind if we don't? It's been a hard day.'

'Isn't that what I'm here for?'

He looked at his glass and give a single shake of his head. Neither of them knew what it meant.

–

'They're asleep, Àlex.'

'I didn't see them this morning.'

Carme, Àlex's wife, sighed and got up from the sofa. She'd got used to the change in the sound of her husband but still couldn't get used to him staying in every evening. She could tell that his voice was slowly returning to normal, the trauma to his neck and vocal chords recovering with time, but she fervently hoped the same would hold true for his mind. For the time being, she'd lost the confident, knowing man who had always driven her up the wall and excited and fascinated her in equal measure.

'I'll come with you,' he told her, following her along the corridor to their sons' bedrooms.

Mateu, the six-year-old, was awake, sneakily reading a comic under the bedclothes.

'You are so like your father,' Carme teased him sadly.

Àlex went to the next room to wake up Jordi, who was just four and lying legs akimbo on the bed, trusting the world.

'Am I allowed to stay up, papa?' Jordi asked him.

'It's an order,' Àlex told him, hugging him close.

Back on one of the armchairs in the living room, Carme sipped at her glass of Rioja and half-watched a programme on TV where a dozen or so people sat around a table and talked about something that appeared to matter to them. Out of the corner of her eye, she studied Àlex playing on the sofa with the two boys, holding them close to him in mock-fight. Her sons could barely keep their eyes open.

–

'Not yet,' Elisenda told herself, looking up at her darkened building reaching into the Girona night.

Instead, she went in through the glass door that led into La Terra, a gentle lively hubbub of a Thursday night in February. Rosa, the young woman behind the bar, smiled at her and pointed to a bottle of red wine. Elisenda nodded and looked for a seat. The tile and cushion benches in the window were all taken, so she sat at a cast iron and marble table under the big mirror. From where she sat, she could still make out her touchstone of the lights on the other side of the river and a steady flow of people strolling over the footbridge.

Looking around her, she saw two people she'd been to school with, so she picked up a newspaper lying on a chair nearby and opened it at random in front of her to fend off company. They saw her and waved, but didn't come over. She wondered when she'd long for them or people like them to come and talk to her.

The rest of the Thursday-night crowd were younger, students or twenty-somethings, earnestly but ineffectually changing the world the way she had when she was their age. Except the world had changed, was constantly changing around us. She was reminded of the old Lluis Llach protest song at the time of Franco, *L'Estaca*, where we were all tied to a stake hammered into the ground, but if you pulled a little on your side and I pulled a little on my side, then one day the stake would fall and we'd be free. Glumly, she felt that all that ever really changed was the nature of the stake.

'Didn't his head cave in?'

She perked up when she heard a teenage girl's voice ask the question on the table next to her. The boy she was with replied.

'No, he had like this brain and everything.'

They were discussing a comic the boy had read. Elisenda couldn't help smiling. They were only about seven or eight years older than her own daughter would be now.

Taking one last sip of her glass of wine, she paid and climbed the stairs to her apartment. Once inside, with the door closed behind her, she heard a child's voice singing.

'Lina, please,' she whispered to the emptiness. 'Grow up.'

Chapter Fifteen

'Zero tolerance for minor offences,' Puigventós avowed at the morning meeting with Elisenda and Micaló. 'I've spoken to the head of the Policia Municipal and he's in agreement with me on this, pledging to clamp down on driving offences in the city.'

Micaló nodded his head vigorously. 'I've set my unit targets in terms of petty crimes. We made four arrests yesterday, one for littering and three for anti-social behaviour.'

And my team is investigating the murders of two men who were impaled on spikes through the head, Elisenda thought wryly to herself.

'Is there any way we could institute on-the-spot fines for these offences, Xavier?' Micaló continued.

'What are your thoughts, Elisenda?' Puigventós asked her.

'Probably a good idea,' she finally told him. And it probably was, she had to admit. The problem was she was struggling with a question of scale. 'Yes, I believe we do have to nip minor issues in the bud to prevent greater ills in the future.'

'I'm glad we all agree.'

The meeting over, Elisenda went to her office to call Jutge Rigau to tell him the leads in the investigation as she saw them.

'*You're running the two cases parallel to each other?*' the judge considered. '*That would make sense. I would want you to focus on suspects capable of committing both murders.*'

'That's one of the avenues. It would put our killer at the age of at least mid-fifties now. The other option is for two killers, the second exacting revenge for the first murder now it's come to light.'

'*Which would probably still put them in the same age range. Keep me in the loop, and let me know what warrants you're going to need. I'll tell you what I need as I need it.*'

Elisenda thought of her constant battles with the fetish Jutgessa Roca in Girona had for petty bureaucracy and form for form's sake.

'You wouldn't consider moving to Girona, would you, Pere? I'm sure you'd be happy here.'

'*Is that an improper proposition, Sotsinspectora Domènech?*'

'Entirely honourable. I'm attracted solely to your willingness to sign endless bits of paper.'

He laughed and they rang off.

Elisenda thought for a moment and called Àlex into her office as she gathered her bag together.

'Josep and I are off to Barcelona soon,' she told him, 'but something the judge has said has reminded me. If one of our alternatives is that the Arbós murder is revenge for the Mascort murder, we need to question Eulàlia Esplugues' son. Find out if he might be someone that would interest us.'

'I'll get on to that. I've started looking for links between Mascort and Arbós, but nothing's come up yet.'

Elisenda explained the situation of Mascort not being the father. 'The son doesn't know, so you'll need to tread carefully for the time being. It will only have to come out by our doing if it becomes necessary for the investigation.'

Josep knocked and came in.

'Ready for the big city?' Elisenda asked him, standing up.

'I've found the second man,' he told her. 'He's also in Barcelona, at the central university. I thought we could see them both today.'

'Good news. Well done, Josep.'

'If you're going to Barcelona,' Àlex said, 'there are two of the students from the 1981 dig we could do with interviewing if you have time. It would save another trip. One of them's also at the central university, the other teaches in a secondary school. They were both there in June 1981 according to the personnel list.'

Elisenda read through all the notes in the car as Josep drove fast along the motorway south towards Barcelona.

'We'll try the retired man first,' Elisenda decided, looking at his name. 'Ricard Soler. Formerly an archaeologist with Barcelona provincial council. He was in his mid-thirties in 1981, he's seventy-odd now.' She looked up thoughtfully. 'Would that make him too old to have committed the Arbós killing? It would have taken quite a blow to penetrate the skull and pin him to a wall.'

'Or several smaller blows,' Josep offered, overtaking a string of lorries. 'If the victim was already subdued in some way. Or if someone else was holding them down.'

'Two people? We'll know more when Riera does the post mortem.'

The pathologist had scheduled the examination for Monday.

'Then we'll go to the university. See the second archaeologist, Jordi Canudas, late-twenties then, so getting on for sixty now. And we can see Àlex's student at the same time. After that, the other student at their school.' She let the folders drop into her lap. 'So nice to get away from it all, don't you find, Josep?'

Her caporal had to glance sideways at her to make sure she wasn't being serious.

Eventually, the motorway bled slowly into the ring road around Barcelona, the traffic dropping in speed to a grudging and fractured flow. Josep jockeyed for position to cut across the three lanes to take the inland section of the road, hugging the hills to the north and west of the city, until they found the junction they wanted, leading down into the Sant Gervasi district and the Parc del Putget.

'I used to come here when I was a student,' Elisenda told Josep. She'd enjoyed the hilly green park above the smog with a view of the Mediterranean in the distance. The temperature in summer was usually a degree or two lower than it was in the city centre, the breeze blowing the humidity away. 'I even lived here for a short time.'

'Very posh,' he said, with a rare smile.

'You're from Hospitalet. Anywhere's posh.'

'True,' he admitted, shrugging his shoulders.

They parked after a couple of turns of the block and found the building they were after, a typical brick and render 1960s low-rise apartment block on a steep road running down in the direction of the sea. There was no answer on the entryphone downstairs, so they rang a couple of the other apartments until someone pressed the buzzer to let them in. Josep checked the battery of post boxes on the wall to the right of the street door.

'Ricard Soler,' he read to confirm. 'Second floor, second flat.'

He peered through the dusty plastic window at the bottom of the box and saw that there was mail waiting to be collected, more than in the others.

'Looking at the other boxes,' he told Elisenda, 'it seems like today's post hasn't come yet. But there's mail in Ricard Soler's. Probably a day or two's worth.'

They climbed up to the second floor, but there was no reply when they rang the bell. Elisenda tried the other apartment on the landing and eventually heard footsteps approaching the door from the inside. A young guy opened, wearing jogging trousers and a thick pullover, fashionably thick-rimmed glasses holding his floppy hair in place behind his ears. She showed him her ID.

'Your neighbour,' she asked him. 'Do you know if he's away?'

'Um, yeah. Night before last. Wednesday.'

'Any idea where he was going?'

'No. I was coming back up the stairs at about six o'clock. I work from home and I'd had to go out to get some printer ink. He was just coming out with a suitcase. Said he was going away for a few days.'

'Did he seem agitated in any way? Was there anything different about him?'

The man considered for a moment. 'No, not really. It was a bit unusual, I suppose. I'd been talking to him over the weekend and he hadn't mentioned anything about going away. He's retired, he doesn't really do anything out of his routine.'

Elisenda gave the man her card and asked him to call her if his neighbour returned home.

'He's not in any trouble, is he?'

'We just want to talk to him, that's all.'

From Sant Gervasi, Josep drove down into the city centre, crossing Gran Via and immersing them in the twisting one-way system of the old Raval district, once a run-down part of town, now home to the contemporary art museum and yet more young men and women in thick-rimmed glasses.

'Is Ricard Soler running scared?' Elisenda had asked Josep as they drove.

The story of the body being found at El Crit had appeared on the TV news on Tuesday and come out in Wednesday's newspapers. There hadn't been much more about the story. For the time being, it was a gruesome curiosity that had little staying power for the press. And no details had been released about how Ferran Arbós had been killed, so the media hadn't stumbled upon a connection. Yet.

'Or is he looking for Arbós?' Josep replied.

On the narrow street, they passed the museum and turned right into the nondescript modern faculty of geography and history building, opposite the salmon and white finery of the centre for contemporary culture.

'This area's changed since I was a student,' Elisenda muttered.

'They have buildings now?'

Elisenda looked sharply at him. 'Very good, Josep, you're learning. You just need to be taken out of your discomfort zone.'

Don't we all, she added for her own benefit.

Chapter Sixteen

Jordi Canudas also went in for the thick-rimmed glasses look, no doubt to appear on-trend to his students, but it was irretrievably hindered by his lack of hair, floppy or otherwise. Instead, he had a salt and pepper goatee and moustache, forming an 'O' around his mouth, which Elisenda thought made him look perpetually surprised.

'Esteve Mascort,' he repeated in wonder. 'I haven't heard that name in years.'

Elisenda and Josep had met the archaeologist, now a lecturer, in his office, but he'd insisted on getting a coffee in the refectory between tutorials. They were sitting there now, each with a large cup of white coffee, surrounded by students who all seemed to be carrying scooter helmets and distinctive folders with the letters 'U' and 'B' in white in separate blue circles. The sight took Elisenda back to her own time in the Barcelona University law faculty, in a different part of the city, the folders having changed little in design.

'He was a complete bastard,' Canudas went on. 'Dreadful man.'

His calm conviction took Elisenda aback. 'Can you think of anyone who would have held a grudge with him?'

'To the extent of killing him, you mean? Most of us who ever worked with him, I'd reckon. I think it would be quicker if you were to draw up a list of the people who couldn't quite happily have throttled him.'

'Why?' Josep asked. 'What was the problem people had with him?'

Canudas thought for a moment before answering. 'I don't quite know where to begin. He was a caricature. He had matinee idol looks, but he should have worn the villain's black hat. Men instantly trusted him, he cultivated a man's man image, but then he'd use your trust against you, steal your research, do anything to further his own career. He'd tread on anyone to get on, he really had no qualms who he hurt.'

'You said "men"?' Elisenda asked.

'He worked women differently. With his looks, and he had an undoubted charm when he wanted, they found him attractive and he used that. They trusted him too, until they found out for themselves what a bastard he was. He'd persuade women colleagues he had their best interests at heart, but he'd simply use their position or knowledge any way that was necessary to feather his own nest. We all pitied his poor wife, he led her a hell of a dance. He made no bones to us about the women he was screwing.'

'Did no one say anything?' Elisenda asked.

'We all occasionally had an argument with him, but he was so thick-skinned, it never affected him. I had a stand-up row with him once, and I was shaking for ages after, but he just carried on as normal, dusting earth off a piece of pottery with a perfectly steady hand, still boasting about his many conquests. He was a complete sociopath.'

'Do you know much about his relationship with his wife?'

'I only met her once. We had a Christmas lunch one year and she came along. She was very quiet, you could see she wasn't happy. I tried talking to her but she was difficult to engage with.'

'Could she have had anything to do with his death?' Josep asked bluntly.

'No one would blame her if she did.' He thought for a moment longer. 'Not the woman I saw, I would say. She seemed resigned to her lot, but you never know what someone would be capable of in a moment of anger or after the years of abuse he must have put her through.'

'Could you have had anything to do with his death?' Elisenda asked, watching his reaction.

'Yes, it was me. I killed him and now I'm confessing.' He laughed. 'As I said, anyone he worked with could conceivably have lost their temper with him. Did I or anyone I know do it? No. Until you told me his name now, I just thought he'd disappeared in search of a main chance. We'd stopped working together anyway as the dig had been called to a halt and were all so happy to see the back of him, no one really thought much more of it.'

'You didn't think he might have met his death?'

Canudas shook his head. 'Not really. He was always going on about some great plan or other to make his fortune and get away from everything that tied him down. I just thought that that was what he'd done. And to be quite honest, I didn't at all care.'

They finished their coffees and Elisenda asked if he had any photos of Mascort and the rest of the team from that time.

'I have in my office,' he told her, checking his watch. 'I can hunt them out for you now, if you want.'

Elisenda and Josep followed him to his room, where he found a ring binder on a shelf, the photos faded and held in place with old-fashioned peel-off sticky plastic.

'That's Mascort,' he said, pulling the film back and removing the photo. 'On the right.'

Elisenda studied the picture. She could see what Canudas meant by matinee idol looks. Mascort had thick black hair, combed with a neat parting on the right and a thin moustache under an aquiline nose and knowing eyes. His lips were parted to reveal perfect white teeth in a smile that, with what she'd heard of him, she now took to be planned to the precise centimetre. Charm with no warmth. He wore a medallion on a chain around his neck.

'A St. Christopher,' Canudas explained. 'He never took it off.'

There were two other men in the picture, which had been taken in a restaurant at the height of summer, judging by the glowing cheeks and open-necked shirts of the three subjects. Mascort was on his own on the right of the table, the other two were opposite him, but both smiling faintly at the camera.

'Who are the other two?' Elisenda asked him.

He pointed to the one on the left at the back, his smile forced, a gentle face and fine, downy brown hair to his shoulders. 'Well, that's me. In the days when I had hair. The other one is Martí Barbena.'

'Martí Barbena?' Josep asked, studying the picture of a young man with gaunt cheeks and a thin nose, his neat, dark hair parted on the right. He was the third man on their list. 'Do you know where he is now?'

Canudas shook his head. 'I lost touch with him years ago. It wasn't a happy dig, I didn't stay in contact with any of them. Mascort had a lot to do with that, but there was a lot of rivalry between the others as well, everyone wanting to make their own name. We were all roughly the same age, towards the start of our careers.'

'Do you know a Ricard Soler?' Elisenda asked him.

'He's the one who took the picture.'

Pity, Elisenda thought. 'You don't have any other pictures with him in?'

'I don't think I do.' He looked through the ring binder but found nothing, so he went back to the photo that Elisenda was holding. 'Soler only got up to take the photo because if he'd stayed sitting any longer, he would probably have taken a swing at Mascort. He hated him.'

'Any reason?'

Canudas gave a wry laugh. 'This is Mascort we're talking about. A woman, of course. Soler was the oldest by about ten years and the leader of the project. Mascort didn't do anything to challenge him professionally because he'd have been on a hiding to nothing. Soler knew far more about his subject than Mascort did. But Soler was seeing a woman, they were serious, I think. So Mascort set out to seduce her, and he succeeded. It was his only way of scoring points off someone who knew more than he did.'

'What happened?'

'Well, she left Soler for Mascort, and then Mascort seemed to have dumped her once he'd done what he set out to do.'

'Do you remember her name?'

'Dolors something. I only met her a few times. Dolors Quintí, that was it. Another archaeologist, although she didn't ever work on the El Crit site. Soler would have taken her back like a shot, but she obviously didn't want to. I remember he was very cut up about it.'

'Do you know where she works now? If she's an archaeologist, you must know of her work.'

'She dropped out. Gave up archaeology. I don't know what she did after that.'

'Do you think Ricard Soler could be behind Mascort's death?' Josep asked.

Canudas seemed to consider it a possibility for a moment. 'I don't know. What is any of us capable of doing? He certainly would have had a reason to, I suppose, but I don't see it somehow. He was quite a gentle man, thoughtful.'

'Have you ever worked with a man called Ferran Arbós?' Elisenda asked him.

He shook his head. 'He's a curator. I switched to lecturing years ago, I've never had any dealings with him.'

Elisenda noted the present tense. He seemed unaware of Arbós's death, news from a village near Girona not filtering to his world in Barcelona.

A student knocked on the door and came in, apologising and backing out when he saw the three of them talking.

'I have a tutorial,' Canudas explained.

Elisenda thanked him and gave him her card, eliciting a promise to call her if anything occurred to him.

'One other thing,' the archaeologist said. 'Soler once accused Mascort of stealing artefacts from the dig. We all thought it was because of the bad feeling between them, but Barbena brought it up a short while after that. He reckoned he'd seen Mascort uncover a brooch, but there was no find like it ever catalogued. I never saw anything I could say made me think he was pocketing the finds, but Barbena reckoned that Soler might have been right.'

Elisenda thanked him and she and Josep went in search of the former student.

'Also working as a lecturer in the archaeology department, according to Àlex's notes,' Josep informed her.

They found him in a hurry between lectures.

'I'm afraid I can't talk,' he told them. 'I'm already late.'

'You worked on an archaeological dig in June 1981,' Elisenda insisted.

The lecturer shook his head. 'I was supposed to be there all summer, but we were sent home at the start of June.'

'What was the reason you were given?'

'None. I'm sorry, I really can't help.'

The secondary school teacher, Àlex's other student from 1981, told them the same thing when they pulled him out of the staffroom at the school where he worked, not far from the ring road.

'No, we were just told one day when we turned up at the dig that it had been cancelled. Lack of money, I heard.'

'When was this?'

'Start of June. I was quite relieved to be honest. There was a horrible atmosphere on site. There was one guy in particular who annoyed everyone because he was so full of himself. In the end, I got a job on the Indiketa site at Ullastret, which was much more interesting.'

Elisenda showed him the photograph she'd borrowed from Canudas and asked him to point out the man he meant. He pointed to Mascort straight away.

On the way back to Girona, they stopped at a motorway services for a quick lunch.

'He wasn't liked, was he?' Josep said once they sat down.

'It is odd. A body gets found, so someone we haven't found a link to yet gets murdered in much the same way, another man seems to have done a moonlight flit, and none of the people we have spoken to are at all worried about saying they'd have happily killed the first victim given half the chance.'

'And there are the accusations of missing artefacts,' Josep said, before tearing a bite out of the chunky cured ham baguette he was eating.

Elisenda finished chewing her mouthful of *fuet* cured sausage baguette and pulled a paper serviette out of the stainless steel holder.

'And there's the fact of the St. Christopher,' she finally said. 'If Mascort never took it off and it wasn't in the trench at El Crit, where is it?'

Chapter Seventeen

'What did you get from Clara Ferré?'

'Nothing,' Àlex told Elisenda. 'She's at a symposium in Paris until today. Due back this evening. Montse and I'll catch up with her tomorrow morning.'

Clara Ferré was the archaeologist on the 1981 dig who now worked at the City History Museum in Girona.

'It's Saturday,' Elisenda told him. 'Don't expect overtime. Any other news, or have you been skiving off all day while I've been working in Barcelona?'

'How was the shopping?'

'All right, don't push it.' No, keep it going, Elisenda thought, we'll soon have you back. She noticed that his voice was just that little bit stronger. It usually sounded more strained by this time in the afternoon.

'Couple of interesting things have come up,' he told her, putting his smile away for another day. 'How did it go in Barcelona?'

She told him about Ricard Soler appearing to have left his flat in a hurry and of all that she'd learned from Jordi Canudas and from the two students Àlex had asked her to speak to.

'I've got Josep to check with Científica if there was a St. Christopher in the trench,' she added, 'but I don't remember one being found. If that's the case, we need to take another look at the dig to see if it turns up.'

'Otherwise, someone took it.'

She nodded. 'It might be nothing or it might be relevant. We need to know. We also have to look into these accusations of Mascort stealing artefacts to see if there's any basis for that and if it might have played a part in his murder.'

Àlex looked pleased with himself. 'I'm so glad you mentioned that. I've been checking up on Ferran Arbós. We knew he was a curator, but it turns out that he left his last job, at the archaeology museum, under a bit of a cloud.'

'Stealing the goods?'

He shook his head. 'Authorising the purchase of artefacts without checking the provenance. Turns out they were genuine, but were stolen from a dig in the Pyrenees, another Iberian site.'

'Isn't that just negligence?'

'I checked up on a few other acquisitions in museums where he worked as a curator. Two other reported instances of a similar event happening.'

'How many others not reported,' Elisenda finished for him.

'Every museum or institution where he's worked, there have inevitably been numerous acquisitions based on his expertise or recommendation. I've also come across over a dozen cases of other museums acquiring artefacts based on his say-so. Now most of them are bound to be legitimate, but it would be easy for him to use his position to include other items that aren't so legit.'

'So Mascort stole them, Arbós acquired them or recommended that others acquire them. They share the profit between them. That's what you're saying?'

'I think it's worth investigating. Look at his house. You don't buy somewhere like that on a curator's salary. And he doesn't sell that many sculptures.'

Elisenda nodded. 'Keep digging.'

'There's something else. I think we can rule out any idea of Mascort's son being involved in Arbós's death. He's in New York, has been since last September, apart from visiting his mother over Christmas. He works for an IT company over there.'

'You know he's there?'

'I skyped him less than an hour ago. He's there all right. And his name doesn't appear on any flights to or from New York since Christmas.'

'That's pretty good as alibis go,' Elisenda had to agree. 'Okay, don't worry about him. Concentrate on the link between Mascort and Arbós, see if any other names jump out at you. I'm particularly interested in Ricard Soler. I'll be speaking to Jutge Rigau for a search order to be put out for him and then I can get Seguretat Ciutadana on to it.'

She went into her office and sat down, unsure what pleased her more, the fact that they appeared to be making progress in the investigation or the fact of her unit looking to be on the path to recovery. She'd been on the point of suggesting to Àlex that she'd interview Clara Ferré the following day, but decided it was better instead to let him and Montse do it. The more she allowed everyone in the unit to work with each other and for each other, the better it would be for them all. She looked at the drawer containing the file with the candidates for the selection panel and opened it. Taking out the folder, she lifted the cover so she could see one side of the details of the candidate at the top of the pile. She closed her eyes for a second and then put the cover back, replacing the folder in her drawer.

'Monday,' she promised.

–

'This is easier than driving out of Girona in the summer,' Elisenda shouted above the noise in the empty car on the road to the coast. She had Sopa de Cabra's *Nou* album as loud on the car CD player as she could take it.

There were none of the summer Friday evening queues to get out of the humidity of the city to the more refreshing heat of the coast. Instead, she'd packed a warmer quilt for the weekend. Despite the best sleep she'd had in months, the night she'd spent at the beach house in La Fosca had been on the edge of chilly and she'd ended up throwing three or four towels on top of the bed clothes to keep warm. Since Catalina only really used the place in the summer, all she had were thin sheets and no blankets. In summer, even a sheet could become too hot.

'That's not the case in February,' Elisenda muttered to herself when she'd bought some food and coffee at the small supermarket on Carrer dels Ciutadans and packed an extra bag before leaving.

The moment she turned off the main road and began to zigzag her way into the incongruous winter land-scape of the summer haven of La Fosca, the music in the car suddenly sounded out of place, a provocation to the ancient peoples who had once lived here in another settlement that had seen out its time and vanished. Almost in a panic, she turned it off quickly, letting the dark silence of the empty streets flood in.

'Too much imagination, girl,' she said out loud, suddenly remembering the legend of El Crit and the woman screaming in her dream. She immediately pushed it into a corner of her mind, glad of the quiet.

She'd left the electricity turned on in La Fosca when she'd returned to Girona on Thursday morning, so all she had to do now was press the remote button on the key fob and the garage door quickly began to rise in front of her, the fluorescent light inside flickering on.

'Trust Sergi to have a turbo-charged garage door,' she muttered, grateful nonetheless for her brother-in-law's love of toys.

The stairs from the garage took her straight into the kitchen and she walked through the house, turning all the lights on, and dumped her bag in the bedroom. Opening the front door, she went outside and stood for a few moments in the garden, breathing in the salt air and staring out at the thin light above the horizon that danced and shifted out of vision the more she tried to catch sight of it.

Back inside, she got the fire in the living room going and cooked a first course of fresh spinach sautéed with pine nuts and raisins, which she ate on the sofa in front of the glow from the grate. The dining table was too large and lonely. Staring at the flames as she ate, she listened to the hissing of the wood as it burned, small sparks spitting off every now and then. The smell of the smoke from the holm oak wood was sweet. There were other deeper sounds underneath, the unknown noises of someone else's house. Afterwards, she quickly fried a piece of sea bass and drizzled olive oil over it, eating it this time standing up by the window, looking out to sea.

Her fork was midway to her mouth when a change in the tone of the light outside stopped her. A fresh cast of the shadows from the house in the meagre moonlight. A door banged shut.

She put her plate down on the table and went to the front door. The noise had come from outside, not inside the house.

Going out into the garden, she saw light thrown from a window in the house that stood next door but one to where she was. Walking on the balls of her feet through the garden, not wanting to be seen on the footpath that ran between the villas and the beach below, she crossed the next-door garden and peered over the wall. The front door was half-open and light from the hallway was spilling out.

Pulling herself over the wall, she quietly approached the front door and gently pushed it inwards, stepping over the threshold. The sound of someone moving was coming from somewhere to the left of her. She tiptoed on the tiled floor across the small hall, careful not to make a sound, to where the light was on behind another door. As she approached, it was yanked open and a man walked out carrying a knife.

Elisenda's reactions were quicker and she grabbed at his wrist, bending it until he dropped the weapon and pulling his arm up behind his back, forcing him to bend forward. He let out a yelp of pain as the metal blade clattered to the ceramic floor.

'Police,' she warned him.

'I live here,' he answered her, breathless.

She released him and made him back off to fetch his ID. He handed it to her and she read the name on it.

'Miquel Canals,' he answered when she asked him to confirm. He also recited the ID number. The address was one in Barcelona.

'Do you have ID?' he asked her, calming down after the shock.

'What were you doing carrying a knife?' Elisenda demanded.

'I was cooking. I'd left my mobile in the living room when it rang, so I went straight from the kitchen to answer it without putting the knife down. I was just on my way back there.' He pointed to the room opposite.

Elisenda looked down to the knife on the floor and saw thin slivers of food that had fallen from it, smearing the tiles. Taking a deep breath, she handed the ID card back.

'I'm sorry, I didn't expect anyone else to be staying here.'

Canals put the laminated plastic card back in his wallet and into his back pocket.

'I have to confess, neither did I,' he replied. 'You still haven't shown me any ID.'

'It's back in my house. I'll fetch it if you want to see it.'

He held up his hand and smiled for the first time. 'Don't worry. Only a cop reacts that quickly. I believe you.'

'What are you doing here?'

'And only a cop asks so many questions. I'm staying here for a while. The house belongs to some friends, they're letting me stay here as I needed some time to myself.' He gave the names of the friends, which Elisenda recognised from summer visits to her sister.

'Any particular reason?'

'You don't get to ask that question just yet. I don't know your name.'

Elisenda reached out her hand to shake his. 'Elisenda Domènech. I'm staying at my sister's house. Next but one to this one.'

'I've opened a bottle of wine. Would you like a glass, Elisenda Domènech?'

She studied him before answering. There was a touch of the Àlex about him when Àlex was Àlex. An undercurrent of leashed power, a strong face and a frank, confident charm. In his mid-thirties, she reckoned. A smile that he knew opened doors.

'Maybe some other time,' she told him and returned to her sister's house.

Chapter Eighteen

The following morning, Elisenda was surprised to find she'd slept until nine o'clock. It was the first time that had happened in as long as she could remember. She collected a kayak from the garage and went out on to the beach. As she'd crossed the path down to the left of the row of villas, she'd seen Miquel Canals standing outside in his front garden. He'd called a greeting and she'd waved back to him.

Making her way along the beach, she turned to look behind her. None of the houses could be seen from this angle, the steep wall of the low cliff hiding them from view. A thin vein of feldspar ran through the parent rock in light contrast to the ancient dark of the stone embracing it. Turning away, she went down to the water and floated the kayak, gingerly seating herself in it and casting off.

A couple of pleasure boats were already out on a winter's Saturday under a cloudless deep blue sky. Used to the roll of the vessel, she settled into a faster pace than the last time she'd tried it and rowed straight out to sea, heading for the horizon. A shape swam under the kayak, knocking the breath out of her for a fleeting moment. A basking shark. A form on which to found endless night-mares but one that was ultimately harmless. She laughed nervously, but paused nevertheless to let it pass on by.

The sound of a plane distracted her. A small private one heading east, away from the coast. A shape and a sound that didn't inspire fear but one that had killed her daughter one summer as her father flew her away across the sea. She watched it disappear over the horizon and turned back for the shore, quickly gathering pace, her arms and shoulders burning with lactic acid.

Nearer land, she turned north and rowed more leisurely along the tiny coves that dotted the shoreline. She rowed below the Agulla de Castell headland, site of another more established Indiketa dig, the point of land jutting out into the sea denuded of pines to aid the archaeologists in its excavation. She looked up at it and wondered if increased funding for the El Crit site would also lead to the felling of trees there. A desire to understand our past temporarily destroying the beauty of the present.

Beyond the headland, she indulged herself and paddled into the sheltered little cove next to it for nothing more than the pleasure of gazing down into the pure turquoise water at the sea urchins on the smooth stones below the surface and rowing under the natural arch of wizened rock. Momentarily out of the sunlight, the air beneath was chill and she gave an involuntary shiver.

The man from the other day was on El Crit beach, picking through the sand for litter near the fishermen's huts. She greeted him as she passed and he looked up at her but made no reply.

'Have a nice day,' she muttered to herself, pausing by the three stone huts next to the foot of the steps leading up to the headland. She saw that towards the rear of the one nearest the steep path, a simple whitewashed storage shed with large twin doors at the front, a thick and rusting metal bracket was jutting out of the wall at a right-angle. She imagined it was used by the fishermen to hang nets or pots.

Stopping for a moment at the stop of the flight of steps, amid the pines and holm oaks, she heard the man's boat splutter into life and gently putt-putt away on to the next cove. Standing still to listen to the sound fade away, she heard another, smaller sound. A rustling from up ahead of her, where the dig lay.

Making as little noise as possible, she crept forward, but her foot caught an old pine cone and it skittered away into the undergrowth. The noise ahead stopped for an instant, to be replaced by a scrabbling, panicked sound. Elisenda immediately ran to the dig, but no one was there. Looking around her through the dense trees, she could hear the sound of steps running away from her, but could see nothing. Choosing the path that ran past the new trench, she followed a trail but the noise she could hear was already diminishing, the whispering of the pine needles confusing the direction the sound was coming from.

Walking back, she wondered if it could have been an animal she'd spooked.

'Only you don't believe that for one moment,' she murmured.

She stood over the new trench where Mascort's body had been found and tried to discern whether it had been disturbed. There were no major movements of earth, but it was impossible to tell. She turned at the sound of more steps coming through the trees. Not stealthy or panicked this time, but with the confidence of someone with nothing to hide.

'Doctor Bosch,' she exclaimed when the archaeologist suddenly emerged. Looking equally surprised, he walked towards where she was standing. 'I didn't expect you to be working on a Saturday.'

'Please, call me Llàtzer,' he told her. He looked around at the site and shrugged. 'I want to get on with the dig. With so much interest after the body was found, I'm concerned people are going to try and steal artefacts.'

'I think I disturbed someone just now,' Elisenda confirmed his fears.

'It happens so much. I thought we'd be safe here because it's so inaccessible, but with it being in the news, we become a target. Did you see them?'

She shook her head. 'Would you mind taking a look at the trench to see if it looks like it's been tampered with?'

He scanned it with a doubtful expression. 'I don't know this trench as well as the other one but it doesn't appear to have been disturbed since you took the body away.'

'Could you look to see if there's a medallion in there? A St. Christopher.'

Without questioning, he began to dust the top layer of earth with a brush. Most of it had been removed anyway when the Científica had conducted their own search, so he only had to work with his trowel for a brief time before coming to the conclusion that it wasn't there.

'Nothing,' he confirmed, standing up. 'But I'd like to check the other trench for tampering.'

'Is there really no way you could have security here?' she asked him as they walked up the incline to the original trench.

He laughed. 'That really would be the end of the dig if we had to pay for that. And the government can't afford to pay for the Mossos to guard it either. Not until we can prove that it's a site of national interest. We're caught between the devil and the deep blue sea, I'm afraid.'

They got to the part of the site where Bosch usually worked and stopped to look down into the pit. 'Well, I can tell you now, that this one's been disturbed. Those scrape marks there and over there are new. I'm the only one who works on this part and I didn't make them. They're not entirely amateur by the looks of them.'

'You wouldn't know if anything's been taken?'

Frowning, he crouched down for a closer look. 'Quite the opposite.' With a puzzled expression, he cleared away some powdery earth that looked like it had been hurriedly thrown over whatever was lying underneath and he picked up a small black bowl with a handle on either side. 'This has been left here since last night.'

Elisenda squatted down to take a closer look. A faint decoration of ivy leaves ran around the edge of the dish, encircling a figure of a man drinking from a goblet at the centre. 'Is it genuine?'

Bosch examined it. 'Oh, it's genuine, all right. But it's not recently excavated. It's been cleaned, for one thing. It's a kylix, by the way, a drinking cup. As you drank, the figure of Dionysos gradually appeared. Sometimes the figures were humorous or erotic. This one would have been traded with the Indiketa by the Greeks in exchange for crops like barley or lentils. I'd say it's fifth century BC, which means it's earlier than the body that was found here. It's completely incongruous time-wise, but I would say it's possible that it could once have come from this site. We've found others here and elsewhere locally.'

'Could it date from the 1981 dig?'

He considered for a moment before climbing out of the trench. 'Possibly. But impossible to say with any certainty.'

'When I was here the other day,' Elisenda recalled, 'I found a piece of pottery that Doctora Fradera hadn't boxed up the evening before. I thought it seemed odd.'

'There was a shard one morning. I did think it strange that she would forget. But I have no idea why anyone would return an artefact to a site.'

'Guilty conscience? Something they took in the past and decided to give back?'

Elisenda stared at the kylix and tried to see how and why someone would be leaving artefacts at the dig. She knew it was significant. She stepped back to let Bosch climb out of the trench.

'Would you care for a coffee?' he asked her, dusting himself down. 'Flask, I'm afraid, which is fairly hideous, but it wakes me up.'

They sat on a large rock near the trench and took turns to sip from the cup.

'You're right,' Elisenda told him. 'It's awful.'

'Pilfering from digs is a problem,' he said, returning to the subject. 'Amateurs visit sites at night, sometimes with metal detectors, and if they don't actually find and take anything that we then lose forever, they can often simply destroy the site through not knowing what they're doing.'

Elisenda wondered at how he could be so different when not around Doctora Fradera. How he could be so forthcoming and pleasant here alone with her in the wood but how the petty jealousy between the two archaeologists could diminish them both, make the pair of them behave like spoilt children. She had seen so often in her job how a bad feeling between two people could make one or both of them act in a way that was so hugely out of character as to lead them to do desperate and appalling things.

'Have you heard of archaeologists stealing artefacts from digs?'

He sighed and screwed the cup back on the flask. 'You do hear of it. There was one a few years ago who was caught trying to sell Roman coins on the internet. But I must say, I've never come across it personally. It would rankle if I ever did.'

'Have you ever had any dealings with Ferran Arbós?'

'Ah, yes, I read about that. Murdered in his own home, wasn't he?'

Elisenda nodded, but didn't offer any more information. The nature of the curator's death had been kept out of the newspapers so far.

'I knew him a bit, but I never worked with him. He took early retirement while I was still doing my doctorate in Barcelona, so I never really coincided. Doctora Fradera knew him more.'

'You and she don't really see eye to eye, do you?' Elisenda tried a direct approach.

He paused some while before answering. 'I suppose it's more of a generational thing than anything personal. I'm younger than she is, I took my doctorate in a less politically emotive age and I was possibly less drawn to the more revolutionary theories that inspired people like Doctora Fradera who studied in the immediate post-Franco era. Archaeology itself evolves, and that's not always such a good thing. We don't always have to embrace the latest thinking as being omniscient.'

'You belong to different schools, in other words?'

'In a very simplistic way, yes. I would probably describe myself as more of a processual archaeologist. Doctora Fradera, on the other hand, is more keen on adopting a cognitive view.'

'Meaning?'

'Meaning, very crudely, that when I discover an artefact, I look scientifically at its function in terms of the way the user of it might have lived. Doctora Fradera believes that when she discovers an artefact, she is looking at the way the user thought.' He pointed at the trench nearby. 'So, when I see a skull severed from the body with a spike through the forehead and I ally that with the history that we know of the peoples who lived here, my interpretation is that it was a trophy of conflict, or a deterrent. All of that is borne out by contemporaneous observers. Posidonius of Apamea and Diodorus of Sicily commented on how the Celts used to display the heads of defeated enemies. So too did Livy. The evidence is too substantial to think otherwise. Doctora Fradera, on the other hand, will try to impose a way of thinking on it, such as the idea of its being a form of veneration or part of a system of beliefs, that we cannot possibly know.' He laughed. 'That is probably the most rough and ready way of describing our ideas that I could have come up with.'

'I'm a very rough and ready thinker.'

'I doubt that very much. You're a detective, you deal in evidence, like a scientist.'

'But as a detective, I also have to try and place a mindset on that evidence.' She looked at her watch and stood up.

'Thank you for the conversation, Llàtzer. And the coffee. But I really have to be going.'

They said goodbye and she set off back towards the beach.

'Haven't you come by car?' he asked her, surprised.

'Kayak. I'm staying in La Fosca for a few days. I might try and get in a visit to the Castell settlement while I'm here.'

'Do, it'll give you a clearer idea of what this village might have been like. And if you're interested in archaeology and you're in Palamós these days, there's an interesting hotel in the old town. When it was being built in the 1960s, they discovered a Roman shrine in what's now the basement. Luckily, they left it intact and the present owner has been very good in showing it due respect. If you tell him I sent you, he would probably agree to letting you see it. Very few people know about it, and it really is worth seeing something so unique outside a museum setting. It gives you a much clearer idea of how a private shrine might have been when it was originally in use.'

'That sounds fascinating. I'll look it up.'

'You should,' he said, turning back to his own temple of veneration.

Chapter Nineteen

'There's little veneration here,' Elisenda muttered after the door closed behind them on the fourth visit.

'Pardon?' Josep asked her.

She explained about her conversation with Doctor Bosch earlier at El Crit. The two Mossos were in Vall-Llobrega, going door to door among the houses neighbouring Ferran Arbós's scruffy villa. Elisenda had driven to the village from the coast, meeting Josep, who had come from Girona.

'They don't come right out and say it,' Elisenda went on, 'but none of them has shown any great affection for Arbós. Or any concern.'

'They're more worried about their own safety,' Josep agreed. 'But he doesn't seem to have been very popular.'

'What would you say, Josep? Do you think any of them's got anything to hide?'

Josep pulled his shoulders back, unfolding to his full height, and sucked in a deep breath of the crisp village air. Elisenda was learning that he did that when he was feeling relaxed and confident. Like most of her team, that had become too much of a rarity in recent months. 'No, I don't. There's no love lost, but not enough to drive a chisel through his head. That takes real anger.'

'Or real coldness.' Elisenda looked at the distant mountains and exhaled. There was the slightest of mists from her breath, ghostly in the rich blue air. 'I agree with you.'

'And they would all have been out when the attack happened, anyway,' Josep added. 'Do you want me to check up on them at the time of the murder?'

'Yes, but don't take too long over it. I don't think we'll find our killer among the neighbours, but best to make sure they really were where they say they were.'

After they'd knocked on the last of the fruitless doors, they went to Arbós's house. Elisenda had called the Mossos station in La Bisbal to tell them she'd be in Vall-Llobrega, and Sergent Poch had sent a Seguretat Ciutadana patrol car with the keys to let her in. The two officers waited outside as Elisenda and Josep entered.

The sculptor's studio was covered in two layers of white dust, a coarser ground layer that had coated the floor and the surfaces near where Arbós had worked for years, with pieces of stone that crunched underfoot and that had steadfastly pockmarked the tiles. The second layer covered any feasible surfaces and handles and was much finer and more temporary, the powder used by the Científica team to search for fingerprints. The forensic team in La Bisbal had already told Elisenda that they'd found nothing of interest.

'Anyone calculating enough to kill someone like this is not going to forget to wear gloves,' the sergent in the unit had commented.

Elisenda and Josep pulled on their own blue gloves and studied the room, dust motes dancing spectrally in the sunlight. Neither of them could help looking at the far wall, crimson bleeding into the plaster and a dried rust tide at the foot of it. Elisenda pulled her gaze away.

'Someone of Arbós's generation is going to have photos,' she explained to Josep as they began to search. 'Especially from that time. We're looking for photos of Mascort with Arbós or any document that would link the two of them. Keep an eye out too for any reference to Ricard Soler. He's gone missing for a reason.'

Shelves lined two of the walls and they took one each, working back and forth along the rows, pulling out folders and dusting off files of correspondence, replacing them when they bore no fruit. There was little from his time as a curator, they both noticed.

'Destroying the evidence?' Josep asked.

'Does it look to you like there are any missing?'

Elisenda stared at a section of ring binders in a row and at what appeared to be gaps between some of them, hastily closed up as though to look like nothing had been removed. Perhaps it was nothing, but she sent Poch a text asking him to send her any photos of the shelves taken by Científica on Thursday for her to check. Renewing her search, she found two binders full of photographs, reminiscent of the one Jordi Canudas kept in his office. She recalled her parents keeping their photos in something similar for years, before everything was kept on a computer. Hunting through them page by page, she was disappointed to see that they both appeared to be for family, with pictures of weddings and first communions, dinners and days out. Stopping at one that looked a more formal affair, she came across a young Fradera in a group around a dinner table.

'Did you miss that one?' she asked in a low voice.

'Got something, I think,' she heard Josep say.

She looked up to see him leaning in the door frame. He led her out of the studio into the living room. She'd been so intent on her own search that she hadn't registered him leaving. Standing in the corner was an old-fashioned bureau that Arbós had evidently used as a desk. The computer that had been there had been taken by Científica, again with nothing of interest being found on it.

Lifting the pull-down flap on which the desktop had stood, Josep pulled out a drawer concealed underneath it. Inside was a flat wooden box with a lid. He took it out of the drawer and replaced the flap so he could place the box on top of it and remove the cover. It was a coin display case, the interior divided into small square compartments, each lined with cotton wool and housing an ancient-looking coin.

'Please tell me the St. Christopher is there,' Elisenda murmured.

'Afraid not.' Josep had already told her that Científica hadn't found the medallion in the trench at El Crit. 'Now, they could be an innocent hobby, but knowing the stories about Arbós, they might not be.'

'We'll take the box to the Archaeology Service, see if they know anything about them.'

'They obviously weren't the motive for his murder,' Josep said. 'Or they wouldn't still be here.'

'No, I think his murder has a far deeper reason.'

Her phone beeped. Poch had sent her two photos taken of the scene on the Thursday. The same gaps she had just found between the photo albums were there already, so at least nothing had vanished since the body had been found. Dissatisfied despite that, she showed them to Josep.

'Inconclusive,' she decided. 'Either it means absolutely nothing or it means that the killer had been looking for something in them and found it.'

Finding nothing more, they took the box away with them and closed up the house, thanking the two uniforms for their time.

'Time for a Saturday, now, I think,' Elisenda told Josep as they each retrieved their cars. 'Anything planned?'

'Lunch with my girlfriend,' he said. He looked at his watch. 'Late lunch.'

Elisenda watched as his shoulders slowly hunched and his head stooped.

–

'He was a bit of a bastard.' The woman laughed. 'But a charming one.'

'And were you charmed?' Montse asked her.

'Good God, no. I was far too sensible to have a fling with Esteve Mascort.'

Clara Ferré had opened the door to Àlex and Montse, a quizzical expression on her face when they showed her their ID, but had been happy to invite them into her chaotic apartment. One of the grand old buildings on Carrer Ciutadans, it had high vaulted ceilings and mahogany panelling to halfway up the walls. The worn but expensive furniture was strewn with clothes from a suitcase lying in the middle of the floor, which looked as though it had exploded in relief, hurling all its contents onto every possible surface in a home already cluttered with books and papers.

'You'll have to excuse me,' she'd told them. 'I got back from Paris late last night, I'm rather exhausted and I haven't finished unpacking yet.'

'No, you haven't, have you?' Àlex commented with a small grin.

Ferré turned and smiled full-face at him, her eyes glinting. Àlex's grin turned into a self-conscious smile and he looked away. Slightly puzzled at his sudden loss of confidence, she cleared a space on the two sofas and invited them to sit down.

Àlex thanked her for seeing them. 'We understand you worked on the El Crit archaeological site in the 1980s with Esteve Mascort.'

She'd sat back in surprise at his words.

'Esteve Mascort. I haven't heard that name in years. He went missing.'

'Yes, in 1981. That's why we've come to see you, Senyora Ferré. We think we may have found his body, so we're now reopening his disappearance as a murder investigation.'

Her mouth dropped open in shock.

'We all just thought he'd run off with some poor woman,' she'd commented.

'Why was that?' Montse had asked.

Which was when Ferré made her comment about Mascort being a charming bastard.

'He tried it on a few times,' she elaborated, 'but that was nothing to feel flattered by. He tried it on with just about every woman within a certain age range.'

'With much success,' Montse pursued.

'Lord, yes. Alarmingly so. He had the looks.' She shot a glance at Àlex as she said it.

As Montse interviewed Ferré, Àlex studied the archaeologist. Her hair was grey, almost white, and worn long,
wrapped around her head in a plait, framing an inquisitive
face that looked like it was never far from breaking into a
laugh. Her eyes, dipping between the two Mossos, were
both interested and interesting, Àlex thought. She wore a
baggy shirt and faded jeans with an effortless and probably
unwitting style.

A key sounded in the front door and it opened. A
young man in his early twenties walked in, who Ferré
introduced as her son.

'Can you wait in the kitchen, darling?' she asked him.
'I'll be with you soon. The police are asking me about
someone who went missing ages ago.'

The son nodded without a word and left them.

Àlex leaned forward. 'Do you know of anyone who
might have wanted to harm Mascort?'

'Plenty of people, I should imagine. One of the other
archaeologists on the dig, Ricard Soler, hated him. Esteve
stole his girlfriend from him and Soler never forgave him.
I didn't ever meet her, so I don't know the whole story,
but there were rumours at the time that Esteve had got her
pregnant and that she'd gone to London for an abortion.'

Àlex and Montse looked at each other in surprise.

'Did you believe the rumours?' Àlex asked her.

'I had no reason not to, but as I say, I never knew the
whole story. Ricard was a bit clingy, so it might just have
been that the girlfriend got fed up with that and dumped
him. The abortion rumour could have been sour grapes
on his part.'

'Do you have a name for the girlfriend?'

She cocked her head to one side in thought. 'Dolors, I think. I don't know her surname.'

'So you wouldn't know where she is now?'

'Not a clue, sorry. I've often thought since that that was one of the reasons why the dig didn't ever really get off the ground. There was so much bad feeling and backstabbing, I think the government was reluctant to throw any money our way.'

'Was that the only reason, do you think?' Montse asked.

'Well, there were the usual professional rivalries, I suppose. Apart from Ricard, the other three of us were at the start of our careers, trying to get a full-time contract. It wasn't a harmonious dig.'

'Nothing else?' Àlex insisted.

'You mean thefts,' she guessed. 'Ricard accused Esteve of stealing artefacts. I think the rest of us just thought it was part of the bad feeling. He desperately wanted Esteve off the project.'

'So you don't think the accusations were founded?'

She began to pick at the stitching on her shirt, staring at the coffee table between her and the Mossos. 'I know I never saw anything,' she said slowly, 'that's a fact. But the notion of Esteve stealing artefacts is not something that would at all have surprised me. He was always on the lookout for anything that would give him an edge, either professionally or financially. He didn't mind how he did it.'

'Do you know if he knew Ferran Arbós?' Àlex asked.

'Oh, Christ, I read about that.' She considered for a moment. 'Not that I know of. I only met Arbós some years later, and both Esteve and I were at a similar stage in our careers, so I don't believe that they would have come into contact with each other. I take it you're asking because of Arbós's dark dealings.'

'He left under a cloud, we understand,' Montse commented.

She laughed. 'He left under a force nine gale. They only had the courage to force him out when it became too obvious that he was up to something. People can make mistakes, but there were just too many in his case. No one's that incompetent. He was lucky that that's all that he got. He should have been investigated and charged. God only knows how many deals he did and how many finds have gone missing.'

'Missing?' Àlex asked. 'I thought it was just provenance that was in doubt.'

'None of us can know for sure, but I'm convinced he was selling to private buyers too. Collectors in this country and abroad.'

They had no more questions, so Àlex and Montse left her to her unpacking and went back down the ornate marble and wrought-iron communal staircase and out into the street, both deep in thought. They had to walk on the road, the narrow pavements teeming with Saturday shoppers.

'How many motives and suspects do we want?' Montse asked, bemusement in her voice.

'Take your pick.'

They cut down past the bright windows of the shoe shops and tailor's and the faded grey of the premises to let on the narrow Carrer Abeuradors and emerged on to the Rambla, teeming with shoppers and strollers idling at the flower stands in the sweet-scented Saturday morning market.

'Any plans for the rest of the day?' Àlex asked Montse.

'Lunch, then haircut.'

Àlex looked at her hair. It was already almost as short as his. 'Not going running today?'

'I ran 5K this morning.'

'You did what?' He stared at her in a mixture of scorn and respect. 'Before meeting me?'

'I'm going to get below twenty minutes this year,' she told him. She tapped him on the stomach. 'You could do with taking a run every now and then, Àlex, you're going flabby.'

'Bit of respect, Caporal.' The grin was nearly there.

She grinned back at him and walked off through the crowd.

Àlex watched her go and turned to head for Santa Eugènia and home. On the big, modern square outside his apartment block, he looked up at the balcony on his flat for a moment and decided to sit for a while on a bench and watch his neighbours at play. Children ran tirelessly around the young trees planted in hollows in the grey paving, their parents deep in superficial weekend conversation with other parents. Elderly men and women sat in groups on benches and talked of age and change, theirs and the city's.

Registering none of the noise and movement around him, he thought about the others in the unit. He knew what they were doing. Elisenda wanted him angry and edgy and was constantly putting him on the spot where he'd react. Montse wanted to goad him through rivalry. And big, tall Josep wanted to look up to him as someone who was strong. All of it was designed to bring him back from the semi-death he'd experienced since his near death.

He reached into his jacket pocket and pulled out an envelope. In it was an invitation to apply for a new post. A desk job in Sabadell. Where no one would ever put a noose around his neck again.

El Crit, 1981

The light blue and white Sarfa bus he'd taken from Palamós dropped him off on the main road a few kilometres north of the town.

'This is the nearest stop to El Crit,' the driver told him, sweating in the sunlight coursing in through his window, his grey nylon shirt open to the waist, the greying hairs on his chest glistening. Hanging from a hook next to him a beige plastic transistor radio was bleating *The Birdy Song*.

The student nodded and climbed down the three steps, grateful to be released from the same bloody tune he'd heard everywhere he went. He watched the bus trundle off into traffic, the cars punching the air in his ears every time they raced past. Smelling the sweet aroma of the asphalt melting in the hot summer air, the student took a deep breath and slowly set off along the small, pock-marked road that would eventually lead to the sea. No wind combed through the tall grass alongside where he walked and he was sweating within moments of getting off the bus.

It was another two hours before he found the cove he was looking for, the path ill-defined through the pines to the headland overlooking the beach. When he got there, he saw two trenches cut into the hard brown earth, signs of trowels scraping across stone.

But not one person was working there.

Mystified, he walked through the archaeological dig. There were no tools, no boxes. In one trench he saw a shard of pottery half buried in the ground. He knelt down and prised it loose and picked it up to look at it. Indiketa, he saw, a thrill running through him despite the mystery of the abandoned site.

From the direction of the beach, he heard voices. Walking to the edge of the headland, he looked down and saw people below, sunbathing or playing in the sea. He climbed down the winding steps to the bottom and walked up to a group of four people. It was only as he approached them that he realised that they were all naked. Looking around, he saw that he was the only one clothed. Unconcerned, he spoke to the four people.

'Do you know anything about an archaeological dig up there?' he asked them, pointing towards the headland.

Equally unfazed, one of the two women in the group answered him. 'There were some people working there a few days ago, but I haven't seen anyone since then.'

The student thanked them and made to leave.

'Where are you going?' the woman asked him.

He told them he was going to Palamós and that he didn't have transport, so one of the men offered to take him.

'We came by boat,' he told him, reaching for a pair of shorts. 'It'll take you hours to get back otherwise.'

In the small Zodiac inflatable on the way to Palamós, the man tried to make conversation but eventually gave up. When he finally dropped the student off at the beach where the fishermen had laid out their colourful nets to dry, he looked relieved to be heading back.

In the town, the student tried ringing the number he had again, but there was still no reply. When that failed, he went to the telephone office and asked for a phone book. He found the numbers he wanted and was directed to one of the grey booths lining the wall of the small office. He picked up the phone and dialled the first of the numbers he'd just found.

'What's happening?' he asked when someone at the other end answered.

Chapter Twenty

It was the perfect day for a dead village.

Elisenda stood alone in the forlorn car park and looked about her. A single cypress stretched proud into the sky, a dark green totem to the past. Loosely swaying pines and stubborn olive trees provided an unnecessary shade from the winter afternoon sun. The bright green oily leaves of a carob heralded her with a lonely arch over the path into the main entrance to the settlement. There were no visitors on a February Saturday. Just a single figure standing between the honey-coloured remains of the walls leading into the ancient village.

'Thank you for agreeing to see me,' Elisenda told Doctora Fradera.

The archaeologist turned and led the way on the steady climb past the initial walls that stood higher than the two women and on into a more open area, where the stones left intact marked out the ground layout of the original dwellings.

'I was going to be here anyway,' Fradera told her. 'Otherwise you wouldn't have seen me.'

Elisenda stifled a laugh. She had to admit to liking the older woman's blunt lack of social niceties. She'd called the archaeologist before leaving Vall-Llobrega as she wanted to get some thoughts straight in her mind. Fradera told her that she was at the Inidiketa settlement in Ullastret.

'I must confess I haven't been here for some years,' Elisenda told her as the path wound up past the skeletons of buildings on either side, framed by a lush and dusty verdancy in contrast to the crystalline sky. Much of the area was excavated, but there was a great deal still to explore, with pieces of land fenced off or marked out.

'Do you always work on a Saturday?' Fradera asked her.

'When an investigation calls for it. Do you?'

'I never stop being an archaeologist,' she replied gruffly. 'The museum is up here. You remember that much?'

They turned off the path to climb some steps, large uneven stones curving like a hillside terrace, leading to a small clearing of gravel and green shoots forcing their way through the dust. Ahead of them stood two tall outlines, timeless and contemporary in stark juxtaposition. The first was another cypress, slender and pointed, the foliage seeming to burst from the layers below like ancient lava. Beyond it, an ornamental lamppost, the two lights suspended from it like twin pearl earrings. Cypress and lamppost were separated by the gnarled form of an olive, the trunk low and clinging stubbornly to the earth, the branches and leaves reaching tentatively to the sky.

Stopping at the top, outside the museum building, Elisenda took the opportunity to gaze out over the plain surrounding the hill on which the Indiketa settlement stood. Flat farmland sheltered by low hills, the knowledge of the sea beyond.

'I'd forgotten how serene this place was,' she said.

'I feel it every time I stand here,' Fradera answered, pausing by her side, her voice suddenly softer. 'At times this would have been an island, the plain here covered in flood water. Perfect protection.'

'That happened a few years ago, didn't it?' Elisenda recalled seeing pictures of the hill surrounded by water, the fields of crops below flooded.

'What you'll want to see is in here,' Fradera said, turning sharply away, back to being bluff.

Elisenda had to let her eyes accustom to the winter glow of the museum after the bright sky outside. The temperature was cool enough to need a coat, but she was instantly reminded of summer visits here, the golden stones and white walls a welcome respite from the hot sun on the exposed hill. They came across the display cases she wanted almost immediately.

'You're lucky there's no school trip today,' Fradera told her. 'This is their favourite bit. We can never get them to move on.'

Huddling close together in the unforgiving spotlight of the illuminated cabinet were two human skulls, a rusted spike thrust through the top of each forehead, seeming to pin them to the stand, redolent of how they might have looked either side of the gateway that Elisenda had walked through just a few minutes earlier. Oddly, Elisenda found them sadder than the Indiketa skull lying in the trench in El Crit. A display in the distant past becoming an exhibition in the present.

'Display,' Elisenda said. 'You questioned Doctor Bosch's idea that these were for display.'

'I didn't question it, actually. I do think they were primarily for display purposes, particularly if there was a spike through them, wouldn't you say? Where I disagree with Doctor Bosch is that he takes a rather narrow view of the reason for the display and he regards the skulls as being solely for that purpose. I do not.' She studied the two skulls for a moment before continuing. 'The problem lies partly in that the most widely-known cases are these ones here with the spikes. They aren't unique, but they are exceptional. We only know of five in Europe, four of which have been found here in Ullastret, these two in 1969, the other two just a couple of years ago.'

Elisenda nodded. 'I remember those ones being in the news.'

'They will be displayed eventually. I'll show you a reconstruction after. As I was saying, though, the problem is that they were found in proximity to the defensive walls or in public places, and that's what's led to their being seen as a token of intimidation. But we've also found fragments of other skulls, and some even intact, in other circumstances, with indications of other practices. The necropolis shows that the usual funeral rite was cremation, but we have also found human remains, predominantly skulls and jaws, in ritual buildings. They all show signs of burial and subsequent retrieval of the skull after skeletonisation. That has to lead us to believe that the answer isn't quite so simple.' She turned to look at Elisenda in the eyes. 'And now, of course, that's all been thrown up in the air yet again with this new find. My body, I mean, not yours. It's the first time we've ever found a whole body intact with a spike through the skull. That has to change our understanding still further. I'm really not looking forward to the day we make this find public.'

Both women turned to look at the two dead and silent faces in the cabinet.

'Come with me,' Fradera suddenly said. 'I'll show you this reconstruction.'

In a calm, honey-coloured office away from the exhibits, the archaeologist pulled up a file on the computer and beckoned Elisenda to take a seat. A short video came up on screen of a three-dimensional computer modelling gradually building up the layers of a skull to recreate a face.

'This was one of the two skulls found recently,' Fradera explained. 'The process goes from a CT scan of the skull, through depth markers showing how thick the layers of muscle and skin would be, to the finished face. But I suppose you know all this. The Mossos must use it.'

'It's extremely rare for us to use the technique, as the technology is still too open to interpretation. We would only use it as a last resort if we were unable to identify a victim by other means. I've never seen it used profession-ally.'

The end of the video showed the face of a young man staring out at them. His eyes set wide apart, the nose flat, long hair hanging lank on his head and wispy down on his upper lip and jaw.

'This is the first time we've ever seen what an Iberian might have looked like,' Fradera said, a slight tinge of awe hiding beneath the bombast. 'This is where we come from.'

Despite herself, Elisenda was enthralled by the face, wanting it to be real. 'What he might have looked like,' she repeated. 'That's the issue for the forensic use of this. It only gives us an idea, it's not infallible. It's too open to interpretation by the modeller to be admissible in law.'

'True,' Fradera conceded, 'but these computer models are becoming increasingly more accurate, more so than the old clay models.'

Elisenda turned away from the young man's face staring sightlessly out at her. 'Coming back to the understanding of what the deaths meant, what might an archaeologist on the 1981 dig have thought?' she asked

Fradera turned the program off, her manner already reverting. 'I couldn't possibly say. There was perhaps a greater belief in the idea of trophy or deterrent in those days, as they would have had less evidence. The Puig de Serra necropolis, for instance, hadn't been discovered back then. They might, perhaps, even have subscribed to the idea of this form of killing being part of a sacrificial rite, in the hope of improved crops or wealth for the village or good fortune in battle. Even now, we don't entirely know, and I couldn't say what an individual archaeologist might have thought in 1981. You've seen how we still disagree on the meaning today.'

'But it's feasible that someone from that team might have seen the ritual killing as an execution? Or as a sacrifice?' Elisenda thought of Ferran Arbós in his villa. 'Or as a warning?'

Fradera tutted dramatically. 'These people lived here for centuries, their society evolved. And with it, their rituals and traditions. We have to presume the rite of the skull evolved also. The common explanation for these practices was that they were intimidatory or religious, but some of us feel that we should also be looking at the possibility of the rites being carried out with both negative and positive intent.'

'Positive?'

'Where there is evidence of violence ante mortem, the skull would arguably be that of an enemy or a miscreant. A trophy or a deterrent, as Doctor Bosch says. There was also the practice of using the skull of an enemy for ceremonial purposes, for libations or offerings. But the fact of skulls being found in ritual buildings or in private dwellings, and not in public places, raises the question as to whether these were high-status individuals who were held in enough respect to warrant a different funeral rite from the usual one. Or they were individuals who were important to the family, and so a symbol of their life was kept in the home as veneration. Not at all as a punishment or a trophy.'

'Is there evidence for that?'

Fradera got up and led Elisenda back to the exhibition room, to another display case, bearing more human skulls, intact this time, and other bones alongside small beakers, miniature amphorae and pots, many with faces carved into them.

'These finds were parts of votive shrines. We think most homes had them. It's conceivable that the skulls were used as part of this rite. And besides these, we've also found similar objects buried in the foundations of family dwellings, indicative of other meanings. To bring luck on the household, perhaps, or the ancestor watching over the family.' She turned away from the case and led Elisenda to the door out of the building into the pale sunlight. 'And we've found newborn babies buried in the foundations too, possibly as an offering or a purification.'

Elisenda was speechless for a moment. 'Newborn babies?' she eventually uttered.

'So your dead man at El Crit could, in most likelihood, have been an execution or even a sacrifice. He was buried, but it's unlikely he was being venerated, wouldn't you say? Or a deterrent or a warning, especially if there was no one to see him?'

The archaeologist turned abruptly and went back inside the dark of the museum.

No, Elisenda thought, but Ferran Arbós probably was.

Chapter Twenty One

'Shortlist, Elisenda. This afternoon. The selection panel is on Wednesday.'

'Wednesday?'

Puigventós looked frankly at her. 'Yes, it says so in the candidate folder I gave you. Remember?'

'Of course.' She gazed back at him. 'I want Francesc Paredes to be added to the list.'

'Paredes?' Puigventós had to recall the name. 'He's a mosso, isn't he? The post is for a caporal.'

'He's eligible for the selection procedure next year. I've no doubt he'll come out among the top candidates in his intake. He knows Girona, I think he's shown himself to be intelligent and resourceful, he's thorough and I believe he has the makings of a good detective. And more importantly, he gets on with the rest of my unit. I'm willing to wait until he qualifies.'

Puigventós shook his head. 'You might be, Elisenda, but Sabadell isn't. If your unit is to prosper, it needs to be brought up to strength. Otherwise I can't ensure that you'll escape scrutiny.' He held his hand up as she was about to speak. 'I'm sorry, Elisenda, but this is non-negotiable. I want the shortlist this afternoon. Without Mosso Paredes.'

Micaló remained silent throughout the exchange.

'Has the composition of the selection panel been decided?' he finally asked.

Puigventós nodded. 'The three of us here and an inspectora from Barcelona. Save a space in your diary.'

At the end of the meeting, Elisenda sat in her office for a few minutes, letting the anger subside. The unusual calm she'd felt on arriving at Vista Alegre that Monday morning had dissipated completely after just fifteen minutes with Puigventós and Micaló.

What had become her morning ritual at La Fosca of a gruelling kayak ride along the coast as far as El Crit before driving to Girona had turned into an unusual moment of peace when she'd spotted a thin whisper of smoke rising into the sky through the pines. It had been coming from somewhere beyond the cove where the archaeological dig lay. On impulse, she'd rowed on and beached the bright yellow kayak on the forbidding grey rocks at Cala des Vedell, scrambling through the sliding stones up the steep face into the tree line. There were no paths worn through the woods here, so she'd had to writhe her way through the dense shade, further into the undergrowth.

Looking up occasionally, she caught brief glimpses of the smoke curling upwards, letting her get her bearings. Expecting to find someone camping in the woods, and to have to tell them to put the fire out because of the risk, she was surprised instead to come across a hut in a clearing. Walking quietly around it, she saw that it was in fact a collection of huts that looked like they'd been tacked on to each other to create a bigger dwelling.

'Very Salvador Dalí,' she muttered to herself, as the whole reminded her of the home the painter had built for himself over some thirty years out of a hotchpotch of fishermen's huts further up the coast.

'Hello,' she called out, listening.

She heard nothing and approached the strange construction. The Mossos had checked out all the homes in the area but had found them all empty, assuming they were summer homes, shut up for the winter, but seeing the collection of old doors that made up one extension wall, Elisenda thought it didn't have the feel of the usual holiday bolthole. It was strange, as she'd never heard of anyone living here.

Pushing against what she presumed was the front door, she let her eyes get accustomed to the dark interior and went in. It was empty, except for the sweet aroma of pine cones burning in an old-fashioned table stove in the centre of the room, the circle of wood with a hole cut in the centre for the stovepipe to emerge, two chairs placed around the table. The sight made her catch her breath. Her grandparents had had one, and she could remember winters in Monells, her knees and legs toasting in the heat that spread from under the table to fill the room with warmth.

Looking around the rooms, she realised that the walls were covered in bookshelves. In fact, the walls *were* bookshelves, thickly coated in old and fraying books, lined up in rows, with more volumes stacked up in front of them. She checked but there was no electricity in the room, just oil lamps, none of them alight. Without her torch, she couldn't take a proper look at the books, but she could see in the light from the open door that they all seemed to be about history. With no exception, as far as she could tell.

Apart from the books and the table stove, the only other piece of furniture in the room was a battered old sofa resting under a window. An open door led into a small kitchen, where she saw a wood-burning stove, presumably for cooking. Her foot knocked into something on the floor. Bending down to take a closer look, she saw it was one of a battery of food bowls, which is when she registered the other scent pervading the room.

'Dogs,' she murmured. 'This is no holiday home.'

No one had returned by the time she'd walked back out into the feeble sunlight filtering through the trees and she heard no dogs barking anywhere, so she'd made her way back to where she'd left the kayak, deciding to return in a more formal capacity later on. Rowing back, she recalled the table stove and remembered her grandparents, a rare feeling of composure accompanying her as she skimmed easily across the gentle surface of the water.

'Elisenda,' Àlex called from the doorway into her office.

Startled, she looked up to realise she'd been lost in thought, recalling the hut in the woods. She was surprised to feel calmer again after the annoyance with Puigventós. She called Àlex in.

'How was Vall-Llobrega?' he asked her.

She told him of the unsurprising lack of any witnesses or leads among Ferran Arbós's neighbours. 'But we did find a collection of coins that could be interesting, given what we're hearing about his shady dealings. I'll be taking them to the Archaeology Service to see if they can shed any light on where they might have come from or why Arbós would have had them in his possession.'

'That is interesting.' Àlex sat down. 'From what Clara Ferré was saying, it seems he wasn't just involved in questionable acquisitions for museums, but in actually selling stolen artefacts to private buyers here and abroad.'

'We need to check up on that. Did you find any connection between Arbós and Mascort?'

'None. Arbós appears to have been too senior to have had much to do with Mascort.'

'I got the same impression.' She checked her diary on her phone. 'Arbós's post mortem is at eleven. You want to take it?'

Àlex nodded. 'How's the shortlist going?'

'Not you too. Puigventós wants it this afternoon.'

'Let's look at it now. I'll help you. Otherwise it'll be hanging over you all day.'

Elisenda considered Àlex's words for a moment and reached for the drawer. 'Why not?'

She pulled the folder out and dumped it on the table between them, not wanting to open it.

'I really don't want to do this,' Àlex said slowly, echoing her thoughts, surprising her. 'May I?'

With a deep sigh, he leaned over and opened the folder, snapping the elastic bands back on the two right-hand corners. The sound seemed to echo in the room.

'There are ten, we have to get them down to five,' Elisenda told him.

'Did I have to go through the same before I got this job?'

'Yeah, but we were a lot less stringent in those days. I pulled your name out of a hat.'

Àlex grinned at her.

'So you were just born lucky.'

He pulled out a sheaf of papers, a thick pile for each candidate and split them into two halves, giving one to Elisenda and keeping the other for himself. The process for taking on a new member of the Serious Crime Unit was another level of selection after the normal lengthy procedure would-be caporals had to go through. To get this far, they'd already had to accumulate up to thirty-three points before they could even submit an application for promotion from mosso to caporal. There were a number of ways of earning points. Candidates got them for being a graduate, for their level of Catalan and for any foreign languages they spoke. They were also awarded half a point for every year they'd been in the Mossos and more points still if they'd received any distinctions or medals.

'No kiddie courses,' Elisenda commented. The more courses a candidate had taken, the more points they earned. 'We want ones who've done investigation courses, not ones for writing press releases or saying their name without falling over.'

The two of them continued to read in silence. Once a candidate had got over the points hurdle, they then had to go on to take written and oral tests, a Catalan language test, physical tests and psychological tests. The moment they failed one stage, they weren't allowed to go on to the next. All along the way, a qualifying tribunal, made up of an equal number of men and women, had the final say on who got to keep going, although candidates could appeal if they felt they'd been hard done by.

'How much do they have to pay to apply now?' Àlex asked.

'Nearly thirty euros.' That was the fee all mossos paid to submit an internal application for promotion. 'What are the piles?'

Àlex had split his reports into three columns. He pointed at them in turn. 'Probable. Possible. Over my dead body.'

Suddenly realising what he'd said, he hurriedly looked down at the next piece of paper and carried on reading. He was mortified, Elisenda could tell, but oddly she saw it as a minor triumph on the road to recovery.

'I've got two piles,' she said to soothe him. 'Don't want. Really don't want.'

He looked up. 'Do you get the feeling we're not going about this with the right attitude?' The grin was back.

After the points and the tests, when the tribunal published a list of the candidates in the order of how well they'd done, came the training course in Sabadell, followed by a three-month placement, working as an acting caporal. If the aspirants got through all that, the tribunal would announce a list of the ones who passed and they got the job, which meant they could be posted to anywhere in Catalonia where there was a vacancy. What was unusual in this case was the invitation to be part of Thursday's selection panel for a place on Elisenda's experimental Serious Crime Unit.

'Any in Girona?' Elisenda asked.

'Not yet.'

They finished their probables piles and swapped them over.

'But none of them appeals to me so far,' Elisenda muttered.

Àlex was silent for a moment. 'It's a tough act to follow.'

They stared at each other across the desk, both of them thinking of Pau, the member they'd lost.

Josep knocked on the door and walked in.

'Sotsinspectora, I've found the last of the 1981 archaeologists, Martí Barbena.'

'Good work, Josep,' she replied, glad of the interruption. 'Where is he?'

'Here in Girona. He's married to Eulàlia Esplugues, Esteve Mascort's widow.'

Chapter Twenty Two

'I told you. We weren't together in 1981.'

Eulàlia Esplugues sat forward on the plastic and metal chair, her arms lying heavily on the bare table, her fingers soundlessly and frenetically drumming centimetres above the wooden surface.

Àlex nodded and looked from her to Montse and back. 'Why didn't you tell my colleagues you'd married one of the other archaeologists who was on the El Crit dig at the time your husband went missing?'

Esplugues looked angrily at him and then at Montse. 'Why should I? I didn't think it was important.'

'Your husband goes missing in 1981, now believed to have been murdered at that time, and you didn't think it was important to tell us that you were having an affair with one of his colleagues?' Montse asked.

'Don't you dare.' Spittle from her mouth landed on the table between them. 'It was my husband who had the affairs. I was the poor, dumb wife who sat at home while he got away with it. Don't you dare tell me I was the one having the affair.'

Àlex studied her face as she answered Montse. Through her anger, he could see deep lines of injustice scored into her. It was his turn to speak. 'Are you saying you began a relationship with Martí Barbena after your husband went missing?'

'You're damn right I am.'

In another room, Elisenda and Josep were interviewing Martí Barbena. He looked strangely like a computer reconstruction of how he might have aged based on the photo they saw in Jordi Canudas' office. The gaunt cheeks more sunken as he'd grown more fibrous into his late fifties, the thin nose accentuated, the hair more sparse with flecks of grey but still with the same neat parting, the same cool expression on his face, the same slightly mocking tilt of the head.

Elisenda watched Josep as he questioned the man. The moment the caporal had told her about Barbena and Esplugues being married, she'd decided she wanted to speak to them both. She hadn't asked Jutge Rigau for any warrants and the couple hadn't been arrested, they were merely being interviewed. Depending on the Mossos' judgement after this stage, Elisenda would arrest them or not and refer the case to the judge for him to instruct the investigation. It wouldn't be until after this interview with the police that they'd be allowed to speak to their lawyer or be assigned a duty one. Things hadn't got to that stage yet, Elisenda mused.

'He was a shit,' Barbena said of Mascort, 'but I didn't kill him. Even if I would ever contemplate taking another life, which I wouldn't, I had no reason to.'

'You were having an affair with his wife,' Josep told him.

'Not in 1981 I wasn't.'

'When did you begin an affair?' Elisenda pushed him.

He turned to gaze at her. 'I didn't. Technically, it was never an affair. I'd met Eulàlia a couple of times socially before her husband went missing, but that was all. We didn't begin seeing each other until more than four years after that, and we got married almost two years after he was declared dead.'

'But you knew Eulàlia Esplugues at the time her husband went missing, now believed to have been murdered?' Josep insisted.

'Evidently. But that would have been some waiting game, don't you think?'

'Maybe it was.'

Elisenda watched Barbena as he spoke quietly with little emotion, his words considered. She could see he'd be difficult to push into admitting anything in the heat of anger. She wondered if he'd be capable of acting in anger.

—

'You felt a sense of relief when your husband went missing?'

Eulàlia Esplugues sighed at Àlex's question and looked at Montse. 'I told you the other day. I felt anything but relief. I was this close to being able to divorce him. The last thing I wanted was for him to run off and leave me in limbo. I wasn't allowed to get on with my life as I was legally still married to him for another ten years until I could have him declared dead, and I could never fully move on at all because I was afraid he'd come back one day.' She looked back to Àlex. 'So, no, at no time did I ever feel a sense of relief.'

'Did you do anything to find him?' Àlex wanted to know.

'The police did.' She shrugged. 'As much as they ever did back then. I was made to feel he was justified in leaving me the way he did because I'd not been a proper wife, not malleable enough. I told them everything I knew, but they didn't break into a sweat looking for him. Neither did I.'

'Where did you think he might have gone?'

'With one of his other women, I presumed. The idea didn't surprise me.'

'Did he know your son wasn't his?'

Esplugues laughed bitterly. 'Good God no. He didn't have the imagination to think I would ever cheat on him. Or the humility to believe I would want to. I can assure you, he had no doubts that our son was his.'

'And you thought him capable of leaving you both so easily?' Montse asked her.

She cocked her head at the caporala. 'What do you think?'

'Would there have been any other reason why you thought he might have left?' Àlex asked. 'Money problems? Anything to do with his work?'

'Not that I know of, but that doesn't mean much. He kept most of his life outside our home to himself.'

Àlex leaned forward across the table. 'So how do you feel now that you've learned of his death?'

–

Barbena considered Elisenda's question. 'Nothing. I feel absolutely nothing at Mascort's death. I couldn't stand him when he was alive, I didn't worry about him once when we thought he was missing and I feel nothing knowing that he's dead. As far as I was concerned, he ceased to exist a long time ago.'

Josep looked directly into his eyes. 'That's interesting. You never worried when he was missing. Not even about him coming back?'

'That didn't concern me in the slightest.'

'Because you knew fully well that he wouldn't be coming back?'

Barbena gave a small laugh and shook his head. 'If you're implying that I knew he wasn't about to return because I'd killed him, you're barking up the wrong tree. I wasn't the slightest bit concerned because he wasn't the sort to show any worries for his wife and son. I believed he was gone for good, of his own accord.'

'Can you account for where you were last Thursday night?' Elisenda asked him.

'Last Thursday?' He didn't once lose his cool or falter. 'What's that got to do with anything?

—

'I was with Martí last Thursday,' Esplugues told Àlex. 'We went out for dinner. Why?'

'You were both together?'

'With friends. We went to Cal Ros with another couple.'

'Can you give me their names?'

Esplugues gave Àlex a couple of names and an address, which he wrote down.

'Until what time were you with them?' Montse asked.

'About midnight, I think.'

'And after that?'

'We went home.'

'Can anyone corroborate that?' Àlex asked her.

'It was just the two of us, me and Martí. Our friends walked with us as far as our car.'

'But they wouldn't be able to say where you went once you left them?' Montse pushed.

'What is this?'

'How well did you know a man called Ferran Arbós?' Àlex changed tack.

She paused for a moment, surprised at the turn in questioning. 'Not at all. I think Martí knows him. Why?'

—

'I'm an archaeologist,' Barbena told Elisenda. 'I met him professionally a number of times.'

'I take it you know that Ferran Arbós was found dead last week.'

'Of course I know. What I don't know is what it's got to do with me. Or Eulàlia. Or Mascort for that matter.'

'What professional dealings did you have with him?' Josep asked.

Barbena sat back, a knowing expression on his face. 'Ah, I see. You think I was part of Arbós's little emporium of forbidden antiquities and that we fell out, so I killed him. Is that it?'

'Emporium of forbidden antiquities?' Elisenda questioned.

'Don't be coy. We all knew Arbós was up to something long before he had to leave his job. Dud finds, fake provenance, artefacts not recorded.'

'But you all turned a blind eye. Why was that?'

'I didn't, I think you'll find. There are reports kept in the archive where I questioned many of his actions. You simply have to look.'

'And that's why there was some enmity between the two of you?'

'Leading to me going to his house and killing him? Because I wrote reports on his misdemeanours over ten years ago? Really? How likely does that sound to you?'

'Quite likely if you had some involvement in his illegal trading,' Josep countered.

'Illicit trading, we call it,' Barbena corrected him, a smile at the edges of his mouth. 'Or more commonly, illicit trafficking. And if I were involved in it, why would I bring it to the attention of the authorities by flagging up Arbós's activities?'

Elisenda stood up. 'Thank you, Senyor Barbena, if you wouldn't mind waiting here a while.'

She signalled to Josep and they both left the archaeologist alone in the interview room.

–

Àlex had one final question for the time being.

'Did your husband own a Sony Walkman?'

Esplugues was taken aback. 'One of those personal stereo things? You must be kidding. They really weren't his style at all. Anyway, were they even around when he went missing?'

'Died, Senyora Esplugues, died. Your husband was murdered.'

Àlex and Montse stood up and left her in the room. Àlex watched Esplugues as they went out, her expression one of consternation rather than concern, impatience rather than panic.

Outside, they found Elisenda and Josep waiting for them in the corridor.

'Well?' Elisenda asked them.

'If they did do it, they're good,' Àlex commented.

'If they did do it. And if they did, which one did they do? Mascort? Arbós? Both? Or did one do Mascort and the other do Arbós?'

'What did the post mortem on Arbós find?' Josep asked Àlex.

'Much as we all saw,' Àlex told him. He'd attended Riera's examination that morning while the others had gone to bring Esplugues and Barbena in for questioning. He'd only had time to tell Elisenda what the pathologist had said, but not Josep and Montse. 'The chisel through the front of the skull is what killed Arbós, but there was also a blow to the back of the head consistent with the hammer, most probably used to knock him out so the killer could position him for the blow with the chisel.'

'Hell,' Montse whispered. 'So cold.'

'Precisely,' Elisenda said. 'Arbós's killing was cold, calculating. Some sort of display or reprisal.'

'Or warning,' Montse added.

'Indeed. But seemingly carried out with complete calm, the perpetrator cool enough not to leave any traces. Whereas Mascort's killing looks like it was done in anger, a heat of the moment attack with the nearest weapon to hand.'

'So you're saying not the same person?' Àlex asked.

Josep nodded at the door to the interview room where Barbena was sitting. 'Guy in there's pretty cold. Nothing seems to get him worked up.'

'He doesn't strike me as the most compassionate of people either,' Elisenda agreed. 'I couldn't see him doing anything out of anger or that he didn't plan, but a cold act of reprisal or warning or whatever we think the motive is. That's possible.'

'And I'd say that after years of marriage to Mascort,' Montse added, 'Esplugues would be capable of losing her temper enough to lash out at him.'

'A lot of people would by the sound of Mascort,' Àlex said. 'But given that she was the one to suffer the most at his hands, it does put her in the frame for his death, despite what she says about waiting for a divorce.'

Elisenda listened to them all in turn before speaking. 'So we think it possible that she could be responsible for Mascort's death, and Barbena for Arbós's death, possibly even to protect Esplugues if Arbós had something on her after Mascort's body was found.'

'Or they were both involved in Arbós's killing,' Àlex suggested. 'Could one person have carried out the attack on their own?'

'We need to consider that,' Elisenda agreed. 'The question is, do we have enough to hold them? We'll have to take what we've got to Jutge Rigau and see what he has to say.'

'You're not entirely convinced, are you?' Àlex asked her.

'Are you?'

Her mobile chimed to tell her an email had come in, and she opened her bag to hunt for it.

Àlex looked over his shoulder at the room he'd just left and shook his head. 'No, I'm not.'

Elisenda read the message that had just come in for her and looked in surprise at Àlex.

'I'm less convinced now,' she told him, brandishing her phone. 'DNA results. The body at the El Crit dig. It isn't a match for Mascort.'

Chapter Twenty Three

Jutge Rigau's office was as bland as her own, Elisenda thought, looking around at the smooth plasterboard walls and ceiling set just too low to feel anything other than steadfastly crushed. The thin windows, which were partially crossed with curious grey strips of concrete that did nothing to enhance the building, inside or out, looked out on to the drab and regimented car park. There were few vehicles left there at this time of the evening. Elisenda watched as two women laden with heavy briefcases emerged from the courthouse and made their way slowly through the gloom to separate identical cars. We all wear uniforms, she thought, looking down at her own brown leather jacket and hard-wearing office trousers. Like her, Rigau had nothing on his walls that revealed anything of him, just the obligatory framed degree certificates and membership of the bar association. No family photos or scenes of past sporting triumphs, not even any of the shop-bought prints that Elisenda used to give nothing of herself away.

The court building was just a few blocks from La Bisbal's charming main drag, studded at one end with the cavernous ceramics shops and potteries for which the town was famed and at the other with faded antiques shops. The two sides met at the river, separated by a bridge and a fine old building with shops and cafés under high porticoes like a benevolent checkpoint. It was a very different world from the legal offices and the new Mossos station in the dusty, modern streets apparently hidden away beyond the old town.

She looked back to the judge, who was raising his eyes at her as he tried to finish a phone call that was evidently heavy going. He bowed his head in exasperation for a moment and she saw for the first time that his hair was thinning, his winter-pale scalp visible through fine black hair. He looked up and she found it hard to reconcile with his childlike face behind the grown-up glasses.

'Sorry about that, Elisenda,' the judge told her once he'd hung up. 'What can I do for you?'

'Eulàlia Esplugues and Martí Barbena,' Elisenda began, going on to explain that she and her team had questioned the two suspects in Girona. 'Nothing in their story wavered at any time. Each corroborated the other, neither incriminated themselves.'

'But?' Rigau added for her.

Elisenda sighed and shook her head. 'That's the rub, Pere. I do have some doubts about their involvement in the two murders, but I think that there is the possibility that Esplugues would have had the motive, means and capability of killing her husband in anger. And Barbena strikes me as being cold enough and arrogant enough to have killed Ferran Arbós in the way in which he was murdered.'

'To silence him? Arbós knew about Esplugues killing her husband and was blackmailing her? He has a record of trying to make easy money.'

'Yes, possibly to silence him if she was indeed involved in her husband's murder. But the staging still suggests retribution or a warning to me.'

'Which would conceivably rule out your theory,' Rigau considered. 'You want me to instruct the investigation in the direction of them as suspects to give you time to turn up anything more?'

'That's rub number two,' Elisenda had to admit. 'We've just learned that the DNA sample we took from Esteve Mascort's father doesn't match the body we found at El Crit.'

Rigau sat back heavily and let out a low whistle through his front teeth. 'Meaning, apart from anything else, that Esplugues and Barbena fall out of the frame if the victim isn't her husband. In that case, Elisenda, I can't really sanction your continuing to investigate them as suspects. Unless you have a strong argument otherwise.'

'Not a strong argument, Pere, but there is a circumstance that I think we need to consider. Esplugues admitted that Mascort wasn't the natural father to their son. Now, we only have DNA from Mascort's father.'

Rigau nodded, a smile on his face. 'And you think that's a precedent.'

'It feels uncomfortable, but we have to consider that just as Esteve Mascort wasn't his son's birth father, then Mascort senior might not have been Esteve Mascort's real father. We only have his DNA to go on to identify the body at El Crit.'

'Visiting the iniquity of the fathers on to the children,' the judge said. 'Only in this case, the mothers.'

Elisenda could feel a flare of irritation rise up in her. 'That's harsh, Pere. Any iniquities of one of the mothers at least seems to me to be more than understandable and far less iniquitous than anything her husband subjected her to.'

Rigau held his hands up in front of him in placation. 'Merely quoting, Elisenda. I agree with you. So what do you want from me for the investigation?'

'I want Esplugues and Barbena to continue to be people of interest, but I also want to find another of Mascort's relatives, on his mother's side, to take another DNA test.'

Rigau moved a couple of folders about on his desk while he considered her requests. 'Yes, of course,' he finally assented. 'Do you have any other suspects?'

'We're following up the other archaeologists and students from the 1981 dig. One of them, Ricard Soler, has gone missing. It's possible the news of Arbós's death prompted that. We want to find his whereabouts and interview him, so I need a warrant for an alert out on him. If Mascort's killing is not related to a domestic issue, or if the body at the El Crit dig really isn't Mascort, we're also considering the illegal trafficking in archaeological artefacts as a motive. Soler's disappearance makes him someone that we're interested in seeing regarding that.'

The judge made a note of Ricard Soler's name. 'Illicit trafficking,' he corrected her absently. 'You think the media might have flushed Soler out in some way? Do you have pictures of him we can circulate?'

'None have come to light. His old employers have nothing, no family, no criminal record and we're not going to get hold of his ID card details anytime soon for the obvious reasons.'

Rigau looked up and grunted. ID cards were a national matter and so their jurisdiction was retained by the Spanish Policía Nacional. The wheels between the two forces were slow and unoiled. 'Okay, I'll do the necessary. Keep me informed of all the avenues and let me know if any more come up.'

'I'd also like a warrant to search Soler's flat in Barcelona.'

The judge thought for a moment and shook his head. 'I can't sanction that until we have evidence of any wrong-doing on his part. If you come back to me with just cause for me to issue a warrant, I'll consider it.' He held his hand up to stop any further argument on the matter.

Not entirely satisfied, Elisenda left the judge in his dark grey basilica and drove on towards the coast away from Girona. She knew that with the interviews for the new caporal later in the week, she'd have to spend a night or so in her own apartment, so she wanted to make the most of her sister's house in La Fosca and the unexpected solid nights' sleep it was bringing her.

'Move to the coast,' she suggested out loud to herself as the car ghosted through the shuttered villages on the main road, but then she thought of Girona and how hard she'd worked to move back to the refuge of her city from Barcelona and her failed marriage and dead daughter. 'Who are you kidding?'

She thought of another death and of the shortlist she'd given to Puigventós after Eulàlia Esplugues and Martí Barbena had been allowed to go home. The inspector had quickly counted them.

'Only one woman out of the five?' he'd questioned her.

'There were only three in the ten candidates in the longlist,' she'd replied, although to be honest, she hadn't realised she and Àlex had only put one woman in their probables lists. When Josep had come in and told them of Barbena being married to Mascort's wife, she'd been grateful to scoop up the applications and stuff them in the folder to give to Puigventós. Another unwanted matter forgotten about for a day or two.

'I want Mosso Paredes to be included,' she'd insisted one more time.

'Forget it, Elisenda.'

On impulse, on the road to the coast from La Bisbal, she kept on going past the turnoff for La Fosca and drove on to Palamós, leaving her car in the public parking area by the port, under the old harbour walls. The sea had receded over the past few centuries and the imposing stones of the medieval dock were now stranded a couple of hundred metres inland, their mooring arches home to boutiques and restaurants. Walking through the tiny Plaça de Sant Pere, surrounded by bars and restaurants, quiet and colourless on a February Monday, she smiled to herself as she always did at the broad canopy of the single pine tree growing out of its raised stone-clad bed. She remembered as a child watching in thrall as cars tried to get round the tree in one go, everyone in the square sitting in cold silence every time a Guardia Civil patrol failed and had to manoeuvre its way around in embarrassment, the entire crowd waiting until the police got fifty metres down the road before breaking into a cheer. That was long ago. The square was one-way now and the area behind the tree paved, the Mossos spared the ignominy of their predecessors.

Climbing the steep street from the little road at the end of the square to the warren of narrow streets between the church, looming over the old town as they always did, and the small balcony overlooking the sea, she found the hotel she was looking for and went in to the warmth of the small lobby. Once a nondescript place for low-cost tourism, its cheap tile floors and mock-Castilian dark wood furniture had been ripped out some twenty years earlier and the whole turned into a boutique hotel that teetered on the edge of being too chic for its own good. In its former life, it would have been closed in the winter, but the canny new owner had seen the potential of a quality place to stay for weekenders from Barcelona and kept it open all year round. One of its attractions was its restaurant, which is where Elisenda was now headed and which was nonetheless quiet despite the hotel's new persona.

It was the owner who served her. Like many of his guests, he too was from Barcelona, Elisenda could tell by his accent. She'd only visited the place once before, with friends, and didn't know him. She ordered and waited for him to return with her wine, a Raimat red from Lleida, one of its recent very good vintages. She'd seen the owner nod in appreciation when she'd ordered it. By the time he brought it, the only other diners in the room, a couple, had paid for their meal and left.

'You're a bit late,' the owner told her. He introduced himself as Guillem Sucarrats. 'It was quite busy earlier. But, hey, Monday.' He smiled, an open, expressive smile that involved not just his face but his shoulders and arms too, all the way down to his long, tapering fingers. It invited a smile in return from Elisenda, despite herself.

Up close, she could see that he was older than she'd first thought, a life of sunlight and lotus flowers by the sea ageing the skin while keeping the eyes and all they saw young. His salt and pepper hair was brushed back in studied untidiness, his face and hands fine and neat, his heavy shirt and trousers a winter's nod to careless fashion.

'Llàtzer Bosch told me about your place,' Elisenda told him after she'd tasted the wine.

He nodded. 'Llàtzer. He's quite a regular visitor.'

'Would you like to share some of this wine?' She gestured to the bottle. 'I can't drink it all.'

Shrugging assent, he fetched a glass and poured himself a measure. 'Good to meet someone else who enjoys the finer things in life. *Salut.*'

'He also told me about your shrine,' Elisenda continued. 'The Roman one in the cellar.'

'Although he might no longer be welcome as a regular,' Sucarrats replied, evidently annoyed at the archaeologist's disclosure.

Elisenda reached into her bag and pulled her ID out. 'Elisenda Domènech. I'm with the Mossos. I'm investigating an old case nearby and Doctor Bosch was helping me. He simply mentioned the shrine in passing.'

Sucarrats looked at Elisenda's ID and took a moment to digest it. 'The body found at El Crit?' he finally asked. 'I wondered what was happening about that.'

'Don't worry, I'm not about to go telling everyone about the shrine. I'm just interested in it.'

'Professionally?'

'And personally. I heard about the Indiketa practice of burying babies in the foundations of homes and I needed to understand it.'

The chef called something from the kitchen and Sucarrats excused himself, coming back straight away with Elisenda's first course. 'Maybe I'll show it to you after you've eaten,' he told her.

By the end of her meal, the owner's irritation had dissipated, to be replaced by his earlier sure composure. Promising her coffee after the tour, he led her to a door to the rear of the dining room and unlocked it with a key on a small chain in his pocket.

'The Romans did it too,' he told her as they descended a steep flight of steps. 'Buried babies in the foundations of buildings. And adults. Usually alive. Although none have ever been found anywhere in Catalonia or Spain that I know of.'

At the bottom, past rows of boxes and bottles of wine stacked on shelves, he unlocked a second door and flicked a switch inside. Half a dozen lights embedded in the ceiling came on, casting a warm glow over old brick walls.

'You know a lot about it?'

He smiled again. It reminded her of Àlex. 'When you have a piece of Rome under your feet, you tend to develop an interest in it.'

He let her in first and she stopped immediately at the sight in front of her. Smaller than she'd expected, the shrine set into the far wall of the small room nonetheless dominated the tiny cell. A woman's face carved in stone peered sightlessly from crumbling and ancient ashlars, the hewn stones in turn set into a modern plaster surround. Below the face were niches for incense or candles, the shadows from the lights in the ceiling creating an unnatural depth to them. Underneath, a small ledge, smooth and worn in the middle over the centuries, held a single red candle, unlit, the one point of colour in the room.

'Minerva,' Sucarrats told Elisenda in a hushed voice. 'Goddess of wisdom, commerce, poetry and magic. And subsequently of war. I'm just her keeper.'

As she stared at it, the shrine seemed to grow with every breath she took and creep towards her in the honeyed radiance of the cellar. She shivered.

'It gets cold down here in the winter,' Sucarrats said.

Elisenda knew that wasn't the reason.

Chapter Twenty Four

'I fucking hate February.'

'You hate every month, Siset.'

Wrapping his over-large coat around his skinny body more tightly, the front buttons reaching around to under his opposite arm, Siset shivered and sniffed loudly.

'And it stinks in here.'

Elena, Siset's on-off partner paused in doing her make-up in front of the greasy mirror in the men's toilets, moving her head up and down to avoid the crack across the bottom half of the glass. 'Well, what do you know,' she muttered absently.

Siset looked up sharply at her. 'I've never hit you once, have I, Elena? Not once.'

'No, Siset, not once.'

'Never even raised my hand to you,' he went on. Of course not, he thought, she's not going to earn much money covered in bruises, is she? And because her pimp would have beaten seven bells of crap out of him, he remembered with a gulp. 'I'm good to you, aren't I? So don't start getting fucking lippy with me. I don't deserve it.'

'No, Siset.'

'No, Siset,' he repeated, his thin lips pulled back over yellowing teeth. He stared at her running her fingers over her eyebrows. 'How much fucking longer are you going to be? I've got business to do.'

Elena turned away from the mirror and looked around. 'Nice office, Siset. You're doing well for yourself.'

He made a gesture as though he was about to slap her, but she stood her ground and stared back at him. She knew he'd never dare hit her, not just because her pimp would have battered him but because Siset knew that Elena would hit him back too. The one time he'd tried it, she'd knocked him out, his eye blackened for a fortnight.

The door to the gloomy toilet in the crummy bar in the Font de la Pólvora part of town opened and a middle-aged man in stained trousers and a grubby nylon shirt came in, tugging at his flies and heading for the least encrusted urinal in the battery of three.

'I'm off,' Elena told Siset. She checked her clutch bag – condoms, tissues, mobile, mace – and walked out of the men's toilets.

'What you got for me?' the man who'd entered the grim room asked Siset, his voice a forty-cigarettes-a-day-for-forty-years growl. Straggly grey and white hair clung damply to his skull, tied in an alopecic ponytail so small it sprouted vertically from halfway up the back of his head. He stood at the porcelain and peed loudly, splashing a fine spray on to his trousers, before zipping up and offering his hand to Siset to shake. Siset took it without a moment's hesitation, his own sanitary regime knowing no better.

Reaching into the battered old-fashioned postman's satchel he'd found discarded on a tip years ago, Siset thrust a bony hand inside and pulled out a pile of DVDs, held together with an elastic band.

'No animals,' the man rumbled at him. 'I don't want animals. Or ladyboys.'

His brows furrowed intently as he flipped through the discs. He had been deprived of cinema, and a great many other privileges, for lengthy periods when Hollywood was releasing its blockbusters, so he evidently had a fair bit of catching up to do.

'Have you got *Toy Story*?'

Before Siset could answer, both men were startled by shouts and a loud bang as the door crashed open and half a dozen figures in uniform suddenly filled the narrow toilets. Siset saw guns being pointed at him and quickly dropped his bag.

'I want to speak to Domènech,' he whispered to the Mosso who closed the cuffs around his scrawny wrists.

Chapter Twenty Five

Elisenda parked in the garage under the house and climbed the steep stairs up into the kitchen, turning the dimmer switch up high and flooding the ground floor of the house in light. After seeing the shrine in the hotel in Palamós, she'd had an irrational urge to get out of the basement garage as quickly as she could, the memories of the sightless face in the little room and of babies buried in cellars preying on her.

She looked around at the dazzling living room and finally laughed. She'd always teased Sergi about his dimmers and embedded sound systems and latest gadgets, all things she would never dream of having in her own home, but she was surprised at herself to find them oddly comforting since she'd been staying on the coast alone. Checking her phone for messages, she found there was no signal. She'd discovered these days that the mobile cover out here slipped in and out quite frequently. As it was a holiday home, her sister didn't keep a landline in the house.

'Sea,' she decided, repelling the silence pervading the house, and walked out of the front door, on to the path that ran along the seafront.

She stood there, letting a cold breeze force its way through her shirt to her skin. She shivered for a second time that evening, only this time it had a strangely warm feel, the sound of the midnight Mediterranean talking to her alone as it whispered back and forth over the stretches of shingle below. A shadow moving in a rectangle of light over to her right distracted her and she looked back to the other houses. The man she'd thought was burgling the next door home but one the other night was standing on his terrace, also looking out to sea.

'Sorry,' he called over to her. 'I didn't mean to disturb you.'

She clutched her arms around herself against the chill wind. 'Not at all. I was just getting some air before bed.'

'I keep forgetting I'm not on my own out here.'

She nodded and tried to recall his name. Miquel Canals, she remembered. 'Me too.'

'I've just made *cremat*. There's too much for one person. Would you like some?'

For the first time, she noticed the sweet aroma of cinnamon washing past her, the scent drawing her in.

'I'd love some.'

She fetched a sweater and joined him on his terrace. On a low table between two solid wood chairs, the middle of the earthenware bowl was already alight. She sat down and watched in silence as the flames illuminated her host's expression of concentration, his lean face calm and controlled in the shadows that flickered across it, his eyes gleaming dark. He slowly stirred the mix of rum, coffee, sugar and cinnamon, the fire burning off the alcohol and releasing the oily perfume from the large slices of lemon peel. Putting the ladle down, he let it burn for a few minutes, the flickering heat a welcome warmth in the cold night.

'I'd never had this before coming to La Fosca,' he told her. 'We don't have it in Barcelona.'

'It was a fishermen's drink,' Elisenda explained, the glow from the flames warming her face. 'To keep warm in the early mornings. It's originally from this part of the coast.'

He blew the flames out and served them both a cup from the ladle. Elisenda closed her hands around the thick porcelain, the heat almost too much to bear but painfully enjoyable. She took in a deep breath of the strong aroma before carefully sipping it.

'It's good,' she told him.

'What do I call you? Inspectora?'

'Thanks for the promotion, but there's no need. Elisenda will do.' She remembered his refusal to answer her question the other night, so she asked him again. 'So, what brings you here at this time of year?'

'You reckon you get to ask me that now?'

'We're sharing *cremat*. That's how it works round here.'

He let out a little laugh and stared silently at his cup for a moment.

'My father died. Just after Christmas.'

Elisenda closed her eyes and cursed her police officer's need to know. 'I'm sorry.'

'I just needed some time on my own, so I came here. My mother died when I was a kid, and I've got no brothers or sisters, so it's just me now. It feels so strange knowing I'm on my own. He and I were all we had, so we were very close.' He laughed, a movement of his shoulders more than a sound. 'So I came somewhere where I'd be even more on my own. That makes sense.'

'I think it does. Only you got stuck with a nosey cop for a neighbour.'

He held up the cup of *cremat*. 'Now I get to ask you. What are you doing here?'

'Not sure it works that way,' Elisenda replied, taking another sip to stall.

She thought of Lina, her daughter, and of the sleepless nights at home, woken by visions of her and the sound of her singing. And of how much she wanted to let go of her daughter and not be haunted by her and of how much guilt that released in her.

'Just for work,' she finally told him. 'It's convenient for an investigation.'

—

Forgoing her now usual habit of an early-morning kayaking out to sea or along the shoreline, Elisenda left the house early and drove the three sides of the square that would take her nearer to where she'd found the hut in the woods the previous day. She parked in a clearing and made her way through the dense trees. There was no smoke spiralling into the sky today to guide her, but she knew the direction to take, the small house two-thirds of the way between the track where she'd left her car and the sea.

Through the thick foliage, she could see the sky was a rich winter blue, cloudless and pure, only a ghost of her breath visible as she walked. The air was much warmer than the previous night, when she and Miquel Canals had soon retreated into their separate homes after sharing *cremat* and confidences.

'Or not, in my case,' she murmured to herself.

A twig snapped like a gunshot in front of her and she instantly ducked, looking keenly around her. Holding her breath to listen, in the distance she heard another sound. Someone or something moving quickly away from her towards the sea.

'And trying not to be heard,' she whispered to herself.

Getting up, she began to run in the direction of the noise, stopping every now and again to get her bearings. The sound appeared to be heading for the little cove at Cala des Vedell, so she gave up listening out and quickened her pace through the trees to try and catch up. As she got closer, she heard the snarl of a motor being hauled into life.

Emerging through the thick pines where they disappeared on to the rocks above the water's edge, she was just in time to catch a glimpse of a boat vanishing around the headland, moving north. It was the one that belonged to the old man she'd met twice on the beach at El Crit. She stared at the wake rippling either side after the little craft had disappeared from view and coming to rest against the rocks.

'So, you're just cleaning the beach?' she questioned in a low voice.

Elisenda turned back from the shore and scraped through the pines inland in the direction of the jumbled house. She slowed down as she approached it and looked around. She heard a dog bark once.

'You might as well come in again,' a woman's voice called out from inside the house. 'You weren't so shy at trespassing on my property yesterday.'

A huge dog emerged from the ramshackle cabin and loped towards Elisenda. A Great Dane, its light grey body came as high as her hip. Wandering up to her, the dog looked up and allowed Elisenda to ruffle its head.

The same voice rang out of the house. 'She likes you. You might not be all bad. Come inside.'

With the dog following her, Elisenda approached the strange building and climbed up on to the stoop running along the front. Stepping inside, she paused to let her eyes get accustomed to the gloom.

'I'm used to it,' the woman said. 'The light. Humans can get used to anything if only we can be bothered. Let me look at you.'

A figure came towards Elisenda and peered closely at her face.

'Name?'

'Elisenda Domènech. I'm with the Mossos d'Esquadra.'

Elisenda's eyes got used to the dark and she could make out a woman in a flowing dress made of a sort of hessian material, held at the waist with an old-fashioned men's fabric belt, fastened with a serpent clasp. The woman's hair was short and grey and looked like she cut it herself, with little tufts sticking out at odd angles and softer locks hanging down at random.

'A woman in the police? Would never have happened in my day, we were too busy protesting against them. And you're Catalan?'

'We have our own police now,' Elisenda answered with a slight smile. 'You haven't noticed?'

The woman looked straight into Elisenda's eyes and grunted. 'You look intelligent. Things really must have changed if they allow that in the police nowadays.'

'May I ask your name?'

'You may, that doesn't mean I'll give it to you. Would you like a coffee? I've got some brewing on the stove. Sit down.'

Elisenda sat at one of the two chairs by the table stove and immediately felt the heat from the firewood warm her knees in the way she remembered from childhood. The Great Dane came and stood next to her for a nuzzle before flopping down on an old wooden rocking chair Elisenda hadn't noticed before. Two other dogs came up and sniffed around her feet, a cocker spaniel and another smaller breed that she didn't recognise.

The older woman returned from the kitchen, holding two mismatched cups without saucers. She nodded at the Great Dane enveloping the chair, which was far too small for it and creaking under its weight. Its front and back legs dangled over the arms either side, resting on a small rug underneath it.

'And Flora seems to trust you,' she said, putting the cups down on the table, 'so you can't be too god-awful. Stupid creature, she thinks she's as small as my other dogs and doesn't realise the chair's not her size. She won't let anyone else sit there.'

'You have three dogs?'

'About a dozen at the last count. I take them in. People abandon them and I look after them. I get the odd busy-body thinking I want more, so they bring me any stray dog they find and expect me to feed it.'

'Which you always do,' Elisenda guessed.

The old woman grunted again and took a sip of her coffee. Elisenda did likewise. It was hot, black and strong, like her grandmother used to make. Another dog ran into the room from outside, its tail wagging eagerly. It was carrying a pine cone in its mouth, which it dropped at the woman's feet. The woman stroked its ears and smiled for the first time, a gentle smile full of warmth, her eyes sparkling in the light cast in through the open door.

'You have an interest in history,' Elisenda commented, gesturing towards the books.

The woman looked at the shelves for a moment. 'I taught history. A long time ago. Before we all decided to abandon our history and revere commerce. That's when I took my own decision that you could all do without my company. And I could do without yours.'

'I have to ask you some questions.'

'My house is legal, if that's what you're after. It's not like other people's houses, but it has more permits and pieces of paper than anyone would ever want or need.'

Elisenda shook her head and looked around at the books and the dogs and felt the comfort of the table stove. 'I'm really not worried about that. I think you have a lovely house, if you want to know. I'm here about a body that was found a short distance away.'

The woman nodded her head slowly. 'Ah, the body.'

'You've heard about it?'

'I might be cut off from society, but that doesn't mean I'm not aware of it. I see what happens in these woods and on this coast, more than most people. So yes, I know about the body.'

'It's a body of a man,' Elisenda explained. 'You might also know that. We believe he was placed there in 1981, at the time of the last archaeological dig. Can I ask how long you've been living here?'

'Well, I wasn't living here in 1981, I can tell you that. I was teaching in Barcelona. I bought this land in 1983.

There was just an old hut on it then, which is now the kitchen, but I didn't start living here for about ten years after that. That's how long it took me to see your society wasn't for me.'

'So you wouldn't have known this area at the time the man was buried here? Have you seen or heard anything unusual in the days since the body was found?'

'Only police and archaeologists tramping everywhere, digging everything up.'

Elisenda thought of the old man on the beach. 'Anyone taking an unusual interest in the woods or in the area of the dig?'

'All human interest here is unusual. Unnatural. There are always people spoiling the calm of this place, no more so now than normal.'

'Have you seen an older man picking up litter on El Crit beach? He gets there by boat.'

'Picking up litter?' She finished her coffee and put the cup down. 'He's been around for years.'

Elisenda drained her cup of thick coffee and stood up. She gave the woman her card. 'If you do notice anything, please let me know.'

The woman took the card and studied it before laying it face down on the table.

'Maria,' she said, gazing up at Elisenda. 'My name's Maria Pujol. You aren't an entirely hopeless case, unlike most. You're free to come back and see me any time you want.'

'Thank you, Maria. I will.'

Out of an impulsive need to check on the site, Elisenda made her way through the pines to the El Crit dig. There was no path to help her and her route along the uneven ground amid the dense trees and sliding carpet of pine needles took her over twenty minutes. Neither of the archaeologists was there when she got to the two trenches. She listened out but heard no movement from the woods around her. Looking closely at the twin excavation sites, she was satisfied that they appeared to be as tidy as she imagined Doctora Fradera would have left them the previous evening. Both were calm. No one seemed to have tampered with anything.

Turning to head back for the long walk to the clearing where she'd parked her car, she stopped dead.

There, facing the new trench and hidden from view as she'd walked down to it, the head of a thick metal spike jutted from an ancient pine. A dark stain of sap coursed down the deep grooves in the aged and peeling bark like dried blood.

Chapter Twenty Six

At Vista Alegre, Elisenda was interrupted as she prepared for her morning meeting with the rest of the unit by Puigventós calling a quick briefing on his low-level crime initiative.

'Twenty-four arrests,' he told her and Micaló. 'From littering to graffiti by the river where the train comes in from the north. It reflects badly on the city, so it's good that we're tightening up in this area.'

'That's excellent, Xavier,' Micaló congratulated him. Elisenda watched her counterpart in the Regional Investigation Unit out of the corner of her eye. The uneasy truce that had sprung up between her and Micaló after the events of the previous year was steadily eroding as Micaló's confidence in the safety of his position slowly returned. It was he who spoke next.

'And for my team's part, we have been targeting petty criminals, primarily those dealing in stolen goods.' He pulled some papers out of his document wallet. 'This graph will show our objectives for this initiative compared with the arrests we've made thus far. You'll see that we're more than fourteen per cent over target.'

Elisenda massaged her temples impatiently and forced herself not to let her head drop in frustration.

'You seem agitated, Elisenda,' Puigventós told her.

'Not in the slightest. I still believe that it's a good initiative. I'm just not sure how it applies to my unit, considering our purpose is to focus on serious crimes. I don't quite see how I'm supposed to contribute to these meetings.'

'We all need to be up to speed with everything that is happening in the city,' Puigventós said, his voice terse.

Micaló nodded in eager agreement.

Elisenda knew when to let it go, particularly if she didn't want to waste any more time on unnecessary lectures, so she acquiesced and let the two men run the clock down. Finally, the inspector called the meeting to a close and she hurried along the corridor to where her own unit was waiting for her. Quickly, she told them all of the spike at El Crit and that the Científica team from La Bisbal were searching the site now, before moving on to other matters.

'Esteve Mascort,' she said to the assembled team. 'I know what the DNA says, but I still want us to consider him as the primary candidate for the El Crit victim.'

'Even if the body is Mascort, do you believe that Esplugues and Barbena are guilty?' Àlex asked.

Elisenda considered for a moment. 'I think they're both still in the frame. Both for the Mascort killing and the Arbós one. But Jutge Rigau won't let us pursue that angle while it's not completely certain that Mascort is the victim. The problem being that we only have DNA from Mascort's father, and we can't simply assume that he was his biological father, in which case, the body at El Crit could still be Mascort. So we need another DNA sample from Mascort's mother's side of the family. Montse, can you get on to that, see if you can find a relative that fits the bill? And that also still leaves Esplugues and Barbena as suspects. I think either would be capable in their way under the right circumstances, but their stories do seem watertight. I've got to go to the Archaeology Service this morning, so I'm going to try and see if this report about Arbós that Martí Barbena claims to have written really exists.'

'I also think that Esplugues' argument about waiting until she could divorce Mascort rings true,' Josep commented.

'Not if she killed him in a moment of anger,' Montse argued.

'Why would she have been at the dig?' he countered, a sniping edge to his tone. 'She's not an archaeologist, she'd have no need to be there.'

'She killed him somewhere else and took the body to El Crit.' Montse couldn't hide her own irritation.

Josep looked directly at her. 'That distance through the woods? You know that's impossible. I see her more as biding her time until she could get a divorce. She had no real motive to kill him.'

Montse shook her head and looked away.

Elisenda glanced at them both and carried on speaking. 'Either way, we do need to consider the possibility of a different victim. Àlex, are there any students who worked on the dig the summer of 1981 who are unaccounted for?'

Àlex shook his head. 'Every one tagged and inter-viewed. And none of them has said anything to indicate that they'd be of interest as the perp either.'

'So, besides Mascort, there's no one we've got who could be the victim. Unless, of course, there was someone involved in dealing in the stolen artefacts who went missing at the time and who we haven't come across yet. We've just been looking at archaeologists. We need to widen the net for possible victims. Museums, collectors, antiques dealers even.'

Àlex groaned. 'So the net just got bigger.'

'And possible killers,' Elisenda added. 'Someone who worked with Arbós and whoever the El Crit victim is and who's now spooked because the first body was found.'

'We also have to consider the possibility that Esplugues or Barbena had nothing to do with either killing,' Àlex argued. 'And that the murders are connected to the trade in antiquities.'

'Illicit trafficking,' Elisenda said, deep in thought. 'As the archaeologists seem to insist on calling it. But you're right. Àlex, could you and Josep dig more into Arbós's dealings, going back in time. See if there's anyone who went missing who might have had dealings with him. And with Mascort, just in case he is our body at El Crit.'

'And anyone who might still hold a grudge now,' Montse added.

'True,' Elisenda agreed, signalling the end to the meeting. 'As well as anyone else who might potentially be another victim.'

With her last observation left hanging in the air, Elisenda let the other three take to their computers to get on with the tasks she'd given them while she picked up a pool car from the basement and headed north out of the city, soon getting caught up in the slow crawl of cars on the Rotonda del Rellotge.

'Tuesday,' she muttered through her teeth.

Market day. She glanced to the Devesa park under the trees while she waited for the traffic lights to favour her part in the ill-tempered dance. Dozens of food and clothes stalls were all but hidden behind the throngs of browsers and buyers shuffling past the wares in their own version of the packed city waltz. They looked to her like a child's model village, too small under the slender plane trees clinging to the height of the sky.

The traffic's slow embrace finally released her and she crossed the river, skirting the foot of Montjuïc, Girona's little mountain outside the city walls, and drove the short distance along the Onyar to the Archaeology Service. The secondary school past the Archaeology Service building was on its break and the low walls along the road were dotted with small groups of teenagers eating baguette sandwiches out of tin foil and pretending not to be impressed by all the other groups similarly feigning boredom.

'Remember doing that,' Elisenda acknowledged under her breath.

Her phone rang. Sergent Poch in La Bisbal telling her that the Científica had found no traces of anything at El Crit that might indicate who had hammered the spike into the tree, the layer of pine needles over winter-hard ground giving away no secrets, the spike itself clean of prints.

'*They'll be checking for DNA back here, but I wouldn't hold out too much hope.*'

She thanked him and hung up, sighing in agreement at his gloomy forecast, before entering the dark vestibule. Taking off her sunglasses after the bright blue sky of the morning, she nonetheless kept on her jacket, the inside of the old building as chill as the air outside. It was only once she was upstairs, in Doctora Fradera's office, that she began to feel warm.

'Your heating's as good as ours,' she commented to the archaeologist.

Fradera looked around her absently. 'Cutbacks,' she finally decided.

Elisenda paused before speaking, recalling the doubts that had kept coming back to her since learning of the DNA test on Mascort's father. Although she'd asked Montse to look into finding a surviving relative on his mother's side, there was nothing in their investigation to indicate such a person existed. She couldn't help thinking it called for desperate measures.

'I wanted to ask you a favour, Doctora Fradera,' she finally said. 'The facial reconstruction you showed me on Saturday. I would now be interested in seeing what modelling of the modern skull might throw up.'

'I thought it was a last resort.'

'It is. I would have to ask you to be discreet about it. I'd make the necessary arrangements with Doctor Riera, the forensic pathologist.'

The archaeologist grunted. Elisenda took it as assent.

'What's in the box?' she asked.

Used by now to the other woman's abruptness, Elisenda placed the display case that she'd taken from Ferran Arbós's house on the desk and removed the lid.

'Good grief,' Fradera exclaimed, visibly taken aback. She took one of the coins out of its cotton-wool padded square. 'This is Phoenician. Where did you find this?'

The archaeologist turned the coin over delicately in her fingers, her expression one of an odd childlike wonder that took Elisenda by surprise. It was very different from her normal studious aloof.

'It was in a drawer in Ferran Arbós's house.'

Fradera laid the Phoenician coin back and looked up and down the rows, occasionally turning a coin over or picking one up, all the while muttering. 'Roman, Greek, beautiful, simply beautiful.'

Elisenda almost felt reluctant to break the mood. 'Would they be from an Indiketa site, do you think?'

'Most definitely. These are the sort of coins we're used to finding in Indiketa settlements.' The archaeologist straightened the box in front of her but didn't replace the lid, preferring instead to continue to gaze at the coins while she spoke to Elisenda. 'Despite the Franco regime's insistence that the various Iberian tribes spent all their time gloriously repelling invaders, they did in fact trade with other Mediterranean peoples for centuries and were colonised by the Greeks and Romans. We're used to finding a great variety of artefacts from their trade with other Mediterranean cultures.' She gestured at the box in front of her. 'But this is a particularly fine collection of coins.'

'Is there a legitimate reason that Ferran Arbós would have had these at his house?'

Fradera tore her gaze away from the collection and looked directly at Elisenda. '*De mortuis nil nisi bonum* and all that, but a collection of coins of this importance would be unlikely to be in the possession of someone in Ferran's position unless it got to them by underhand means. The fact that he was a museum curator makes it doubly distressing.'

'Distressing?'

'We all had an idea that some of Ferran's methods and procedures weren't entirely rigorous. Museum acquisitions that later proved to have been looted. He was forced to leave his job because of a string of items that he'd acquired without due diligence. At the time, I preferred to think of it as incompetence, but keeping artefacts in this way for himself is another matter completely.'

'Could he have been trading in them, do you think?'

'I really wouldn't know. I know that some of my colleagues felt that he might have misappropriated some artefacts.' Fradera absently picked up one of the coins from the box and gazed at it. 'As the least of all evils, I would like to think that if he did take them, they were for his own use, not to sell on. Selfish rather than self-serving.'

'Who would he sell them to if he did? A private buyer? We understand that some of the acquisitions made by museums based on his recommendation have turned out to have problems with provenance.'

Fradera looked coldly at the coins and then at Elisenda. 'I'm afraid you possibly have your answer there. Ferran's links with numerous museums and the good reputation he had with other curators and institutions before his fall from grace would suggest to me that he would most likely be selling them to museums.'

'How would that happen? Surely he couldn't approach a curator with a bag of coins and ask them to buy it.'

The archaeologist shook her head. 'I imagine he would be providing the provenance. Fake certificates, anything that would give the artefacts an air of respectability.'

'Would a museum be convinced by that?'

It was time for a withering Fradera look and Elisenda got one. 'Some of the finest museums in the world have been taken in by looted artefacts. Others have turned a blind eye. Even today, there's a culture in some museums of having the biggest and the best displays of material culture, no matter the cost to archaeology.'

'Is it common?'

'I've heard it said that around 80% of Roman and Etruscan artefacts that are on the market at any one time are looted or false. So I think you can say it's common. Perhaps less so since the 1970 UN convention on illicit trafficking in cultural property, which forced museums to be more rigorous in their checks, but it still happens much more than we'd like to think.' She paused for a moment, her face darkening. 'The colonising countries have long had a culture of collecting through their museums that has always sought to justify the theft of artefacts from other cultures. Many of the objects in many museums all over the world have been acquired unethically. Despite everything, that continues to be the case.'

'I thought we'd returned some items.'

Fradera snorted. 'The Peruvian amphorae from the Archaeological Museum in Madrid, you mean? Yes, they were returned, but others haven't been. The courts here refused to return other artefacts because the original crime occurred outside the country, which is the most stupid argument they could ever have come up with for looting cultural goods from another country.'

Elisenda let the older woman calm down a little before continuing. 'Ferran Arbós?'

The archaeologist sighed heavily and put the lid on the coin box. 'I suppose if you wanted to give these curators the benefit of the doubt, what someone like Ferran, and whoever he was working with, would do is lay a trail of false certificates and a string of sales at successive auctions that would effectively confuse the provenance, so the curators would feel that they were buying a genuine item.'

'Whoever he was working with,' Elisenda commented, voicing her own thoughts rather than asking Fradera's opinion. 'Are we looking for a third person? Someone between the archaeologist or whoever stole the artefacts and Arbós, who provided the respectability for the item to be accepted? A dealer, someone who was actually the person who traded in the artefacts, who dealt with the museums and the auction houses?'

Fradera shrugged. 'I'm sure I wouldn't know, but I imagine it would make sense.' She pulled the box of coins towards her. 'I should probably keep these.'

Elisenda leaned forward and retrieved the collection. 'Yes, you probably should, but not just yet. We still need them as evidence.'

The archaeologist grunted in annoyance and watched as Elisenda picked up the box and walked out of the office. Downstairs, in the entrance hall, Elisenda ran into Gemma.

'I'm still looking for more documents from the El Crit site,' Gemma told her, her voice not quite as thick with her cold, but her eyes still red. 'It's ever so exciting.'

'Thank you. There is something else I'd like you to look for. A report by Martí Barbena about Ferran Arbós. Do you think you'd be able to find it if it existed?'

'I can look into it,' the younger woman promised eagerly.

Elisenda thanked her but was cut short by her phone ringing. It was Jordi Canudas in Barcelona, the archaeologist on the 1981 dig that she and Josep had interviewed.

He was calling to tell her that someone had broken into his office.

'Anything taken?'

'*Just some photo albums.*'

–

Elisenda scanned the shelves in the lecturer's office. Jordi Canudas stood next to her, the greying circle of surprise around his mouth accentuating his consternation.

'I didn't expect you to come,' he'd told her when she'd turned up at the university in Barcelona an hour or so after his phone call. 'I just thought I should let you know what had happened.'

'Do you know exactly what's been taken?'

Canudas pointed to a gap in the folders. 'Just the albums I showed you the other day and a couple of others. Nothing I would've thought would be of any importance to anyone.'

Elisenda looked back at the empty spaces and thought he was probably wrong. Something he had was obviously important to someone. Or they thought it was.

'You mentioned the other day that you suspected Esteve Mascort of stealing artefacts. Were there any other archaeologists you worked with that you also suspected of doing the same?'

Surprised at the question, Canudas had to stop and think. 'No, not at all. Since that time, I've worked mainly as a lecturer. I go on digs with my students, so it's not really something that's ever been an issue. They're still too idealistic,' he concluded with a wry smile.

Thanking him, Elisenda left the university and on impulse drove through the slow traffic to Ricard Soler's apartment block on her way back to the ring road. The missing archaeologist's trendy neighbour wasn't in and there was no porter in the building to open the door for her. She considered for less than ten seconds.

'I'm pretty certain you don't need a warrant for breaking and entering,' she muttered to herself, thinking of Jutge Rigau's words and working at the locks with two picks that Siset, one of her informants, had taught her how to use.

The door opened surprisingly easily. The lock was one of the old ones where you normally had to turn the key three times to secure it, but it clicked open quickly, as though the last person to close it had simply pulled it shut behind them and failed to lock it completely with their key. Elisenda was sure that Soler would have closed it more thoroughly if he'd been going away for a few days.

'Which I would say means he wasn't the last person to leave this flat,' she murmured. She knew that when she left, she'd also simply be pulling the door closed behind her as she didn't have a key to lock it properly.

Opening it, she looked up and down the staircase before going into Soler's flat. It smelt musty and had the clutter she'd expect of an academic who lived alone. The small, dark square of a tiny hallway led into a narrow kitchen, its walls tiled in greasy white squares. She checked the room, but nothing looked like it had been used in some days. Opening the fridge, she sniffed at an open carton of milk and recoiled at the smell. Soler evidently hadn't been back at all.

In the bedroom, his bed was made, old-fashioned sheets and blankets spread over it like a rumpled tent. The living room revealed little more. Divided by a faded sofa, it had a small dining table and two chairs on one side and a coffee table and ancient TV on dark wood shelves on the other. There were no books on the shelf. They were all in the study, the only room with any hint of a personality. An untidy and seemingly chaotic one but that no doubt meant something to its creator. All four walls were covered in shelves, in turn covered in books, standing precariously in rows and stacks, some of them holding loose pages and bulging files in place, others failing, as a white flood of paper attested. Stacks of books stood in ranks on the floor like the stones in a hypocaust.

Elisenda stood and stared intently at the four walls in turn, trying to decipher the mess, until she recognised a similar shape emerging on the shelves to the one she found at Ferran Arbós's house. Gaps here and there where something looked like it had been taken, the spaces closed up. Impossible to say with any certainty that anything had been removed but she knew deep down that someone had been here and taken folders.

'More photo albums,' she said to herself. 'Someone looking for someone.'

She also looked, but failed to find any files with snap-shots in, either on the shelves or in the drawers of the large and ancient desk that stood next to a shuttered window. There was no computer either, just the small lozenges on the leather desktop where a laptop's pads would normally have stood. Whether Soler took that with him or whether the other visitor stole it, she had no way of knowing.

Roaming through the flat again, she found nothing to identify Soler, no photos, no documents with his picture on, just two faded oblongs in the living room wall where pictures normally hung. Elisenda had a fleeting moment where she doubted his existence and had to shake the thought out of her head.

'Another buried ghost,' she muttered.

Her phone rang, breaking the cold silence of the empty flat. It almost felt like a relief. Answering, she heard the whine in the other person's voice before he got his first word out, an odd synchronicity given how she'd got into the apartment.

'Elisenda, I've been arrested.'

'You're a petty criminal, Siset. It's what happens.'

She pressed disconnect and put the phone back in her bag, taking one last look around her and pulling the door closed as she left.

Chapter Twenty Seven

Like most victims, Raimon Boldú had soon become invisible.

Glancing up briefly, he saw that it was unlikely to rain today. It was a relief, although the February cold had long since seeped through his suit and cut into his skin with the insistence of a thousand needles. His legs felt it the most, protected only by the thin material of his once-smart trousers, now fraying at the heels where they'd slipped, loosened by the weight he was losing, the cloth over his knees and thighs shiny with age.

A council employee left the Town Hall, one of his former colleagues, and hurried past, unwilling to make eye contact. The same as every day, Raimon Boldú didn't say a word, but simply watched the younger worker walk past. In a reflex action, he hefted the banner he was holding, the words painted thickly in black paint on a large piece of brown cardboard from an old packing box.

Standing between the wrought-iron gates of the small side entrance and the larger archway into the Town Hall, he watched and hefted his sign as two other employees left on their morning coffee break. Neither stopped or paused to acknowledge him. He was invisible to them. They merely walked straight past under the stone arch leading past the tiny Les Voltes bookshop that only sold books in Catalan towards the coffee and *xuixo* aroma of La Vienesa. He could remember quite clearly the last time he tasted one of their long, custard-filled doughnuts and sat in the window with a large *café amb llet* and without a care. It was exactly one hour before he'd been called into his superior's office and told that he was now part of the recession.

'We just can't afford to keep you on,' his manager had told him, his thick salt-and-pepper moustache shielding his mouth.

Had Raimon Boldú's former colleagues stopped to read his notice, they would have seen a tidy, well-ordered list of figures. The years of experience of all the other people like him who'd been made redundant, the difference in salaries of the younger, cheaper people kept on, the price of the contracts awarded to a handful of businesses, the costs cut on other services and the pay rise given to himself by the superior who had let Raimon Boldú go. No one looked at them anymore.

A car drove slowly towards the archway. A new one, one he hadn't seen before. It stopped to let two pedestrians walk past, a couple deep in conversation, taking books they'd just bought in Les Voltes out of a bag to look at them. The car revved, the driver impatient. Raimon Boldú crouched slightly to look through the passenger window and saw his old boss in the driver's seat, staring straight ahead to the haven of the courtyard past the gateway.

'You,' he said.

His boss didn't turn to look at him, so he leant forward and tapped on the window. Still he got no acknowledgement from the other man, so he knocked again, harder this time. And again. And again. Until he finally took a step back and kicked out at the side door, the metal folding luxuriously under his foot.

Chapter Twenty Eight

'Haven't any of your clients ever heard of the internet?'

Elisenda examined the scrawny figure sitting opposite her. Looking deeply sorry for himself, Siset was one of her main informants, regularly swapping tales of the big boys in the playground for small change and minor tolerances. Staring back at her, he shrugged and sniffed back a pearl of mucus that had been dangling from his nose. Elisenda fished out a paper tissue and gave it to him. Looking uncertainly at it, he used it to wipe the corners of his mouth and made to hand it back to her.

'You can keep it, Siset, I've got plenty more.'

He nodded, staring at the strange item one more time, and put it in his trouser pocket. A second tear of snot dribbled on to his upper lip and he sniffed it back up once more. She closed her eyes and tried not to laugh. He looked as empty, grey and miserable as the interview room they were sharing in Vista Alegre.

'I've been arrested, Elisenda,' he told her for the third time, his voice metamorphosing progressively from self-pity to petulant umbrage. 'Arrested.'

'You were selling bootleg DVDs, Siset. It's illegal. The city's trying to clamp down on petty crime and you got caught.'

She had to admit, she was enjoying herself.

He pointed a chewed and grubby finger at her. 'I've got protection, Elisenda. I tell you things, you don't let them arrest me.' A thought struck him, his eyebrows creasing in indignation. 'What do you mean, petty?'

Elisenda stood up. 'I'll see what I can do, Siset. You'll be my number one priority. In the meantime, have you got anything for me? Something that might work in your favour?'

She watched his mouth turn upwards and his eyes frown as he racked his brains to think of something. Reluctantly, he shook his head. 'Nothing. Quiet right now, what with your lot busting everyone.'

'Ah, you see, Siset. You want protection, you tell me things. That's how it works, you said so yourself.'

'Petty,' he grumbled as she went to the door. 'Pity I wasn't selling drugs when they caught me. Then who'd be laughing?'

'Who indeed?' Elisenda replied, shaking her head and leaving him alone in the bare room.

Outside, she spoke to the sergent in charge of the custody cells.

'Take him back to a cell and keep him there. Let him sweat a bit.'

The sergent grinned. 'Always a pleasure.'

A uniformed mosso held the door to the staircase leading up to the offices open for her and glanced down bashfully as she walked through. He looked about fourteen years old, she thought, the fine, downy hairs on his chin a contradiction with the subtle scent of after shave. She thanked him with a smile and climbed the stairs to Puigventós' office.

'I have an informant who's been arrested,' she explained to the inspector when she got there. 'He's been caught selling bootleg DVDs as part of the low-level crime initiative. He's more use to me out in the street than cluttering up a cell.'

Puigventós held both hands up in front of him. 'Sotsinspector Micaló's arrest, I'm afraid. You'll have to speak to him.'

'But it's part of your drive against petty crime, Xavier.'

Puigventós looked at his watch. 'Roger is actually on his way here now on a disciplinary matter. I'm sure you could raise it with him. Briefly.'

'Disciplinary? What's he done?'

'Not Roger, one of the uniformed Mossos.'

Elisenda had to hide a smile. She'd been under no illusion it was Micaló on a charge, he was more usually on the giving end, but she could always dream. She watched Puigventós sort a few papers out on his desk while they waited for the other sotsinspector to come along.

'Any news on the Arbós murder?' the inspector suddenly asked without looking up, his voice too casual for Elisenda's liking. She'd learned to be wary of the question in passing.

'Two angles,' she told him, choosing her words. 'We're looking into the possibility of a connection with Eulàlia Esplugues, Mascort's widow, and Martí Barbena. And we're also pursuing a connection with a trade in illicit antiquities. Both are feasible at this stage, and possibly connected.'

He looked up and gazed at her. 'Good. Keep me up to speed.'

She steeled herself. She'd called in on Riera at the Institut de Medicina Legal on the way back to Vista Alegre.

'Facial reconstruction?' the pathologist had blurted. 'Fucking useless.'

'Doctora Fradera feels it might help.'

'A fine woman.'

Leaving him after he'd promised to get the skull to the university for the CT scan and modelling, she'd asked him to keep quiet about it for the time being.

'Budgets, eh?' he'd commented. 'I do so love insubordination.'

For her part, she felt, she couldn't help herself. She looked at Puigventós now and spoke.

'I want to order a digital facial reconstruction of the skull at El Crit. I know it's a last resort but the DNA test seems to show that the body isn't Mascort, and I think it's flawed. If we're unable to find another relative, I think we need to find another way of trying to identify the victim.'

Puigventós let his pen drop onto the desk with a clatter and began to shake his head. Elisenda could see the refusal forming, but before he could speak, there was a knock on the door and Micaló entered, telling someone to stay outside until called. A genuine first, Elisenda thought, relief on seeing Micaló not an emotion she often felt. He in turn looked surprised to see Elisenda waiting in Puigventós' office.

'You're holding one of Elisenda's informants,' the inspector explained to him.

'Siset,' she added, turning to face Micaló.

'Siset,' Micaló repeated, nodding slowly, an unpleasant knowing smirk turning the edges of his mouth down.

Everyone knew Siset by his street name, so much so that only the Mossos who filled out the occasional charge sheets for him ever remembered what he was really called. 'And what do you want me to do about it?'

'He's more use to me on the outside, telling me what's happening. I want the charges against him dropped.'

Micaló sat down on a chair and looked Elisenda up and down. 'So you disagree with the initiative to nip low-level crime in the bud, Sotsinspectora Domènech?'

Elisenda stifled a sigh. 'Not in the slightest. I just agree more with an initiative that also prevents serious crime. I need people like Siset to help make sure that happens.'

Micaló shook his head rather too dramatically to be sincere. 'Ah, another one who knows best how the law is served,' he commented cryptically. 'We have to be seen to be tackling anti-social crime, Sotsinspectora. I'm sure the people of Girona wouldn't be happy to know that the Mossos are releasing petty criminals simply because you believe you and your pet informants are above the law.'

'He's been caught selling bootleg DVDs,' she argued, her voice calm, the anger kept in check, 'which is infinitely less of a crime than the ones he helps prevent or clear up. Arresting and sentencing him will serve no purpose to anyone.'

'So you decide what is and what isn't important enough a crime. Wasn't that the problem in the first place? Didn't you lose an officer precisely because of that?'

Momentarily stunned, Elisenda leaned towards him to speak, her breath measured, her knuckles clenching as she struggled to stay in control, but before she could say anything, she heard a loud crack and saw Puigventós out of the corner of her eye slamming a folder down on his desk.

'Roger, that's enough,' he interrupted before Elisenda could continue, taking her by surprise. 'Do not push my patience. You are not immune.'

Elisenda could see the shock on Micaló's face, his newly-rediscovered confidence wilting. The room was silent, waiting for Puigventós to calm down before continuing.

'This is not about being above the law,' the inspector finally carried on. 'It's about best serving the community. I'm inclined to agree that Elisenda has a point. Combating low-level crime is very important, but we mustn't lose sight of policing the city as a whole.'

Elisenda slowly backed away from Micaló, standing up straight, her eyes not leaving his once. When she trusted herself to speak, her voice was strained. 'You will drop all charges against my informant.'

Micaló looked from Elisenda to Puigventós. Elisenda could see by the dull glint in his eyes that the corporate politician in him had already calculated that this was no longer a battle worth pursuing. He nodded his head once and turned away to call through the closed door.

'Mosso, come in now.'

The door opened and a uniformed cop walked into the room, his cap in his hand. Elisenda looked on in shock.

'Mosso Paredes,' Puigventós uttered, his disbelief echoing Elisenda's.

Elisenda watched as Paredes came to attention and thought how the nervous young mosso with butterfly fingers she'd first met some six months ago had given way to an assured cop, his cold stare resolute, even now.

'What's this about?' Elisenda asked.

'A disciplinary matter,' Micaló replied. 'Not your area of authority, I'm afraid.'

Puigventós pulled his gaze away from Paredes and turned to Micaló. 'I don't think any of us would have any problem were Elisenda to stay,' he told him.

Grudgingly, Micaló assented with a nod of the head. He was visibly nonplussed by Puigventós' apparent lack of support for him and gathered himself before continuing to speak. He glanced once at Elisenda before doing so.

'Mosso Paredes also appears to be above pursuing low-level crime,' he began, his voice steadily strengthening. 'He was seen refusing to arrest a member of the public as part of your initiative, Xavier.'

'Paredes?' Puigventós said to the mosso.

Paredes looked at Elisenda before replying. She gave him the slightest of nods in encouragement. The mossos' dark eyes seemed even more intense in the oppressive atmosphere of the inspector's office.

'It was the man who stands on Plaça del Vi, outside the Town Hall, the one with the banner protesting about council spending.'

Puigventós nodded. 'I know who you mean. Boldú. He was made redundant a few years ago.'

'That's him, Inspector,' Paredes answered. 'He kicked his old boss's car this morning and dented the passenger door.'

'Criminal damage,' Micaló interrupted. 'Which Mosso Paredes failed to arrest him for.'

'With respect, Sotsinspector, he's unemployed. He lost his temper at the person who fired him. I felt it was better to give him a warning rather than arrest him.'

'Why so?' Puigventós asked him curiously.

'Because he's having a hard enough time as it is, Inspector. He's never been in trouble with the police before, but if we charge him with an offence, he then has a criminal record, which will make his chances of getting another job even slighter than they already are. I believe we serve him and the city better by giving him a warning and nothing more.'

'You do understand why we're pursuing low-level crime, I take it.'

'Yes, Inspector.' Paredes glanced at Elisenda for support. 'And I've been true to it, but I feel that we should be allowed some leeway to make sure the campaign doesn't hurt the people it's supposed to be protecting.'

'So you feel you have the right to decide,' Micaló commented, 'not your superiors. Not the law.'

'I feel I have the duty to exercise restraint, Sotsinspector.'

Micaló looked in disbelief at Paredes and tried to find words. Elisenda broke in before he was able to.

'I think that's exactly the way we should be tackling this initiative,' she said, addressing Puigventós. 'We have to be selective in how we approach petty crime.'

'Selective?' the inspector questioned.

'Using our judgement. Not at the expense of creating antipathy towards the Mossos, or of victimising individuals we should be protecting, but dealing with the crimes that really do have an effect on the majority of the people in the city.'

Micaló snorted. 'For pity's sake.'

Puigventós stared at Elisenda and at Paredes for what seemed to Elisenda an age.

'All right, Mosso Paredes,' he finally said. 'I'll accept your argument for now. I agree with you that we have to observe the correct spirit while targeting low-level offences. But I will insist on you exercising restraint in exercising restraint. This initiative is important to the city.' He turned to Micaló. 'I trust you'll be satisfied with that, Roger.'

The politician's mask was in place. 'Of course, Xavier, and I shall make sure my unit observes the spirit, as you call it.'

The inspector dismissed Paredes, who managed to leave the room without letting out a huge sigh, and Elisenda waited until Micaló left before she spoke again.

She pointed at the closed door. 'You see why I want Paredes in my unit. He has the right character traits to work in my team.'

Puigventós sat down. 'He has seventeen credits, Elisenda. He's at least a year away from qualifying for promotion and he's much too inexperienced. Give him time.'

'He can learn as he goes along. You've seen how quick he is, how he reasons. He has the right sort of mind, the right sort of intuitive logic, for the Serious Crime Unit.'

'I'm sorry, Elisenda, it's simply not going to happen, and that's final.'

She turned to leave, but Puigventós had one more thing to say.

'And don't think that I will always take your side, Elisenda.' He signalled for her to go. 'Because I won't.'

'No, Xavier,' she answered in the room.

'No shit,' she added outside.

Chapter Twenty Nine

There was an email waiting for Elisenda back in her office. From Gemma Cardoner at the Archaeology Service. She read it and called Àlex in, telling him first about her visit to Barcelona.

'I've got something too,' he told her when she'd finished and signalled to him to read what was on her screen.

He put down some papers he was holding and angled the monitor towards him, quickly scanning first the email, then the attachment. When he finished, he looked at her once and sat down on the chair opposite her.

'So he did try to blow the whistle on Arbós,' he finally commented.

Elisenda nodded. 'Martí Barbena was telling the truth.' She checked the date on the document on screen. 'Eleven years ago, he wrote a report about Ferran Arbós, just as he said he had, accusing him of trading in stolen artefacts and faking provenance.'

'So where does that leave us with him and Eulàlia Esplugues?'

One last time, Elisenda quickly skimmed through to the most salient parts of the report that an evidently angry Barbena had written. 'Not so cool when he wrote this, was he?' She thought for a moment. 'It simply means he wasn't working with Arbós, so therefore Arbós's murder wouldn't have been a falling-out between partners.'

'Or a warning to a former partner.'

'But if it does turn out to be Mascort in the grave at El Crit, then we still have to consider both of them for that murder at least. And it still leaves the possibility of Arbós blackmailing Esplugues after Mascort's body was found.'

'That's if there was anything to blackmail her for and Arbós knew about it.'

Elisenda sighed heavily and rubbed her eyes. 'Everything seems to bring people and motives into focus while moving them out of it at the same time. Who's the first victim? Why is he a victim? Why was Arbós killed? And from that, who had the motive and means to kill one or the other or both? There's something else. Something that Doctora Fradera told me this morning made me think that we should be considering a third person, one who's nothing to do with Mascort's ex-wife or with the original team of archaeologists at El Crit.'

Àlex leaned forward and picked up the papers he'd left on her desk.

'That's what I had to tell you. I've been going through Arbós's bank statements. His bank has released his accounts for the last ten years to us.' He laid the papers out on the table, printouts of a current account statement in Arbós's name, and pointed at a number of entries highlighted in yellow marker. 'Up until six years ago, he received payments from a company based in Andorra. Not regular, but substantial when he did get them.'

'Andorra?' Elisenda commented, one eyebrow raised.

Àlex nodded. 'Precisely. A tax haven. I've got Josep looking into it too, but we've been running around in circles. As far as we can ascertain, the company folded a little under six years ago.'

'Any names of directors?'

'That's the problem. So far, all the directors we've found were other companies, all of them offshore. And the directors of the one company of those that we've been able to track down so far are also other companies. I think we're going to find that across the board. No individual's names have come up yet. Evidently, if it were an honest business, that just wouldn't happen.'

Elisenda scanned the papers. 'So you think this company was masking the intermediary who Arbós worked with to traffic the antiquities?'

Àlex uncovered another piece of paper. 'We've only just started looking at this, but we think we've found a link between one of the shareholder companies of the original company that made the payments and a bonded warehouse in the Zona Franca customs zone in Barcelona that was raided six years ago. All we've got at the moment is that it was called Serveis Art. Josep and I are still digging, but so far, its name has turned up as the importer of three archaeological artefacts subsequently sold at auction, two in London, one in Berlin. All of them now known to have been stolen.'

'Part of the trail of fake certificates and auctions that Doctora Fradera was talking about to give legitimacy to the artefacts.'

Àlex nodded. 'And Arbós was the one providing the legitimacy. Mascort stole them, Arbós faked the provenance.'

'Which just leaves the person trading in them. Most probably the person behind the company paying Arbós.

And possibly the person behind the murder of Mascort or Arbós or both.' She looked at the print-outs. 'Of course, if Mascort died in 1981, there would have to have been other archaeologists since who were involved in stealing the artefacts for Arbós and our mystery dealer to then sell on.'

'They don't necessarily have to be archaeologists,' Àlex commented. 'After Mascort's death, if he is dead, the goods could have been acquired in other ways. Metal detectorists. Or even more organised: gangs stealing to order from unattended digs or from museums.'

Elisenda shook her head in frustration. 'We just keep widening the field. And either way, Arbós's murderer could be any one of them.' She thought for a moment. 'You'd better call Josep and Montse in, they need to know the latest. That's if they can bear to sit in the same confined space as each other.'

Àlex looked out at the two caporals in the outer room and sighed. 'So much changed with Pau's death.'

He opened the door to call the other two in, giving Elisenda a moment's grace to hide the sadness that had caught in her throat at his comment.

The two caporals came in and sat at opposite ends of the desk. Àlex sat down between them and shot a glance at Elisenda. Composed, she explained the theory that she and Àlex had been discussing about a third person who would have been involved in the chain.

'Which also makes them a suspect for one or both murders,' she concluded, 'whoever they are.'

Josep looked at Àlex before replying. 'Have you mentioned the payments to Arbós?'

'And the bonded warehouse,' Elisenda interrupted before Àlex could reply. 'Yes, it's an interesting lead. Keep looking into it. The problem is I want to spring another likely avenue on you all.'

'More?' Àlex sighed.

'More. Jutge Rigau in La Bisbal made some comment about the sins of the fathers. Perhaps we're looking at the wrong generation. Mascort's killer would be at least in their fifties if they're still alive, and that's what we've been concentrating on, but just as Arbós's murderer doesn't have to be the same person, neither do they have to be the same age. Maybe we should be looking for someone younger, the next generation.'

'Presuming Mascort is the first victim,' Àlex insisted.

'I haven't found any maternal relative yet,' Montse added.

Looking at all three of her team in turn, Elisenda told them of her decision to arrange for a facial reconstruction of the skull.

'And Puigventós agreed to this?' Àlex asked her.

She thought for a moment. 'He didn't refuse.'

'So if it's not Mascort in the grave,' Montse asked, coming back to Elisenda's original comment, her voice doubtful, 'the victim's son knows who he really is and is looking for revenge on the murderer? Is that what you mean?'

'We've ascertained that Mascort's son is out of the frame for killing Arbós as revenge,' Josep added, not looking at Montse. 'He has a watertight alibi.'

Elisenda shook her head. 'Not necessarily the victim's son. Or daughter. But the child of the original killer, out to cover up their parent's crime.'

'Either of which would put Arbós's murderer in their twenties or thirties,' Montse replied.

Àlex let out a long breath and looked at his watch. 'Hell, Elisenda, it's just got even more complicated in the last five minutes,' he complained.

'That's what makes it all so worthwhile,' she answered him, a light smile creasing the corners of her mouth.

Chapter Thirty

Clara Ferré poured a glass of red wine and watched her son in idle curiosity for a few moments before turning back to the article she was reading. He was held in thrall by a computer on the dining table at the other end of the large, old living room, his earphones on, watching some streamed broadcast of an opera. She smiled wryly. At his age, she recalled going out most nights discussing the end of Spanish rule and having sex with a string of earnest young men in wispy beards and cheesecloth. Taken in all, she imagined her youth was rather more fun than her son's.

Turning back to her article, she imagined either would be more enjoyable than any more time wasted reading the modish cant the writer appeared to revel in, the latest in a long line of anti-establishment academics stead-fastly seeking to become the establishment. She threw the journal onto the coffee table and took a sip of wine.

The doorbell rang.

Not the harsh buzzing of the intercom downstairs in the street, but the two-tone chime of the door to the apartment. That was odd, she thought. It was either one of her neighbours, and she couldn't remember the last time any of them had emerged from their homes at this time of night to come calling, or it was someone who'd found the street door open and come straight in. She hadn't heard anyone going up or down the stairs, so it wasn't a case of someone taking advantage of the door being opened by one of the residents entering or leaving the building, in the way that door-to-door sellers did. Looking at the clock above the fireplace, she couldn't think of anyone who'd call at this time of night without phoning first. Her son hadn't heard the bell over his Verdi, so she got up from the sofa with a sigh and crossed the hall to the front door, listening for any sound from outside.

As ancient as the building, the original door had an old-fashioned Judas window, a metal grille at head height that opened or closed like a dial to allow the owner to see out, but it had seized up long ago. Instead, she'd had a spyhole put in underneath. Crouching down slightly to look through, she was startled by her son's voice behind her, asking who it was. Instinctively backing away from the door and turning to face him, she immediately flinched at the heavy sound of metal hitting metal and wood splitting violently.

Looking back at the door, her right eye was less than a centimetre from the pointed end of a metal spike, thrust through the spyhole, the deep mahogany around it splintered and cracked. She heard her son gasp and tried to move her head back from the sharp tip, her movements slow in her panic.

She heard the same sound again of metal on metal powering through the spike as a second hammer blow came from the other side of the door.

Chapter Thirty One

'I hope this is all going to be worthwhile,' Catalina complained, holding one hand on her stomach and watching Elisenda.

'You wanted to come here.'

'It doesn't mean you have to enjoy it so much.'

Elisenda looked at the ice cream she was holding in either hand and shrugged. 'I think you'll find it does.'

She'd left Vista Alegre, the last one of her unit to go. Turning the lights out on her office before closing the door on the still unknown killers of Mascort and Arbós, she'd walked out of the modern building into the cold evening air, the gloom and the brume of the riverside failing to wash away her own darkness. She'd followed the Onyar towards the Rambla, a damp night promising. A seething chill rose off the river, whispering through her coat, her breath dancing multi-coloured before her in the shop-window neon as she walked quickly along the edge of Plaça Catalunya. Catalina was waiting for her on the corner of the Pont de Pedra stone bridge and the Rambla, her own coat pulled tightly around her, her face shrouded in her own damp breath.

'You want an ice cream?' Elisenda had asked her sister after Catalina had made her demand. 'In February?'

In reply, Catalina had flapped open her coat to reveal her bulge.

'You want an ice cream,' Elisenda surrendered.

'Rocambolesc,' Catalina clarified.

'Where else?'

Elisenda held on to her sister's arm and walked with her along the Rambla. No terrace cafés were open at this time of year, but light from the shops and cafés and restaurants spilled out onto the promenade, washing them both with a winter pallor. The bookshops and shoe shops and clothes shops, the old and the new, would be closing in less than half an hour, but there were still plenty of people hurrying in and out of them in clouds of warm breath.

At the end of the Rambla, they crossed the river on the narrow Pont de les Peixateries footbridge, built by Eiffel. Stopping to stare a moment at the bombazine water through the red iron lattice that embraced them, Catalina looked up and sighed.

'I hate it when they turn the cathedral lights off,' she commented. 'It looks so sad.'

'Winter sad,' Elisenda agreed.

The solid shape rose reassuring but sombre above the city, its one tower obscuring a blackening sky. In an hour or so, you'd only know it was there by its absence, a darker shadow over the old town.

'You're looking better, mind,' Catalina told her. 'Not so tatty. Like you're sleeping better.'

'Ice cream,' Elisenda reminded her sister, bundling her across the bridge towards the other side, their shoes clattering loudly on the wooden floor.

They'd ordered a cornet inside Rocambolesc, amid the fantasy red and white striped pipes, choosing a different topping each, and taken them back out on to Carrer Santa Clara to eat them.

'I can't eat it,' Catalina had said after her first mouthful. 'It's too cold.'

'It's ice cream.'

Catalina gave hers to Elisenda, who stood helpless with a cone in each hand in the biting evening chill. With both hands full, she hung her head at the shrill sound of her phone clamouring for her in her pocket. Looking pointedly at her sister, she slowly placed both ice creams in a bin and reached inside her jacket.

'I'll be glad when this baby's born,' she told her.

—

The apartment door was wedged halfway open when Elisenda got there, two Científica examining either side of the split wood, dusting the long steel spike impaled in it and the area around the front and back of the door and the bell for fingerprints.

'Clean so far,' one of them told her.

Gingerly, Elisenda stepped inside the flat and studied the sharp end of the pin where it came through the spyhole. With the force of the hammer blows, it had burst through the fisheye glass inside the little metal frame, which now lay on the floor some distance into the hall next to a small plastic marker. She imagined Clara Ferré looking through it and couldn't help wincing.

'Through there,' the second forensic officer told her, gesturing behind to the interior doors beyond.

The archaeologist was sitting on the sofa next to her son. She was holding a glass of wine, taking small and insistent sips from it. Her son stared at the wall opposite, his

231

hands fluttering in his lap. She looked up when Elisenda walked in and sat down in an armchair at a right-angle to the sofa.

'It only just missed me,' was the first thing Ferré told her. She sounded more angry than frightened.

Elisenda listened to the woman's account of what had happened and asked her if she knew of anyone who might want to harm her.

'No one. Two of your people came to see me to ask about Esteve Mascort, but I really don't know anything about that. It was all a long time ago.'

'We think this might have more to do with Ferran Arbós,' Elisenda told her. 'We believe that there's some relationship between his death and that of Esteve Mascort.'

'But they barely knew each other as far as I know. Esteve and I were at the same stage in our careers when he went missing, and I know I had no contact with Arbós at that time, so I doubt Esteve did. You can't think it was anything to do with that, can you? After all this time?'

The sound of footsteps came from the hall and Àlex walked into the living room. He nodded at Elisenda and sat down in another chair.

'Can you think of any connection between you and the two of them that anyone might make?' Elisenda continued.

The archaeologist's hand began to shake slightly, and she put the glass down on the coffee table. Finally showing some reaction, her son reached across and held her hand.

'I'm sorry,' Ferré said, 'but I really can't think right now. I don't understand why anyone would want to attack me. I don't know anything.'

Elisenda saw that they weren't going to get much more out of her for the time being, a delayed shock setting in, so she asked her if there was anywhere else she could stay for a few days, but Ferré shook her head vehemently.

'I'm not being forced out of my own home. We're staying here.'

Àlex was about to argue, but Elisenda stopped him. 'We'll make sure you have protection from uniformed officers,' she told the archaeologist.

'We're not going to get any more sense out of her tonight,' Elisenda told Àlex on the staircase after they'd left Ferré and her son. 'She's told us all we need to know about tonight's attack, so we'll make sure there's a watch on her and question her again about Arbós when she's calmer.'

'You think it's safe for her to stay here?'

'If this were a genuine attack, he wouldn't have just smashed a spike through her door. This killer's efficient, he would've got inside the apartment and done the job properly. This is intimidation, another display to warn people that he's out there and to tell them to keep quiet about anything they might know.'

'So why kill Arbós? Why not just a deterrent with him?'

'Because Arbós really did know the dealer. He worked with him for years and could have incriminated him or blackmailed him with Mascort's murder after his body was found.'

Àlex nodded his acceptance of her argument.

'If the dealer is our murderer, that is,' she added, still uncertain.

Chapter Thirty Two

Tentacles of mist slithered across the surface of the river, slowly reaching into the gaps between the overhang of the houses and the water, probing the underside of the Pont de Sant Agustí, poising to curl over the top of the footbridge and wrap itself around the ankles of the young man walking in dawn tiredness across it. Elisenda rested her head against the cold kitchen window and watched the wintry brown of the Onyar disappear under a grim white shroud as the gelid air rolled down from the mountains. Closing her eyes, she yawned, her eyes so tight for a moment she remembered all the times she'd thought in fear as a child that they'd never open again.

Struggling to raise her eyelids, she focused on the city waking up along the river and was surprised to see Àlex on the bridge, walking towards her side of town. She'd barely had time to put away the duvet she'd wrapped around herself on the living room sofa in the fractured night and close the door on her unslept-in bed before the downstairs doorbell rang.

'It's Àlex,' he called up on the intercom when she answered. 'Come for breakfast.'

'Be down now,' she told him, keeping the tone of wonder out of her voice. It was the first time he'd ever called on her before work.

She laced her boots up and put her warm jacket on, taking one last look behind her before closing the door. She thought she saw a shadow flit across the living room beyond the small hallway and felt a moment of sorrow at her relief at the thought of spending that night away from home.

'Home,' she muttered wryly and trotted downstairs.

Àlex was waiting for her on the narrow road in front of the door to her building.

'No chance of getting run down in the metropolis,' he commented.

'Yeah, so Barcelona has traffic,' she teased him. 'What are you doing here? Can't keep away?' They'd only parted outside Clara Ferré's building a few hours earlier.

He looked uncertain for a moment before replying. 'Interviews today. I thought you might want some support. Go for breakfast.'

She nodded. 'Going to be a tough day, I suppose,' she admitted. She was touched but didn't want to show it. 'You're buying, I take it.'

He grinned, one of the quiet grins she was beginning to get used to. 'You look terrible, by the way. Didn't you sleep?'

She paused the briefest moment. 'Bad dream.'

'What about?'

She recalled the nightmare she'd had a few nights ago and gave him a sanitised version of her vision of a woman on the beach at El Crit. She didn't say the woman looked like how she imagined her daughter would have been as an adult.

'Why's it called El Crit?' Àlex asked her when she'd finished.

They were crossing Quatre Cantons, a cold wind from the river suddenly catching them broadside. A small plane flew overhead, briefly visible above the rooftops. Looking up, Elisenda almost missed her step on the pavement. She caught herself just in time and answered Àlex's question.

'The scream? You really want to know? It's a legend.'

Àlex shook his head angrily. 'Hell fire, Elisenda, are you lot in Girona capable of seeing anything or doing anything without attaching a legend to it? For Christ's sake.'

She let his anger subside before continuing. 'Some say it's a true story. A Moorish ship raiding the coast took shelter there in a sea fog one night. The next morning they heard a cock crow and thought there must be someone living nearby. They found a house, tied up the owner and stole everything and set fire to the barn. As they were leaving, they heard a cry and discovered the owner's daughter, but when the captain tried to take her back to the ship, she began to scream at him to let her go and bit his finger. So the captain drew his sword and cut her head off. That's it. When the wind blows, it whistles through the cove, supposedly the daughter's screams.'

Àlex didn't speak for a few moments. 'As long as that bullshit doesn't come back to haunt us,' he finally replied. He refused to talk any more about it, and Elisenda showed him in through a door into the welcome warmth of a café. They took a stool each at the bar.

'This place used to be called Granja Mora,' she told him, coaxing him to speak again. 'It had been here for sixty-odd years before it closed. It had a ruler running up the wall over there showing how high the flood water came up when the river overflowed. I used to love it as a kid.'

Àlex grunted. 'I'd never smelt damp in the air before coming to Girona.'

'You see, new experiences. What more could you want? My father used to have a beard years ago, but he shaved it off one winter because he was so fed up with it being sopping wet with the humidity all the time.'

Àlex waited until he'd been served his black *café sol* and turned to face her. 'That dream is bullshit, Elisenda.'

'It's a legend.'

'No, the dream. You didn't have one. Something's up when you stay here in Girona. You don't sleep.'

Elisenda took a slow sip of her *café amb llet* and tried to show nothing of what she felt. 'This is support?'

'Yes, Elisenda, it is. I saw the plane just now. You think we don't notice, but you're always looking up when you hear one. I know it's about your daughter.' He finished his coffee in two gulps the way he always did and put it down on the counter. Absently, he prodded at the small breakfast cheese roll in front of him. 'When I… When I nearly died last year, you insisted that I had counselling.'

'It's standard procedure, Àlex.'

'Yes, but you insisted. You thought I needed it.'

'Are you saying you didn't?'

He took a deep breath. 'Yes, I did. I didn't appreciate it at the time. And I resented you telling me I needed it, but you were right. The problem is that now it's my turn to say the same thing to you. You need to talk to someone, Elisenda.'

'Talk to someone? Why? Where's your counselling left you, Àlex? I can sort my own problems out.'

'Elisenda,' Àlex insisted, his voice cold but urgent, 'you need to talk to someone.'

She put her cup down on the counter and asked for the bill. She didn't wait for him to eat his breakfast.

'We both do, Àlex.'

She picked up her bag from the floor and left for Vista Alegre.

'I'm afraid we're going to have to put the first interview back at least half an hour,' Puigventós told Elisenda when she went to his office. 'The inspectora coming from Barcelona has rung to say she's stuck in traffic. An accident on the motorway, apparently. The candidates have been told.'

Elisenda nodded, faintly relieved at the stay of execution. Checking her watch, she saw she was still early for work.

'Breakfast,' she told herself. The rumbling in her stomach was telling her that she hadn't eaten yet. She hadn't even finished her coffee before leaving Àlex in the café.

Seeing that none of her team was in the office yet, she walked out of the building and past the two cafés by the station to avoid having to get into conversation with other Mossos and went the short distance along the river away from the centre to a tiny little café on the corner of a narrow street.

Micaló was in there, and it was too late for her to back out. He saw her and gestured half-heartedly to the chair opposite him at the red-topped table.

238

'Not the sort of place I'd expect to find you, Roger,' she told him, ordering a *café amb llet* and two croissants from the café owner.

'Precisely why I come here,' he replied. 'I'm usually left to my own thoughts. I take it you've been told the inspectora from Barcelona's running late? It must be a relief to you.'

'A relief?'

Micaló studied her before continuing. 'I have to apologise for what I said yesterday about your unit and the death of your officer. I was perhaps too zealous about the low-level crime initiative and I took Mosso Paredes' actions too personally.'

Elisenda was taken entirely by surprise and had to gather her thoughts before answering. 'Apology accepted. Thank you. But why do you say it must be a relief?'

'I've never lost a member of my team, or any colleague I've worked with, for that matter, so I can only imagine what it must have been like to lose your caporal last year. I should imagine that anything that puts off having to replace him would feel like a reprieve.'

She could only stare at him, stunned by his insight, shaken by his sympathy. She looked for any sign of insincerity, but Micaló's face was blank, unfathomable.

'Do you know anything about her?' she asked, wanting to move on. 'This inspectora from Barcelona.'

'Fast-track, tipped for a senior post before she's forty, that's all I know. I read an article she wrote for La Vanguardia on modern policing, which I found very interesting, but I've never met her. I must admit I'm looking forward to it.'

'Right.' Another career politician, Elisenda instantly thought. She'd already decided that she was probably not going to like her.

'Only one woman on the shortlist, I noticed.'

Elisenda shrugged. 'I chose the best five.'

She had to admit to herself that she wasn't entirely sure that that was true. In her reluctance to take on a new member of the team because it finally meant accepting Pau's death, she knew that she hadn't looked at the applications as closely as she had done when taking on the original officers in her unit, the excitement she felt then in stark contrast to the deep aversion to change she felt now. Her only choosing one woman to go forward for interview was unintended. When the Mossos took over policing in Catalonia, one of the ways in which they wanted to sever any connection with the past was in recruitment. Apart from police finally being from their own region, something that didn't happen under the old Spanish system, the Catalan police took the decision that it wanted to attract more women and more graduates. But instead of having quotas, they adopted a solution that Elisenda had to admit to finding quite neat, on the whole. Rather than an equal ratio of candidates, it was the people taking the decisions in the selection process that had to fulfil quotas. At every stage in the procedure, including all the tests and all the decisions as to who went on to the next stage, and all the interviews, the panel that chose who was recruited or promoted had to be made up of an equal number of men and women of an equal rank. This was why they were waiting now for the inspectora from Barcelona. Elisenda and Micaló were the two sotsinspectors, Puigventós and the officer now stuck in traffic were the two inspectors. The idea was that, ultimately, the Mossos chose the best possible candidates, regardless of gender, while reducing the possibility of the gatekeepers only letting their own sort into the club. For the want of anything better, Elisenda felt it worked quite well.

'I'd better be getting back,' Micaló suddenly said, getting up. 'I'll get this.'

'No it's okay, thanks. I'll get mine.'

He paused before leaving and picked up a newspaper from the adjacent table. 'You probably need to read this.'

She watched him go before picking the paper up. The first double spread inside was an account of how Ferran Arbós had died. Elisenda cursed and read on. Despite the space given over to it, the article was mainly conjecture, but dangerous conjecture, demanding to know why the curator would have been killed so savagely and making the obvious connection between his death and the body found at El Crit.

Sighing, she folded the paper up and made to leave, when her phone rang. It was Gemma Cardoner from the Archaeology Service.

'*Elisenda, I've found something more for you.*'

El Crit, 1981

'I want to find a skull.'

'Grow up.'

The student knew he was on a hiding to nothing, but he couldn't stop himself. 'I want to find a skull with a spike,' he insisted. 'Something that changes what we know about the Indiketa.'

Esteve Mascort stood up from where he was digging in the trench at El Crit and grinned, a mocking gash of white picked out in the cold spotlight under the parallel line of his dark moustache.

'Believe me, I know what you want and it's not to find some ancient bones.' He walked forward under the harsh glare of the arc lamps set up next to where they were both digging and pushed his face right up to the student's. His smile increased as the student flinched. 'Money. That's what drives you. Wealth, position.'

'You're wrong.'

'Wrong? So, go. What are you doing here if it's not money you want? Go, tell everyone what we're doing.'

The student knew he'd lost and bent down again to carry on digging. Mascort looked scornfully at him and went back to his part of the trench, both of them word-lessly scraping away at the earth beneath them.

'Want to make some real money?' Mascort had told him when the student had phoned him the other night.

The student was grateful at first that Mascort had been the first name on the list of archaeologists he'd tried phoning.

'They've cut the funding for the dig,' Mascort had told him. 'But that doesn't mean they've cut my funding. I could do with a hand from a kindred spirit.'

The student wasn't sure how he felt at being described a kindred spirit by someone like Mascort, but he'd listened to what the archaeologist had had to say and he'd gone along with it. It was better than the thought of going back to his course in Barcelona and scrimping and saving for every last thing.

Feeling something under his mattock in the carbon light of their illegal dig on the secluded headland in the deep of night, the student leaned forward to see what it was. It wasn't the skull with a spike through it that had fuelled his childhood desire to become an archaeologist. He was almost relieved.

He was yet to see the real money that Esteve Mascort had promised him.

Chapter Thirty Three

Elisenda recalled a time not so many years earlier, when she was living in Barcelona, before she joined the police, or indeed had any inkling that she ever would. The Mossos d'Esquadra had taken over policing in Girona and a number of other areas as part of the piecemeal handover of powers, but not yet in the Catalan capital, where the old Spanish Policía Nacional and Guardia Civil were still running things.

Someone had stolen her ex-husband's car number plates and they'd had to report it to the Policía Nacional before he could apply for replacement plates at the traffic department and get them made at one of the official centres. She recalled going to the small police station in a leafy street of fine houses and affluently ageing apartment blocks in Sant Gervasi, the district of Barcelona where she and her ex were living at the time. The cop on duty, a wheezing bureaucrat who only spoke Spanish, laboriously typed everything out on an ancient typewriter, which he clunked around unhurried on a huge metal trolley. She'd watched impatiently as he'd slowly loaded a piece of carbon paper sandwiched between two printed forms and steadfastly tried to type his report in the spaces provided. Her undying image of pre-Mossos bureaucracy was carbon paper and corrector fluid, neither of which served a purpose other than to add to the sea of paperwork that inexorably drowned the country.

She thought of it again now.

'Have you seen Àlex?' she asked Josep when she got to the unit's offices. She'd been told that the inspectora from Barcelona had arrived in Girona and was on her way to Vista Alegre, so she had to sort things out quickly.

'I haven't seen him, Sotsinspectora,' Josep told her.

'OK, I've had a call from Gemma Cardoner at the Archaeology Service offices, out on the Pedret road towards the prison.'

'The one who found all the documents for the first El Crit dig?'

'That's the one. Well, she's just called me to say that she's found some more documents in another box that should have been holding artefacts. They're all carbon copies of other documents, so we might find we've got them all anyway, but we need to check through them. Can you go to the Archaeology Service now and pick them up, then start checking them against the documents you've already looked at. See if anything new turns up in them. I don't hold out much hope. Carbon copies never did anyone any good, but we have to be sure.'

Josep nodded his head. 'I'll do that.' He sounded more eager than Elisenda felt.

She thanked him and made her way to the meeting rooms where the selection panel interviews were to be held.

–

Martí Barbena opened his front door in jeans and a floppy sweater. Àlex had stood waiting at the front door for some time, listening to the sounds inside. A man's voice, Barbena's, had called to say he'd only be a minute. Àlex had absently pushed the dead leaves that had wedged themselves against the front step of the house with his feet, first one way, then the other, clearing a small path through the middle. They left a damp stain on the toes of his shoes. Barbena finally opened the door, evidently without bothering to look through the spyhole.

'Sorry about that, I was showering,' he began, but the look of expectation on the thin lines of his taut face quickly gave way to a mocking smile. 'You?' he finished.

'Expecting someone else?' Àlex asked him.

'A colleague, if you must know. We're working here today on a paper for a journal. Am I being harassed again today? Only I'd like your name first, if you don't mind.' His mouth curled in a vulpine grin. 'I don't believe we were properly introduced the last time we met.'

'Sergent Àlex Albiol. May I come in? I'm here to ask you some questions about Ferran Arbós. You're not under suspicion in any way.' Not now while it suits me, Àlex failed to add.

Barbena looked doubtful for a moment, but curiosity appeared to overtake him and he beckoned Àlex inside.

'I can't give you long,' the archaeologist told him. 'As I said, I'm expecting someone.'

He led Àlex through to the kitchen, where small logs were spitting in the fire burning blue and green on the water pipes in the grate. The room was soporifically warm after the chill wind of the street.

Àlex explained that they'd read Barbena's report on his suspicions of Arbós's illicit activities. 'Do you have any ideas how he might have traded in the artefacts?'

Barbena sat down at the kitchen table in the window and invited Àlex to take the chair opposite. 'I think it was there in my report. It's so long since I wrote it, I really can't remember everything I said. I recall that two museums I worked with had acquired items on Arbós's recommendation, which were purportedly found at sites where I'd worked. I catalogued or saw the catalogue records of every artefact that was discovered at those digs, and I knew for a fact that the items simply weren't from those sites.'

'Why would that be?'

'I can only surmise that they were taken either from the sites secretly, which would have involved an archaeologist stealing them without cataloguing them, or they were from other sites altogether. The items in themselves were genuine, their provenance wasn't. I had good cause to suspect that it was Arbós who was faking the provenance to secure their sale to the museums.'

'Would Arbós have been the one to sell the artefacts to the museums? Or to other buyers?'

Barbena shook his head. 'Extremely unlikely. That really would have aroused suspicion. No, they would have been presented through other channels, either already with Arbós's recommendation or his support of the provenance or through his subsequent approval. Both of the museums I worked with acquired the pieces at auction, which effectively muddies the route they took to get to that stage.'

'Do you know of anyone that Arbós worked with for that purpose? Any dealers?'

'No. I was always pretty certain that Mascort was stealing for him from the digs he worked on, but I don't know of any other archaeologists after Mascort's death that

Arbós might have worked with, although there must have been someone. And I don't know of anyone else he might have worked with to sell them on. That wasn't what I was interested in, to be honest. I thought I had enough to get Arbós removed from his post just through the fake provenances and the artefacts stolen from digs. I didn't look into how they were sold.'

'Does the name Serveis Art mean anything to you?'

Barbena thought for a moment but shook his head. 'Nothing.'

They were disturbed by the door bell ringing. Barbena got up to answer, leaving Àlex with his disappointment that the archaeologist knew nothing more than what he'd already said in his report. Barbena returned into the room with his colleague. Àlex looked up at her in surprise. Looking much more composed than she had the last time he'd seen her, she was back to wearing her hair in the same grey, twisted plait as she had the first time, a smarter pair of jeans under a long woollen coat that looked expensively warm.

'Sergent Albiol,' Clara Ferré commented. 'What a pleasant surprise.'

'Àlex, please. Actually, I was just on my way to see you.'

She took her coat off and sat down. 'That would have been a pleasure.' The smile that had been missing the previous night now gleamed mischievously in the kitchen's warmth. As Elisenda had predicted, she was much calmer and more willing to talk, a quiet resilience firmly back in place. Àlex asked her the same questions about Arbós that he'd put to Barbena.

'Years ago, my predecessor at the history museum was offered an artefact that we both had a bad feeling about,' she told him after a moment's thought. 'I was a junior curator at the time.'

'Was this through Arbós?'

'No, there was no mention of Arbós, and my boss told the guy that he wasn't interested long before it even got to the provenance stage. Something wasn't right, so we got rid of him as soon as we could.'

'Do you have a name for the man who tried to sell the item?'

She shook her head. 'I can't remember. This was some years ago and most of his dealings were with my boss. I've never seen him since. Creepy, though, I remember that. He had a baby face but dangerous eyes, not someone I'd want to meet in a dark alley.'

'Can you describe him?'

'Not really. I only recall his eyes being cold, calculating. Otherwise, slim, normal height, balding, nothing special. I suppose he'd be in his sixties now. He was about ten years older than I was. But that's all I remember. Sorry.'

'Might your old boss remember him?'

'I'm afraid he died some years ago. He was already ancient when I started working with him.'

Àlex thanked them both and drove moodily back to Vista Alegre, his knowledge no more complete than it was before talking to the two archaeologists. He recalled Elisenda's words about the investigation moving in and out of focus. He disagreed. To him, it was constantly out of focus, something indiscernible just beyond their field of vision that no matter who they talked to or what they found refused to mould itself into a distinct shape.

Chapter Thirty Four

'Where do you see yourself in five years' time?'

Most probably on a charge for punching you to the ground, Elisenda thought, the first time she heard the inspectora from Barcelona ask the question.

The woman had wafted into the interview suite, borne in on a sea of self-confidence that threatened to drown everyone else in the room. Elisenda had caught Puigventós looking aghast at her air of entitlement at one point, but then hurriedly try to hide it when he'd glanced over at Elisenda. Micaló looked like a puppy with a new owner.

'Alícia Comas,' she'd introduced herself, holding her hand out limply and looking at the next person in the meet and greet chain. Elisenda had been tempted to withdraw her hand until the woman made eye contact with her.

The same age as Elisenda, Comas was of the type that was always going to prosper in any organisation more than Elisenda ever would. With short brown hair and sharp black eyes and a grey suit that was straight out of the corporate manual, she asked the candidates questions that were an inconsistent mix of textbook cliché and jargon clique. Oddly, Elisenda found the interviewees' reactions to the questions telling of their characters, although probably not in the way Comas might have imagined. In a moment's irreverence, Elisenda had decided she was going to wait for the first one to show irritation and offer them the job. Neither of the two they'd interviewed so far had.

'I think we'll call a break now,' Puigventós suggested wearily after the second candidate had left the room, 'and reconvene back here in half an hour.'

Elisenda could have kissed him.

–

'Anything?' Elisenda asked, walking into her unit's outer office, temporarily sloughing off the lethargy the selection panel had nourished in her.

Josep sat and stared at the flaky mountain of wafer-thin papers in front of him and shook his head. To Elisenda's eyes, the bruised blue lettering that had bled into the flimsy carbon copy paper over the years was already dancing giddily in front of her eyes. Josep must have been well on the way to a bureaucracy migraine.

'Nothing yet.' His earlier eagerness was evidently wearing off. He gestured to the sturdy cardboard box from the Archaeology Service sitting on his desk. 'It was full to the brim with papers, and they're so thin, there are so many of them.'

'Àlex in?'

'He went out to see Martí Barbena and Clara Ferré to ask them if they knew anything about the antiquities dealer.'

Josep looked in dismay at another, smaller pile of documents on the table opposite him, the one that Montse used to use but that she'd now swapped with Àlex. They were the files in the paper chase for the company that used to make payments to Ferran Arbós.

'Enjoy,' Elisenda told him. 'Get Montse to help you if you need to.'

He shot her a glance that told her he wouldn't be doing either.

Elisenda's half-hour respite immediately vanished when a call came in from the sergent in charge of the cells, telling her they were just discharging Siset.

'*He wants to see you.*'

'Couldn't you have kept him in a bit longer?' she asked the sergent when she got there.

He looked at her over half-rim glasses. 'Not if the whining little shit wanted to live another day.'

Elisenda nodded, a smile on her face. 'He's a challenging taste, isn't he?'

Siset slouched in front of a caporal through the two sets of doors to where Elisenda was standing. He was fighting his usual hopeless battle of tucking his shirt into his trousers and moaning something incomprehensible.

'I don't want to be arrested again, Elisenda,' he told her. 'It's not right. I've got immunity. I'm a public service.'

'Well, I'll bear that in mind, Siset,' she replied, trying not to notice the other two Mossos smirking. She walked with him out of the cell area. 'And your next public service is to find out what you can about someone selling fake antiquities.'

'Antiques?'

'Antiquities. Things people find at archaeological sites. Old coins, pottery, bones. I want to know who's selling them on the sly.'

He snorted and looked scornfully at her. 'Blue-collar shit. Nothing to do with me. I'm street.'

Elisenda nodded meaningfully at the door to the cells. 'Public service, Siset. Find out what you can.'

She watched him go, knowing he was unlikely to come across anything that would be of use to her. 'Hopeless,' she muttered.

Checking the time, she saw the half-hour was up and so she quickly made her way back to the interview suite, where she waited while Comas finished a call. The inspectora from Barcelona had applied a fresh layer of deep red lipstick like an angry wound and was pursing her mouth in irritation at whoever was on the other end of the phone. She hung up and shot a politician's smile at the other three members of the panel, who were sitting in silence. Some of the lipstick had come off on her teeth.

'Where do you see yourself in five years' time?' Comas eventually asked the next candidate, a thickset guy who was currently posted to the Ebro Delta region, the wetlands at the southern tip of Catalonia.

Elisenda watched him try but not fully succeed in hiding a look that was a blend of disbelief and disdain before he replied. Covering her smile, she glanced down at his file and checked his name. Manel Moliné. Originally from Lleida, she read, the provincial capital some two hours west of Barcelona. She watched him and listened to what he had to say in the deliberate, almost Spanish-sounding vowels of his accent.

–

After lunch, Àlex sat down opposite Josep and took over the files dealing with the bonded warehouse. But not for long.

'Any news from the selection panel?' he asked Josep.

The caporal looked up briefly from the wall of thin papers either side of him and shook his head. 'They broke for lunch over an hour ago. Elisenda had to go with them. She didn't look too pleased.'

Àlex grunted. 'She didn't say anything about how the interviews were going?'

'Nothing. She just told me that there were still two more left to do.'

Montse came in, shaking her heavy coat down off over her arms, and looked at the two men working through the papers. She pulled up a chair between the two of them, where their desks met, and sat down. 'How can I help?'

Àlex looked up and gestured to the piles of documents stacked up around Josep. 'His need is greater than mine.'

Montse nodded, not making eye contact with Josep. 'Okay, what do you want me to do?'

Josep pointed at a pile to his left. 'You take these. Most of them are copies of what we've already got, but some are new. We're looking for anything we haven't seen yet that might be important for the Mascort killing.'

'Or for Arbós,' Àlex added. 'Or the trafficking. There could be anything.'

Montse gazed at the tower of flimsy and yellowing paper and took a deep breath before picking up a small wad from the top and scanning through the first one.

Àlex's phone rang. He answered it absently, but sat up sharply after the person on the other end began speaking, his free hand flexing as he searched for pen and paper. Montse and Josep couldn't help exchanging a look before both hurriedly turned back to face him. While he was talking, Àlex wrote something down and went searching on his computer screen. Thanking the other person, he hung up and made another phone call, introducing himself to the person on the other end and arranging to meet them.

Standing up, he pulled his jacket off the back of the chair and put it on. 'That was a sotsinspector from Barcelona getting back to me,' he explained to the other two. 'He was a sergent at the time that Serveis Art, the bonded warehouse, was raided. The owner was arrested and imprisoned.'

'You going to see him?' Josep asked but Àlex shook his head.

'He died last month, apparently. He was in prison for four years at La Roca, and discharged just over a year ago. Diagnosed with cancer when he was still at La Roca. I'm going to see his widow. She lives in Palamós.'

'So he couldn't have been responsible for Arbós's death,' Montse commented.

Àlex shrugged. 'My gut feeling is he's not our dealer, just a link in the chain. I'll see what I can get from his widow.'

'Want me to come?' Montse asked him.

Àlex glanced at the desk sinking under the papers from the Archaeology Service and shook his head. 'Better if you both stay here working together through all this lot.' He looked pointedly at the two caporals. 'Better for us all.'

Chapter Thirty Five

The house stood between the small Palamós football ground and the pitted old main road running from the new dual carriageway to the neighbouring town of Sant Antoni de Calonge. The old road still busy, a relic of a less affluent past, the new buildings and highways a reminder of a more confident, more recent history, now also gone. A tall hedge of bamboo and rushes shielding the short terrace of modern houses from the road whispered in the cold wind, now and then chattering angrily in the wake of a car speeding past on the other side before settling down once more into idle winter gossip.

Àlex parked the pool car in front of the house he was after and rang the bell. An elderly woman answered, an old-fashioned nylon housecoat spread tightly over a faded sweater and cardigan, a small and ancient bulldog wrapped between her stout legs. On her feet were frayed fleece-lined slippers, scant protection from ceramic floor tiles thought more for the heat of summer than February's chill. She pulled the coat and cardigan tightly around her and looked quizzically at Àlex.

'Thank you for seeing me,' he told her after introducing himself.

'Why now?'

'May I come in?'

Nodding in curious resignation, she turned and led the way along a corridor to the rear of the house. The dog waddled snuffling ahead, turning from time to time to keep a rheumy eye on the newcomer. Àlex followed, closing the front door behind him, conscious of his shoes resonating on the incongruously cheerful honey-coloured floor. It was a building meant for summer.

'Why now?' the woman repeated after she'd shown Àlex to an old and expensive leather chair at one end of a mahogany and marble coffee table. A similar chair stood empty at the other end. The woman sat down on a long sofa of the same pattern. Glancing around, Àlex saw that the room wasn't crammed with bric-a-brac as he'd first thought, but with a jumble of tasteful pieces of sculpture and figurines, the refinement of the individual items undermined by the over-indulgence of the whole. The paintings on the wall were originals, some of them by Catalan artists that Àlex recognised. Old money. A lighter, oblong patch on the wall opposite gave away the woman's financial straits. Old money that wasn't growing any older.

'It's in connection with another investigation,' he told her. 'We aren't reopening anything to do with your husband's conviction. I'm simply here to ask you about that time.'

'Conviction,' she spat out bitterly. 'Scapegoat.'

'Why scapegoat?'

'I lost the last five years of my marriage, Sergent Albiol. My husband died here in this house but he was killed in prison. Before he even went to prison. The worry killed him, and the fear. That man killed him.'

At her last words, Àlex remained calm. He recalled the notes that the sotsinspector in Barcelona had given him on

Joan Canyellas, the woman's husband and owner of the bonded warehouse through which illicit antiquities had been traded before it had been closed down. Àlex had had a suspicion all along that Canyellas had been a minor player, and the woman's words seemed to be confirming that. He needed to know who the man was that she'd referred to, but he knew he had to tread carefully if she wasn't to clam up.

'What was he afraid of?'

'The devil.'

Àlex stayed silent, simply looking at the woman, who suddenly seemed a lot smaller, engulfed in the heavy brown sofa. Seated on the floor in front of her, the dog sensed something and moved closer. She reached down and stroked its head.

'The devil,' she repeated quietly. 'With the face of an angel. Joan was so frightened of him, he didn't know what to do. He couldn't get away from him. He said he felt he was strangling the life out of him.'

Tears began to run down her lined cheeks. Àlex seemed uncertain for a moment, staring unsure at the woman. At once the room seemed hot, the sparse garden through the French windows crowding at the glass, the air thin. Àlex could feel the breath catching in his throat, his neck burning, his mouth unable to form words, a silent noose closing around him. He had no idea how long he sat stock still before a jolt appeared to go through him and he hurriedly leaned forward to take the woman's hand. She squeezed his tightly and his lungs filled with air, the sound of life in his chest filling his ears with a cleansing rush, like water over pebbles.

'What was he afraid of?'

'I never knew his name. Joan wouldn't let me know. He said he didn't want me to know who the man was so that I'd be safe from him. Joan was so afraid. The man made him keep all these things in his warehouse and sell them through his business. Those things the police found when Joan was arrested weren't his.'

'But you saw him once? You said he had the face of an angel.'

'I went to see Joan at his office one day, but before Joan realised I was there, the man showed up. I knew it was him by the terror in Joan's voice, so I hid. Joan never knew I was there that day, I never told him. But I saw him and I heard him speak. He was the devil with the face of an angel, and the coldest voice I've ever heard. He could say things you wouldn't think were threatening, but they somehow sounded so horrible in that voice.'

Àlex knew the answer, but he had to ask it. 'Why didn't your husband tell the police the truth when they arrested him? Or at his trial?'

The woman shook her head, grief and anger fighting each other for precedence. 'He was terrified. He knew what the man would have done to him, but he was more worried about me. He made me swear never to breathe a word about it to anyone, not even when he was in prison or when he was dying.'

'Do you know where the man is now?'

She shook her head. 'After Joan was imprisoned, I never knew any more about him. Joan wouldn't speak about him, and after he came home, the man didn't ever come back. Joan had lost his business then and he wasn't well, so he had nothing the man would have wanted. He finally left him alone when he was already dying.'

Àlex went to the kitchen and made them both a cup of coffee, sitting with her and talking about her and her husband's shared love of art and antiques until she was calmer. He knew he wouldn't get any more out of her of help to the investigation, so after a time he stood up to leave.

'I will do what I can to find this man,' he told her. If he's still alive, he thought to himself. At the door, he asked her if there was anyone who could sit with her for a time.

'My neighbour is very good, but I'm all right. I'm used to being on my own now.'

'Do you have any children?'

'No.'

So no sins of the fathers revisited on the child, Àlex couldn't help thinking on the drive back to Girona. He thought, too, of Clara Ferré and her description of the man who'd tried to sell artefacts to her boss when she was a junior curator. He had no doubt it was the same person Joan Canyellas' widow had been describing.

Imperceptibly, he pushed harder on the accelerator as he drove on the return journey, speed and urgency filling his head.

—

'This guy's new.'

'Show me,' Josep said.

Scanning through the page again, Montse handed him the flimsy piece of paper. While he read it, she drained the last of the coffee that Josep had gone to fetch about half an hour ago. She shuddered at the cold, grainy feel of the drink and threw the cup into the bin.

'Ivan Morera,' Josep read, shaking his head. 'He hasn't come up before. Not in the personnel listings. Or anywhere else.'

Montse took the piece of paper back from him and checked the details. It was the carbon copy of a letter from the Archaeology Service in Girona to Morera at an address in Barcelona, giving him the details of how to get to El Crit, where he was apparently to be working as a volunteer for the summer of 1981, and an address in Palamós where he was going to be staying.

'They even give his National ID number,' Montse commented, pointing to the reference bit by the address.

Josep looked at her and nodded. 'What do you want to take?'

'I'll do the ID if you want to check up the addresses in Barcelona and Palamós.'

'I'll also double-check with the other student volunteers that summer, see if anyone remembers him.'

Montse nodded. 'Okay, and we'd better look into the person who signed it, see if they're still there. They might remember something. I'll take that.'

'This is looking good,' Josep said. He leaned back and stared at the paper Montse was holding, a deep breath of satisfaction after hours of bureaucratic slog escaping from him. He sat forward again, tentatively. 'Want to go for a coffee first? This could be a long haul.'

She stared at him and thought for a moment. 'Sure. Why not.'

Chapter Thirty Six

'I've never liked that name,' Josep muttered darkly.

'Good to see you going into this with an open mind,' Elisenda told him.

For a morning meeting with so much news, it was proving to be surprisingly heavy going. Elisenda had got home to her apartment in Girona late the previous evening, too wrung out even for a *licor de café* while watching the lights in the river from La Terra, and she'd lain awake thinking of the day's selection panel to the murmuring undertone of Lina's nursery rhymes floating by in the dark.

Each of the panel had had a different first choice, so everyone's subsequent choices were totted up, the candidates given a descending mark according to their position in the ranking. The classic decision by committee, Elisenda thought as the scores were added together to find the overall favourite. In the end, with the result being a two-way tie and the discussion looking like it would never end, the other three panel members had given her the final say. After yet more argument and a sleepless night, she'd come in that morning and the first person she'd seen had been Paredes. Stifling a sigh, she'd hoped she'd made the right choice.

'Manel,' Josep repeated. 'Bit old-fashioned.'

'His full name's Joan Manel if that suits you any better,' Elisenda told him. She knew that telling her unit about the new member of their team was a difficult moment for everyone and she was determined to go easy on them.

'You could call him Joanma,' Montse offered. Surprised, Elisenda caught the lack of any antagonistic tone in her voice.

'Compound names,' Josep muttered. 'They're even worse.'

'As I said,' Elisenda told him. 'Good to see you keeping an open mind.' Two thoughts struck her. The first was that she knew that she was also struggling to be positive about the idea of an outsider joining the team and had to suppress that. The second was a stirring in her mind, triggered by Josep's comment about compound names. About how Joan Manel could have chosen to call himself by any combination of those names. About how anyone else could do the same and so be perceived to be a different person.

'Manel Moliné,' she repeated for them all, putting the last thought away for another moment. She looked pointedly at Josep. 'From Lleida, so don't complain about his accent. You Barcelona types sound odd to those of us who speak proper Catalan.'

Àlex and Josep exchanged a wry smile. Elisenda paused before carrying on. 'Now I know we're all reluctant to have an outsider coming in to replace Pau. Pau can't ever be replaced and we have to accept that.' She saw Àlex turn away to hide his expression. Montse and Josep both looked down, their faces impassive. 'But we're stretched enough as it is. We need new blood. And most of all, we have to be fair to Manel, none of what happened is his fault, we have to accept him as a new member.'

She heard Montse take a deep breath before looking up. Josep continued to stare at his lap.

'When does he begin?' Àlex asked.

'Tomorrow.'

The one word was met with silence.

'We found something last night,' Montse finally said, cracking the thin ice that lay over the room. 'In the carbon copies. A student on the 1981 dig called Ivan Morera who doesn't turn up anywhere else in the records.' Between them, they explained what they had found to Elisenda and Àlex and the paper trail that they were pursuing. 'But he seems to have vanished into thin air before he even appeared,' Montse concluded.

'We called all the other students who worked on the dig that summer and the previous Easter,' Josep told them, 'but none of them had heard of him. I've tracked down the address in Barcelona. He was fostered by a couple, who are still living there now. We can go and see them tomorrow. As for the address in Palamós, it turns out he was going to be renting a room from an elderly widow who lived there. She's now died, so I don't know if he ever showed up there, but I'm trying to track down any family members who might be able to tell me something.'

Elisenda was about to praise him, but decided it was better to keep silent. It was Montse who took up the reins.

'The copy of the letter we've got was signed by the then director. He's also died now, and I can't find anyone there who remembers anything about the student. There's no record of an Ivan Morera working on any dig before or after that. But what we do have is his ID number. It was at the top of the letter.'

'Good,' Àlex commented. 'That should give us the answer.'

Both Montse and Josep shook their heads in unison. Elisenda forced herself not to smile.

'The ID was due for renewal in 1985, but it was never renewed. It simply expired without anyone doing anything about it or reporting anything. No loss or theft. No death certificate, no record of emigration, nothing. He just vanished and no one appears to have noticed. I'm going to check social security records today to see what that turns up, but I don't think I'm going to find anything.'

'And we're hamstrung as always with missing person records from that time,' Elisenda commented, 'even if anyone did report him missing, which doesn't sound likely.'

'One thing,' Montse added. 'By the date of birth on his ID, he would have been a mature student at the time, about the same age as Esteve Mascort and the other two junior archaeologists. It might be significant, it might not.'

Elisenda nodded her head slowly, taking it all in. 'Good work, you two. Keep chasing the various leads up. Since none of the students on the dig knew him, see if you can find anyone who was on his university course in Barcelona. Someone from there might remember him.'

Checking her mobile when the others left the room to carry on with their searches, she saw that she had four missed calls, one from Poch, the sergent in charge of the Local Investigation Unit in La Bisbal, and three from Doctora Fradera. She rang Poch first. He told her of a man and a woman caught in the small hours of the morning nighthawking at Ullastret.

'Nighthawking?'

'*Using metal detectors to steal archaeological artefacts. They were looking in the area to the west of the main site, inside the complex. Someone living in a house nearby saw the light from their torches and called the Mossos. It was Caporal Fabra from the Palafrugell station who found them, but we've got them in custody in La Bisbal. I thought you might want to see them.*'

'You thought right. Thanks, Jaume. I'll be with you as soon as I can.'

Grabbing her things, she phoned Fradera. The archaeologist had called her with the same news.

'I'm on my way to La Bisbal now to question them,' Elisenda told her and hung up.

Out in the main room, she looked at the other three and took a decision.

'Àlex, come with me to La Bisbal. There's been an attempted theft at Ullastret. It might have some bearing on the Arbós case.'

Àlex logged out of the computer he was on and picked up his coat. 'Keep us posted,' he told the other two.

They drove in silence out of the city and past the Devesa, which had a naked air today compared with the bustle of the market the last time Elisenda took this road.

'Are we stopping to see Doctora Fradera?' Àlex asked as they passed the Archaeology Service.

'She's in Ullastret. She wanted to meet us in La Bisbal. To lynch these two we're going to see, I imagine, so I told her it wasn't a good idea.'

Àlex made a noise that could have been a laugh. They still hadn't spoken properly since their argument the previous morning.

'Micaló apologised to me yesterday,' she finally told him.

Surprised, he took his eyes off the road for a moment to see if she was being serious.

'For a comment he'd made about losing a member of the team,' she added.

A muscle in Àlex's cheek twitched. 'So he should, the prick.'

'Show some respect, Sergent Albiol, he's a senior officer.'

'And a prick.'

'And a prick,' she agreed.

'I wouldn't trust him. He'll see his apology as being in credit until the next time he tries to pull one over us.' He accelerated a moment to pass a Sarfa bus, all but empty on the winter morning run to the coast. 'You're not expecting me to apologise, are you? You still look terrible, by the way. I take it you spent last night in Girona.'

Elisenda stifled a laugh. 'Well, I'm not apologising, either.' With which, she knew, they'd both apologised. 'For your information, I didn't sleep because I was trawling the internet until the wee small hours. Checking up on the Indiketa and these skulls with spikes.'

'I saw a piece on the news a year or so ago how they'd reconstructed one of the faces. I checked it out again. It was fascinating. I take it that's what we're doing.'

'Just to try and get some idea. See if it looks like the picture we've got of Mascort.' She looked out of the side window, the undulating green of the Empordà hinterland blurring past them. 'Fradera seems to be out of step with most of the theories I found. The general consensus seems to agree with Bosch. The skulls were trophies of war displayed to intimidate other tribes and invaders and show how great the Indiketa were. They talk of the skulls of ancestors or village elders possibly being used for veneration, but not necessarily in these cases.'

'You find it odd that she should be going for the veneration idea?'

'I don't know. Perhaps. Or she's just brilliant and sees what no one else does.'

Àlex told her of his visit the previous afternoon to Palamós to question Canyellas' widow.

'She spoke of the man who worked with her husband the same way Clara Ferré described the man trying to sell dodgy artefacts to her boss. But no name anywhere. He hid himself well with his fake companies. And now he seems to have vanished. Just like Mascort and just like this new student.'

'And Canyellas' widow lives in Palamós,' Elisenda muttered. 'Do you notice how everything keeps coming back to there?'

Àlex was silent for a moment before speaking. 'And if this guy has vanished, maybe he just died. Which comes back to the theory of Arbós' killer being the original murderer's son or daughter.'

Which also brought the sudden image to Elisenda of her temporary neighbour at La Fosca, Miquel Canals. Whose father died just the previous month and who came to stay on the coast at the same time the body was found at El Crit.

Chapter Thirty Seven

'We're not common thieves,' the woman told Elisenda, her tone aggrieved.

'We're collectors,' her husband told Àlex in the interview room next door.

'They're a waste of time,' Elisenda muttered to her sergent as they swapped rooms to take a turn interviewing the other suspect.

Àlex had to agree. 'They're not exactly what I had in mind when I thought of organised gangs stealing antiquities,' he conceded with a faint grin.

What they were was a couple in their mid-forties with a metal detector, a plastic shovel and a battered Seat Ibiza. They also had two cats at home that needed feeding, the husband had protested to Poch when he'd held them in separate cells overnight.

'You're collectors?' Elisenda asked the husband when he repeated the claim he'd made to Àlex. 'At night, when no one's around, the other side of a fence on a protected heritage site.'

'You are thieves,' Àlex told the wife. 'We will be charging you with theft.'

She'd looked at him more in effrontery than fear when he gathered up his papers and left the interview room.

'Except there is no theft,' Elisenda reminded him in the corridor between the two doors.

By the time the Mossos patrol car had turned up in the middle of the night at the corner of the Ullastret site to find the husband blissfully unaware under his earphones and the wife absently pointing her torch at the earth by his feet, the couple hadn't yet found anything. They had no items in the bag slung over the wife's shoulder or hidden in the large plastic DIY box in the boot of their car.

'This is outrageous,' the husband had complained to the Mossos who'd arrived at the scene. 'We've got plenty of finds at home. There's never been any problem.'

He was now denying he'd said such a thing, and while Elisenda and Àlex were interviewing the couple at the station in La Bisbal, Poch and his team were searching their house in the neighbouring village of Cruïlles thanks to a warrant from Jutge Rigau.

'The wife tried to justify it by telling me that these things they find belong to the nation,' Àlex told Elisenda as they walked the short distance to the court buildings to see the judge, 'and that as they are part of the nation, they're only taking what's rightly theirs. What an attitude.'

Elisenda let out a small laugh. 'When I was a kid, we heard a huge crash from the upstairs flat. It turned out it was a Romanesque statue that the man living there had simply taken from a church out in the sticks because he liked collecting them. It was so heavy, it had pulled the shelf down off the wall and broken. When my dad said it was a tragedy, the guy said not to worry, he could always go and get another one. He then complained bitterly when his flat got burgled a couple of years later and they were taken. Some people have an ambivalent idea of what property means.'

They found Rigau appeared to have his hands tied by the same attitude.

'They took nothing,' he told them. 'They were found with no stolen goods on them, so we can't charge them with theft. Unless Poch turns up something out of the ordinary at their house, I'm going to have to order their release.'

Elisenda was dumbstruck. 'They were attempting to steal archaeological artefacts.'

'That won't stand up. Who says they were attempting to steal? Any half-decent lawyer would get that buried in five minutes.'

'Trespass, then. Criminal damage. They can't be allowed to get away with this.'

'No criminal damage,' Rigau told her. 'Trespass, yes, but I for one don't want to see my court clogged up with petty cases like that. I think you'll just have to accept, Elisenda, that they're small fry. I know they're annoying, but they bear no relation to the illicit antiquities investigation, either in terms of a direct connection to it or of scale. I'll get Sergent Poch to put the fear of god into them, that's all I can promise.'

Elisenda stood up to leave. 'The fear of god? In Girona, we're running a low-level crime initiative to stop offences like this, maybe you should consider it here too.'

She calmed down on the way back to the car parked at the police station.

'It's not even like I particularly welcome the low-level initiative Puigventós is doing,' she muttered to Àlex. 'But we have to be able to do something about these two.' She noticed him keeping silent. 'What?'

'Siset. You had him released. His crimes are no different. Or his attitude.'

'I had him released for the greater good, Àlex.'

'And what would charging these two with trespass do for the greater good when we've got someone running around sticking spikes through people's heads?'

'Hell, Àlex, you're getting me to defend Puigventós' petty crime campaign.' She shook her head in anger. 'Let's take a drive out to Ullastret. If only to calm Fradera down. And me. I want to see the site, and I'd also like to see if other artefacts have been taken from there before now.'

Retrieving their car from the side of the pavement, they left La Bisbal and drove across the plain, past idling crop fields and rambling farms either side of the fast minor road that stretched in a relentless straight line towards the Iberian site at Ullastret.

'Wrong angle to see the pregnant woman from here,' Elisenda broke the silence at one point.

Àlex glanced at her as he drove. 'The pregnant woman?'

She pointed up ahead of them at the low-lying mountains in the distance.

'Get those mountains at the right angle and it looks like a pregnant woman lying on her back. Other people see a bishop, but I prefer to think of them as a pregnant woman.'

'You people in Girona really do have a lot of time on your hands.'

Elisenda rang ahead as they passed the medieval upstart of the new town some two kilometres away from the ancient settlement. By the time they reached the car park, Fradera was waiting for them at the entrance. Walking towards them, she motioned them to stop and climbed into the back of the car.

'We need to take this track here to the left, outside the settlement,' she told them, slamming the door shut. 'It's the quickest way to get to where these people were digging.'

Elisenda stole a look at Àlex, who seemed slightly fazed by the archaeologist's dispensing with any greeting. For herself, she'd got used to the other woman's ways and quite welcomed the lack of small talk. Equally to the point, she told her about Jutge Rigau's argument and the probable release without charge of the couple.

'Oh, for heaven's sake,' Fradera replied. 'How can we ever hope to know our history when it's constantly being hijacked by a bureaucracy that works in its own favour, not that of the rest of us?'

In silence as Àlex drove gingerly through the potholes of the dirt track, Elisenda had to agree with her. She allowed the archaeologist to continue her rant amid the car's constant sliding and jarring on the worn surface.

'While we're kept waiting for funding, sites deteriorate and people like this have pilfered so many artefacts over the years that could have afforded us far greater knowledge of ourselves.' She tapped Àlex on the shoulder. 'You need to pull over here to the right and park where you can. We've got to walk the rest of the way.'

She didn't let up as they climbed over the low fence and trudged across the hard earth to the place where the couple were found detectoring.

'But these people aren't the real problem,' she insisted to Elisenda. Despite herself, Elisenda found it fascinating, and she could see Àlex taking in every word. 'Politicians and business have been the bane of our history. Officially, Franco's lot never used archaeology to create national myths the way other fascist regimes did. They justified their centralist, authoritarian arguments on a perverse view of an imperial past that they chopped and changed to match the political situation that they were imposing on the rest of us. So at best, they simply didn't bother funding archaeology in this country because it wasn't expedient for their purposes. At worst, they swept any archaeology that didn't fit in with their ideology under the carpet. In their view, Spain ceased to be a collection of tribes after the Roman conquest and became a single imperial entity, a vision of false unity that they tried to hold on to for forty years, and heaven help any piece of evidence that proved otherwise. God knows how many physical manifestations of our past were destroyed over the years. And even now, we're constantly at the mercy of political and economic policies that see us as a luxury and that still determine how much of our heritage we're allowed to unearth and so understand. And that's why there are still people who think that this is acceptable.'

She showed them to an area of dusty ground that had signs of footprints and scraping, but little more as evidence that anyone had been there. Elisenda had to admit that Rigau was right, it couldn't be called criminal damage, despite Fradera's anger and her own frustration.

'You're certain they took nothing?' she asked the archaeologist. She was fighting an urge to confide in the other woman that new policing often felt the same.

No matter how bad the past was, the lack of continuity with it made piecing together present crimes and their historic antecedents a constant struggle.

'The Mossos found nothing on them, and looking at this, there doesn't appear to be anything removed. Fortunately in this circumstance, these people were amateurish at best and didn't do too much damage. That is not always the case.'

'How much does go missing from here?' Àlex asked.

Fradera glanced at him and turned to Elisenda to reply, impervious to his dark charm. 'Extremely rare. Any thief who knows what they're doing thinks we're more protected than we are because of our status as a heritage site. It's the opportunists like these who tend to target us and even that's very uncommon. It's places like El Crit that suffer, isolated sites with no security of any sort. Fortunately for El Crit, it's so isolated and so arduous to get to that it's largely been left alone.'

'Except for finds being added to the dig,' Elisenda commented.

Fradera snorted. 'Doctor Bosch and his mysterious artefacts turning up. He claims another one appeared this morning.'

'You don't believe it to be genuine.'

'Of course it's genuine. But it's probably just something he forgot to catalogue in the first place.'

Elisenda recalled how clean the kylix that she saw with Bosch was and found herself disagreeing with Fradera. Again she thought how the ill-feeling between the two archaeologists diminished them both.

'Do you think he could have been keeping them for himself and returning them now there's so much scrutiny at the dig?' Àlex asked her.

Elisenda applauded her sergent's question and studied Fradera's face when she answered.

'I am not suggesting that for one moment. Merely that he might not be as organised as he should be.'

'You knew Ferran Arbós,' Àlex persisted. 'Do you know of anyone that he had dealings with in trading in the artefacts?'

'If I had, Sergent Albiol, I would have told you before now. I knew him as a curator, my dealings with him, as you call them, began and ended there.'

She had little more to tell them, so Elisenda and Àlex drove her back to the entrance to the settlement and headed back to the main road.

'She's got something to hide, or she thinks Bosch has?' Àlex questioned out loud, accelerating on the old, straight roads that squared the triangle back towards Girona.

'More pettiness than accusations,' Elisenda mused. 'Or absent-minded confessions. It's hard to discern anything other than rivalry through their points-scoring off each other. Which just goes to show how easy I am to work with.'

Àlex tugged his forelock. 'Yes, Sotsinspectora.'

'It's in the papers,' Elisenda said, changing the subject and telling him about the article she'd read in the previous day's newspaper.

'I saw. Do you think someone's leaked it? Poch's lot in La Bisbal, the courts, the Archaeology Service?'

'It could have got out anyhow. Arbós's cleaner could have told anyone in the village, any of the neighbours

276

could have got hold of it. It's the effect that worries me more than the cause. Who knows what it'll flush out. The attack on Clara Ferré might even have been a result of it.'

Her phone rang as they neared the last stretch of road leading to the city. She listened for a moment before answering.

'No, best if you stay there and keep looking. We're on our way back to Girona, we'll go and see her.'

She hung up and waited until a chime told her a text had come through.

'Address in Girona,' she told Àlex. 'That was Josep. He's found someone in Girona who was on the same university course as Ivan Morera, our missing student.'

—

Anna Espriu lived in one of the old apartment blocks in Santa Eugènia. Old in this case being from the 1970s, one of the frequent boom periods in the jagged timeline of construction in the city. It stood at the other end of the sprawling suburb from the modern block where Àlex lived, nearer the city centre, the relic of another vanished spike in confidence. Drab on the outside, the interior of the flat was furnished in blond wood and abstract paintings, a welcome light in the narrow streets of this part of the neighbourhood. Two walls in the small living room where Espriu had brought them coffee were filled with books.

'Ivan Morera,' she repeated. 'He was a loner. I never really knew much about him, which was as much as any of us did. He was a mature student, about six or seven years older than the rest of us and he didn't have anything in common with the other students. Or any desire to, from what I remember.'

'Can you remember any friends he did have?' Àlex asked her.

'None. As I say, he was a complete loner. He was friendly enough, he wasn't stand-offish or anything and he'd sit and have a coffee with us, but that was as far as it went.'

'And you didn't think it odd that he didn't return for the second year?' Elisenda questioned.

The woman, in her mid-fifties and dressed elegantly in black trousers and a ribbed sweater, looked to be casting her mind back to a time over thirty years ago. She spoke in what Elisenda's mother would have called a forty-Ducados-a-day voice. A deep, rasping sound supposedly caused by the fashion when Anna Espriu was young of smoking black tobacco. It was a type of voice you rarely heard these days.

'I think I was surprised he'd lasted the whole of the first year. Which was sad, because he was good, he was fascinated by Iberian history, he knew a lot more about them than the rest of us did. But he had issues. For one thing, he was obsessed with money and possessions. He always had to have the latest thing before anyone else. He had this saying that we all thought made him a bit odd. If there was someone who was a bit hard up, or even that he wanted to criticise, he'd say they were poorer than a beggar's wallet. It sounded old-fashioned even then.'

'Possessions,' Elisenda commented. 'Did he have a Walkman?'

'I really don't remember. Were they around then?'

'What about his tastes in music? Any favourite band?'

Espriu shook her head helplessly. 'I really didn't know him well enough. No one did. He never talked about things like that. He didn't have small talk. If it wasn't money or possessions, it was his other obsession. He'd been put up for adoption as a baby, but he always lived with a succession of foster families from what I could gather. The one thing about himself that he would talk about was that he wanted to find his real mother. There were rumours before the summer he left the course that he'd found her. He'd always said that if he did, he'd change his name and take hers.'

Elisenda and Àlex exchanged a glance. Yet again, the investigation had thrown up another obstacle, a new name to be found. As Espriu had nothing more to add, they left her and headed back into the city centre, crawling along the bright red conveyor belt of frustrated brake lights. At Vista Alegre, Montse and Josep had one good piece of news for them.

'We've been looking for the landlady where Ivan Morera was supposed to have stayed in Palamós,' Montse told them. 'She died some years ago and the house no longer belongs to her family, but we've tracked down a granddaughter, who still lives in the town.'

'We don't have a mobile number,' Josep added. 'Only a landline, and there's no answer, so I've left messages for her where she works for her to get back to me.'

'Good news,' Elisenda told them. 'He might never have shown up at the house, and the granddaughter might know nothing, but it's worth pursuing. Keep me posted.'

She told the two caporals about what they'd learned from Anna Espriu.

'So we need to do what we can to go through any adoption records left from that time to see if we can get a possible name change.'

'That'll be impossible,' Montse complained.

Elisenda sighed. 'I know, but do what you can.'

Leaving the others to find what they could, Elisenda drove back out to La Bisbal and the court building.

'I've had to order the two detectorists to be released without charge,' Jutge Rigau told after he'd shown her into his office.

Elisenda shook her head angrily. 'What about the search of their house?'

'Tat,' the judge said simply. 'Nothing of any worth. Nothing we could ever hope to prove they took from an archaeological site. Poch has given them a warning and told them they'll be charged if they're ever caught again, that's all we can do.'

'So much for stopping low-level crime.'

Rigau held his hands up. 'I'm sorry, Elisenda, I understand your frustration.' Seeing her anger, he changed tack. 'How are the other areas of the investigation going?'

She told him of the news about Ivan Morera's possible name change and about the landlady's granddaughter in Palamós. 'We're unlikely ever to be able to find his adoption records.'

'Not now,' the judge agreed. 'Madrid's being even more obstructive than ever with coordinating investigations.'

Elisenda laughed wryly. The Catalan and Basque police had only recently been excluded from another supposedly pan-Spanish criminal investigation initiative. 'We're on our own, Pere.'

'If only. Any news on Ricard Soler?'

She shook her head and thought of the other archaeologist from the 1981 dig. 'Vanished without trace. Not seen since he left his apartment in Barcelona. And we still don't know what we're looking for with him, whether he's a potential victim because he was another archaeologist who dealt with this trader or if we suspect him of being the killer.'

'Well, thanks for coming all the way out here, Elisenda. I'm sorry we don't have more promising news for each other.'

'Not to worry. It's on my way. I'm staying in La Fosca these days, it's more convenient for the El Crit scene, here and Palamós.' She explained about her sister's apartment on the beach.

He checked his watch. 'I'd invite you to dinner,' he told her, 'but I'm afraid I've got another engagement tonight.'

'Not to worry, I'll probably go to Palamós.' She told him of the hotel and of the votive shrine in the basement. 'But the owner doesn't like too many people to know about it,' she warned.

'I'm sure he doesn't.'

El Crit, 1981

The landlady's granddaughter, a snot-nosed little kid in a summer dress and T-bar sandals, eyed him warily. He'd had to tell her off for touching his things and she kept quiet now when she was there to spend the day with her grandmother.

'Property's property,' he told her, but she ignored him and went back to drawing a picture of Naranjito, the kid in the shape of an orange to be used as a mascot for the following year's world cup. She was forever doing the same picture.

Giving up, he went out early and waited with a beer for Esteve Mascort to turn up, who came along half an hour late as usual in his brand-new bright-red Ford Escort, the new model that everyone seemed to want that year. His pussy magnet, Mascort called it. Together, they drove out to El Crit and parked another hour's walk from the site. It was deserted when they got there, as it always was. If anyone were to come along, they'd tell them they were part of the official dig.

'That's new, isn't it?' Mascort had said, pointing at the Walkman, the first time he'd seen it. 'Let me have a go.'

Reluctantly, the student had handed it over and watched the other man stab heavily at the buttons. Mascort's face registered disgust.

'What is this shit?'

'Orquesta Mondragón.'

Mascort had handed the machine back. 'You want to listen to some proper music, not this rubbish.'

That evening, Mascort took the Walkman from the student and put a cassette of his own into it.

'El Puma,' he told him. '*Pavo Real*. Real music, not that nonce shit you listen to.'

The student kept his face impassive as he watched him listen to another of the summer's dated commercial abominations. He'd decided that if Mascort didn't let him in tonight on what his plan for making money was, he was going to walk.

When they'd finished working, and as if picking up on the student's mood, the archaeologist insisted on the student staying with him at the dig after night fell and he'd turned the arc lights on. It was gone eleven o'clock and the student had missed his dinner at his lodgings. The student couldn't help feeling annoyed as he'd paid for it.

'Watch and learn,' Mascort told him. 'You'll be able to afford to eat in the best places.'

So the student watched, and what he learned was that the super-cool Esteve Mascort was thoroughly in fear of the man with the cold eyes and baby face who came to inspect what they had to offer him that night.

'You just have to get into bed with the devil,' Mascort told him after the man had gone, trying to regain some of his composure.

I already have, the student thought.

Chapter Thirty Eight

Elisenda could see Montse and Josep stealing glances at the fourth person sitting in her room on Friday morning. Àlex was too canny to be caught looking at him, but she knew he was summing the new addition up all the while.

'This is Manel,' she'd introduced him to the members of her team at the morning meeting. 'And today's his first day with us. I'm sure you'll welcome him warmly and help him settle in with us in every way you can.'

Àlex said a good morning, Montse smiled at the newcomer and Josep nodded once. Manel looked at each one in turn, appearing to size them up, and greeted them, a new accent in a room used to voices from Girona and Barcelona.

'We touched on this at your interview, Manel,' Elisenda told him, 'but we'll bring you up to speed on the investigations we have in hand at the moment.'

She quickly explained of the thirty-something-year-old body at El Crit and the murder of Ferran Arbós and how they believed that the two killings were linked. She then let the other three tell him of the specifics of the two investigations and how they were tackling them. As the others spoke, she watched his reactions, hoping he'd get to fit in, knowing at that moment that the dynamic of the months since Pau had died was now gone. She wasn't so sure that that wasn't such a bad thing.

She watched Manel nod along with the comments made in turn by Àlex, Montse and Josep, but say nothing in return. Where Pau had been slight but had under-pinned the group with his off-the-wall intellect, Manel filled the room physically but remained silent, his bulk straining under an old-fashioned leather sports jacket, his presence yet to be known. His was a different, ostensibly more powerful build from Àlex's lean muscularity, but no more imposing for it. She closed her eyes for a moment and hoped that he would complement the others in her team.

Elisenda tuned back in as Montse began to speak of the latest developments in the case. She'd been trying to find social security records for Ivan Morera, but had found nothing since July 1981.

'What we don't know now,' Montse added, 'is whether that's because he is the body at El Crit or because he changed his name and has been living his life since. What we do have is the address in Barcelona where the Archae-ology Service in Girona wrote to him. It turns out that that was the last couple to foster him. It's strange that he was still using it as an address for correspondence in his mid-twenties, but the couple who fostered him are still alive and still at the same place. We can see them today. Besides that, I've also been trying to find a maternal relative of Esteve Mascort to see if he's the El Crit body once and for all, but that's turned up absolutely nothing. No dental records, either. I checked, his dentist died years ago, nothing on computer.'

'The facial reconstruction might tell us something there,' Elisenda commented.

'No luck with Morera's name change, either,' Josep continued. 'I'll keep digging, but I can't see us getting anywhere with it. What I do have is the granddaughter of Morera's landlady in Palamós. I've spoken to her, and she remembers a student called Ivan staying there at that time, so it does look like he made it to Palamós that summer.'

'Which means he could be our body at El Crit,' Àlex commented.

'We can see her this morning,' Josep told him. 'Anyone want to come with me?'

'Actually, Josep,' Elisenda interrupted him, 'I'd prefer you to carry on digging into Morera's name change here. I could also do with you having a word with Martí Barbena again to see if he remembers Morera. It'll also let him know that we've still got him and Esplugues in our sights. Manel, you and I'll visit the granddaughter to see what she remembers. Montse, you and Àlex visit the foster parents in Barcelona.'

An unhappy Josep looked about to say something, but a look from Elisenda told him to leave it.

'OK,' she said to close. 'We all know what we've got to do. Josep, show Manel where he can take a desk. Manel, we'll be leaving in ten minutes.'

Àlex hung around as the other three filed out. 'Doesn't say much, does he?' he murmured.

'Give him time, he's got to find his place.'

Àlex looked directly at her. 'He's got to make his place.'

—

'Why the cold case?' Manel asked Elisenda on the road to Palamós.

Elisenda drove because she knew the way better than he would and she felt that driving would be less distracting than giving directions while she got to know the new member of the unit. As it was, she found the creaking of his jacket every time he moved rather disconcerting. She was hoping it wouldn't end up irritating her.

'I thought we were a serious crime unit,' he carried on. 'I don't see why we've got the cold case.'

'The two are connected. To solve one, we have to solve the other. The order doesn't matter. Neither does how old it is.'

'It was over thirty years ago, Sotsinspectora. The Mossos weren't even around then.'

Elisenda used the roundabouts on the outskirts of Palamós to help her keep cool. 'It's a murder, Manel. A victim. How old do you think it has to be to cease to matter?'

He thought for a moment as a delivery lorry trundled past. 'Five years? Ten years tops?'

'That was a rhetorical question. It never ceases to matter. Not to the victim's family, not to the law, not to the Mossos and not to me.' She pulled out into traffic. 'And not to you, either.'

He nodded his head slowly as she drove. 'OK.'

She tried another way to get the feel of him. 'Do you know this part of the coast?'

'No.' He laughed wryly. 'The coast again. I thought I'd had enough with the Ebro Delta, now this.'

'Miss Lleida, do you?'

'I miss the mountains. You don't have mountains here.'

Elisenda pointed to the peaks visible far away in the distance in the blue winter sky. 'Those are the Pyrenees over there. Mountains enough for you?'

He shrugged. 'Hardly on the doorstep.'

She parked the car and decided not to ask him any more questions. The less he spoke, the less of a hole he dug for himself. They were in the streets behind the old Guardia Civil barracks, oddly still in use as an excise post, one of the powers to have stayed with the old Spanish police forces after devolution of most police duties to the Mossos d'Esquadra as it had national security implications. The town was turning out to be the latest to fall foul of the batting back and forth of politics between Catalonia and Spain. The port was supposed to be turned into a Schengen external border port, with a Guardia Civil and Policía Nacional complement for customs and immigration. That would allow cruise and cargo ships from outside the EU to stop off, bringing revenue into the area, but the renewed calls for Catalan independence had led to the Spanish government constantly deferring any decision in retaliation. In the meantime, nothing got done while lots of money was spent on things that might never happen and the Mossos still only ran a temporary station in the town in the summer. And they wonder why we want to go, Elisenda always thought.

The old lady's granddaughter let them into a stylishly furnished two-storey house in a quiet lane at the end of the steep street that climbed between the hospital and the barracks.

'My grandmother used to live on the same street,' she explained. 'A little nearer the town centre, but we decided to sell it when she died because we didn't want the Guardia Civil as neighbours.'

'My colleague said that you remembered Ivan Morera, the student who stayed with your grandmother in the summer of 1981,' Elisenda asked her after they'd been shown into a small but airy living room overlooking a narrow rear garden. 'Is that right?'

The woman, slim and in her late thirties and wearing a dogtooth check skirt and dark blouse, set down a tray with coffee and dry Maria biscuits on. Elisenda could imagine the grandmother doing the same thirty-odd years ago for her tenants.

'I remember him. I was very young at the time, six years old, but he was mysterious, so he stuck in my mind.'

'Why mysterious?'

'He only stayed a week, which was odd. He was supposed to have been here for three months, but he just left.'

'Did he take his clothes with him?' Manel asked her. Good question, Elisenda thought, as she was about to ask the same one. 'Did he leave anything behind?'

'No, he took all his things away with him. I didn't see him when he left, but my grandmother told me that he left with the bag he'd come with. He just told her after a week that he was leaving. He'd paid a month in advance, but when my grandmother offered to pay him back, he told her not to worry, he'd send her the details of how to pay him, but he never did. She told me all this years later, when I was older. She never heard from him again.'

Elisenda recalled the words of Ivan Morera's fellow student the previous evening, about how he was obsessed with money. It didn't tie in with his apparent lack of concern for a month's rent, which would have been a lot of money to a student.

'It was definitely Ivan Morera who left with the bag, not a friend?'

'It was definitely him, my grandmother said. No doubt about it.'

Elisenda couldn't get a picture of what must have happened. The signals were too confusing.

'What else did you find mysterious about him?' Manel asked.

'Well, I only met him about three or four times. I used to spend a lot of time here when I was little as both my parents worked. But he was always very nice to me, until one day, he really shouted at me. My grandmother wasn't there to hear it and I never told her because I was worried I'd done something wrong.'

'What had you done?'

'He had one of those personal stereos. A Walkman? I'd ever seen one before and he was always listening to it. So when he went out of the room one day, I tried it on and he caught me. He screamed at me and told me never to touch his things again. I was terrified. I'd never seen anyone so angry over a belonging before.'

'Can you remember what tape was in the Walkman?' Elisenda asked her.

The woman laughed. 'I've never forgotten. Orquesta Mondragón, it was. I've never liked them since.'

Chapter Thirty Nine

Àlex walked out on to the bustling square in front of the central university building in Barcelona and took a deep breath. The air was warmer than in Girona. The sun's meagre heat was convected by the buildings and pavements, mingling with the throngs of people herding past, vapour from cars and humans rising in a hidden and toxic mist around their heads. The atmosphere wasn't as fresh as the moist Girona morning they'd left just over a couple of hours ago but it was still fresher than the stifling sensation of confused loneliness of the small flat he and Montse had just visited.

Montse was waiting for him on the kerb, the slow traffic an arm's length from where she stood. 'We didn't get much, did we?' she commented when he joined her.

Àlex shook his head, ignoring the pedestrians shuffling irritably past them.

'Who'd get old?' she added, instantly kicking herself in case it affected him.

'Who indeed?' He looked at his watch. 'Fancy a coffee? I could do with changing chip.'

He took her to a small and faded milk bar in the enclosed streets behind the square, where they both ordered hot chocolate. It felt comforting.

They'd been to visit the elderly couple who had fostered Ivan Morera as a boy at the address given on the copy of the letter sent to him as a young man. The two people were a couple caught out of time in a crumbling apartment where the old now only stayed if they couldn't afford to move.

'Ivan Morera,' the husband had repeated slowly, dredging up a memory from a tangled web. 'Was he the one who wet the bed?'

'No, he was the one with all those toy spaceships,' his wife corrected him. 'He grew up and worked in a bank.'

'You're probably right,' he told her, tucking a blanket under her, down the sides of an armchair, its design so faded that Àlex and Montse couldn't tell what the original colour might once have been. The whole apartment was glacial. There were no radiators anywhere, just a single old butane heater in the middle of the dark room. It was switched off, the ceramic elements grey and cold.

'Do you have any records of that time?' Àlex asked them. 'Any letters?'

The husband brightened up. 'We've got photos.'

He led Àlex to a box room down a dark corridor that held a wall of ancient picture albums. No dates on the outside, Àlex noticed, pulling one at random off a shelf. He scanned through it to find a selection of photos of days out and school portraits with various children of all ages. None of them had a name on it.

'Can you remember who this boy is?' he asked the elderly man, pointing to a sepia-faded photo of a child that must have dated from the 1960s.

'Is that Ivan?' the man asked him.

Àlex flicked through a few more albums, but saw that it was pointless. None of them had names or dates or any information written anywhere. They returned to the living room to find Montse asking the wife if she remembered any of the children they fostered coming back as adults. Montse looked up at Àlex and shook her head slightly.

When they left, Àlex thanked them, letting Montse go first. When no one was looking, he took out his wallet and left a fifty euro note on the flaking wood of an old sideboard. He knew they'd find it and think they'd forgotten leaving it there.

In the milk bar, sipping at the childhood memory of piping hot chocolate, he decided he'd visit his parents one weekend soon. He thought again of the desk job with the Mossos. It would be much nearer their home, he knew, even if he didn't particularly like Sabadell.

'He doesn't say much, does he?' Montse interrupted his thoughts. 'The new guy. Manel.'

Gathering himself, Àlex considered her words. 'He's new. He's seeing how the land lies. Give him time.' A ghost of a grin crossed his face. 'You didn't talk much when you first started. Now look at you.'

'I hope so.'

'Talking of talking much, you and Josep seem to have sorted out your problem.'

She looked up, surprised. 'Problem?'

'You think no one noticed?'

Montse ran her spoon back and for through the thick chocolate, staring at the wake it left. 'It never quite happened after Pau died. Probably no bad thing.' She glanced up at Àlex. 'Did Elisenda know?'

'One of the best detectives you know? What do you think?'

'What would she have done about it if Josep and I had...?'

'Who knows? As long as it doesn't affect your work, which it has done lately, she would probably have let it ride.'

She took a long sip of her drink. 'Well, we'll never know now.'

Àlex looked at her, a wry smile on his lips. 'Yeah, sure.'

–

On the way back from Palamós, Elisenda stopped at the Institut de Medicina Legal and introduced Manel to Albert Riera.

'Ugly place, Lleida,' Riera told the new recruit. 'People talk in a strange accent.'

'We at least talk with our mouths open,' Manel countered, 'unlike the Gironins.'

'We talk with our mouths closed?' Elisenda asked him, her voice fizzing.

'Everyone knows that. Gironins talk with their mouths shut, can't understand a word they're saying.'

Riera looked from him to Elisenda. 'See someone's going to make themselves popular here. What was it you wanted?'

Secretly pleased that Manel wasn't intimidated by the pathologist, although not entirely happy with the reasons why, Elisenda asked Riera how the facial reconstruction was progressing.

'I'll call the university for you.' He looked at Manel. 'Out of the way, young man, I have to use the full force of my lips to talk on the telephone, otherwise I imagine the person at the other end won't know what I'm asking them.'

Enunciating more carefully than usual, all the while staring at Manel, he spoke to the technician at the university and hung up.

'She's sending a video through now. The reconstruction's still at the depth marker stage, apparently, but she says she'll be working over the weekend and should get it to us by early next week.'

After a few minutes, Riera's computer bonged to tell him an email had arrived. Opening the attachment, he showed the two Mossos a 3D image of as much of the model that had been created so far. He turned his screen towards them and a raw face stared out at them, coloured markers where the cheeks should be and around the nose and mouth showing the calculated depth of where the skin would come to. Layers of muscle had been superimposed on the upper part of the face, and blindly staring eyes filled the sockets. The hole where the mattock had been embedded was now covered in blood-coloured tissue, but it was still a stark portrait of a dead face yet to come back to virtual life.

'Far too early to make any assumptions,' Riera announced, closing the file.

He was right, Elisenda knew, but she also knew what she wanted to see.

'Thanks, Albert,' she told him, signalling to Manel that they were leaving. 'Keep me posted.'

'God, does he ever stop talking?' Josep demanded, wide-eyed.

'Who?' Àlex asked him. He and Montse had returned from Barcelona just a few minutes earlier and were getting warm by a radiator.

'Manel. The new guy. He doesn't shut up.'

'Are you serious?' Montse asked him. She was hanging her coat up next to Manel's leather sports coat. He'd gone to the toilet just before the other two had arrived, giving Josep the chance to let off steam. 'He barely opened his mouth this morning.'

'Elisenda's had me showing him the systems all afternoon. I couldn't get a word in edgewise.'

Elisenda came out of the room and the three of them immediately stopped talking. She eyed them all in turn. 'Any joy in Barcelona?' she finally asked Àlex and Montse.

'Nothing.' Àlex explained a little of the couple they'd been to see.

She turned to Josep. 'How about Barbena?'

'I went to see him at his home this morning. Eulàlia Esplugues was with him. Neither of them reacted when I mentioned the name Ivan Morera. Barbena said he didn't know him and that there was no one of that name among the students he'd worked with on the dig. It seemed genuine.'

'OK. When Manel returns, can you all come in?'

Once the fifth member was back and all her team were seated in her room, Elisenda told them of what they'd learned from the landlady's granddaughter.

'He had a Walkman?' Àlex repeated. 'In that case, we've really got to consider that Ivan Morera's the body at El Crit.'

'So where's Mascort?' Montse demanded. 'Did they both die and we've only found one of them? Or Mascort just ran off, like everyone thought he did.'

'If the body is Morera,' Josep asked, 'how come he packed his things and told the landlady he was leaving?'

'That's if it is Morera at El Crit,' Elisenda commented. 'I'm keeping an open mind until we see the reconstruction. There's still a possibility that it was Mascort buried there. Either way, we've just posed ourselves yet more questions.'

'If it's Mascort buried there, why's the Walkman there and why haven't we found the St. Christopher medallion?' Àlex asked. 'Hell, Elisenda, it's like nailing a shadow to the ground.'

'The dealer,' Manel piped up. The others stopped talking. 'We still don't know who he is. Could he be whichever of the two is not the body at El Crit? My money would be on Mascort being the body and Morera being the dealer. We've been told he loved money and possessions.'

Elisenda stared at him, slowly nodding her head. 'So, instead of digging up artefacts for a living, he trades in them to make the money he was obsessed with. Good possibility.'

'If either of them was the dealer, he also seems to have vanished,' Montse commented. 'Or died. So did either of them have a son or daughter?'

'Or partner of some sort?' Elisenda asked.

'More people,' Àlex muttered. 'Because it wasn't complicated enough.'

Chapter Forty

'Llàtzer, how are you?'

'Good evening, Elisenda. Would you care to join me?'

She hesitated the merest fraction before replying. 'I'd love to.'

She looked around the hotel restaurant, busy on a Friday night in the second half of the month. With what everyone traditionally called the 'January climb' now over, the Christmas bills paid, bank balances topped up with a month's salary, and a week still to go to Carnaval, which was normally the starting pistol for renewed frivolity in the new year, people were tentatively starting to go out again.

Sucarrats pushed the chair back under the table he'd originally shown Elisenda to and laid another place at Doctor Bosch's table. In tribute to the changing spirit of the month, the hotel owner was wearing a brighter winter wardrobe than the other day, his hair more studiedly casual, his eyes gleaming more brightly.

'I'm honoured,' Sucarrats told her. 'Palamós is a long way to come from Girona for dinner.'

'I'm sorry to have to confess that I'm staying in La Fosca, at my sister's house. It's more convenient for the current investigation. But you can be sure I will be making the trip especially when I'm back in Girona.'

He gave a half-bow. 'Thank you. We have sea urchins as seasonal specials today, by the way, caught by my own fair hands between here and Palafrugell.'

'That's what I'm going for,' Bosch interjected.

'I'll stick to good Girona veal,' Elisenda told him.

'I'm with you,' Sucarrats agreed. 'I'm not a sea urchin fan. You've got to respect an animal that has five gonads, but I'm not sure I want to eat them.' He wafted off to another table to attend a moneyed party of four local couples.

'Follow that,' Elisenda told Bosch with a smile. She was already enjoying herself, the enforced socialising probably better for her than the thoughtful isolation she'd had in mind.

'Are you here to see the shrine?' Bosch wanted to know. His voice was hoarse and he also seemed to be struggling with the flu bug that was laying everyone low these days.

'I saw it last week, after you told me about it.'

'It's quite haunting, isn't it? And quite amazing it survived, when so many other pieces were destroyed.'

'How do you mean?'

'The tourist boom. Ancient sites up and down the coast were bulldozed to build hotels and apartments in the sixties and seventies. Yet one more thing for which we have Franco to thank. When he and his minister of information and tourism, propaganda and tourism as we all called it, decided to boost tourism in the country, they didn't bother to put any controls in place, so anyone could throw up hideous building after hideous building with no regard whatsoever for what lay beneath. So it's remarkable that whoever built this place back then had the foresight to save the shrine, and subsequent owners have had the ability to respect and preserve it.'

Sucarrats returned with their bottle of wine, the same Raimat red that Elisenda had ordered before. He replied to Bosch with a mock self-deprecating smile. 'Thank you for the part of that praise that relates to me. It's fully deserved.'

'I have to agree,' Bosch told him, his expression more serious. 'Many wouldn't have kept it intact. Many haven't.'

Sucarrats shrugged. Bosch's words had got through to a more sober side to him. 'We all owe a debt to the past. My repayment is to continue what others before me started.' He glided away to another table, his movements effortless.

'Was so much really destroyed at that time?' Elisenda asked Bosch. 'I know about all the stories of the Franco regime wanting to cover up anything that disagreed with their view of Spain's past, but were there really so many artefacts destroyed because of the tourist boom?'

Bosch took a sip of his wine and nodded thought-fully. 'I would say that the uncontrolled construction boom of that time wreaked more damage than any ideology of Franco's. So much so that we can't begin to imagine what was lost. I'm sure Doctora Fradera would disagree, but Spain was so poor by then, after the Civil War and isolation, that the regime desperately needed to make money from tourism, which it did any way it could, so it simply turned a blind eye to the excesses of commerce. There was a wholesale practice of throwing away archaeological finds and hiding discoveries to ensure that nothing stood in the way of making money. When I was a teenager, I heard of a necropolis near Lloret that was completely destroyed, burials of children and adults simply thrown into a skip, the entire site flattened and built on. Our history lost forever, our ancestors held in disdain.'

'Is that why you studied archaeology?'

'Partly. My parents both had a passion for ignoring the official history to which we're all subjected and getting through to the real story. I imagine that rubbed off onto me.'

Between dessert and coffees, Sucarrats led them both down to the cellar on Bosch's urging for another look at the shrine. Elisenda saw it as small this time, a more private being that no longer threatened. She was struck by its simple and timeless beauty in a way she hadn't the first time she'd seen it.

'Have you been to see the Indiketa settlement at Castell?' Bosch asked her. 'It's not far from you in La Fosca.'

'Not this time, but I have visited it in the past. I know the importance of the site, but I find the loss of the trees there so sad.'

Pragmatic as always, Sucarrats shrugged off her words. 'They'll grow back. You're probably too young to remember, but Platja Castell was one of the first triumphs of local democracy after Franco died. The whole area was about to be developed and turned into a holiday marina, which would have destroyed not just the trees and the ecology supported by them, but the settlement as well. But the local council held a popular referendum and the people voted to save it. It's thanks to that that the archaeology is still intact.'

'And the beach,' Bosch added. 'And the wetlands sanctuary.'

'That's why all this is important,' Sucarrats murmured thoughtfully, gesturing towards the stone face at the end of the small room. 'It's how we right the wrongs of the past.'

—

In Girona, Manel was eating dinner alone at a restaurant near the hostal where he was staying in the old town until he found somewhere more permanent to live.

'The artichokes we have in Lleida are much bigger,' he told the waiter. 'More succulent.'

'Is that right?'

After dinner, he walked back to the hostal and rang a friend in Lleida, who could barely hear him over the music in the bar where he was with all the people he and Manel grew up with.

He hung up and lay back on the bed, staring at the ceiling until he turned the light out.

—

Across the river, in the new town, at the café where Josep had met his girlfriend the last time, he sat on the same stool, his legs cramped under the counter, and stared at the half-empty glass of beer in front of him.

The door opened, letting a rush of cooler air in past the fan blowing hot air down over the entrance. He turned to look, but it was a couple, no one he knew. He sighed and took a drink of his beer. He wondered if his girlfriend was going to come back in. It was now quarter of an hour since she'd gone.

'This isn't working, Josep,' she'd told him, her voice calm but insistent below the thrum of the other drinkers. 'And it's not me, it's you.'

She'd picked up her coat and bag and walked out, leaving behind her the glass of beer that now stood untouched next to his. He hadn't followed her or even watched her go.

The door opened again and he turned, hoping it wasn't her.

—

Montse watched the herb-infused ice slowly melt in her gin and tonic and listened to the guy sitting beside her. He'd told her about his work and was now on to his moisturising routine. Fortunately, she hadn't yet been asked to elaborate her lie of the previous week of working in an office. She had a feeling she wasn't going to have to.

The lights in the bar were low, perfect for a small winter city, and the music was loud enough to melt into the warmth of the hubbub rising from the other drinkers.

When he asked her if she wanted to go for dinner, she reached for her coat and went with him, texting her mother that she'd met a friend and would be late home.

—

Àlex stood outside the bar on the new side of town near the river and watched.

Two toughs walked past him, the usual wildlife to be found at that particular bar on a Friday night. They recognised him and nudged each other as they went past. One of them spat on the ground near Àlex's feet and

303

looked him in the eyes. Àlex looked back but said nothing. Getting the reaction they'd learned to expect these past few months, the toughs leered at him and muttered something, turning to walk across the cold square into the bar. Loud music and low laughter burst out for a brief moment as they opened and closed the door.

Debating, Àlex stood there for a few moments longer, clenching and unclenching his fists, waiting for the anger to come. His cheeks ached from the muscles twitching closer and closer to the surface.

Turning, he walked back to Gran Via and to one of the old burger bars, still open and serving food. Sitting alone at a table with a beer, he reached into his jacket pocket and took out the letter with the form for the desk job in Sabadell. A formality, the letter told him. Wiping food crumbs off the table with his hand, he spread the form out and reached into his pocket again for a pen, studying the first question to be filled in.

–

Miquel Canals was in when Elisenda called on him at the beach house in La Fosca.

'*Lumumba*,' she told him, preparing two tall glasses. 'Another fisherman's drink from the region. Brandy with hot chocolate for the winter, like now, and with cold chocolate and ice for the summer. Either warming or refreshing.'

'These fishermen knew how to look after themselves,' Canals replied, gingerly holding onto the piping hot glass as they toasted on his terrace. Both were wrapped up warmly against the sea cold.

'So how come you can take so much time off?' she asked him. She knew the answer, she'd checked up on him.

'Are you a cop now?'

'I'm always a cop.'

He laughed gently. 'I sold my company last year. When my father was ill, I decided I'd had enough. I also had enough money and I felt it was time for a change. I'd started it when I was a student, and I'd done with it everything I'd wanted to.'

'And do you have to work again?' The idea of not needing to work both intrigued and disturbed her.

'Depends what you mean. Financially, probably not. Mentally, yes. I'm starting to miss having a purpose.'

'How did you manage to get the money to start it when you were a student?'

'My father lent it to me. I told you we were very close. He told me he'd loan me the money as long as I paid it back inside five years. I did it in three. He knew business and expected the same of me.'

Elisenda looked at him over the top of her glass and nodded. She realised as he was speaking about money and business that just as her interest in him as a man waned, her view of him as a potential suspect waxed. The moon disappeared behind a passing cloud, one of the few she'd seen in the sky for weeks, and his face was clothed in shadow for a brief moment.

'What was the company?'

He told her a name. It was one she'd recognised even before she'd checked him out. 'We gave head massages to people on their lunch break or their way to or from work or when they were out shopping.'

And very successfully too, Elisenda knew. She'd seen the franchises all over Barcelona. Small premises, each with ten or twelve ergonomic chairs and a team of young assistants giving ten-minute head massages in a fixed formula for thirty euros a shot. Not much for the customer to pay, low overheads and a steadily accumulating profit for the franchisees and for Miquel Canals, who'd thought of it. It was the perfect business idea for a pre-recession city. Even with the downturn, he'd sold it for millions.

'Here, I'll show you,' he told her.

Without giving her a chance to object, he got up and stood behind her chair, gently beginning to knead her scalp in light, circular movements. She had to admit to herself that she could see why someone would want to fit a sensation like this into a fraught day's work. She might even have found the hypnotic effect of his fingers skilfully working her head relaxing were it not for the images she couldn't shake out of her mind of the skulls at Ullastret, huddled together sightless under the shocked gaze of the people who paid to come to see them. And of a dead man lying forgotten in a trench and an ageing curator pinned to a wall in his house by the spike that someone had buried in his forehead.

'Cold?' he asked her when she shivered.

Chapter Forty One

El Crit.

The scream.

Only it was more of a yelp that Elisenda heard from the top of the headland. One of pain. And it was coming from the direction of the dig.

Her feet still wet in her trainers and her body drenched in sweat from the Saturday morning kayaking, she skittered across the floor of dead pine wishbones towards the cry. Shouting a warning, she ducked and raced through the sharp points of the green needles on the trees that scratched her arms as she ran. Over the noise that she was making she could hear no other sound from ahead.

Emerging into the small clearing, she saw a figure leaning back against the deeply-furrowed bark of a holm oak, its legs stretched out along the ground in front. Quickly looking around as she approached, she saw no one else nearby, no movement in the branches to betray someone fleeing.

The figure groaned.

Kneeling down, Elisenda saw that it was Doctora Fradera.

'What happened?' the archaeologist asked her, her voice slurred.

'I was about to ask you that.'

She tried to help Fradera to her feet, but the older woman cried out in pain and sat back down heavily again. She held her left hand to her right shoulder, by her neck and closed her eyes.

'Something hit me,' she told Elisenda. 'Behind me. I was bending over to look at something in the trench. I heard something. And I stood up and I felt something hit me on the neck. That's all. What happened?'

Supporting the weight of the woman's arm, Elisenda pulled back her collar to reveal a bruise already forming on the top of her shoulder.

'The skin's not broken,' she told Fradera, who gingerly begin to rotate her arm. 'Or the bone by the look of it.'

Scanning the area around her, Elisenda spotted a glint on the ground from the sunlight filtered through the trees. Leaving the archaeologist for one moment, she went over to take a look. Lying on the pine needles was a metal spike, the tip covered in light brown dust where it had landed in the earth and fallen back out again. Someone had evidently dropped it, probably when they heard her running through the woods. Staring closely at it, she made her mind up and went back to where Fradera was lying.

'Now you tell me what happened, Doctora Fradera. Why would this person attack you?'

The archaeologist was silent for a long moment and Elisenda thought she wasn't going to say anything. When she did speak, Elisenda couldn't help feeling shocked.

'Six years ago I agreed to give someone an artefact from a dig I was working on. I know, I'm vociferous about the theft of our culture, but he had something on me. An indiscretion from years before that would have damaged my reputation as an academic. It's pointless you asking me what it was as I have no intention of telling you. Suffice to say that I'm not proud of any of it.'

'Who was it?'

'I don't know. A man but I never met him, I only ever spoke to him on the phone. I took the item, a votive statue, and waited for him where I was supposed to, but no one ever showed up. So I went home and waited for my career to end, but I heard nothing more, ever again. I felt I'd earned a reprieve. Until now.'

Elisenda studied the archaeologist's cold expression and thought. Six years ago. That was when the dealer, whoever he was, seemed to vanish without trace, when his heavily-cloaked business folded, when his victims and cohorts appeared to have been released from their servitude. She wondered if there was one more body buried in a shallow grave somewhere, or if the dealer had simply died a peaceful, anonymous death and his machinations had died with him. Until now, prompted by the discovery of Esteve Mascort at El Crit, and someone had taken over his mantle.

She was interrupted by the sound of movement coming from a way to her right. She looked up to see Doctor Bosch appear along the faint path from where they always parked their cars.

'Mireia,' he worried. 'What's happened?'

He rushed up to her and helped her get to her feet.

'Did you see anyone on the path?' Elisenda asked him, but he shook his head. She took her mobile out of the waterproof pouch slung around her neck, but there was no signal. She turned back to the two archaeologists. 'You're going to have to leave. This place isn't safe.'

'Nonsense,' Fradera told her, irritated. 'No one's going to come back now.' Bosch was pouring her a cup of his execrable coffee from the flask. She took it and slowly drank, wrinkling her nose at the taste.

'I have to insist.'

'You can insist all you like, dear,' Fradera told her, 'but I'm staying here. I have work to do.'

'Me too,' Bosch added, his voice rather less certain.

Giving up, Elisenda picked up the spike with a plastic bag folded inside-out that Bosch gave her and sealed the bag, tying it to her pouch. Leaving them, she retrieved her kayak and rowed north, deep in thought. She was still off the shore when she finally got a phone signal so, balancing on the gentle waves, she called Caporal Fabra in the station in Palafrugell and explained what had happened. She asked him to come down to meet her in Calella, one of Palafrugell's beaches. When she got there, she beached the kayak to an audience of coffee-drinkers in overcoats and sunglasses watching her in idle curiosity from the café by the low sea wall. Fabra was waiting for her. She handed over the spike and told him to get it to Científica in La Bisbal.

'And I want patrols out to El Crit as often as you can.'

'I'll check it out now,' he promised, 'but realistically we'll only be able to get there once a day, twice at most.'

Having to be satisfied with that, she refused his offer of a lift and paddled back out into the sea. Slowly, she rowed north along the edge of the coves for a short distance before turning to head back for La Fosca. She was looking for a little motor-boat and a middle-aged man supposedly picking up rubbish on a beach.

Chapter Forty Two

Canals was on the beach on Sunday morning when she was pushing the kayak out into the water. He was wearing a wetsuit and carrying a spanking new kayak of his own over his head.

'Top of the range,' Elisenda commented to him. 'Have you met my brother-in-law? You'd get on.'

'I've seen you doing this other mornings,' he explained. 'It looks fun. Can I join you?'

Elisenda looked straight at him. 'Yeah, why not?'

She waited for him to get comfortable in his sleek new toy and they slowly paddled out into deeper water. He rolled precariously from side to side as he got used to the movement, and he had to grab hold of her kayak to steady himself.

'What's in the bag?' he asked to hide his embarrassment, nodding at a waterproof rucksack fastened in front of her.

'Dog food. Don't ask.'

Without waiting for a reply, she dug her paddle into the water and led him at a leisurely stroke northwards to the neighbouring coves. He quickly found his balance and was able to keep up, providing she went slowly. She veered to the left into the small cove at the foot of the Castell headland and came to a halt in the clear blue water glittering over the rocks below. She spotted a colony of sea urchins clinging under the surface to the sides of the stone arch reaching out from the land.

'Castell,' she told him, pointing upwards.

'Indiketa,' he replied, looking at the bare rock of the settlement thrusting up out of the water, crowned by the concentric rings of a necropolis.

'You know about the Indiketa?'

He shrugged. 'Only a layman's interest.' He turned away and rowed under the arch, emerging around the other side of the rock with a huge smile on his face. 'I see the attraction.'

'I've got to press on,' she told him. 'We'll do this again another time.'

'Sure. I don't think I could go much further anyway, my shoulders are already aching.'

Deep in thought, she shifted her position in her kayak and dug the paddle far into the water, gaining momentum immediately. She could feel the power in her shoulders and upper torso having strengthened over the last couple of weeks, despite not having gone out on the kayak for a few days. She made good time along the shore now she was on her own. In contrast to the denuded headland at Castell, the trees standing along the coastal footpath threw long, still shadows away from her as the sun steadily rose above the horizon to her right.

Maria was in when she got to the cabin in the woods, a second cup of coffee waiting on the table as though she were expecting Elisenda.

'You'd be surprised how far sounds travel through the trees,' the older woman told her.

Elisenda placed the waterproof bag she'd tied to the kayak for the journey on the table and pulled out two large bags of dried dog food. 'I don't know how easy it is for you to buy food for them,' she explained. 'Or for yourself.'

'Supermarket bins,' Maria told her. 'They throw away enough waste to feed all the people forced into using food banks. Another system that has failed us. They've discarded it, so I take it. It's no longer their property.'

'I imagine the supermarkets may have a different view from yours.'

'I imagine they would. Unfortunately for them I have little regard for their opinion.' Getting up from her chair, she cut open one of the bags with a knife she fetched from the kitchen and poured it out into bowls for the dogs, which all ran skidding into the cabin, enticed by the smell. 'But you didn't come to bring me food for my dogs or ask about my dietary requirements.'

Elisenda waited until she sat down again. 'Why are you leaving artefacts at the El Crit dig? Where are they from?'

Maria looked over to where Flora lay on the tatty old rug where the rocking chair usually stood. The chair had been pushed into a corner of the room. The Great Dane was moaning balefully and the woman beckoned her over, buying time. Flora looked up at her trustingly as she absently stroked her head. 'Finds go missing from these places,' she eventually said. 'I find them, I return them.'

Elisenda took a sip from the strong coffee and savoured it before continuing.

'I have a new member of my team, Maria. His name's Manel. His full name's Joan Manel, to be precise, and he could have used any combination of those two names to present himself to the rest of us. Joan. Or Manel. Or Joan Manel. Or even Joanma. But he chose Manel.'

'You're rambling, Elisenda. Why should this interest me?'

'It should interest you because by simply choosing which part of a name someone uses, it changes their identity. It can even change who they are. I've been told of a Dolors Quintí, an archaeologist on another site who was Ricard Soler's girlfriend until she left him for Esteve Mascort.'

She saw Maria sit rocking on her chair, looking intently back at her.

'Dolors is part of another compound name,' Elisenda continued. 'Like Joan Manel, although women rarely use the two parts of that specific name together. Which is why it took a little time for it to click. Maria Dolors. That's your full name. And Quintí Pujol are your two surnames. So the woman whose full name is Maria Dolors Quintí Pujol and who was once known to everyone as Dolors Quintí…'

'…is now Maria Pujol. What of it?'

'You were in a relationship with Esteve Mascort when he went missing. You had an abortion when he refused to recognise your child.'

Maria looked at Elisenda before breaking suddenly into laughter. A full, round outburst of joy that ended as quickly as it began.

'An abortion? Oh, that is rich. Were those the rumours? That I had an abortion?'

'Didn't you?'

314

'I can assure you, Elisenda, that I have never ever had an abortion. Yes, my full name is as you say it is and I had an affair with Esteve Mascort, but it was over long before he disappeared. Those idiots on the El Crit dig had more time on their hands than the wit to know what to do with it. If they hadn't been so busy bickering with each other and feathering their own career nests, they might have spent their time more profitably finding all the history there is to be told by this wonderful place rather than on making up stories about each other. And about me.' She shook her head in disbelief. 'An abortion? Simply wonderful.'

Elisenda drank from her cup to gather her thoughts, considering where her questions were to go next. 'Why did you keep who you were a secret from me?'

'I didn't. I am Maria Pujol. I am no longer the woman I was over thirty years ago. If you'd wanted to know my full name, I would have told you happily.'

'When exactly did your relationship with Esteve Mascort end?'

'He went missing in the summer of 1981. I broke off my relationship with him at the end of 1980, over six months before he disappeared. I was old enough to have seen through him by that time. Despite what the idiots he worked with might have told you.'

'Did you know he was stealing artefacts?'

'Not when I left him, no. But when I learned, it didn't surprise me.'

'I take it the pieces you've been returning to El Crit are ones he stole from there all those years ago. How come you have them?'

'I found them. He'd left them in my apartment and I only discovered them after we'd split up.'

'Why wait this long to return them?'

She thought for a moment. 'I didn't know what to do with them at the time. I knew they were stolen. I didn't want to get into trouble. And by the time I'd found them, I couldn't return them as the dig had been closed down. I've had to wait until now that they've started working on it again to give them back.'

Elisenda studied the other woman's face. She knew that something didn't ring true with her story. 'So if you knew nothing about it, you wouldn't have known anyone he might have sold the artefacts to?'

'I wouldn't have the faintest idea. I tell you, when we separated, I had no idea of what he was up to.' She got up and went into the kitchen to fetch the *cafetera* to refill the cups. 'In your position, if I were trying to find who killed him, I would be more interested in the professional jealousy of the other archaeologists on the dig. Esteve might have been amoral, but he knew the Indiketa, he had a feeling for the history. The others were politicians, interested only in their reputation.'

Unwillingly, Elisenda immediately recalled the report blowing the whistle on Ferran Arbós written by Martí Barbena. Maria's final statement set it further on its way worming into her doubts.

'All history, all archaeology, is written by the victors. Perpetrators become heroes, victims become villains.'

All the way back to La Fosca, Elisenda felt punch-drunk. In the cabin in the pines with a woman who conversed almost exclusively with herself and with her dogs, Elisenda had felt more confounded than at any time during her career in the Mossos. The older woman had seemed able to predict Elisenda's train of thought, shrugging off her revelations as though they were common knowledge, rebutting her theories with more feasible truths.

She was still going over Maria's words when she got back to the beach by her sister's house. Canals' kayak was pulled up onto the pebbles under the small cliff, but he was nowhere to be seen.

'Trusting,' she muttered to herself.

Showering quickly, she drove inland towards Monells, stopping at Xidors to buy one of their chocolate and custard cakes. Once by the side of the road, the stylish patisserie now found itself tucked away behind the busy dual carriageway, although that never put off people in the know, as the Sunday morning queue she found herself in proved.

The first thing she saw when she got to her parents' house in the small village they'd moved to some years earlier, to the house once owned by her father's parents, was an amphora standing in a rusted iron frame. It was Greek, from a wreck, and it had stood in the family home in Girona throughout Elisenda's childhood. After kissing both her parents on the cheek and hugging them both warmly, she paused in the hall and let them go on into the kitchen. Not even the aroma of softly-remembered coffee was enough to move her. Instead, she stood and stared at the ancient amphora. Its cylindrical shape tapering at the bottom into a point, held in place by the simple stand, and at the top into a heavy lip for pouring, the harmony broken by a small circular handle. The whole of the body dark and stained and encrusted with the remains of sea creatures. She'd known it all her life, but it was the first time she'd properly seen it.

'Where was this from?' she called through to the kitchen. 'This amphora. Where was it from?'

Her father came back out into the hall. 'We've had it for years, Elisenda, you've seen it thousands of times.'

'I know. I want to know where it's from.'

Puzzled, he told her it had been a present from a client. 'One Christmas years ago, when you were still a child. It was a company that was a regular client of the firm I worked for in those days, before starting my own practice. They gave us all one, all the lawyers in the team who'd worked on their affairs through the year.'

'Where did they get it?'

'The sea, Elisenda, how would I know? It was a gift.'

'It's theft.' She reached out to touch it. 'It's our history, they had no right to give it to you.'

Her mother came out to join them, to see what the fuss was about. Elisenda saw her father look quizzically at her mother. 'They were different times,' he told her.

'How can we ever know our past?' she demanded. 'It's criminal. It's no different from ordinary people stealing from archaeological digs or petty criminals selling bootleg DVDs. Or Franco robbing us all of our history.'

'It's an amphora, Elisenda,' her father argued. 'They're ten a penny. Hundreds turn up in the sea every year.'

She looked at him. 'Until they don't. Until there are no more left to turn up. Then what happens?'

Her mother came forward and took her hand. 'Come and have a coffee, Eli, please, and tell us what you want us to do about it.'

Elisenda allowed herself to be led into the warm of the kitchen. 'I want you to give it back. To a museum.'

'We will, Eli, I promise. Just come and sit down. You look tired.'

'It's this job,' her father muttered.

'Don't start, Enric,' her mother warned. 'Leave her alone.'

'You could have been a judge by now,' he told Elisenda, unable to let it go. 'If you'd worked in law.'

'I'm a sotsinspectora,' she told him. 'One of the first women to get there. That should be enough for you.'

'But you could have been a judge. Like this Rigau you're working with now. He's the same age as you and he's a judge, one of the best we've got. And he didn't have any of the privileges you did. He had to work for it all with no family to help him.'

Elisenda stood up and put her coat back on. 'And I'm having to work for it all to be a police officer, and I've got no family helping me.' She walked to the front door, past the amphora on her way out. 'I want you to give this to a museum. Or I will investigate its provenance.'

'Eli, please,' her mother called to her.

Elisenda turned and hugged her mother before leaving the house. Closing the door behind her, she strode to her car and drove back to La Fosca.

Chapter Forty Three

'I've been arrested.'

'I'll be with you now.'

Elisenda hung up her mobile and considered. For once it wasn't Siset calling her, moaning about his latest skirmish with the Mossos. It was Maria, ringing from the police station in La Bisbal.

'She was caught taking food from a waste bin belonging to a supermarket in Palamós,' Sergent Poch explained to Elisenda when she turned up there half an hour later on Monday morning. He looked terrible, his voice heavy with a thick cold.

'Belonging to a supermarket? A waste bin?'

Poch took her to visit Maria in the cell where she was being held.

'I was taking food from the rubbish bins,' Maria said. 'Like I told you I've done for years. Yesterday evening, when the shop was closed and no customers were around. I don't see what harm I was doing.'

'Why didn't you call me sooner?' Elisenda wanted to know.

'I didn't expect to be here this long. I didn't think for one minute they'd arrest me and keep me overnight.'

Elisenda got up. 'I'll go and see the judge. He's normally amenable, he should be able to sort it out.'

She walked the short distance to the court, where Rigau agreed to see her immediately. He had some notes in front of him.

'The supermarket owners want to press charges,' he told Elisenda, who was momentarily dumbstruck.

'For taking food they've thrown away?' she was finally able to say.

'Trespass.'

'Trespass? They're rubbish bins at the back of the building.'

'Legally, the bins are on land belonging to the supermarket. They have a case.'

'Oh come on, Pere. They simply don't want someone getting something for nothing. Even if it's stuff they've discarded and that was heading for landfill anyway.'

'I know what you're saying, Elisenda, but they have a right not to want the accused to get something for nothing. She'll simply get a fine, I can promise you that. I'll order her release now so that she can go home. She'll be issued with a summons in due course.'

Elisenda got up, exasperated. 'So all she'll get is a fine. That's one fine more than people stealing from a heritage site got.'

'They didn't take anything,' he called after her, but she was already out of the room.

After all the paperwork at the police station had been sorted out, Elisenda drove Maria back to her home in the woods by El Crit. On the way, she vented her frustration and told the older woman of the detectorists who had been released without charge.

'The wrong people always get caught for the wrong crimes,' Maria told her. 'No one cares about the past, anyone can alter that with impunity. But the twin idols of commerce and corporatism have to be protected by any means, no matter how amoral. And your Mossos haven't made a blind bit of difference there.'

Elisenda wanted to tell her that they were making a difference, but she was too pent-up to try to reason with her. Instead, she spoke of the shrine in the hotel in Palamós.

'Not everyone is driven by greed,' she concluded. 'The owner could easily have chosen to use the room for something to make money, but he's preserved the shrine intact.'

Maria snorted. 'And I thought you were brighter than the usual bunch of idiots running things, Elisenda. I know the hotel you mean. And I know the owner. Sucarrats. I also know that he was a town councillor for years, most of which he spent vetoing any proposals to renew work on the El Crit dig because he said the money could be better spent elsewhere to bring revenue into the town. That's the extent of his altruism.'

Shocked, Elisenda glanced over at her and back to the road. Processing what she'd just heard, she decided to change the subject. She asked Maria again about Mascort's dealing in illicit antiquities.

'You're sure you never knew about it until after he disappeared?'

'Not until after we'd separated,' Maria corrected her. 'By which time, I could do nothing about it.'

'And you really have no idea who he was passing them on to? Do you know of any other archaeologists who you'd suspect could have been trading in artefacts?'

'You forget I gave up archaeology to work as a teacher. I lost all touch with who was doing what in the profession. I found it too backbiting a world.'

Elisenda drove as far into the woods as the track would allow and pulled over. 'The present El Crit dig doesn't appear to be the most fortunate work environment,' she agreed.

Maria snorted. 'Fradera and Bosch. Each one wants to be the other's iconoclast. Why? So they can become the icon instead. Such is the way of all self-appointed critics.' She got out of the car. 'I can find my way from here. No need to come with me.'

Elisenda watched her disappear into the pines and began the laborious manoeuvring to turn the car to head back along the track.

'So if you lost touch with archaeology,' she muttered as she finally headed back to the main road, 'how come you know who Fradera and Bosch are and how they get on?'

She knew where she was heading next, and turned left for the short drive to Palamós, parking in front of the old harbour wall again. She could smell the salt in the air. The raucous clamour of seagulls told her that a tuna fishing boat had come into the port behind her. Hurrying into the old town, she had to blot out the squelching thud of the hooks being smashed into the flesh of the huge fish to lift them to the quayside.

The hotel receptionist, a young guy with joyously unruly hair and a bright voice, told her that the owner had gone out but would be back shortly if she wanted to wait. He showed her to a table in the temporary extension, a stylishly decorated glass and white wood shell placed for the winter where the open-air summer terrace would be, and asked if she wanted a coffee.

'*Cafè amb llet*,' she requested. 'And a small mineral water.'

As she waited, she stared out at the tiny square and narrow streets running beyond it. Four people at another table in the corner, bathed in gentle sunlight, got up to leave, each one greeting her with an automatic *Bon dia* as they passed.

Elisenda sat up with a start. Through the window, she saw Sucarrats walking towards the hotel and stop at the end of the square to shake hands in goodbye to the man walking alongside him. Miquel Canals smiled warmly at Sucarrats and hurried away along the street heading towards the port. Approaching, Sucarrats saw her through the window and waved.

'You know Miquel Canals?' she asked him when he came in to say hello.

Surprised at the question, he nodded. 'I've known him since he was a kid. He used to come and stay here with his father every year. The last time he was here was when his father was ill. One last time. Very sad.'

He excused himself and went to fetch a round aluminium tray to clear the empty cups from the other table. When he'd done, he came back and stood over her, the full tray resting effortlessly on his left forearm.

'I was talking to a woman called Maria Pujol this morning,' she told him. He shook his head to show he didn't recognise the name. 'Dolors Quintí,' she tried. She saw a faint flicker in his eyes before he again shook his head.

'Two women?' he asked her.

'Same woman, two different names. She mentioned that you'd been a councillor and had regularly vetoed funding for the El Crit dig.'

'I have no idea who she is, but she's quite right, I did.'

'She said you felt the money would be better spent on other ways of bringing revenue into the town.'

He laughed. 'That's not entirely right. An archaeological site requires constant and steady funding. A town council simply wouldn't be able to sustain that and maintain it to the standard it would require. Besides that, it's potentially a major heritage site. Funding for that has to come centrally, from the Catalan government, as part of an overall strategy to protect our history. Otherwise, it becomes a mess. We've had enough of that in the past. That's why I vetoed it.'

'Are you sure you don't know the name Dolors Quintí?' she asked suddenly. She saw the same flicker in his eyes before the repeated denial. 'One other thing, I hope you don't mind, but I mentioned the shrine in the cellar to a colleague, Pere Rigau, he's a judge in La Bisbal.'

Staring out of the window, Sucarrats looked like he'd been stung. The tray fell from his arm with a clatter, the coffee cups crunching on the wooden floor, two glasses shattering loudly. Following his gaze, Elisenda looked across the square and saw the man that she'd seen picking up rubbish from the beach at El Crit. Jumping up from the table, she ran outside, but he'd seen her and had hurriedly turned away down one of the lanes leading past the church and away into the old town. She searched for him in the little streets around the church and the square but he was gone.

Returning to the hotel, where Sucarrats was sweeping up the debris, she asked him who the man was.

'What man?' he insisted. 'I didn't see anyone. I just dropped the tray because it was heavy, that's all.'

He turned away from her to kneel down and began picking up the larger pieces of broken glass, placing them carefully on the tray.

Chapter Forty Four

Elisenda's phone rang as she was getting back into her car. It was Albert Riera, telling her that the facial reconstruction was complete and that he would forward it to her by email.

'That's good time,' she told him. 'How's it looking?'

'*Like some fucking serial killer who's missing his mother. They always do.*'

She hung up and rang Àlex in Girona to tell him that she was on her way from Palamós.

'Can you be there when I get back? Riera's sending the file with the facial reconstruction. I want you to see it as well.'

She drove to Vista Alegre, where she found not just Àlex, but the other three members of the unit waiting for her. Gathering them all into her office, she opened the file and turned the screen for them all to see. An image of a face came up and her heart sank. She could sense, too, the disappointment in the others. Used to the more creative productions for archaeology, the technician had added an impression of hair, which they couldn't know from the skull, and left the face clean-shaven with full lips.

'It's impossible to tell,' Àlex complained.

'The hair is distracting,' Elisenda agreed, framing the face with her hands to try to blot out the top of the head. 'But at least the facial structure and features will be accurate, except for the lips and the ears.'

Manel leaned forward and took the keyboard. 'Can I?'

Using a image editing program, he opened another file with the scanned photo of Esteve Mascort that Jordi Canudas had given Elisenda and Josep when they'd interviewed him in Barcelona, and created a similar 3D image to the reconstruction. Using the mouse to size the photo of Mascort to the right dimension and to rotate the two images, he slid the photo over the reconstruction, superimposing one over the other. Lining up the eyes, the nose and the mouth, Mascort's hair now appeared over the image produced from the skull. Opening the original Mascort photo, he then lay them out on the screen side by side. The five of them leaned forward, rapt. The same face stared out at them. The same B-movie assuredness, the same slender nose, the same confident turn of the cheeks and jawline.

'It is Mascort,' Elisenda whispered.

One by one, they all looked and considered and agreed. It could only be Mascort in the trench at El Crit.

'So where's Ivan Morera?' Àlex asked.

'And why did the killer bury Morera's Walkman with Mascort?' Montse added. 'Was Morera the killer and he dropped the Walkman when he buried the body?'

'It still doesn't answer the question of what happened to him after,' Àlex insisted.

Sitting back, Elisenda gave them a quick rundown of what had happened that morning with Maria and her conversation with Sucarrats. 'I don't believe that Maria didn't know anything about Mascort stealing from the dig,' she concluded. 'And she knows more about El Crit past and present than she lets on. Also, Sucarrats reacted when he saw the man from the beach outside his hotel. He knows who he is, even though he denied it. The question is, who is the man from the beach and where do Sucarrats and Maria fit into it all?'

'Well, if Ivan Morera is still alive, I'd say the man you've seen on the beach has to be him,' Àlex surmised. 'He's Morera, the missing student. He's the one who killed Mascort.'

'And Sucarrats?'

Josep snapped his fingers. 'Sucarrats was the dealer. He's the one who was selling the artefacts.'

'He's had the hotel for about twenty-odd years,' Elisenda argued. 'The dealer appears to have stopped working six years ago.

'He could have run both businesses alongside each other. He bought the hotel with the profits from the illicit antiquities and used it as the respectable front. He stopped the illegal side when the legal side made enough money for him to become completely above board.'

Elisenda stood up and reached for her coat. 'Either way,' she told the others as she put it on, 'we need to have another word with Sucarrats and we need to find the man from the beach, whether he really is Ivan Morera or not. Àlex, you come with me, the rest, look again and track down anything you can about Morera. Look for anywhere we might have missed him resurfacing.'

'I'll go back to the adoption records,' Josep said, his voice betraying his lack of confidence.

'If you've seen him in Palamós,' Manel offered, 'he might be registered there under whatever name he's using. We could go through land registry and voting register records between 1981 and the next five years to see if something comes up.'

'Try it,' Elisenda told him, 'but it'll take forever.'

'I'll give medical records from the time he might have been born a go,' Montse said, 'but that'll be as impossible as the adoption records.'

Elisenda and Àlex left the three of them looking at each other, all equally daunted by the task facing them, and picked up a pool car from the underground garage for the drive out to Palamós.

'It's hopeless,' Àlex commented as he picked his way past the Devesa park and the traffic. 'They'll never find anything in the records.'

In Palamós, they parked by the port and hurried into the old streets to the hotel, where the receptionist told them that Sucarrats had gone out and that he didn't say when he'd be back. Elisenda went into the dining room, to the door that led down to the cellar room.

'Do you have a key for this?'

The receptionist fumbled through a chain attached to his belt and opened it for them. Pushing it open, Elisenda switched on the light. She and Àlex slowly descended the stairs into the anteroom, the receptionist following a few paces behind them, his curiosity overcoming any fear he might have felt. There was no sign of anything out of the ordinary among the stacks of wine bottles and boxes on the shelves. Noticing the receptionist behind them, Elisenda asked him if he had a key for the second door.

The young man shook his head. 'Only Senyor Sucarrats had a key to that door.'

Elisenda glanced at Àlex once and made her mind up. She told the receptionist to go back upstairs and not let anyone past. Standing square in front of the frame, she lunged sharply with her foot next to the handle. The door burst open, the wood of the jamb splitting, part of the metal lock clattering loudly to the floor. She quickly jumped to one side and peered cautiously around the jamb. No sound came out of the room. Reaching for the switch on the wall inside the room, she flicked it on and peered in. She entered and Àlex followed her into the small room. Coming to a halt next to her, he turned to look at her, a puzzled expression on his face.

Embedded in the plaster above the bust of Minerva was a spike. The dust from the hole gouged violently into the wall had wept in white over her blank features.

'I think we've missed him,' Elisenda commented.

Chapter Forty Five

'I'm not going anywhere.'

'Maria,' Elisenda cajoled her. 'We can't keep you safe here. I need you to come with us to somewhere we can keep you out of harm's way.'

'This is my home. I'm safe here. And I'm not leaving my dogs. I don't know why you should think I'm in any danger.'

'Please, Maria, I've told you. We think that Guillem Sucarrats might be responsible for the murders of Esteve Mascort and Ferran Arbós. He's gone missing and I think that you are in danger.'

'Why would I be in danger from him?'

Elisenda looked in frustration at Àlex and back at Maria. 'Because you have consistently lied to me about how much you know about the events at El Crit and the sale of illicit antiquities. We think Sucarrats might be the man that Mascort traded with and that he thinks that you can incriminate him. We think that might have already killed again to protect a secret from 1981. We don't want you to become the next victim.'

'Nonsense. I'm staying here.'

Elisenda was distracted from saying any more by the sound of Flora, the Great Dane, pricking her head up from her usual place on the too-small rocking chair and keening in a low moan at a noise from outside. Àlex went out to look, coming back in almost immediately, telling Elisenda not to worry.

'It's the others,' he told her. 'They've arrived.'

When Elisenda and Àlex had seen the spike in the wall at the hotel in Palamós, Elisenda's first reaction had been that it was a setup.

'If Sucarrats really is our killer, he's done a runner, and he's trying to put us off the scent. The spike is in the wall, not in the face. Sucarrats loves that shrine, he would do nothing to damage it. Anyone else would have buried the spike in the head to mirror the Indiketa practice.'

Àlex had looked at the stone and shaken his head. 'Too hard. Sucarrats or anyone else would have had a problem getting a spike through this stone. And it would have made too much noise.'

Looking more closely, Elisenda had had to agree with him. 'Either way, we need to find Sucarrats. And we need to protect Maria Pujol. I think she's at risk.'

Àlex had called the Mossos station in Palamós to organise protection and a Científica inspection of the hotel cellar, while Elisenda called Vista Alegre. She told the other three members of the team to meet her and Àlex at the cabin in the woods by El Crit. And to come in two cars.

She'd hung up and considered another angle. 'There's also Ricard Soler. He's been missing for some time. We don't know if he's already a victim, or if he's the one responsible for this.' She'd gestured at the spike casting a thin shadow over the stone face from the light embedded in the ceiling.

In Maria's cabin, Josep and Montse filed in, followed at a short distance by Manel, between them filling the small room and increasing the sensation of darkness in there. Elisenda explained to them what had happened and told them that Maria refused to move.

'I want Montse and Josep to stay here to protect her until we can get a Seguretat Ciutadana patrol from Palafrugell or La Bisbal out here. Àlex, you and Manel talk to Poch in La Bisbal and organise the search for Sucarrats. I'll go and see Jutge Rigau to get him to authorise that. I also want to have a word with someone in La Fosca called Miquel Canals, who appears to know Sucarrats. He might know where he'd go.'

'No, judge, I need the three authorisations.'

Rigau had a harassed air about him and was proving to be more of a stickler than usual.

'And I will issue them, Elisenda, I just need to go over them with you. I don't understand why you need another one for Ricard Soler. We already have an alert out for him.'

'Okay, Pere, he's not the most important. I just wanted to make sure that the efforts to find him were renewed.'

He held his hands up. 'That's a Mossos matter, surely. You don't need my authorisation for that.'

'I need it updated and upgraded. I think it's become more imperative that we find him. He's either implicated in the whole matter, whether it's the murders or the illicit antiquities, or he's another victim. Or potentially another victim.'

He opened a document on his computer. 'Okay, Elisenda, I see your concerns. I can do it. Now, Maria Dolors Pujol Quintí…'

'It's the one for Guillem Sucarrats that's the most pressing. At the moment, he's our main suspect for the murders of Ferran Arbós and Esteve Mascort.'

'The same perpetrator for both crimes? I see.'

'I want a search and arrest warrant out on him, now. It is extremely urgent that we find him. The warrant for Maria Pujol is for her safety. I want Seguretat Ciutadana patrols at her home.'

'Can't she be taken to a safe place?'

'She refuses.'

He paused to consider Elisenda's requests and finally agreed. 'They'll be with Sergent Poch within the half-hour,' he promised.

'Thank you.'

Outside, it was already beginning to get dark, even though it was only mid-afternoon, but it heightened her sensation of time being wasted. She jogged from the court to the police station and went in to see Poch to tell him to expect the warrants from the judge.

'The one for Guillem Sucarrats is by far the most important,' she told him. 'Priority is to be given to that. And I need Seguretat Ciutadana with Maria Pujol as soon as you can, so I can free up two of my team.'

'I'll see to that as soon as the warrants come through,' he promised.

'I'm sending you a copy of the photo of Sucarrats now.' She emailed a file from her phone to his. 'And here are the details about his car. Can you circulate those to your team and the ones from the Palamós station?'

The Mossos only had a small station in Palamós, but she wanted everyone available to be out searching for the hotelier.

'Will do.'

She left him and drove to La Fosca. She tried Miquel Canals' door but there was no reply, even though she could see a light on in the house. She gave up after a few rings and went back to her sister's house while she decided on her next move. She checked her phone, but the signal was down again and she shoved it in her jacket pocket out of frustration. She stood up again just as the doorbell rang. It was Miquel Canals.

'Sorry I didn't answer,' he explained. 'I was in the shower and didn't get out in time. What was it you wanted to see me about?'

'Come in.'

He looked puzzled and followed her in. 'That had an official ring to it. Is this official?'

She showed him to one of the sofas and took another one opposite him. 'Not at all. I just wanted to ask you something.'

He sat back and studied her. 'Can I ask you something? Are you ever not a cop?' His voice was cool.

'No, probably not. I wanted to ask you how come you knew Guillem Sucarrats. I saw you with him in Palamós this morning.'

'Following me?'

'No. Following Guillem Sucarrats.'

'Ah, judge me by the company I keep. I've known him pretty much all of my life, although I suppose in a very superficial way. My father and I used to stay at his hotel when I was a kid. We took our summer holidays up here.'

'When did you last stay there?'

'Last autumn, if you really must know. My father was dying and I took him there one last time. And if you're really interested, it was one of the saddest moments of my life, when my father and I reversed roles and he became my child and I became the one looking after him.'

She watched him closely as he spoke. He suddenly sounded drained.

'I'm sorry,' she finally said. 'I'm a cop. I have to question everything. Everyone. Your story is exactly the same as Sucarrats'.'

He stared at her coldly. 'Well, lucky me, Elisenda. I take it that's all we have to say to each other.'

'I'm sorry, Miquel, I had to be sure. I don't want to suspect you.'

'Well, now you don't, can I go? I have things to do. I have to get back to work.'

She sighed. 'I can't apologise any more.' She tried to think of something more to say to repair the situation. 'Back to work? Have you had enough of the quiet life?'

He seemed to calm a little. 'I need to work. I'm getting bored. And I don't want to end up as poor as a beggar's wallet.'

Chapter Forty Six

'Are we going to tell Elisenda?' Josep asked Montse in a whisper.

Montse looked at him, unsure. 'I don't know. Not yet. Maybe we should keep it to ourselves for the moment.'

'What about Àlex?'

'Let's see.'

Josep got up to help Maria in the kitchen. She was making a cup of coffee. She seemed to him to live on it. He wished they'd brought some food as they had no idea when the Seguretat Ciutadana patrol would turn up to relieve them.

'Do you never worry about not being able to communicate while you're here, Maria?' he asked her, looking in dismay at the barren columns on his mobile phone.

She looked sternly at him over the steam rising from the blackened *cafetera*. 'I would be more concerned at being able to be disturbed by people. You all talk far too much as it is, without all your mobile phones and computers to give you even greater opportunities to be a nuisance.'

She poured the coffee and put some milk that had been warming on the stove into a jug and placed the lot on an old tray. Josep took it from her and carried it through into the living room.

'My grandmother had a table stove like this,' Montse commented when they brought in the tray. 'It's lovely and warming.'

It was her turn for a stern look. As there were only two chairs by the table, Josep picked up the rocking chair and pulled it over. Flora immediately loped across from where she'd been sitting by the front door and growled at him.

'That's her chair,' Maria told him. 'I'm afraid you're going to have to put it back where it was. There's a stool in the kitchen you can use.'

Josep did as she suggested and finally sat down on the stool, his knees tucked up uncomfortably against the side of the table top as they wouldn't fit underneath. Flora went back to her post by the door. A gust of wind rattled the old timber frame and whistled down the flue leading up to the ceiling from the stove.

'There's a wind blowing up,' Josep commented.

'There is,' Maria agreed. 'But that's not what we need to worry about.' She pointed to Flora sitting by the door. 'She only sits there when she can sense something. Long before we ever do.'

–

'Do you ever get used to this, Sergent?'

'Used to what?' Àlex asked.

'All this,' Manel said, gesturing vaguely out of the window. 'Girona. The sea. The people.'

Àlex glanced across at the new recruit. He was driving as Manel still had to get to know the region and they were in too much of a hurry for him to have to learn that evening. 'They also have to get used to you, Caporal. It works both ways. Never forget that.'

Manel grunted, evidently dissatisfied with the answer.

They pulled into the police station in La Bisbal and went to see Sergent Poch. Àlex introduced him to Manel.

'Any sightings of Sucarrats?' Àlex asked him.

Poch looked at him. 'We've only just had the authorisation from the judge. I've got the photo and the car registration circulating now among uniforms here and in Palafrugell, but it's too soon to hear anything back.'

Àlex checked his watch and shook his head in irritation. Elisenda had seen the judge an hour ago.

'What about relief for my two caporals? I need them out searching for Sucarrats.'

'Elisenda mentioned that, but I haven't heard from the judge. As soon as I do, I can arrange it, but I'm having to recall Seguretat Ciutadana officers who are off-shift as it is, and I've got two of my own team down with this flu, and one of the Palafrugell team is off sick, so it's going to take some time anyway.'

Àlex looked aghast. 'You haven't heard from the judge?'

'They're in the same boat as we are. Half the staff there is off with this bug.'

Àlex and Manel left the building and walked to the court.

'See what I mean?' Manel commented. 'Girona. Can't get anything done.'

Àlex grunted and led him into the court building, asking at reception for Jutge Rigau.

'He's out, I'm sorry,' the receptionist told him. Her voice was hoarse and her eyes were streaming.

'Is his secretary in?'

'He's off sick, I'm afraid. Jutge Rigau is only working today because the other duty judge is at home with flu.'

Àlex thanked her and asked for the judge's mobile number. On the way back to their car outside the Mossos station, he tried ringing the number she gave him but it went to voicemail.

'Girona,' Manel muttered darkly.

Àlex stopped in his tracks and waited until the caporal registered it and turned around to face him. When he did, Àlex approached him to close the gap, his face close to Manel's.

'One more comment about Girona, caporal,' he told him, 'and I will make sure that you are shipped off to some forsaken desk job in the back of beyond. Now shut up and do your job.'

Manel turned away from Àlex just that moment too soon not to be insubordinate.

'Yes, Sergent.'

–

Elisenda stood at the sink in the kitchen, her hands leaning heavily either side of the zinc, and looked out at the darkness below.

'Let me get you a drink,' she'd told him, 'so I can make up for being a cop all the time.'

Canals was still in the living room. She'd offered him a drink to buy time while she thought.

'Poor as a beggar's wallet,' she whispered to her reflection in the window. The phrase that was Ivan Morera's favourite and not at all a common one. 'So who are you? And who is Ivan Morera to you?'

Because of the split-level house, the room was one storey up at the rear of the building and gave an unusual view over the trees and ill-lit and deserted roads. This was when life in a summer resort was less desirable, she thought. Her phone lay on the draining board next to her. It had no signal.

'Was he your father? And if he really is dead, who's the man on the beach?' There were constantly more questions, more doubts, more dead-ends.

'Everything all right?' he called through.

'Fine,' she called back. 'Won't be a moment.'

A set of car headlights approached the end of the road, travelling slowly as though it were looking for something. She watched as it slowed down and turned into the area below the house where the entrances to the garages were. She lost sight of it as it stopped directly below the window, outside the garage to the house where she was.

'Out of wine,' she called again. 'Just going down to the cellar to fetch a bottle.'

Cursing that she'd left her service pistol in the bedside table, like she always did at home, she picked up her car keys from the bowl on the kitchen counter and went down the stairs into the garage, turning the light on. Someone was gently trying to turn the backup manual handle on the outer door, but it was locked and wouldn't open. Unlocking her car and taking out a baton that she kept in the door pocket, she stood back and pressed the wall button inside the garage that operated the electric door. Once again, she thanked her brother-in-law's need for the best and most expensive, and the shutter raised quickly and silently.

A man was waiting outside, his face turned away from her. Before the door had opened fully, he turned back and ducked down to get under the door, bringing him into the full unforgiving light of the garage.

'You?' she gasped.

Chapter Forty Seven

'Maybe we should tell Àlex,' Montse decided.

She glanced around. Maria was in the kitchen, washing the coffee cups, Josep was at a window, peering out into the gloom. Flora hadn't once left her post at the door.

Josep looked across at her. 'Maybe we should,' he whispered.

He cast his mind back to the morning at Vista Alegre searching through the records to try and find some sign of Ivan Morera, before Elisenda called and told them to get out to Maria Pujol's cabin. Of how Manel had ceaselessly tried to order them about.

'For Christ's sake, leave that and start looking for the land registry records,' he'd told Montse, the final command that had made her lose her temper with him.

'In case you hadn't noticed,' she'd told him, 'you're a caporal, the same as us.'

'And we've been here longer,' Josep had added. 'You don't get to tell us what to do.'

'Just trying to get some order into this,' Manel had replied, his closing words before an ill-tempered silence fell over the room.

Josep was brought back suddenly from his musing by a sound outside. Through the keening of the wind was an undertone of something scraping on the earth and twigs. Flora got to her feet sharply, her nose pressed up against the door. Josep and Montse exchanged a look, and Montse turned to see where Maria was. She'd evidently heard it too and was facing out into the living room from the kitchen.

'That's not an animal making that noise,' Maria told them. 'That's some dumb human stumbling in the dark.'

'I'll go and look,' Montse told Josep. 'You stay here with Maria.'

'Not a chance,' Maria told her, striding forward. 'This is my home. I'm going to look.'

She was at the door and out of it, with Flora bounding ahead of her into the dark, before Montse or Josep had time to react. Drawing their guns and holding their torches at head height, the two of them left the warmth of the cabin and followed their charge out into the night.

'I'll go this way,' Montse told Josep above the wind, pointing with the beam of light at the path leading to the sea. 'You check around the cabin first.'

He agreed and quickly made a circuit of the outside of the chaotic structure, coming back to the front door. He looked inside and closed the door before turning back to the path that Montse had taken. He couldn't see the light of her torch or hear any noise other than the wind beginning to chant its lament in the trees on the edge of the beach at El Crit.

–

'No news,' Àlex told Manel as he got back into the car. It was pulled up in the old streets of Palamós as near to the hotel as he could get it. He'd just gone into the building to see if Sucarrats had returned. The receptionist had heard nothing from him. It was the only address they had for the owner as he lived in a suite on the top floor, so there was nowhere else they could try.

'Is there anyone he might have gone to stay with?' Àlex had asked the young guy behind the desk.

'No one. I never saw him with anyone close.'

As Àlex was negotiating the narrow lanes back down to the port, his phone rang. He stopped the car to the annoyance of a couple of pedestrians behind them and answered. It was Poch in La Bisbal, calling to say that they'd had a sighting of Sucarrats' car. The driver matched his description.

'*It was by the turnoff for La Fosca*,' Poch told him.

Àlex banged the steering wheel with his fist. He tried calling Elisenda's mobile, but the number was unavailable. He knew that if she was in La Fosca, she would be unlikely to get a signal. Thinking, he called her sister in Girona to ask for the address of her beach house.

'There's no problem, Catalina,' he told her. 'I just need to contact Elisenda.'

With the address memorised, he moved the car forward, putting the blue light on and honking at the same irate pedestrians to get out of the way. Down in the port, he put his foot down and cut through the newer backstreets of the town on the way to La Fosca.

–

'Please, close the door,' he said urgently. 'Quickly. I don't know where he is.'

Instinctively, Elisenda did as he asked, but she kept her eyes on him all the time.

'We've got half the Mossos out looking for you,' she told him.

'I don't care,' Sucarrats said. His normally stylish hair was dishevelled with sweat and his clothes were more on the shabby side than the usual chic. 'Better you than him.'

'Who?'

He was about to speak when the lights went off and the room was plunged into a more complete darkness than the winter streets outside. She tried the door button as it was closest to her but it wasn't working. The electricity had blown. Or been switched off at the mains, upstairs where Miquel Canals was.

As her eyes grew used to the dark, she could sense that Sucarrats hadn't moved either. She could just make out the vaguest shape where he'd been standing before. Reaching forward, she opened the car door and the courtesy light came on. He was standing where she'd last seen him, looking even more terrified than he had been less than a minute earlier. She was about to say something when a huge metallic clatter rang through the house, ringing on the tiled floor above their heads and echoing through the gloom of the garage. Someone had dropped something heavy to the ground. Like a hammer. Or a spike.

Taking her heavy police torch from the car and ruing once again having left her gun in the drawer in her bedroom, Elisenda told Sucarrats to stay where he was. She saw from the look on his face that he had no intention of moving anywhere away from the relative safety of the garage. Moving sideways so she could still see the hotelier out of the corner of her eye, she quickly climbed the stairs, making as little noise as possible. Pushing the door into the kitchen open with a rapid movement, she held the torch so the beam would dazzle anyone facing her in the room. There was no one there. No Miquel Canals, no one.

She quickly went into the living room, moving the light cast by the torch rapidly about to catch any movement or anyone hiding in a corner. Seeing no one, she made her way to the small hall at the top of the three steps and found the mains switch. Turning it on, she looked first back at the living room and then out into the dark beyond the front door, which had been left open. Whether it was by someone entering or leaving, she wasn't sure.

For the first time, she noticed the blood on the wall by the front door. A hand that had smeared across as someone left in a hurry. Taking one more quick look at the room behind her, she ran out to the path in front of the house. The same light that had been on in Canals' house earlier was still on, but from below she heard the sound of someone running across the shingle and splashing into the sea. Going to the edge of the low cliff, she looked down to see a figure pushing Canals' beached kayak out into the water. The moon was behind a cloud, whipping quickly past in the rising wind, and she couldn't make out who the person was. She shone her torch at them but they were too far away for the beam to penetrate.

As the figure steadied themselves in the kayak and began to paddle, she ran back into the house and down to the cellar. Sucarrats was still there and had locked himself in her car, although the exit was blocked by his own vehicle slewed in front of the door. Ignoring him, she grabbed a kayak from the wall and ran out into the night and towards the beach.

Pushing the craft into the water, she could just make out the person she was pursuing rowing north. Finding her position on the seat, she rammed the paddle into the black foam and pushed away from the shore. The other person had a big start on her, but the wind finally favoured her, blowing the clouds away and keeping her target in her sights. She felt her shoulders strain with practised ease and she cut through the night water, her eyes never leaving the person ahead of her.

Only then did she remember that she hadn't fetched her gun.

Chapter Forty Eight

'Stop there.'

The man on the beach at El Crit turned to face Montse and raised the spear-gun, pointing it directly at her face. She shone the torch in his face, dazzling him.

'Put the torch down, or I will fire this,' he warned her.

She could see that despite being caught in the glare, he hadn't wavered in the direction he was aiming the spike. Reluctantly, she angled the torch at the ground in front of him, but she didn't turn it off. She could see him through the light reflected on the tiny pebbles, a ghostly glow under his chin, casting eerie shadows up his face.

He was old, she could see that. Wiry, with grey hair combed back in waves from a high forehead, which was accentuated by the meagre beam of light.

She heard footsteps behind her. On the edge of her vision, she saw Maria come and stand nearby, parallel to her but a short distance away.

'Put that down,' Maria told the man.

He looked at her and then back at Montse.

'I can't,' he told Maria.

Sucarrats' car was pulled up in front of the garage at the beach house and the large door was open, flooding the small area in front of it in halogen light.

Àlex and Manel got out of their car and approached. The first car was empty. Àlex recognised the second, the one inside, as a Mossos pool car, the one that Elisenda had been using. It was also empty.

There was no one there. Drawing his gun, Àlex told Manel to go around the outside of the house and approach the house from the front. Watching him hurry out. Àlex quickly climbed the stairs into the kitchen. Checking the downstairs rooms, he saw they were empty, but lying on the floor behind one of the large sofas was a large metal spike, the sort used on construction sites. He also saw the blood on the wall by the front door. At that same moment, Manel ran in, also looking at the stains, careful not to touch them.

'There's someone in the water,' Manel told him, his voice gasping.

Running out, they peered over the cliff and saw a figure paddling a kayak hurriedly away from the beach.

'There's another,' Manel said, pointing further away at another craft caught in the moonlight.

'That's the direction of El Crit,' Àlex told him.

Going back into the house, they found a dishevelled and frightened man waiting for them in the living room.

'Sucarrats?' Àlex said, recognising him from his photo. 'Where's Elisenda?'

Visibly shaken, the hotelier pointed towards the stairs down to the garage. 'She took a kayak and went outside. There was someone upstairs.'

'What are you doing here?'

'I came to ask Elisenda for protection. I know who it is you're after. I think he's after me.'

'Who is it?' Àlex demanded.

Sucarrats told him a name.

'Who?' Àlex couldn't hide his disbelief.

Taking a decision, he told Sucarrats to come with them. Quickly putting him in the back seat and handcuffing his hands to the stanchion at the base of the front seat, Àlex turned on the blue light and floored the accelerator. In the passenger seat, Manel tried his phone, but there was no signal.

'Where are we going?' Sucarrats asked.

'El Crit.'

'No,' the hotelier wailed, his head hanging down to his lap.

–

Elisenda could see that she was catching the other person up. She paused once to shine her torch at them, but they were still too far away for her to see who it was and it only slowed her down, so she thrust it back into the top of her jacket and renewed her paddling. She couldn't help asking herself all the while she rowed, her mind chanting in rhythm with her paddle, who it was that she was chasing. An hour ago, she would have said it was Sucarrats, but that was before he turned up at her sister's house. An hour ago, she had decided it wasn't Canals, but that before his use of the missing student's odd phrase. And if it wasn't him, where was he now and whose blood was it in the hall? She also still wondered if she had Ricard Soler in her sights. Or the man picking up litter from the beach. And if he really was Ivan Morera.

Whoever it was that she was chasing also seemed to sense that she was closing the gap on them, and they suddenly veered in towards the shore. Elisenda followed them, knowing in the black that she couldn't worry about the rocks lying below the water's surface.

Then she heard the scream.

A woman's scream cutting through the sea-black night, filling the darkness and pulling her inexorably back to El Crit.

–

Àlex drove the car further along the track towards the sea than he should have, only stopping when a rock brought them to a halt with a loud grinding crack underneath. Getting out, he left Manel to keep guard over Sucarrats and he ran through the trees, following the swathe cut by the beam of his torch and ignoring the needles flaying his face and hands. Up ahead, the wind rising from the sea curled through the night, whispering a dark lullaby in his ears.

Crashing through it, another noise tore into his head, recalling Elisenda's legend of the beach. A woman's scream, shrill in the void.

–

A woman's scream.

It stopped Josep momentarily in his tracks, before spurring him on. He was at the top of the ragged steps down to the beach at El Crit. Below him, he could see a faint light on the stones. He took the steps as quickly as he could, their tortuous course taking the three figures he'd spotted on the beach in and out of sight as he descended them. The lull left in the aftermath of the scream brought another sound through the wind's song. The rippling of water, of someone in the sea approaching land.

Jumping the final steps, by the fishermen's huts, he ran out onto the beach to see Montse, Maria and a man in an uneven triangle. Montse was looking in shock at Maria. It was the older woman who had screamed. A pent-up scream born of anger and frustration.

'Let me go.'

As Josep drew up to them, Maria walked ahead and placed herself between the man and Montse. 'Put it down,' she told him, her voice calmer now.

Montse saw Josep and signalled to him to move around to the other side of the man.

'Drop your weapon,' Josep told him, following Montse's lead.

'Put it down,' Maria repeated.

Hesitantly, the man bent forward and placed the spear-gun on the ground. Montse walked up to him and removed the weapon. She handed it to Josep, who gingerly placed it at the foot of the steps, fearful its mechanism would suddenly go off.

'Ivan Morera?' Montse asked him.

'Who?' he looked puzzled.

Maria walked up to where they were standing. 'I don't know who your Ivan Morera is. This is Ricard Soler. The silly old duffer still thinks he has to protect me.'

'That's all I've ever wanted to do,' he told her, the pleading evident in his frail voice.

'You are joking,' Montse told them both in frustration.

The rippling of the water that Josep had heard became louder, and they turned to see a kayak grind across the surface of the water, scraping against the rocks, and beach on the pebbles at the far end of the shore from where they were held in thrall in the weak torchlight. A figure clambered off the craft and ran ashore, splashing through the thin surf. Seeing them, the shape ran to the edge of the cliff towering over the beach and vanished into the darkness. Reacting, Josep and Montse shone their torches to try and pick out whoever it was, but the beams weren't strong enough.

A second kayak came ashore, a second figure stumbling through the water onto the pebbles. Josep ran from the steps to where the other three were still standing. Montse continued to keep an eye on Ricard Soler while Josep moved forward, his gun raised, to try and make out who the newcomer was.

'It's me,' an exhausted voice called across the beach. 'Elisenda. Stop that person.'

Josep immediately turned back to the darkened cliff, shining his torch, but a movement at the foot of the steps caught his eye and he turned to see the figure pick up the spear-gun and start running up the steps.

Elisenda ran to join the four people gathered in torch-light, trying to catch her breath. 'Give me your gun,' she told Montse.

She and Josep chased after the shadow turning back on itself up the rough steps. As they reached the bottom, another light appeared at the top, descending towards them, at each turn momentarily catching their prey in its spotlight.

'It's me, Àlex,' a voice called from the top.

The figure stopped, hesitating, caught between pursuers top and bottom. In the gloom and at a distance, Elisenda still couldn't make out who it was. It ran first up the steps, then down, evidently in two minds what to do. Finally, it ran down to the first bend in the flight of steps and leapt off towards the protective shadow of the fishermen's cottages.

They heard a wet thud that reminded Elisenda of the grappling hooks being embedded in the tuna brought ashore at the port in Palamós. A second scream rent the darkness, a man's scream.

Àlex ran down to the bend in the steps and called down to Elisenda and Josep, who had descended once again to the bottom to make their way to the rear of the huts.

'I know who it is,' Àlex told them.

Elisenda led the way cautiously to the back of the nearest hut to the steps and shone her torch at a figure standing with his back to the wall. Held fast by the rusted iron bracket for hanging nets that Elisenda had spotted a few days earlier was a man, the thick spike of the metal arm thrust through the back of his skull and projecting out of his forehead.

'No,' Elisenda whispered.

Caught in the sharp beam of three torches was Jutge Rigau, sightless through his thick-rimmed spectacles as ancient skulls in a glass case.

El Crit, 1981

The student watched as Esteve Mascort scraped away at the earth in the trench. The heavy rain falling incessantly since earlier that night instantly washed almost everything he scraped back, but he kept going. He had to. The dealer would be there shortly and he had to feed the man's need for artefacts. The student knew that Mascort was as afraid of the dealer as he himself was of Mascort. He watched the archaeologist in annoyance, wearing his Walkman, listening to his music. Just one of the prices Mascort had demanded for allowing the student in on his scam, although he'd scored a petty victory that night, swapping the other man's El Puma for his own Orquesta Mondragón.

'Go and get me a coat?' Mascort called to the student now, his temper evil.

'There isn't a spare one.'

'Give me yours then.'

The student had handed it over without any complaint and retreated to the shelter of a low pine for a brief respite from the downpour. While he was standing there, a figure emerged from the path to the other side of the dig. The student gasped, keeping the noise to himself, as the dealer wasn't expected for another couple of hours. He'd be furious if they hadn't found enough items for him to sell.

The student saw Mascort stand up. Through the rain, he saw him tense up, startled at the newcomer, but then relax and lean back against the side of the trench. His laugh, mocking and unpleasant and by now so familiar to the student, sniggered through the trees. The other figure said something that the student couldn't hear through the rain, and Mascort laughed again, louder this time, and longer.

The other figure jumped down into the trench and picked up something from the ground. A mattock. The student watched it swing in an angry arc, whistling through the rain. Under the sound of the torrent, he heard a second noise, a sickening thud as the mattock buried itself in Mascort's forehead. He fell instantly, like an animal poleaxed in an abattoir, the tool so firmly embedded in its victim that it was wrenched from the attacker's grasp.

The student thrust his hand into his mouth to cover up any noise he might make. He watched the other figure stand over Mascort for a few moments and then simply walk away, oblivious to the rain thundering down on them.

The student waited under the trees for a good half an hour after the killer had gone to make sure they didn't return. When he was certain that no one was going to be coming back, he cautiously left his shelter and walked over to where Mascort lay face-up in the trench, the mattock jutting out of his forehead, his eyes seeming to stare at the student. He tried closing them but couldn't.

Angling the light away, the student was struck by another clearing further down the incline from where the dig was. Looking back to the dead man in the trench, he thought.

He'd found his skull.

He'd also made his decision.

Chapter Forty Nine

'I buried him,' Sucarrats told Elisenda in the interview room in the Mossos station in La Bisbal. 'I don't know who killed him, but I didn't. I buried Mascort in a grave I dug at the bottom of the slope, and when the dealer came, I told him that Mascort was no longer working for him and that I was. The problem came when they realised that the site was more extensive than they'd first thought and Mascort's body suddenly reappeared.'

'Which is why you'd used your position as a councillor for years to veto plans for funding the El Crit dig.'

'I had no idea when I buried him that the settlement was going to be so important.' He shrugged. 'Ah, well, such is life.'

'When did you change your name?'

He smiled at her, the slick hair back in place, the clothes cool once more. 'Ah, my name. Poor old Ivan Morera, as poor as a beggar's wallet. He had to go.'

'So you found your real mother's name and changed to that instead?'

'Not at all. I never found out who she was. But I used that confusion of the time to change my own. I just picked a name out of the phone book and claimed I'd lost my ID card when I was working abroad. For all the mind-numbing bureaucracy in those days, it really wasn't as difficult as you'd think.'

Despite herself, Elisenda was enthralled by Sucarrats' casual telling of his story. 'Why did you react when you saw Ricard Soler?'

'I tell you, I don't know who Ricard Soler is. I recognised the name as one of the archaeologists who was supposed to be on the dig, but I never met him. The only one I ever knew was Mascort. What startled me was when you mentioned the judge who you'd told about the shrine in the cellar. You told me his name. Rigau.' He shivered involuntarily. 'He was the scariest person I've ever met. Rigau senior, that is. He had a killer's eyes and none of the scruples.'

'But you still you took over Mascort's business to trade with him?'

He shrugged. 'I wanted the money. I have fine tastes, you've seen my hotel. And I only worked with him for as long as I needed to until the hotel started to make enough for me to live well. It was a huge relief not to have to work for Rigau anymore. And a bigger relief when the old bastard died. I slept easier in my bed after that. Until Mascort's body was found. But even then, I thought I was safe. I'd forgotten Rigau had a son. I only saw him once, when he was a kid. Rigau doted on him. Little wonder he grew up to be the killer his father wasn't.'

Wasn't, Elisenda thought. We'll come back to that.

'And the son doted on the father,' she told him. 'We're certain now that Jutge Rigau killed Ferran Arbós and we think he did it to protect his father's name, and consequently his own position as a judge. Because his father had killed Mascort, he was afraid that Mascort's body being found would lead the investigation back to him. It was his form of veneration.'

Sucarrats laughed wryly. 'Which is ironic, when you think of it.'

'Ironic? You said the son is the killer the father wasn't.'

He considered for a moment. 'I couldn't see who it was that night because of the rain, but Mascort didn't react to his killer in the way he would have to Rigau. He was scared stiff of him. He wasn't scared of the person I saw that night. And Rigau always came by boat. The killer came from the other way, along the path that led to the road. I'd stake everything I own on Rigau senior not having killed Mascort.'

Elisenda got up to leave. 'You know you'll be charged with not reporting a crime, illegal burial, trading in illicit antiquities and faking your identity?'

He gave her his most charming smile. 'It all happened a long time ago. A different country in a different age. I can afford good lawyers. I'll be all right.'

She went outside and stood in the corridor.

'Yes, you probably will,' she muttered to herself.

Another of her jobs that night was to go and see Miquel Canals in hospital in Palamós.

'I'm sorry I didn't believe you,' she told him.

He stared back at her. One eye was covered by the heavy bandage wound around his head. 'You're a cop. It's what you do. That much never changes.' He was silent for a moment. 'Did you catch him?'

'We caught him.'

'Who was he?'

She told him as much as he needed to know. 'You were just in the wrong place at the wrong time. Luckily he knew it wasn't you he was after.'

Canals gestured to his head. 'Very lucky.'

He had been lucky, though, the doctors had told Elisenda. It had been a glancing blow with the hammer. Had it been a more direct hit, the outcome would have been very different. She didn't tell him that.

'How did you get away?' she asked him.

'I don't really know. He just didn't come after me a second time. So I ran out and into my house. I barricaded the door and didn't come out until your lot came to find me.'

Elisenda nodded. She'd sent Àlex and Manel to find him. She didn't tell him that either.

With nothing more to do that night, Elisenda spent what she knew would be her last night in La Fosca, drinking a *lumumba* alone on the chill terrace and watching the phosphorescence glitter on the Mediterranean.

Chapter Fifty

She drove the next morning. It seemed more official than taking the kayak, no matter how much she wanted one final view of the land from the sea.

Maria was making coffee. A second cup was on the table waiting for Elisenda.

'Ricard Soler not here?' Elisenda asked her.

Maria shook her head irritably. 'That man never knew when something was over. He told me he came when he read about the body being found at El Crit. Old fool thought I needed protecting.'

'You did. Why didn't you tell me who he was when I first mentioned him?

'Not important. I thought he'd get the message and just go. He didn't.'

'Especially when he read about Arbós's murder in the paper,' Elisenda muttered. She'd realised as she was watching the sun come up at La Fosca an hour or so ago that it must have been Jutge Rigau who'd given the details to the press in an attempt to flush out anyone who might be of interest to him, to his own need for protection. Of himself and of his father's memory. Picking up the piping hot coffee, she let out a slow sigh. Flora was stretched over her favourite rocking chair, the noise it made as it moved softened by the rug placed underneath it. Elisenda leaned across and stroked the dog's head.

'I spoke to the judge this morning,' she told Maria. 'A different one. The supermarket is refusing to drop the charges against you for taking food from the bins. You'll still be fined.'

Maria shrugged. 'It's to be expected. You might think you've got your new police and your new judges, but nothing ever really changes. At least in my day you knew where you stood. The cops and the justice system and anything that came from the Franco regime were rotten to the core and made no bones about it, the rest of us just had to put up and shut up. How's all this going to leave your lot looking now?'

Elisenda wanted to argue otherwise but didn't have the energy. She knew she had to remain focused. She'd asked Puigventós the same question late last night when he'd turned up at El Crit beach with Albert Riera and a Científica team from La Bisbal, her own question to the inspector searching under the glare of the arc lamps set up at the scene. She and Puigventós had been watching the forensic team and the pathologist working under the body of the judge hanging from his own shrine. The town's other judge was standing silent some distance away, pulled from his sick bed and pale in the spotlight.

'This could kill my unit,' Elisenda had worried. 'Between what happened last year and this, I don't see how we can survive the scrutiny we're going to come under now.'

'Quite the contrary,' Puigventós told her in a quiet tone. He half-gestured to the dead man on the wall. 'This will be the saving of the Serious Crime Unit. Judges are such powerful, high-profile figures, the media will delight in the downfall of one of them. And what a downfall. And the public doesn't necessarily equate them with the police. All this will serve to do is take attention away from us and point it at the legal hierarchy, the whole system of instructing judges and courts. The Mossos are the ones who stopped an abuse of power, brought a killer to justice and solved an old crime. We'll finally be painted in a good light.'

At the time, Elisenda found it hard to think he was right, but the calm of the sunrise over the sea began to make her see that there was a lot of truth in what Puigventós said. She hoped so.

Although the inspector couldn't help the sting in the tail.

'But don't forget you're a unit, Elisenda. At least you're supposed to be a unit. Sergeant Albiol left a new officer alone in a car with a prisoner, excluding him from the team, from the moment of victory, if you like. I don't want to see a recurrence of that.'

'The moment called for it,' Elisenda argued, although she had to admit that she'd also questioned Àlex's motives in leaving Manel in the car. She knew she'd not only have to speak to Àlex and the rest of the team, but also find a way to smooth Manel's rough edges. She hoped that wasn't going to become the next threat to her unit.

'Elisenda,' Maria called to her, bringing her back to the moment. She could see the older woman studying her with concern. 'I have something for you.' Maria went into the bedroom and came out with a box of artefacts. 'They were taken by Esteve. It's about time they were given back.'

Elisenda looked at the items in the old wooden fruit crate lined with newspaper. Most of them were broken shards of something Elisenda couldn't identify. People had been killed for them, she mused, putting the box down on the table.

'Is that all that's left?'

Maria busied herself, her back to Elisenda. 'That's all. Now, if you'll excuse me, I have to go and put food out for the dogs.'

'Please do,' Elisenda told her.

She watched Flora unfold herself from the rocking chair and follow the woman out into the fresh air. The previous night's wind had died down to reveal a splendid blue sky. Elisenda sighed and got up. Glancing out through the front door, she moved the rocking chair back and folded the rug up. There were no rings embedded in the floor, or latches. Just a square of loose boards that came away when she prised them up with the end of a coffee spoon.

Elisenda shone her torch into the space left. A bracelet glittered back at her, Indiketa she imagined, or Greek. In the centre was a kylix, more humble than the one that had been returned to El Crit. The design in the middle was of a man and a woman holding both hands together. The border was simpler than the first one she'd seen, with just a curved line snaking around the edge. Something else glittered in the torchlight. She reached down to pick it up. A St. Christopher medallion, still shiny.

'Oh, Maria,' she whispered.

In the space in front of the kylix was a small bundle of material. Reaching in, she carefully unfolded the fabric and breathed out deeply. Wrapped inside was a skeleton. A baby.

'I told you I'd never had an abortion,' Maria's voice came from behind her. 'That much was true. I had a baby. But she died four hours after she was born. No one worried about an unmarried mother leaving a hospital without being discharged in those days.'

'The baby in the foundations,' Elisenda said. 'The Indiketa custom.'

'He wouldn't accept that it was his. He said it could have been anyone's. He told me to have an abortion. He just laughed at me when I told him I'd given everything up for him.'

'So you killed him.'

'It was a moment of anger. I thought he'd be found the next day and I'd pay for what I did. I never understood what had happened to him until his body was discovered all these years later. What will happen to me?'

Elisenda gently wrapped the tiny bones up again in the blanket and stood up, she looked directly at Maria.

'I have to do what is right,' she told her.

Chapter Fifty One

Àlex stood outside the bar on the nondescript modern square by the river and stared at the door. The two toughs who'd muttered something to him on the Friday night walked past him again, and again they spat on the floor and made some comment. Again, not so loud that Àlex could hear what it was. They still weren't that confident. Àlex watched them open the door and disappear into the dingy bar.

Waiting just one moment longer, Àlex walked slowly to the bar and pulled the door open, letting the lights of the square illuminate the harsh faces of the men standing at the counter. He walked up to the bar, the two men behind it sneering openly at him, the bigger one with his arms folded across his broad chest. The smaller, dangerous one turned to wink at the two toughs, standing at the bar. One of them lit up a cigarette.

His eyes fixed on the young tough, Àlex reached out and pulled the cigarette from his mouth, mashing it out in the ashtray picked out in the halogen beam pointing down at the scuffed wood surface of the counter.

'Smoking in a public place is illegal, boys,' Àlex told them.

He picked up the lighter, resting on the flimsy packet of cigarettes lying on the bar, and reached into his inside jacket pocket. He looked from one to the other. They all watched in silence as he took out an envelope and slid a piece of paper out of it. The form for the desk job in Sabadell. Holding the lighter underneath the form, he watched the flames take hold on the paper and engulf it before he dropped it into the ashtray.

In the swollen silence, The Birdy Song suddenly played mechanically on a one-armed bandit, the only sound apart from the crackling of the paper smouldering on the bar.

Looking at each of them in turn, he unleashed the full power of an old Àlex grin.

'I'm back.'

Chapter Fifty Two

Elisenda climbed the stairs to her apartment, carrying two bags of her clothes and some leftover food. She'd gone one last time to the beach house and packed away all signs of her stay there, washing the bedclothes and folding them away, cleaning out the grate and covering the army of ornaments once again. She'd looked around and turned the electricity off at the mains before closing the door. With the investigation at El Crit over, there was no longer a need to stay at La Fosca. There was no longer an excuse to stay at La Fosca. It was time to go home. Outside, on the path, she'd said goodbye to the sea. Glancing over at the house where Miquel Canals had been staying, she'd seen that it was empty. He said he'd be returning to Barcelona to carry on mending.

Opening the front door to her own home, she sensed a shadow flit across the hallway into the living room. The air was stuffy and silent. Without turning any lights on, she put the bags down and went into the kitchen, opening the windows that looked out onto the colours in the buildings across the river. Her home seemed so small after her sister's house.

Below her, the Onyar winked a reflection of coloured lights at her, glittering on their way to the sea. The slow knell of the water gently running by whispered a lullaby, one that she'd taught her daughter so many years ago.

It was her baby buried in the foundations.

Leaning her head against the window frame, she looked out, her head dropping only slightly.

'I'm back.'

Author's Note

Before you go looking for an archaeological site at El Crit, I have to tell you now that I made that bit up. Everything else is really there. The little cove with the underwater rocks, the fishermen's huts, the steps winding up from the beach and the headland and woods do exist and are among the most tranquil and beautiful spots you might find anywhere, but there is no dig there or any evidence of an Indiketa settlement that I know of.

If you are interested in the Indiketa, however, the extensive settlement at Ullastret and the dig on the Agulla de Castell headland do exist, as do the skulls with the spikes embedded in them in the museum at Ullastret. Both sites are fascinating pools of calm.

Acknowledgements

As always, there are so many people to thank for their help and support with this book. I've been bowled over by the generous response to the first story in the Elisenda Domènech series, and I'd like to thank all the wonderful readers and reviewers who have left such kind reviews and sent me such positive messages, including a number of readers from Girona, which was particularly gratifying.

I'd like to give a very belated thank you to my students at the Archaeology Service in Girona, to whom I taught English many years ago. That experience and the behind-the-scenes glimpses of digs and historic sites that they gave me fired a deep fascination with the history and archaeology of the region, which I have no doubt ultimately led to this book. Credit must also go once again to the lovely city of Girona and its beautiful surroundings, which are at all times inspiring.

I'm tremendously lucky to have a great publisher in Canelo and I'd like to thank everyone there once again for their vision and for their faith in Elisenda and in me: Michael Bhaskar, Iain Millar, Nick Barreto and Simon Collinson. A huge and heartfelt thanks also to Ana McLaughlin for all her hard work and skill in promoting City of Good Death, to Helen Francis for her masterful copy-editing, and to Chris Shamwana for the extraordinary and atmospheric cover designs for my books. And a hello and thank you to Maisie Lawrence, who I'm looking forward to working with.

My agent, the brilliant Ella Kahn, is officially a star and a trailblazer, to which I can wholeheartedly attest – they simply don't come any better. Thank you as always for all the support, encouragement, patience and belief.

And finally, I want to thank my wonderful wife Liz for everything. And for keeping me in wine.